REMNANTS IN THE MIST

Remnants in the Mist

*Divine Trials
Series
Book 2*

MEGAN EINARSON

Contents

Prologue

AT THE BASE of the towering mountain, standing in solitude against thousands of his brethren, an angel lied.

I will make it out of this alive.

In his heart, he knew this wasn't true. A single angel could not oppose the overwhelming strength of all of Spira's soldiers. He felt the thunderous shaking of their march down the mountain in his very bones. The sword of flames held proudly by their Commander announced his impending doom. And yet, he lied. He could win. He had to win. For the sake of the demon that he loved so dearly, he had to lie. For the sake of her freedom, he had to hold on to hope.

"Samael, do you truly intend to oppose us? To oppose all of Spira?" the Commander asked, voice echoing down the mountain. "You would give up this life for that unnatural beast?"

Samael's body glowed like an emerald in moonlight. His form shifted and grew into a colossal, serpentine beast. "You are giving up your own life for far less," he growled, slitted eyes burning with protective fury. "You believe her to be a beast? That her desire for freedom is a sin punishable by death? You fools have accepted the Archangel's deceit as fact."

"Their words are law."

"Their words are born of their own cowardice."

The army gathered at the mountain's base. The valley held its breath. Angels Samael had once considered brothers and sisters now readied their weapons, no mercy in their hearts, no hesitation in their eyes. Samael had been deemed a traitor, and for the mighty soldiers of Spira, that was enough to strike him down.

Samael was fine with this... That's what he told himself. He did not need to win, he simply had to buy her enough time to flee. He would allow her to escape without bloodying her own hands. They believed her to be a monster, and he would not let them force her into proving it. Raising himself high in his monstrous serpent form, he shouted out to his opponents.

"We live in paradise! What right do we have to steal her chance to find her own? The Archangels fear what she has become. They fear the might of a fellow Celestial."

"Hold your tongue before I tear it from you, Samael," the Commander warned. "To speak against the Archangels is-"

"Freedom. That is what it is. That is what she wants. And so, I will fight so that she might have it."

"So be it."

The divine army roared; the valley's silence released in a violent exhale. Even against his own, the fallen angel fought fiercely. He couldn't afford to hold back. Not when they wouldn't grant him the same mercy. Over and over, he used his ability, pushing the limits of his magic until his body began to crack. His magic, his very life, leaked from the fractures, yet still he fought on. Even when his energy was spent, he could feel the land itself empowering him. As if Archas and Adoil, the Celestials of the earth and the heavens, were driving him forward, pushing him further and further, urging him to come undone just as they had.

But the power of the divine realm is immeasurable, and before long the angel's opponents landed a killing blow.

Samael's form shifted from serpent back to angel. As he felt the ground's embrace, he could swear he heard a voice whispering beneath the earth.

I have watched... I have witnessed... I am moved...

He felt a connection, a promise to remember his bravery and loyalty. To never forget his strength of will or his desire to be with the one he loved. A thank you, for defending their sister.

As these words accompanied the angel's repose, the demon he'd fought so hard to protect reached the base of the mountain. Despite his efforts to hide it from her, she'd realized the plan he'd hidden. She'd rushed in vain to stop him. She saw his crumbling, bloodied body lying lifeless on the ground. Emerald lights drifted from his wounds to the heavens. The crimson flooded her mind, blinding her sight and reason with bloodlust and anger boiling beyond control. The angel she'd loved was gone. They had taken him away.

T h e y   h a d   t a k e n   h i m   a w a y.

They would pay with their lives.

In a bloodthirsty frenzy, she turned against the divine once more. She pushed through injury after injury. Deep gashes from the angels' blades, scalding burns from their torches, limbs torn from her body in slashing blows; each one healed from her powers and she returned their attacks in kind. The ground fractured and split around them, just like the body of her love. She killed angel after angel. Murderer after murderer. Their blood and magic flowed from the wounds, blending with the miasma escaping from the cracks in the earth. Once the final angel fell, the demon ran to her lover's side, clutching his body in her arms.

As she let out an anguished scream, the earth burst open. The lifeless husks that had once been angels, the nearby mountain that had stood since the creation of Terrael, even the immortal demon herself were all claimed in the blast, leaving behind nothing but a perfect, spherical cavern of smoldering stone in the side of the mountain. Even centuries later, the forest that grew in the crater remained a deep red, still stained by the angel's final stand and the demon's furious vengeance.

The events of that fight were never recorded, taking place when the concept of history was not yet known to humanity. For the Archangels, it took little effort for them to cover up the tragedy. Everyone involved had perished at the hands of the angel, the demon, and the mysterious explosion.

But when we hide our mistakes, we are doomed to repeat them. Even though the humans that settled in the crater centuries later never learned the truth behind the abnormal shape of their home, the earth never forgot.

The earth never broke its promise.

Chapter 1

ONE WOULD THINK that a graveyard would be a place drowning in bitter truth. A mire of loss, despair, loneliness and regret. After all, the bodies laid to rest beneath the soil will never again smile. They'll never stroll down a beach with the people they love. They'll never greet their coworkers with cheerful stories, share a drink with friends, or lift their giggling child high into the air. And yet, in a poetic irony, the graveyards of Terrael are a place filled with life thanks to the Resting Gardens. A beautiful lie to soften the cruel truth of our mortality.

Magic is life itself, and when we die the magic that we still had within us erupts into the world. From our death, new life is born in the form of a Resting Garden around the body. A flowerbed for the deceased, bringing comfort in their eternal slumber. These gardens are often brought with the body to their grave, carefully moved and replanted by the Church or the departed's loved ones. And so, the graveyards that you would expect to be void of life instead become vibrant, natural mosaics of colors, scents and vitality.

Never was this beauty more evident than in the graveyard of Ritae Dazael. It had always been especially breathtaking.

A gem hidden away amidst the dry, dusty badlands surrounding the city. A veritable oasis of harmony between life and death. As the angel Azazel placed his hand against the hot metal of the front gate, he left the barren dust behind, and entered the beautiful garden with a rusted *crreeeeaak.*

The early hours of night were fast approaching, leaving the graveyard nearly empty, just as he'd hoped. But the angel stopped as he saw a small, hunched figure by the water pump only a short distance from the entrance. For a moment, Azazel hesitated. His foot slid back against the stone path, hoping to hide before he could be seen. Even if his wings were currently hidden by the enchanted paper tucked into his coat, here his face alone would give away his secret. But his memories held him still. He recognized the figure struggling to lift the weighted watering can wavering in her arms. Of all the people he could have encountered, he knew there was no risk in lending her a hand.

Water spilled from the top of the watering can, landing on Azazel's yellow long coat and leather boots as he extended a hand to steady it. "Here, let me help you with that," he offered, causing the elderly woman to jump.

"O-Oh! Sorry deary, I didn't hear you come close," she said, allowing the watering can to be taken away. "Thank you."

"It's no problem at all. I'm not the kind of guy that can just sit by and do nothing while a beautiful lady is struggling."

"Oh, you charmer." The older woman chuckled. A slight flush colored her cheeks. "I'm sorry I can't honestly repay the compliment. Though I'm sure you must be quite the handsome young man by the sound of your voice." Her flattery faded to mild confusion. "Though, you sound somewhat familiar. Have we met before?"

"I doubt it," the angel lied. "I'm just a Pilgrim visiting the city. Haven't been here long enough to run into anyone just yet."

"Ah, then let me be the first to welcome you to Ritae Dazael. My name is Zilla."

Azazel took Zilla's outstretched hand, easily carrying the weight of the watering can in his other. "You can call me Gregory. It's a pleasure to meet you, Miss Zilla." After placing a gentle kiss on the back of the older woman's hand, Azazel pulled back his own. "If you'd like, I can help you carry this to wherever you're heading."

"Such a kind young man. That would be lovely, thank you." Zilla grabbed her white cane, the aid leaning safely against the pump. Once she had it firmly in her hand, the two set off.

"So, you're a Pilgrim then," Zilla said, making her way down the graveyard path. A statue of an angel, weeping for those lost in the First War, watched as they passed. "Are you here for work? Or is this a personal visit?" The woman's body tensed. She receded somewhat, as if trying to pull back the words. "Oh my, that was a rather nosy question, wasn't it. You don't need to tell me if you wouldn't like to."

"It's fine," Azazel reassured. "And a bit of both now, it seems. There's someone I'm hoping to visit while in town, but I wouldn't be a very good Pilgrim if I didn't stop to help someone in need."

"So dedicated. Though, I'm afraid I don't have enough to cover a commission fee," she admitted, her steps slowing.

Gregory chuckled. "Good thing I won't be charging one then. The pleasant company of a delightful young woman is payment enough."

"Oh my," Zilla blushed once more. "If you're trying to flirt, I'm afraid I'm taken." She let out a chuckle, but her wrinkled smile fell as she recalled her husband, taken too soon. Alone as she was, her loyalty would outlive even the memory of her love.

A soft metallic song filled the air, the breeze gently dancing with the windchimes that hung from a post in the soil. Zilla stopped, turning to the modest headstone next to it. The golden, circular emblem of the Church protruded from the peak of its arched shape. "Ah, here we are," Zilla said, holding out her hands for the watering can. Azazel obliged, kneeling down to support the can from underneath until Zilla had poured enough to carry it herself. Eye-level with the grave, Azazel finally noticed the name carved into the stone.

Kuno. He'd assumed Zilla had been there to visit the grave of her husband. The name of her son was the last one he'd expected to see. A mournful veil shrouded his expression. "...How did they pass? If you don't mind me asking?"

"Oh, I don't mind, deary. It's been some time since I've had the chance to talk about him." Zilla continued to water as she spoke. "This grave is my son's. He was killed by that horrible anti-Church group. He'd only just graduated, but those brutes didn't care. They murdered him without even a shred of guilt."

The final drops of water clung to the spout of the watering can like Zilla's tears clung to the past reflected in her eyes. The grieving mother placed the tool onto the path beside her. "It was awful, what they did. Whatever *greater good* they're always shouting about can't be worth the lives of the people they kill to get it." She reached out, placing a hand on Azazel's arm. "Please be careful, deary. They were willing to kill an innocent man just because he was a Priest. I wouldn't be surprised if they were willing to kill a Pilgrim as well."

"I appreciate the concern, miss. I'll do my best to stay safe." Nostalgia washed over the angel. Memories of a young child, Kuno, eagerly bragging about his father the Inquisitor to anyone who'd listen. He'd had such a distinct giggle whenever Azazel had ruffled his hair. Had it truly been that long?

"How about you, dear? You said you were here to visit someone as well, right?"

"I am. She..." Azazel hesitated, not wanting to add to the elderly woman's woes. "She died of natural causes. Happened when she was asleep."

"I see. At least it was a peaceful passing then." Zilla wiped the tears from her eyes, closing them as she placed her hands over her heart. "Would you like to join me in praying for them? I'm sure Kuno would be happy to have the support of a fellow man of the Church up in Spira."

"Yeah, I can do that," Azazel replied. The Pilgrim folded his hands on his chest. As a pensive silence overtook them, he turned his gaze back to the tombstone. No prayer filled his mind. His words would do nothing. All he could do was hope that Zilla could be spared further pain here in Terrael.

"Thank you, Gregory," Zilla said once she finished. Her hand returned to the grip of her white cane.

"I'm happy I could help," the Pilgrim replied. "Do you need me to walk you back to the gate?"

"No, no. I know the way well enough by now. Thank you dear."

"Then I'll let you head home before it gets too late." Azazel crouched down, lifting the empty watering can off the stone path. The metal felt warm against his skin, like the lingering heat of the setting sun. "As for me, I should get going. Don't want to leave a lady waiting, after all." Parting ways with Zilla, Azazel wandered further into the graveyard, stopping at another water pump along the familiar path.

The owner of the grave Azazel had come to visit had hardly been wealthy during her life, but nevertheless, her grave stood out amidst the headstones that surrounded it. Towards the back of the graveyard, it sat atop one of the smaller hills, a short distance away from a tree rocking gently in the warm breeze. At this height, the wind carried the faint scent of metal and oil from the city, blending with the pastel sweetness of the flowers.

On the grave itself, visitors could see their reflection in the steel plaque attached to the smooth marble base. *"Adina Veramor. Her light outshone even the angels of Spira"* was embossed neatly into the metal, surrounded by a border of decorative steel ribbon. True to this claim, the polished marble of the grave's life-sized statue shined like gold in the light of the sunset. The statue depicted a woman in a long, elegant dress. She sat comfortably, leaning somewhat to the right as she smiled at anyone that came to visit. Beautiful, orange daylilies surrounded the base of the statue, drops of water clinging to their petals and leaves as Azazel gently watered each one with a loving smile.

The yellow of the sky matched the yellow of his jacket. The same jacket he'd worn nearly every day since he and Adina had first made it together. Though Azazel did have an eye for the aesthetic, Adina had been the one to design it. Yellow coloring to match the angel's bright personality. Various stripes, buttons and belts that gave the garment an almost armor-like appearance. This metallic detailing matched the sheen of Azazel's many rings, all of which currently caused light to dance across the ground with each tilt of the watering can.

The jacket drifted somewhat in a warm breeze, blowing some of the abrasive badlands' dust at Azazel's face. His long, white, loosely pulled back hair soon followed, tickling his cheeks with the end of the ponytail. Azazel quickly closed his eyes. From dust or mourning, he'd never liked how he looked when he teared up. Of course, it wouldn't be uncommon for someone to cry at a graveyard, but he didn't want Adina to see him like that.

Normally, just as Zilla had, when one finished watering the flowers around a grave they would then offer a prayer to the Archangels. You would ask that they guide the soul of the departed to a better life in Spira. Azazel wouldn't follow this tradition. He knew the Archangels had no interest in whatever prayers he had to offer. He knew that Adina wasn't waiting for him in the divine realm no matter what the humans believed, or how much he wished it were true.

"Sorry I'm late," he apologized, smiling up at the statue of Adina. "Things have been pretty hectic lately, and I slept a little too long back home after the flight." Shielding his eyes with his hand, Azazel glanced towards the sunset with a judgmental look. "Only flying at night is as much of a hassle as always. But I couldn't risk someone recognizing me in the city. You know how it is."

After ensuring no one was there to see, Azazel set down the watering can and lifted himself up onto the gravestone.

His movements were gentle and calculated as he took the utmost care to avoid trampling the surrounding flowers. "Though, I'm sure Enoch would be happy that the flight helped work off the cake I ate the other day," he continued. "Kinda his fault though, since it was a thank-you cake for both of us and he didn't want to eat more than one slice of his half." Once he was up, Azazel made himself comfortable next to the statue of Adina. "Oh! But I guess I haven't told you about him yet, have I? I swear, you two would've gotten along like a fish and water."

With the distant, energetic clattering of the city melding with the pensive rustling of leaves, Azazel told Adina the story of how he'd met Enoch in the capital. How the young Scribe had had a vision of Azazel in danger, and sought him out to warn him. How Enoch had saved his life when a demon's attack brought him to the brink of death. As well as how Enoch had faced even more demons to save his mentor Cyrus, but had to break the law to do so. Azazel, with his unending modesty, also made it quite clear that it was thanks to the angel's intervention and hard work that Enoch had managed to get a lessened sentence. Just three months of community service under the supervision of a licensed Pilgrim. It had seemed quite the unbelievable blessing to be spared from harsher consequences, but he wasn't the type to deny a given gift.

"We were told to go to Civionis for it. I guess they figured a town with so many strong Priests would be a difficult place to cause trouble in. But honestly, I approve. It's a beautiful place, and Archangels know the kid could use a break after all the craziness back in Courciel." Azazel stretched, looking towards the silhouettes of the hoodoos north of the graveyard, his mind drifting to the city far behind them where this had all begun. "Just two more weeks and he'll be heading back home... I'm a little sad to see him go, but that's just how things have to be, I suppose. I'll just focus on keeping him safe until we part ways."

The angel slowly swung his legs as they dangled off the marble base. With a pensive smile, he leaned to the side, resting his head on the statue's shoulder. "I really wish you two could've met. He sews too, actually! Not nearly as well, but he's pretty good for a kid his age." The final words seemed to strike a nerve as they escaped the angel's lips, his thoughts jumping to the darker parts of his mind. A quiet guilt crept onto his face, as gradual as the sun lowering on the horizon. Even with no one there to see him, the angel forced a smile.

"Everyone else still seems to be doing well," he continued. "I haven't gotten to check in in a bit, but I'm sure Semyaza is keeping them in line. Or at least as in line as those guys can get."

The words he meant to say stuck in his chest, the breath escaping as a sigh instead. The forced smile faded completely, Azazel's legs slowing to a halt. "Still no news of him, by the way. But I guess that's good. That was the whole point after all." With a darkened expression, Azazel's posture slowly straightened. He put some distance between himself and the statue, turning to face the graveyard instead of his marble company. "...please continue to watch over us, wherever you are."

As Azazel managed to get out the words, he noticed a light approaching on one of the distant graveyard paths. With the sun now hidden behind the rocks surrounding both the graveyard and the city, Azazel couldn't quite make out who it was holding the lantern. That didn't make much of a difference though, since when it came to the people of Ritae Dazael, he knew he always had to take extra caution.

The angel hopped off the grave, using his hidden wings to add some distance and make absolutely sure the daylilies would be safe. "Sorry. Guess I'll have to head out a little early," he said. "I'll tell you more about Civionis next time though. Enoch had a pretty awkward start to all the Pilgrim work, so I've got some hilarious stories." He returned the statue's smile with a melancholy one of his own, before taking a moment to test the direction of the warm night wind. "See you next month, Adina. Love you."

As quiet as his whispered farewell, Azazel spread his wings and took off into the night sky, leaving Adina behind, his falling tears hidden by the darkness.

Chapter 2

THOUGH THE THREE Realms are filled with many strange and wondrous locations, Civionis had always been a hidden gem. A city of secrets. A city of power. A city of loss and reunion. The mountain city was the first step in a journey that would eventually change the course of history itself. But even if Enoch's visit hadn't ended the way it had, the location would have undoubtedly still left an impact on his mind.

In the Northern Mountains, nestled inside the base of Mt. Morus, was an oddly shaped cavern. A perfect sphere carved into the ground and mountainside. The surrounding stone curled around it like two hands gently grasping the city from above and below. Despite the unstable shape, the remaining rock above had never broken or eroded. The top of the sphere kept out the rain and snow, while the mountain offered natural defenses against any forces that might wish the citizens of Civionis harm. Within the sphere itself, those who visited were transported to what could only be described as a fairytale.

Azazel and Enoch re-entered this fairytale as they closed the door to their bed and breakfast behind them. Though the sun had already risen, the mountain blocked most of the light, leaving the city in an extended night until sunset. In fact, the final hours of the day were the only time the sun lowered enough for the citizens to bask in its glow. Until this golden hour, the city got most of its light from streetlamps, firepits and one of its most beautiful natural features, the starlight stones.

Golden, luminescent clusters of adolium lay scattered throughout the top of the sphere like stars in the night sky. Though this gemstone of solidified magic would normally harm anyone exposed for too long, the size of the cavern kept the people far from its effect, instead allowing them to admire the gems' natural beauty and light from a safe distance. This is exactly what Azazel and Enoch stopped to do before heading to their work for the day.

Their bed and breakfast sat towards the edge of the cavern. As he left the warmth of the building behind, Enoch's dark, curly, asymmetrical hair swayed in a cold draft, the fresh, sweet scent of the surrounding Everred Forest still lingering in the air. He shook off the cold, just as he shook off the uneasy feeling prickling at the back of his neck. The feeling that someone was watching him. The Scribe pulled his dark brown trench-coat closer to his body, dismissing the discomfort as he had every other time. "Does it seem colder than usual today?" he asked Azazel.

The angel looked over from the metal railing he'd been leaning on. "Not that I can tell," he said. "But then again, you grew up in mid-Terrael, right? Anything up here will probably seem colder to you."

"I guess?" Enoch replied, rubbing his arms to warm them up. He joined Azazel at the railing, eyes drawn to the crystal-like waterfall pouring from the far side of the cavern. The reflection of the starlight stones sparkled in the water, turning the lake beneath them into a rippling night sky. The dark-haired Scribe held the railing a little tighter. Dreamlike as the view was, the dangerous reality still nagged at is mind. He hoped that the stone pillars holding up each district of the city would hold out. The idea of constantly being above such deep, icy water was one he'd likely never get used to.

Azazel chuckled. "I told you they fix up the stone stilts every winter. The city isn't going to sink while we're here."

"Well, *I* still will if I don't watch where I step." Enoch argued, body feeling colder just from looking at the undoubtedly freezing water.

"Better pay attention then." Azazel patted Enoch's back before heading to the bridge branching off of the residential district platform. "Let's get going. That stage isn't gonna build itself."

Enoch nodded, carefully hurrying to follow Azazel across the bridge. The two walked in silence for a while, listening to the sounds of the city. The distant rumble of the waterfall. The gentle lapping of the water against the stone pillars below. The rhythmic thuds and creaks of the wooden lifts, carrying Church workers and their families to the upper district homes built onto the side of the cavern.

The crackling of a large, grated fireplace grew louder as they approached the nearby terminal platform. Several of these circular platforms could be found throughout the city, connecting the different districts and offering a brief respite from the cold. The drifting warmth in the air brought that topic to mind just as Azazel noticed Enoch still shivering. The angel gestured to the group gathered by the fire. "I'm feeling a little chilly too, actually. Mind if we stop for a bit?"

"I wouldn't turn down a breather," Enoch replied, following Azazel over to the crowded stone bench surrounding the covered firepit. For a moment, they worried they may have nowhere to sit. After all, they were hardly the only tourists seeking solace from the cold. However, before the duo could give up, a young couple offered their seats. Azazel thanked them with a smile, Enoch did the same with a nervous wave, and then the two sat with satisfied sighs.

Even through the grate, the heat managed to warm the stone. Enoch leaned as close to the metal as he safely could, trying to shake off the chill running through his body. "So... How did your trip go, by the way?" he asked. "Did you get that paperwork delivered in time?"

Azazel hesitated for just a moment, caught off guard by the question. He'd nearly forgotten the excuse he'd given Enoch for his two-night absence. "Yeah, I got it in," he replied. "Hopefully you weren't too bored stuck in the B&B. If I was allowed to let you run around on your own I would've, but you know the situation."

"It was fine. Kinda nice to actually get some time to myself for a bit. No offense."

"None taken. I know I'm a handful." The angel sent a cheeky smile Enoch's way. He did admittedly feel a little bad lying to Enoch about where he'd gone, as well as shirking his responsibilities as Enoch's temporary caretaker for personal reasons. But the kid had dealt with enough death in his life already, and the angel didn't want to add his own losses to the boy's list of worries. All he wanted to do was help Enoch hold onto the small spark of confidence he'd found during the incident in the capital. The angel's own problems were exactly that, his own.

"Enoch! Gregory! Heeeyyy!" From the closest bridge, a short, elderly man called out. There was a rasp to his voice despite the volume, like how one would imagine an old book to sound if it could speak. Hearing their names, or in Azazel's case, the false name he used when disguised as a human, the duo turned to look. Next to the canal, 'Old man Gozan' as he was known, waved excitedly. "Good morning! You two wouldn't happen t' be free t' help carry some luggage to the station, would ya?"

Azazel waved back with an apologetic smile. "Sorry Gozan, much as I wanna help, we aren't taking street commissions today. We're helping with ceremony set up!"

Old man Gozan nodded at the reply, his waving hand returning to his decorative cane. "Ah, I see. Feels like every Pilgrim and craftsman in th' city's been roped into that. Can't be helped, I suppose." Despite the turned down request, Gozan still hobbled over, hoping to chat while the two young men were warming up. Picking up on this, Azazel sent a smile his way.

"You mentioned luggage though. Going on another vacation?"

Gozan returned the smile. "We are indeed! Me and my fella are gonna head up to Novaetis for the weekend this time around."

Enoch kept his gaze glued to the ground as he spoke, still not completely used to the social side of Pilgrim work. "It still surprises me that everyone can afford to go on monthly trips here. It sounds nice."

The old man blinked a few times in confusion. "It ain't a matter of affordin', sonny. The Church handles all that finicky financial stuff. Well, unless ya want somethin' real fancy, then ya pay the rest outta pocket."

Azazel's eyes went wide before wandering to the High Cathedral in the center of the city. "You don't say! That's awfully generous of them."

It was no secret that the city was well funded. The polished, fantastical architecture and peaceful atmosphere were enough to see that. There was a natural talent to the folks recruited from Civionis, and the families of effective Church workers were often well compensated. Going so far as to fund the travels of these family members still seemed excessively generous, but perhaps the recruits' talents truly warranted such special treatment.

"The Church takes care of us here," Gozan replied. "A healthy city is a happy city after all!" A mischievous spark lit up the man's eye, and he leaned in closer. "But if ya ask me, I think it might just be t' make room for all the tourists. The platforms can only hold so much weight, y'know?" Across the canal, a somewhat rounder man waved to Gozan. Gozan waved in return before tipping his hat to Enoch and Azazel. "Well, suppose I should go track down some other Pilgrims t' help out. Must be at least one free out there. You two take care!"

"We'll do our best!" Azazel replied. "And we should be good to help clean the windows again once recruitment is done!" The old man nodded with a smile before returning to his partner across the bridge. Once he was out of earshot, Enoch crossed his arms.

"Guess he thinks I'm an official Pilgrim then?" he said. Azazel let out a chuckle.

"Well, a Pilgrim's assistant does the same work as a Pilgrim, right? So, you can't really blame the guy. Plus, I never really did let anyone here know why you were helping me out. Well, other than the people that legally needed to know." The angel nodded to the center of town. "You warmed up yet? Don't wanna be late after having to miss a day of work, and it looks like you've gone from chilled to sweating."

Enoch rubbed the moisture off his brow, realizing the angel was right. Somewhat confused, he wiped his hand off on his dress pants before nodding, following the angel to the site of the recruitment ceremony. Gozan's misunderstanding still hummed in the back of the Scribe's mind as they walked. Him, a Pilgrim... He hadn't considered the thought until then. Unfortunately, even if Azazel had kept it to himself amidst their Civionis friends and clients, his criminal record still existed. Just like the fairytale city, once he returned to the capital his time as a Pilgrim would be nothing more than a dream.

Chapter 3

IN THE CENTER of the city, beneath the elevated High Cathedral, Church workers hurried to decorate the city's largest terminal platform. Every stone surface had been polished to a dazzling gleam. The candles in every streetlight had been replaced, with any excess wax cleaned away. Even the protective grate around the central fireplace had been removed, cleaned and repaired several times as the smoke and ash continued to soil the metal.

Just a short distance away from the warmth of the fire, Enoch and Azazel helped several other Pilgrims with assembling the stage. At that moment, Azazel's hands emitted a golden, magical light. He pressed them against the plain steel railing of the stairs, fully focused on the job at hand. The golden glow spread throughout the metal, the end curling and splitting into a spherical version of the circle and cross of the Church's emblem. Embossed tree branches appeared along the railing, wrapping around it like ivy. Once he'd finished, the angel took a step back to check over his work. Basa, a beautiful and brash young Pilgrim with blonde hair brushed to a shine, did the same as she approached from behind.

"Nice touch with the everred branches, Greg," she complimented, throwing her weight over the Pilgrim's shoulder with a swing of her arm. "I'll never get over how useful that ability of yours has been with the set up." The golden-haired Pilgrim noticed Enoch hurrying by. Having no experience or training in construction, the young Scribe had been assigned to tool and material delivery. The box of nails in his hands rattled as Basa pulled him over. "Where were you two hiding before you came out here? The extra help would've made things loads easier at last year's ceremony."

Basa ruffled Enoch's curls with a smile, like an older sister teasing her brother. Enoch receded a little out of habit, but knew there was no use fighting her affection. "So... this is a yearly thing?" he asked, gaze glued to the ground. Azazel chuckled.

"You're asking that this close to the actual day? It's been a full week, bud."

"I thought it was an anniversary or something," Enoch replied, cheeks flushed as he tried to defend himself. "Y'know, since the Church usually just recruits through schools or drafting."

"Yup. *Usually.*" Basa shrugged, resting her chin on the back of Enoch's head. The temporary Pilgrim's assistant felt warm, and if he wasn't going to make eye-contact anyways, she was going to take advantage of him not pulling away from the half-hug. "But Civionis is a special case."

"Enoch, you have those nails ye–" Hopping off the wooden stage, Thistoron, or Tory to his friends, noticed the small group. The Pilgrim had dark brown hair, shaved and cut into branching patterns on his head, revealing the dusky skin beneath. His cheerful demeanor and inability to say no to people made it feel like having a second Azazel around. However, Tory was certainly more grounded than Enoch's caretaker. Perhaps it was due to the lack of wings. "Oh! Sorry! Did I interrupt?"

"Nope! Just telling Curls here about the ceremony!" Basa replied, giving Enoch a soft squeeze for emphasis. Tory noticed Enoch's muscles tensed like a wrung cloth, raising an eyebrow at his golden-haired friend. Basa took a second before realizing what this meant, promptly and reluctantly letting Enoch go. Having rescued his young friend, Tory leaned against the stage.

"Right. I suppose the ceremony isn't too well known outside the city. Makes sense you'd have a question or two," Tory said. He smiled before looking over the terminal platform with a sparkle in his eye. Though the city was known to be one of the most beautiful in all of Terrael, the extra work really made the place more dazzling than ever. The polished platform shined as it reflected the starlight stones. The streetlamps and firelight shimmered on the lake like melted sunlight floating on its surface. Tory let out a wistful sigh.

"Civionis is the hometown of a lotta really powerful magic users in the Church. Since so many of the folks here end up big shots down the line, recruiters paid more attention. Then the old Bishop started making a big spectacle of picking the people that'd represent us, and that became the recruitment ceremony. Big heroes deserve big beginnings after all!"

"Most of the money that comes into the city is from bigshot Church workers picked in older ceremonies," Basa added. "The set up and cleaning can be overkill for sure, but if it means we get to live the good life, I don't mind decorating a stage or two."

Tory nodded in agreement, glancing over to a young man currently bent over the side of the terminal platform, kept in place by a leather safety harness attached to the railing. "We got the easy work though. I heard they're making *him* scrape off all the algae and mildew on the platform." The energetic Pilgrim let out a sigh, happy he hadn't been the one picked for the job. "Poor guy. The recruiters aren't even gonna see that, but they've got him doing it anyways. He's gonna smell like mold and lake water for weeks."

As the three and a half Pilgrims mourned the man's unfortunate fate, Morael, a gruff, older gentleman, cleared his throat from atop the stage. His Pilgrim emblem swung from his neck with the impact of his hammer. "Commander Ocudolis is here. Sure you wanna be caught chattin' on the job?"

"Th-The Commander!?" Tory nearly toppled himself over as he pushed off the stage, replacing his casual lean with painfully perfect posture. "Where?"

Gently, Azazel turned Tory's head to the edge of the terminal platform. A group of children stood gathered on the bridge, surrounding a far taller figure clad in an elegant, red cape. Though it was hard to tell with the darker tone, Tory's face went half a shade redder. He took Enoch's arm, leading him towards the stage stairs. "C'mon Enoch, let me, uh... Let me show you how to properly fasten a podium!"

"Oh, uh... Sure?" Enoch followed Tory's lead, nearly spilling the box of nails in his hands from the speed of the dark-haired Pilgrim's escape. Basa watched the two with a smile before waving to Azazel.

"Guess that's my cue to get back to work too. Wanna help me set up the ribbon, Greg?"

"Actually, I think I'm gonna take a break real quick," Azazel replied, earning a nod and farewell wave from Basa. She turned to follow the others.

"Don't hog Curls for too long! I'll need his help too in a sec!"

The sight of Enoch being so popular with the Pilgrims brought a smile to Azazel's face. Against his social nature, the angel had taken a step back to let Enoch interact with the others. However, despite knowing he should continue to help out, he didn't want to let this new opportunity go to waste. It wasn't every day he got to chat with a Circlet Guard Commander, after all! He headed towards the crowded platform bridge. As he got close, the excitement of the children surrounding the Commander pushed through the sound of the construction.

"Pleeeease Iris! Just one trick!"

"Please please please *pleeeeease!*"

Iris' dark pink ponytail bounced with the turn of her head as she smiled at the children. "Okay, okay, I'll do a few tricks." A chorus of youthful cheers filled the air until Iris raised a finger. "But if I do, you need to promise you'll keep away from the construction site. It's dangerous here right now."

The chorus of cheers faded into a mumbled agreement. Having made her deal, Iris patted one of the kids on the head. "Oh, don't be so grumpy. After all..." With a flick of her wrist, Iris pulled a gold coin out from behind the child's ear. "I have presents!"

Yet again, the atmosphere shifted. This time the playful wonder remained. Iris plucked coins out of more and more ears with the same performed surprise and resounding applause each time. She made them appear and disappear in her palm. She ate them. She sneezed them out. She rolled them over fingers and caught them mid-toss so quickly they fully vanished! Eventually the show came to an end, earning the dispersal of her audience, and applause from Azazel.

"Expertly handled!" he complimented once the children had left. Unsurprised by the Pilgrim's sudden conversation, Iris turned back to the platform with a smile. As she approached, Azazel realized that his head barely made it past the woman's chest. The Pilgrim blushed, quickly looking up to avoid being rude.

Much like the recently tidied city platform, Iris' uniform was spotless. Not a single thread frayed from the black and gold tunic. Her hand rested on the handle of her Church-issued rapier, a casual reminder that she was currently on duty despite her relaxed stance. When combined with the gentle billow of her long, red cape, the pose felt like standing in the presence of a fairytale prince. Azazel nearly felt the urge to bow.

"It isn't the first time they've tried sneaking in to see the set up," Iris replied. "Kids... Always so curious about what they think they shouldn't know."

"Can't argue with that. But they're no match for the bargaining skills of the great Iris Ocudolis, it seems."

Iris' eyes went wide, a slight flush coloring her cheeks. "Oh, you've heard of me, then?"

Azazel nodded. He hadn't met the high-standing woman until then, but he'd certainly heard of her since their arrival in the city. In fact, he'd been told that many of the jobs he and Enoch had taken during their time in Civionis would usually be handled by her when she had the time. If she was willing to help out the people of the city, on top of the numerous responsibilities she would have as the Bishop's right-hand, she was a good person in his eyes.

"I have indeed," Azazel replied with a smile. "The kids called you the magic giant. Said you make gold appear out of thin air. Seems that was more than just a rumor."

His reply earned a chuckle from the Circlet Guard. She lifted her hand from her rapier, holding it open for him to see. The angel stayed still as she reached behind his ear, miming a plucking motion before revealing another gold coin. "So that's what I'm known for these days, eh?" she said, rolling the coin over the back of her fingers. Azazel smiled at the trick.

"Among other things," he replied. "I'm happy to have a face to put to the good reputation."

"So am I." Iris tucked the coin away before shaking his hand. The movement felt somewhat stiff and formal compared to her more casual demeanor. "You're Gregory Veramor, correct?"

"The one and only! But I *am* surprised to find out a Circlet Guard Commander has heard of me." The angel fidgeted with his earing, a flush framing his smile. "Hopefully I'm not in trouble?"

"Not at all," Iris reassured. "The Judicial High Inquisitor gave a description when you and your young charge arrived. She needed the Bishop's permission for you to stay longer than the city's visiting limits."

"Oh right, I almost forgot about that," Azazel replied. "I'll admit, the concept surprised me. What's the reason? Some kind of safety thing?"

"Well, the platforms can only handle so much weight," Iris explained, lightly placing a hand on the nearby railing. "But we have quite a few people eager to experience our beautiful city. Limiting how long they can stay helps us keep under capacity while making sure everyone still gets a chance to see the sights." A loving glow filled the woman's eyes as she looked over the water; the distant platforms silhouetted by the dim, golden light; the people walking atop them with smiling faces. Silence betrayed her reverence. "Civionis is a gift. I– ...*We* want as many people as possible to experience it, even if we have to keep their visits short to give everyone a chance. I'm sure you can understand, Mr. Veramor."

"Of course. It's a breathtaking view, after all." As he so often did with first meetings, Azazel decided to up the charm, his smile shifting to a playful smirk. "Oh, and it's just Gregory to my friends. So, feel free to drop the rest if you'd like, Miss Ocudolis"

"Alright then, Gregory it is." With a flattered grin, Iris' fingers once again rested on her blade as she turned her attention back to Azazel. "And I'm glad to hear you've enjoyed your time here. You and your charge have been quite helpful since your arrival, or so I've heard. The people of this city are very dear to me, so on behalf of the Bishop and as a citizen of Civionis myself, I'd like to thank you."

"Oh, that's not necessary. That's just what Pilgrims do." Azazel dismissed the comment with a casual wave of his hand. Continuing the motion, he gestured to the workers scattered throughout the terminal platform. "You have a lot of great Pilgrims here already. We were just working hard to match their pace. The set up has been a lot more complicated than I thought it'd be though. I knew you guys go all out, but..." he trailed off, trying to find a way to say *"this feels like too much"* without coming across as rude. Before he could, Iris found it for him.

"I'll admit it can be a bit excessive, all things considered." The Circlet Guard Commander ran a finger along the polished platform railing, finding not a single speck of dust on the metal surface. "But with everything going on in the world right now, isn't it nice to pretend things are better for a day? The recruits deserve a happy start to their time with the Church. We can't change how rough the work will be, but we can give them one day in the sun." She hesitated for a moment, rethinking her words. "Or, starlight stones, rather."

Azazel chuckled, his warm smile catching the Commander's eye. She took the moment to look him over. The jacket. The jewelry. The hum of energy that had radiated off of him since the conversation started... "By the way, thanks to the special permission you were given it's been nearly three months since you two arrived, correct?" The pink-haired Commander's expression hardened like water beginning to freeze, the colder attitude hidden beneath a smile. "How are you and your assistant feeling?"

"How are we feeling?" Azazel repeated, somewhat confused. "Can't speak for Enoch, but I'm feeling fine! Hard not to when everyone is so excited for the ceremony."

"I see..." the Circlet Guard held her gaze on Azazel a moment longer, before–

"Commander Ocudolis! There you are!" Next to the Commander and Pilgrim, the city's Bishop approached in a huff. The elderly man gripped the fabric of his purple robes, doing his best not to trip at his brisk pace. Compared to Iris' regal demeanor, the city's leader looked more a fool than a prince. Nevertheless, Iris straightened her posture at his arrival.

"Yes. Sorry for wandering off, Father Paras."

"We have business to attend to at the cathedral. Have you finished checking in on the ceremony set up?"

"Of course, Father Paras. Everything appears to be progressing smoothly." Iris placed a hand on her chest, bowing in the Bishop's direction. "If you are ready to leave, I'll follow your lead."

The Bishop nodded before noticing Azazel next to them. The old man adjusted the golden circlet on his head and nodded in the Pilgrim's direction, nearly knocking the headpiece out of place again. "Thank you for your hard work, uh... sir?" The Bishop eyed Azazel, the angel's androgynous appearance admittedly causing some uncertainty. Brushing this dilemma aside, he turned with a sway of his robes, marching down the platform with a wag of his finger. "The ceremony is a very important event! Take pride in the work you're doing to bring prosperity to our beautiful city!"

As is the custom when parting ways with a Bishop, Azazel repeated Iris' earlier bow, along with a two-hand salute, crossing his wrists to form wings with his fingers. Unfortunately, the influential man was already too far to notice the formality. Still close enough to see, Iris replied with a small farewell nod before following her boss, the two boarding the wooden lift leading to the High Cathedral above.

Azazel tracked their movement, fascinated by the mechanisms of the lift, as well as the majesty of the cathedral. The building's base and buttresses sprouted from the stone like a statue from its pedestal. The darkened stilts supporting the upper platform gave the illusion that the cathedral was floating in the air. Once again, Azazel found himself mesmerized by the city's beauty. However, a sudden panic pulled him from this fairytale.

"Curls? Hey, Enoch! You okay?" Basa's voice broke through the sounds of the lift and construction. Azazel turned just in time to see Enoch collapse to the ground, caught by Morael just before impact. With a quick slide of his foot, Tory stopped the spool of ribbon Enoch had dropped before it could roll right off the edge of the stage.

"What happened?"

"I dunno! He just passed out outta nowhere!"

"How long has the kid been here, again? A month?"

"N-No, longer than that I think."

"Damn. He must've been hidin' symptoms."

For a moment, it felt as though the terminal platform had shattered beneath Azazel's feet. His stomach sank as he rushed forward, a terrifying memory shooting through his mind and heart, causing both to race. *Healer... We need to get him to a Healer!* He leapt onto the stage, sliding to a halt as he knelt down and took Enoch from Morael.

"Hey tough guy, stay with me! I promised Cyrus I'd get you home safe and sound!" Feverish heat radiated off of the Scribe's body. Sweat dripped down his face. A chill ran down Azazel's spine.

When had Enoch gotten so sick?

How had he not noticed?

Chapter 4

THE HEALER QUIETLY closed the door to the examination room. The repetitive tapping of Azazel's pacing came to a halt as the angel swiftly turned to face her. "How is he? Is he okay? He's dying, isn't he? Please tell me he's not dying!"

Surprised by the sudden panicked onslaught, the Healer leaned away before letting out a light chuckle. "The kid's fine, Mr. Veramor," she reassured. "It's likely just a case of everred fever."

"Everred fever?" Azazel's head tilted in confusion. He knew that everred was the name of the uniquely crimson trees that grew around Civionis, but he hadn't heard of them causing illness. "I could've sworn it was magical overflow. Figured the stones must've caused it."

The Healer shook her head. "The symptoms are similar, so I can't blame you for thinking that. But I promise the stones are far enough to be safe. We wouldn't be living here if they weren't."

"I see..." Azazel took a breath, releasing the anxiety from his body and voice. "Right, that makes sense. But then, what's everred fever?"

"It's an illness unique to this part of north Terrael. Researchers think it's caused by something in the everred trees, hence the name. But as long as you distance yourself from them time to time, it's harmless." The Healer gently moved the too loud Pilgrim away from the examination room. Enoch needed rest, and volume control clearly wasn't the man's strong suit. "Different people have different tolerances to it, so I guess he just reached his limit."

Azazel raised an eyebrow. *I've been here just as long, but I haven't felt odd at all. Is my tolerance higher because I'm an angel? Or was it the trip to Ritae Dazael that helped?* The Pilgrim brushed these theories aside for now. All that mattered was that Enoch wasn't suffering from something worse. Relief washed over him, the wave not quite strong enough to remove the remnants of anxiety lingering in his stomach.

"If the forest is making people sick, why risk living so close to it?"

"Well, it's a beautiful city, and the free vacations are definitely nice," the Healer answered with a chuckle. "But honestly, with how easy it is to treat it, and how peaceful it is to live here, most folks just think it's worth the risk."

Azazel fidgeted with his earring. "Taking a risk for a comfortable life, huh? Well, no one in town ever even mentioned it."

"We only get the occasional case nowadays, thanks to the limits on how long folks can stay. I find that a lot of the locals treat it the same as you'd treat a cold, when they even remember it's a thing at all." As she began opening the door to the reception area the Healer glanced back to Enoch's room. "Actually, people rarely ever reach the point your friend is at. You two really should have come in sooner."

Noticing the immediate panic in Azazel's face at her words, the Healer gave his shoulder a reassuring pat. "But like I said, it's an easy fix. Just take him out of town for a day or two and he'll be back to normal in no time. He should be able to head out in an hour or so once he's rested."

"Right. Thank you." Azazel let out a heavy sigh, releasing the tension growing in his chest. At the behest of the Healer, he returned to the reception area. *Doesn't feel right to leave him behind like this, but I guess I don't have much of a choice.* Heading to the exit, he began to plan his next move. *Enoch was supposed to stay here the full three months, but I'm sure the Judicial High Inquisitor will understand if we leave early for the sake of his health. Plus, Cyrus would never forgive me if something happened to him on my watch.*

Outside of the House of Healing, a cold wind carried the smoky scent of a nearby fire pit. Flickering embers drifted past the starlight stones before their warmth faded in the chilled air. Azazel took a moment, leaning against the platform railing as he let his remaining anxieties fade with them. He was glad that Enoch's condition could be remedied so easily, but it was a shame they had to cut their time in Civionis short. He'd seen the way Enoch's eyes had sparkled at the view each morning. That youthful sense of wonder warmed the angel's heart. The young Scribe had even started getting along with the locals. Or as close as he could get with his current lack of social skills. A little longer and maybe he would have actually been able to call the rest of them friends...

Azazel lightly tapped the railing, sending a judgemental glare towards the Everred Forest, as if intimidating it could halt the trees effects on his charge. On this particular platform, only a single bridge stood between him and the edge of the city. As a group of three hikers reached it, he quickly wiped the glare from his face, not wanting them to think his negativity was directed at them. However, as he looked a little longer, it seemed their frantic waving *was* intended for him. The Pilgrim stood up straight, straining to get a better view of the trio. He saw the cause of their strife before he heard their cries for help.

With the usually blue uniform stained red, it had been difficult to recognize, but Azazel now noticed the familiar black and gold helmet held by the shorter of the two hikers. The man supported on the other's shoulder was no civilian, he was a Priest.

"Heeeyyy! Somebody! Please! This man needs help!" The wind nearly swallowed the young woman's voice. Azazel rushed down the bridge, meeting them halfway across. Once he was close, he showed them the Pilgrim emblem hanging around his neck. The shorter girl broke down at the sight, tears of panic and relief mixing on her cheeks now that they'd finally found someone that could help.

The two teens were shaking, their clothes and hands red as the forest behind them. Quickly looking them over, Azazel couldn't see any obvious injuries on either of them. The ragged, middle-aged Priest was another matter. He clung to life as weakly as he clung to the taller girl's shoulder, gashes bordered in blood covering his uniform. His gruff face looked as pale as the ash drifting through the city air, a slight gleam to it from the sweat coating his skin. Nearly hidden behind his large, scruffy beard, his mouth hung open. Weakened breaths managed to push through, far fainter than ideal.

The shorter girl spoke through heavy sobs. "We... We found him out in the forest. He was– We were just hiking,

I– I don't know what happened. There was so much blood, I... I..." Her fingers gripped the helmet so tightly it felt like it could crack. The tears fell harder after Azazel placed a hand on her arm.

"Hey, it's okay, it's okay," Azazel gently reassured. "Deep breaths, in and out. You're okay. Everything's okay." As the teen tried to slow her breathing, Azazel gave her arm a comforting squeeze. "There you go. You two did good, but I can take him from here. It's gonna be okay."

Noting the taller girl's shaking hands, Azazel took the Priest from her, supporting the man on his own shoulder. Once they were free, the taller hiker hid her hands beneath her arms, not wanting to see the frightening color staining her fingers. Though tears were stinging her eyes as well, for the moment she was holding things together far better than her friend. Azazel began heading back towards the city, glancing in the taller girl's direction. "I'll help you get him to the House of Healing. Could you run ahead and tell the Healers we're coming?"

"Y-Yeah. I can do that." The taller hiker ran off, grateful for the chance to leave the gruesome sight behind. The shorter girl clung to Azazel's jacket sleeve with both hands, too afraid to trust her own feet. Azazel lifted his arm a little to make it easier for her.

"What's your name?" he asked.

"...Melody," the hiker replied softly.

"That's a beautiful name, Melody. You and your friend did a good thing. We're gonna get this guy some help and then he'll be good as new!"

The teen nodded, the movement barely discernable from her own shaking. "What's yours?" she asked, looking for any way to drown out the wheezing breaths of the Priest.

"Gregory."

"R-Right. Thank you, Mr. Gregory," Melody whimpered.

"...*Veramor*..." The sudden, strained voice of the Priest caused Melody to scream. She cowered away from the dying man, crouching at the edge of the bridge. Azazel couldn't quite make out her muttered words of fear between the sobs that had returned with a vengeance. Even if he could, his attention had been fully claimed by the man now glaring at the ground with a rage burning like a torch in the wind. The man that somehow knew who he was.

"He... said that name..." the Priest wheezed. Blood gushed out of his wounds from the effort. Though Azazel wanted to tell him to stop, he knew it would make little difference at this point. Maybe he could at least get some information, some clues to lead him to the man's attacker.

"Who did this to you? Who said my name?"

"He's looking for you... Man in... metal mask..." With the last of his strength, the Priest grabbed Azazel's collar, his grasp as weakened as his voice. *"This is... your... fault..."*

Azazel's balance lurched as the Priest's weight fully fell into him. The man's words, broken and weak as they were, echoed so loudly in the angel's mind that every other sound found itself swallowed by the sinking feeling of recollection.

A man in a metal mask...

A man looking for him...

A man willing to kill to find him...

Panic replaced the Priest's grip, reaching further in, clutching the angel's heart.

This was his fault...

His fault...

Once again, there was blood on his hands.

Chapter 5

WHAT IS THE purpose of a lie? Do we use them to protect ourselves? To protect others? To find hope in a hopeless situation? Is a lie a shield to defend us from the gnawing fangs of painful truths? Or is it a weapon we use to hurt others when the pain we carry overflows into our very words?

The common belief is that lies are inherently wrong. Dishonest children are scolded for hiding the truth from their parents. Deceitful companions are accused of betrayal and are cut off from their friends. Those in power lose the trust of the people for failing to keep their word. But if lies are truly a language of pure evil, then why is it we have all told one at some point in our lives?

"I'm fine, I promise."

"It was like this when I found it."

"It isn't you, it's me."

"I love you."

"I'm doing this for your own good…"

Some lies are told to spare another from pain. Some lies with harmful repercussions were told with good intention. Some lies are simply the result of someone believing them to be the truth. And so, why is it that lies are vilified? That one dishonesty is a kindness while another is a betrayal?

As Azazel closed Enoch's suitcase, the luggage straining to contain everything within it, he struggled to choose between the truth and a lie.

The Priest's words... The description of his attacker... This wasn't the first time Azazel had been warned of a man in a metal mask. A little over two months prior, Enoch had told Azazel that a figure in a metal mask would attempt to ambush and kill him, losing their own life in the process. Normally, the words of a stranger approaching and claiming such a thing would be dismissed as the insane ramblings of a madman, but Enoch's prediction held more weight than that of the average person. After all, as Azazel had learned back then, Enoch was a Seer.

Though a Seer's visions are linked to magic, they don't quite fall under the nine categories used to define various magic abilities. This is because unlike an ability, which is powered by an individual's own magic, a Seer's visions come from a unique sensitivity to the magic flowing through the world. Using this connection, a Seer can gain insights and glimpses into potential futures or unknown information. Some Seers simply have strong intuition when it comes to decision making, while others may be able to receive answers to specific questions under the right circumstances. Using this information, Seers can alter the course of fate itself, leading many into influential and powerful positions, at times against their will.

Enoch's visions came to him in the form of silent dreams. He could watch the future play out before his very eyes, with figures unknown to him appearing as silhouettes. Though being able to visibly see the future unfold was an enviable ability even among Seers, Enoch had kept his gift suppressed and hidden for most of his life. Nevertheless, unique circumstances at the time had led to his vision of the masked attacker. The same attacker that had likely assaulted the Priest now fighting for his life in the House of Healing.

If the masked killer was targeting people that potentially knew Azazel, then Enoch was in danger. This was of course in addition to the everred fever already trying to drag him to an early grave. There was no doubt in the angel's mind that Enoch had to leave the city. His health and safety depended on it. But... *If the killer sees him with me, will that make him a target?* Azazel wondered, fidgeting with his earing as he thought. *I know I'm supposed to keep an eye on him, but that would do more harm than good here...*

The angel stood, beginning to pace about the small room. The path wandered as much as his thoughts. *I can't tell him the masked killer is here. Absolutely not,* he decided. *After what he did in the capital, I don't think Enoch would just hop on a train and leave if he knew the situation.* Azazel sighed, sitting next to Enoch's suitcase on the bed. *Maybe I'm overestimating how much he'd care though. I'm not exactly Cyrus, after all. But if there's even a chance, I can't risk it. I can't let Enoch put himself in harm's way.*

"He needs to leave alone..." he whispered. "...for his own good."

Creeeeeaaaaak. The hinges of the door to their humble little room announced Enoch's return, and sent Azazel's heart into his throat. The Scribe placed his key back in his jacket pocket as he shut the door with repeated protest from the metal fastens.

"I'm back. Sorry for the trouble," Enoch said. "The Healer said I just need to–" he froze, noticing his already packed suitcase on his bed, and the train ticket next to it. "Ah. I guess she told you the same thing then."

"Yeah, you're all packed and ready to go!" Azazel replied with a smile, lightly patting the suitcase with his hand. The lid popped open with a *click!* "Ah, whoops!" The angel scrambled to get it shut again. "Sorry, I was planning to head back and pick you up, but... I must've lost track of time."

While Azazel fretted over his poor packing skills, Enoch scanned the apartment from the door. Aside from the wooden furniture that had been provided by their host, his side of the room was now bare. Azazel's side, on the other hand, was as busy as always. The angel's make-up and hairbrush still sat haphazardly atop the dresser. His jacket still laid on the side of the bed where Azazel always carefully placed it upon his return. Though, the garment seemed somewhat damp, leaving an unfortunate, jacket-shaped puddle on the sheets. The empty suitcase that had stubbed both his and Azazel's toes on several occasions still poked out from beneath the angel's bed, eager to add another tally to the injury count. Taking all this in, Enoch turned back to Azazel, the Pilgrim successfully getting the Scribe's suitcase to latch again.

"Do you want some help packing your own stuff?" he asked. Azazel's moment of triumph faded into a meek uncertainty at the question. He shrugged, still staring at the suitcase despite having won his battle with it.

"Actually, I'm not coming with you. Sorry," he replied. "I only bought one ticket for the train today. I... can't leave before the stage is set up, right? Wouldn't be fair to leave more work for the others."

Enoch raised an eyebrow at this, an expression Azazel was all too familiar with at this point. "I mean, that's true, I guess. But aren't you supposed to make sure I complete my community service?"

"Don't worry, I wrote a letter explaining the situation. It should make sure no one gives you any trouble over this. Just don't break the seal before you deliver it." The angel patted the suitcase again, immediately regretting it as another *click* replied in turn. Azazel sighed. "Oh, c'mon you stubborn little—"

"Azazel, is there something going on?" Enoch asked. "I mean, I know the Healer said I have to leave, but packing my stuff for me and buying the first ticket out of here is a bit of an overreaction, don't you think?" Enoch walked over, casually turning the suitcase away from the angel. Pulling the lid to the side a little, he closed it once again with a heavier click than before, lightly patting the top once it properly locked. Having removed the distraction, he turned to his friend once again. "What aren't you telling me?"

Admittedly, the ease at which Enoch fixed the suitcase caused Azazel's eye to twitch, but he quickly brushed the embarrassment aside. It seemed he and Enoch might have spent a little too much time together if he was already this good at reading him. Not that he'd been doing all that great a job at hiding his anxiety. The angel sighed.

"Look, I just freaked out a bit when I saw how sick you were," he replied. "The Healer said people don't usually reach that point." Azazel finally looked to Enoch. The man's crossed arms and stern expression were reminiscent of a parent scolding a misbehaving child. "But on the topic of not telling people things... How long were you planning on hiding your symptoms from me?"

With the turn in the conversation, Enoch turned himself, sitting on the side of the bed. "Not long. I just didn't feel like it was worth mentioning." The Scribe let out a sigh, his lingering exhaustion hitting harder now that it was the topic of their discussion. "I'll admit that I should've brought it up sooner though. I didn't think it would get that bad so quickly.

"And that's why I'm sending you home so soon, even if I can't join you just yet," Azazel said, his own expression softening somewhat at Enoch's reply. "I just have to clean up some loose ends here before I can. Paperwork and such. You know how it is."

"Right." Enoch let out a soft chuckle, followed by a poorly hidden cough. "Y'know, I didn't expect Pilgrim work to involve so much paper. Feels like I'm back in the library sometimes."

"Oh yeah?" Azazel did his best to ignore the cough Enoch had tried to conceal. With a smile of his own, he gave the Scribe's hair an affectionate ruffle. His fingers nearly getting caught in the tangled curls. "Maybe I'll get you to handle the forms when I'm back in Courciel then." Enoch half-heartedly pushed the Pilgrim's hand away before standing up with a slight sway.

"Yeah, I don't think that's legal," he argued, another small chuckle accompanying the words. "I'm not a Pilgrim after all." He glanced down at the train ticket still sitting next to the suitcase. While not close enough to cause panic, the departure time was still sooner than ideal. If he didn't want to strain himself, Enoch knew he should probably start heading to the station. With a slight sigh, he picked up the ticket, gently waving it in the air. "I wouldn't mind having the Pilgrim discount on travel fees though." Tucking the ticket into his pocket, Enoch lifted his suitcase. His arms shook somewhat from fatigue, but he pushed through it. "Time to get going then?"

"Yep!"

Enoch headed to the door, hesitating as Azazel didn't move to follow. In fact, the angel seemed far more focused on the room than the Scribe's departure. He lingered a moment longer, before reluctantly turning to the door. If Azazel was no longer monitoring him, then it seemed his job, as well as their time together, was done. That truth swirled uncomfortably in the Scribe's stomach.

"See you in Courciel then, I guess."

"I'll try to not make you wait too long," Azazel promised with a smile, watching as Enoch made his way back to the door. "And besides, you probably want a little more alone time anyways. I'm sure you could use a break from me by now."

Once again, Enoch hesitated. His feet stuck on the floor, and his words stuck in his chest. The Scribe quickly recovered, pulling the door aside with his foot once he got it open. "Yeah, there'll be more than enough of that back home, I suppose." he said quietly.

The door swung shut before the angel could reply. Glancing down, Azazel noticed Enoch's key sitting on the bed where the ticket had been before. With the Scribe now on his way to the safety of the train, Azazel allowed his mask to slip, falling onto the bed with a heavy, muted *thump*.

"Sorry, tough guy," he said softly. "It's for your own good, I swear."

Chapter 6

HOLDING ONTO the railing at the edge of the platform, Enoch contemplated the dream that surrounded him. The crystalline waterfall in the distance; the golden starlight stones above, their lights reflected in the pitch-black water of the lake. The residential district platform stood above the night sky, the starlight stones rippling with the water close enough to reach out and touch. Soon, he would board the train and leave it all behind him. He would return to the ground, the sky too far to reach once again.

Soon, he would have to wake up.

It began to sink in as he looked to the site of the recruitment ceremony. In the center of the city, the light of the firepit danced across the base of the High Cathedral above. He could almost hear the others laughing and chatting cheerfully as they worked. Tory, Basa, Morael... Enoch hardly needed grand fanfare or some sort of farewell celebration, but it still would have been nice to say goodbye to everyone. It was a strange feeling, to have people in his life to say goodbye to again.

The Scribe did his best to shake off the sentimental thoughts. *They were just coworkers...* he lied. *It's time to go back to my old job. Back to the library, and the book deliveries... and the silence...* His eyes stung a moment, but he blinked away the dull discomfort. He couldn't think like that anymore. He had to look for the positives. *I'll also get to spend more time with Cyrus! It shouldn't be as awkward after what happened, hopefully... That'll be nice, right?*

Enoch knew from the start that all of this had been temporary, so there was no reason to grasp at an ending dream. In fact, this was probably for the best. Fates could change so quickly. It would be better to leave before the memories could turn bitter; he knew better than most how dangerous a dream could be. And perhaps once he left, the prickling paranoia at the back of his neck could be left behind as well. Beautiful as it was, something about Civionis felt unnerving. Once again, he wondered if he was being watched. Once again, he found no eyes turned his way.

Still though, Enoch's stomach twisted, fighting his body on which way to go. With a deep breath, the Scribe did his best to settle himself. Perhaps, his hesitation was simply anxiety. He would be boarding a train bound for the capital, after all. But he was old enough to overcome that fear now, even if he had to do it alone this time. "It's fine. He just needs to wrap up some loose ends," Enoch reassured softly. The spoken words failed to bring him peace of mind. "If he didn't, he'd be out here for sure. You know that."

At the thought of his mentor and friend, he turned back to the bed and breakfast, still a short distance away. A figure caught his attention, standing on the path by the entrance. Their dark-grey, mottled cloak blended with the cavern shadows, making it hard to focus on them. This didn't matter much though, since Enoch was more interested in the door to the building that had been his home for nearly three months. A door that still hadn't opened since Enoch had closed it behind him. It seemed Azazel really wasn't going to join him on his walk to the station. His twisting stomach sank, and the Scribe followed, leaning down to grab his suitcase.

It was time to wake up.

As his finger brushed against the handle of his luggage, Enoch froze. A metallic glint glimmered at the edge of his vision. Twice, he looked its way, wanting to make sure he hadn't imagined it. But there was no mistaking the familiar sight within the cloaked figure's hood.

In an instant, Enoch found himself within a reawakened nightmare. It had been over two months, but the memories of his vision came flooding back. A figure of crimson flame attempting to kill Azazel. The spiked pillars of fire emerging from the ground. Azazel's sword slipping, the blade driving straight through the attacker's stomach. He remembered the firelight burning through the figure's incandescent metal mask; the same angular mask now surrounded by a dark hood and cloak rather than crimson flame.

Is it them? Enoch wondered. *The mask matches, but maybe it's a uniform, like with the Soldiers of Lilith.* His gaze darted to the window of his and Azazel's room, the lights within still lit. Even if it wasn't the masked attacker from his vision, with Azazel's life on the line, as well as the life of the attacker himself, Enoch didn't have the luxury of dismissing this as coincidence.

Enoch silently watched the masked figure, his mind and gaze focusing as intently as his fever would allow. Neither of them had moved an inch since Enoch had first seen them. Instead, the stranger simply stared at the building in front of them, as if their feet had been fastened to the platform.

From the shape of the cloak, Enoch assumed their arms were crossed. The fabric shifted somewhat, a quick, rhythmic bounce as the stranger tapped their finger. Was it in frustration? Anticipation? A nervous tick? For nearly a minute, the scene remained frozen this way. Then, the stranger took a single step. Enoch tensed.

I should do something, right? If the vision was showing this moment... If they get inside to Azazel, both of them could be in danger! The Seer's heart pounded in his chest. Could the stranger hear it? *What's the best thing to do? Should I confront them? Shout and warn Azazel? Or could I try talking to them? Maybe they'd only be murder-y if it's Azazel.*

The stranger stopped. The Scribe held his breath, terrified that they might have heard his thoughts. Like a deer caught in the gaze of a hunter, Enoch stayed as still as he could. He stared as the stranger uncrossed their arms, a hesitation lurking within the shadows of the cloak.

A tension built in Enoch's chest, and dread filled his mind as he realized it wasn't solely out of fear. Holding his breath had strained his lungs, and the everred fever decided to fight back with a building discomfort. He could feel the cough crawling its way out of his lungs, claws climbing up his throat. How would the potentially murderous stranger react if they were startled? Enoch didn't want to find out.

The masked figure took another half step towards the building. The cough climbed higher and higher. *Stop. Stop!* Enoch begged, and then, with a force that rattled Enoch's ribs, the violent barrage of coughs escaped.

Instantly, the stranger glanced towards the platform's edge. They reached a hand into their cloak, readying something inside. When they saw nothing but the sickly, coughing Scribe, the stranger released the hidden weapon and took a step back.

"H-Hold on!" Enoch struggled to say. Unfortunately, his insistence worked against him. The masked figure turned and fled down the street. Once he'd recovered, much to his own surprise, Enoch followed.

The Scribe's mind pushed through the feverish haze to question his course of action. Aside from the fact that they were going to attack Azazel with lethal intent, Enoch knew absolutely nothing about this person. He was in over his head, but knowing what might happen if he didn't intervene, he couldn't bring himself to just board the train and run away. It was risky, yes, but if he could learn more information, perhaps he could stop the fight from happening in the first place. This would likely be his only chance to even try, so he couldn't afford to wait.

Enoch's breath fogged in the air. He could feel his heartbeat reverberating through his body, the quick, repetitive beat begging him to abandon his chase, to rest and let it recover. He wondered if it would be best to tell Azazel first. *Do I have time to stop and warn him?* The ever-shrinking silhouette of the masked figure gave him his answer. Even if he did choose to let the figure get away, to warn Azazel instead of giving chase, nothing would change. The attacker would still be a stranger. Their motive would still be unknown. The ambush could still come at any time. If he wanted to change the future he'd seen, he needed to know who he was dealing with, even if that meant putting himself in danger. Scared, yet intent on solving this mystery, he continued to run. He ran through the residential district. He ran past the curious and concerned expressions of the people watching in the street. He ran until the sweet smell of the Everred Forest filled his straining, struggling lungs.

The surrounding forest sat just a short distance away now. A narrow bridge connected the elevated platform to the solid soil. A blur of mottled gray crossed the far end of the narrow, pedestrian path, rushing into the cover of the treeline. Enoch's chase slowed as he reached the edge of the city. The forest sounded so quiet, so isolated. His hand rested on the metal railing as he watched the distance between him and his mark grow.

Should I go? Following him alone into the forest doesn't seem like the smartest thing to do...

Enoch thought of the alternative. Turning back to warn Azazel. Being ushered out the door, and sent away on the first train out of the city. Back to the capital. Back to how things were. Back to the life beyond the dream.

Tap Tap Tap Tap Tap Crunch Crunch Crunch... The stone of the bridge ended. The forest soil crumbled under his feet. Enoch had spent enough of his life running from dangerous dreams.

He wasn't going to wake up just yet.

Chapter 7

RATHER THAN THE earthen, emerald shade one would expect from an evergreen, the trees surrounding Civionis were instead a rich crimson hue. The aptly named Everred Forest only grew within and around the canyon. Its perpetual autumn drew many tourists eager to explore the hidden jewel of the Northern Mountains.

All kinds of unique animals lived beneath the arching canopies. Deer with jewel-toned fur, birds with horns sprouting from their heads, winged fish swimming through not only the small, sparkling streams, but the swirling mists above them as well. These uncommon creatures were anything but to the people of Civionis.

A small family of yellow-furred foxes scuttled away in a panic as Enoch stumbled by. From a safe distance, they turned to watch the visitor, a curious sparkle in their small beady eyes. Enoch's own eyes had nearly glazed over. The everred fever had already drained much of his energy, and his sprint had slowed to more of a feverish, drunken stagger. He'd long since lost track of the masked figure. Between his blurred vision, the figure's camouflaged cloak, and his own exhaustion, he hadn't stood a chance at catching up. Now, the Scribe simply wished to regain his bearings, hoping to stumble his way back to the city safely. After all, trying to find the masked man now would be as difficult as finding the Progenitor Garden in the desert. He'd tried his best, but it seemed he wasn't quick enough.

One would think getting back to Civionis would be as simple as turning around, but with his head spinning as wildly as it was, Enoch felt he'd already done this far too many times. Luck seemed to be on his side though as the trees thinned ahead of him. Excited, he rushed forward as quickly as his tired legs would carry him, only to have his hope pulled out from underfoot. The edge of the forest turned out to be nothing more than a small clearing.

The crunch of the ashen grass beneath him shifted into smooth stone. The steep rock of Mount Morus created an impassable wall on the other side. Flickering shadow and sun painted the ground, most of the light blocked by the mountain and trees. But compared to the perpetual night Enoch had lived in for over two months, he might as well have been standing in a snowfield at noon.

With a sigh, Enoch entered the clearing. He took a moment to sit on one of the flatter rock clusters and fill his struggling lungs with the sweet-scented air. His short, soft laugh broke the silence.

How did I think this would go? Surviving the attack in Courciel doesn't mean I magically got more stamina. Wanting to help Azazel doesn't make me strong enough to fight someone that may be a murderer. And running right into the forest that's making me sick was a stupid thing to do. Regardless of his good intentions, strength of will wouldn't make his actions any less foolish. Blaming his condition for the lapse in common sense, Enoch tried to rein rationality back to the forefront of his mind. He still had to get back to Civionis.

He pushed through the fatigue chaining his feet, stumbling over to the sheer stone of Mt. Morus. From the clearing, he could hear the distant rumble of the waterfall. All he had to do was follow the base of the mountain, and eventually he'd find the luminescent cavern city. The young Scribe had no idea if his energy could hold out that long, but what choice did he have? Before he could take a single step forward though, a young man's sullen yet assertive voice interrupted the steady song of the forest.

"You wanna tell me who you are, and why you chased me all the way out here?"

Enoch turned around, finding himself face to face with the masked stranger. His vision continued to spin even after his body stopped, staggering the young Scribe. The stranger took a step back, the unexpected movement startling him as well. Within his cloak, a silver blade slipped into his hand. Even after Enoch recovered, the figure remained alert, his deep red eyes watching with an unbreaking stare behind the mask.

"I–" The Scribe's mind skipped like a carriage wheel caught in cobblestone. *When did he start following me instead? And how did he get so close without me hearing?* His gaze darted down to where he'd seen a flash of steel in the stranger's hand, the hand now empty. There were no claws at the tips of his fingers, no jewel-toned color in his skin. Enoch could only assume this meant he was human. The thought eased his anxiety, if only a little. But he would need to know much more if he wanted to discover the man's identity.

Slowly, Enoch held his hands up in front of him, showing he had no ill intent. The stranger watched the Scribe silently as he moved. A quiet scoff sounded from within the mask. "You don't look like you're with the Church," he said, eyeing Enoch from not nearly far enough away. "And I don't recognize your face. So, why are you looking at me like you know me?"

"I don't."

"So, chasing folks you've never met before is just a fun hobby of yours?"

Enoch couldn't move, his mind fully focused on finding a response. He couldn't exactly say *"Oh! I saw in a dream that you're going to die trying to murder my friend!"* without making the situation far worse, or far more complicated. The stranger waited for Enoch to speak, letting out a sigh when the silence failed to meet his expectations.

"You look *awful* by the way." Enoch tensed as the stranger lightly swatted one of the curls dangling in front of the Scribe's face. He began to circle, lightly poking and prodding, assessing the potential opponent. A defensive tenseness permeated the outwardly casual demeanor. "You're clearly sick, so what made you think you could do whatever you followed me out here to do? Stupidity? Delusion?"

"Hope, actually," Enoch muttered. The masked figure stopped in his tracks. Both Enoch answering, and the answer itself, seemed to catch his attention. Realizing he'd said that out loud, Enoch couldn't stop his own panicked ramblings. "But you're right. I... I lost track of you so quickly, so maybe I am just stupid. I shouldn't have come out here in the first place." The words had just slipped out, Enoch's insecurities worming their way from his mind to his tongue.

The Scribe felt a tightness in his chest, forcing himself to stop talking.

The stranger took a moment. The crimson eyes beneath the mask trailed Enoch's. Subtle as it was, he could see them starting to water. Was he really that scared? No, that didn't seem to be it. The Scribe was clearly afraid, but those tears carried something else entirely. Frustration? Or maybe disappointment?

"Well, it took guts either way, so maybe that's why I feel like giving you a chance to explain instead of kicking your ass right here." Crossing his arms, the stranger took a step back. His small reassurance felt empty as it rolled off his tongue. "But you better not let that chance go to waste. I'm not generous enough to give you more than one."

"R-Right..." Slowly, Enoch's fingers clasped his wrist. "I... After I coughed, I saw you run. So, I thought that maybe..." The Scribe's gaze lowered, seeking solace in the grey-toned grass. "If you were running, maybe you were doing something you shouldn't be, so... I chased you."

The world swayed as the stranger pulled Enoch forward, the blade in his hand brushing against the Scribe's throat. The cool metal fogged from the heat. "Don't lie to me," the young man spat. "I warned you that you only get one chance."

The sudden force threw all sensible thoughts from Enoch's mind. He found himself back at the cathedral in Courciel, pinned by the bloodthirsty form of his mentor Cyrus. Struck by the gargantuan fists of the Priest Asir. Threatened by the deadly points of Furcus' trident. Panicked, he tried to pull away, too weak to escape the stranger's grip. His heartbeat echoed through his skull like an off-tempo drum. His hands trembled. The air felt thinner. A sharp pain, like a jab from a needle, pressed into his neck, a trickle of blood running down the edge of the stranger's blade.

The masked man himself held a second longer before tossing the Scribe away. He'd seen that expression before. He'd seen how people looked when panic and fear drowned out their own minds. The Scribe was somewhere else. He'd get nothing from him in this state.

"Could you be any more useless?" The stranger moved away, leaning on the cluster of rocks at the base of the mountain. "Guess I'll just have to figure it out myself." Once he'd stopped, he pulled a familiar paper out from within his cloak. The eyes of the mask almost seemed to narrow as his head tilted downward to get a closer look. Had Enoch been capable of perceiving his surroundings in the midst of his panic, he would recognize this paper as the train ticket Azazel had bought earlier that day. The stranger had plucked it from his pocket while poking and prodding before, almost amused by how unperceptive his target was.

The young man skimmed the contents of the ticket for useful information, allowing Enoch a moment to collect himself on the forest floor. The Scribe was doing his best to slow his breathing, nails digging into his arm as he crawled away. Muttered reassurances filled the clearing, almost too soft to understand.

"A train ticket, huh?" the stranger asked, despite knowing Enoch wouldn't respond. "Guess I can at least get your na–" Like he'd seen a ghost, the figure froze. The paper ticket creased in his hand. It couldn't be. Fate wouldn't be so kind. Or perhaps, so cruel. And yet there it was, printed clear as day in front of him. With a slow, intense glare, he turned to Enoch.

"This ticket," he growled. "Did you buy it?"

The Scribe was currently clutching his chest, having managed to ground himself somewhat in the midst of the panic attack now that the stranger had walked away. Still sitting in the dirt, he turned towards the masked man. "Huh? N-No, I... I didn't." The sudden intensity radiating from the young man felt like a wall pushing him back, while the fury in the figure's eyes demanded he keep still. Though Enoch couldn't tell if it was real or not, it felt as though the ground itself shook in fear. At the Scribe's response, the stranger looked between him and the ticket, his thoughts like leaves caught in a hurricane. After an eternity in his mind, and seconds in reality, he managed to snatch the right one from the swirling chaos.

"You know him..."

The emotions seeping through those three words could not be described in the number it would take to tell this tale. They carried an accusatory weight heavier than the depths of the Ring Sea, and a liberating relief lighter than the floating isles of Spira. Fear. Joy. Anger. Confliction. I could fill an entire novel with the thoughts that cascaded through his mind in that moment. Innumerable words in his head. Three spoken aloud. Two written on the ticket. One man, the center of it all.

Gregory Veramor.

The stranger moved before Enoch had even processed the words he'd said. The Scribe's recently healed ribs struggled against the force of the steel toe boot kicking him fully to the ground. His vision tripled. A steel spike aimed at his chest, then shoulder, then his chest again, dancing back and forth in a blur. His ears rang like a boiling kettle, drowning out the stranger's frantic voice.

"Did he tell you to chase me off? Is that why you followed me out here?" The stranger didn't wait for a response, pushing down on Enoch's shoulder with his free hand. He heard a cracking sound beneath. "Gregory Veramor. He actually *was* in that building, wasn't he? But then you–" His red eyes flared in anger. *"You..."* The blade pulled back, anger aiming it towards Enoch's chest. But the stranger's thoughts interrupted his attack. Through heavy breaths, he glanced up, looking over towards the sound of the distant waterfall.

Slowly, as if he'd forgotten Enoch existed at all, the masked stranger stood up. He stared through the forest, through the mountain, through the distance between him and his target. Each disjointed, subconscious step forward beat against the brittle stone with a metallic *thud*.

He was in the city this whole time... the stranger realized. *Is... Is he still there? Or did I miss my chance?*

"No. I can still find him," he muttered to himself, an uncertain reassurance to drive his feet forward. "Before he can leave. I... I'll–"

C-C-Crack! Beneath the two young men, the stone fractured like the ice of a frozen lake. The world shook violently beneath them. The sound dragged the masked stranger out of his tunnel-visioned desperation, his pursuit halting as he glanced around him.

Hisssssssssssss. Emerging from the cracks, a red, swirling mist surrounded them. It seeped into Enoch's lungs. His legs shook as he struggled to stand and escape it, the crimson miasma clawing at his skin and chest. His vision swayed. Focused, blurred, focused, blurred. He tried and failed to find a semblance of balance amidst the tremors. But even with unsteady feet, he kept his gaze locked on the stranger. After what just happened, Enoch couldn't let him reach Azazel. He had to stop him somehow.

The masked stranger turned to Enoch. "Are you doing this?" he asked, pulling his cloak up to stop the mist from flowing beneath his mask.

"N-No…" Enoch stuttered, choking on both the mist and the words. The stranger tightened his grip on the steel blade in his hand, watching the ground continue to crack around them.

"Don't lie to me, if this is you, I'll send this through your chest before your magic can affect me." One look at the Scribe was enough to prove his innocence. Like an injured animal, he tried again and again to stand, each attempt ending with him falling back into the thickening mist. Realization pierced through the stranger's mind like a blade. He'd seen the faintest traces of this mist before, back when he'd interrogated the Priest that found him in the forest. At the time he'd thought it was the man's ability, but he'd be long dead by now. So then… what was it?

The dense, suffocating crimson burned Enoch's body. His muscles gave out, and he collapsed to the stone again. The masked attacker's form faded into the choking mist. Using the last of his strength, Enoch reached out, begging his body to move forward, to stop him. If he could hold the violent figure back, unravel himself to reach a little farther… For a moment, he pictured it; a faint ghost of a thread, a lifeline, a snare to catch the dangerous masked man. And then, crimson faded to black, his head and hand falling limply to the ground.

As if waiting for Enoch to lose consciousness, the breaks in the stone finally gave way. *Crack! C-c-crack! Crack!* Parts of the ground began to collapse and crumble away. The masked stranger stepped back towards the safety of the tree line, his gaze fighting him on which way to go. *Go! Just go!* He couldn't stay there. He didn't have time to waste. He was so close, but...

"Damn it!" he growled, turning back to the clearing. He rushed forward, sliding along the shifting stone towards Enoch's unconscious body. With each new fissure, the mist burst into the air like spores around him. As quickly as he could, he lifted Enoch onto his back.

The ground fell away beneath each step. He sprinted towards the trees. The stone inclined. Empty air replaced the unstable foundation beneath him. The stranger watched as the edge of the sinkhole flew upward. He reached out, out towards the tree-line, out towards the distant waterfall. Then the two fell down beneath the earth, a gleam of silver swallowed by the crimson mists.

Chapter 8

EVEN MOUNTAINS crumble when placed under enough pressure. Perhaps not all at once. A rock dislodged here. A crack forming there. A stream eroding the stone so slowly that even the peaks fail to realize they're shrinking. Or perhaps the damage could come from a quake deep within the ground, shaking loose pieces of a cavern that had stood strong for centuries.

Small stones landed with soft *clicks* and *taps* on the Civionis platforms. The water rippled with quiet *plip plip plips* as others dove into the lake. These stones went mostly unnoticed, the debris too small to warrant attention. Even those unfortunate enough to have them land directly on their heads failed to realize, far more focused on the quake rumbling throughout their home.

Up in the city's cathedral, Bishop Paras steadied the ink bottle on his desk as it rattled along with the rest of his office. The ink that already spilled soaked through the notes he'd been looking over, the contents covered before he'd even had the chance to dispose of them. Behind him, one of the paintings of the city's previous Bishops toppled to the ground, knocked fully off the nail. Paras glanced over to his fallen predecessor. With a subtle sneer, he chose to leave him there on the floor for now as he placed a lid back on the ink. Then the Bishop hurried to the door, eager to get to the bottom of this sudden tremor. Never before had such an event affected the proud city of Civionis, and he would not let it go ignored under his watch. Not if he couldn't get away with it.

Outside, just a short distance away, Iris caught a young woman that had lost her balance in the swaying, wooden lift leading up to the cathedral. The Circlet Guard took a moment to reassure the panicked passengers. She smiled, telling them the supports were strong enough to hold. Though, even she couldn't help but feel unsteady at the sound of the creaking wood and jangling pulleys. Nevertheless, she maintained her composure, ensuring every passenger disembarked safely onto the platform below. With the lift empty, Iris watched the rolling water underneath. She wondered what might have caused such violent shaking. A chill ran down her spine. An answer whispered in the back of her mind. She turned away, doing her best to ignore it as an Investigative Inquisitor waved to get her attention. After a short exchange of words, Iris followed the Inquisitive's lead, leaving the central terminal platform behind for matters in need of her attention.

And as Bishop Paras sought out answers; as Iris set out to complete her work; as Enoch and the masked figure fell to what would likely be their deaths; Azazel felt his stomach sink as well, as if the ground had fallen away underfoot.

By the time he'd reached the door of the bed and breakfast, the tremor had come to a halt. The lake water continued to lap against the platform pillars, the waves trying their best to cling to the far sturdier stone, hoping to regain some semblance of stillness. Pedestrians clutched their chests and caught their breath, wondering what had just happened. What could have possibly caused Mt. Morus to shudder so? Concerned mutters filled the streets and canals. Though Azazel had hoped to begin his search for the masked attacker after ensuring the safety of his temporary neighbors, something else caught his eye. Enoch's luggage sat next to the platform railing, toppled over by the force of the earthquake.

"Enoch?" Azazel cried out, running over to the railing. *Why is his suitcase here, but not him? Did something happen? Did he fall into the water during the quake?* The angel nearly fell in himself as he grabbed the railing with more momentum than he should have. Holding on tightly, he leaned over the edge, searching for any sign of his friend. "Enoch! Are you down there? Answer me!"

Only the turbulent water replied. Taunting him with its silence. Hiding its secrets beneath its darkened surface. Azazel took a step onto the bottom of the railing. The angel hadn't even realized he'd done so until a hand gripped his shoulder.

"Woah, easy does it. Is everything alright, sir?"

Azazel turned around, finding himself face to face with a well-dressed man walking a large, fluffy, white dog. Concern and curiosity swirled within the man's amethyst eyes. Azazel stared back, confusion and unease in his own. "Huh? What do you–" The angel put two and two together, realizing what this looked like. "Oh, no. I'm not– I'm okay, don't worry." Stepping down from the railing, Azazel grabbed the man's shoulders. "More importantly, did you see a guy with curly black hair near here? Or did you hear a splash during that shaking?" The sudden grip took the man aback a moment. Hearing the dog growl, Azazel let go, taking a step back. "Sorry. I... Sorry. He's a friend of mine, so I'm a little panicked right now. Any information would help."

"Well, he certainly didn't fall in. I can tell you that much." The man flattened his clothes with a brush of his hand. He noted the Pilgrim's entire body relaxing at the news, as if he'd suddenly sank into a warm bath. Scratching his dog's head, the man tried to recall more details. "A younger man, correct? Wearing a... brown trench coat?"

"Yes! That's him! You saw him?"

"When Snowy and I started our walk, yes." The man gestured to his dog, the pooch lazily sitting on the ground now that Azazel had backed off. "Normally I wouldn't pay folks much mind while out and about, but he'd coughed so loudly it was hard to ignore."

The reminder of Enoch's condition felt like a cold bucket of water dumped over Azazel's head, yet his throat felt suddenly dry. The angel held his tongue, waiting for the man to finish.

"After he'd stopped coughing, he ran after some fellow in a cloak and mask that way. That was about an hour ago. Figured the lad would have come back by the time Snowy and I finished our walk, but it seems that wasn't the case."

"Some guy... in a mask?"

The man's confirmation and rambles about odd accessories went unheard as Azazel could think of nothing but the injured Priest on the bridge. The wounds perforating his body. The blood that had nearly stained the angel's jacket. The words that had escaped his lips in a dying murmur.

He's looking for you... Man in... metal mask...

Had this same man targeted Enoch despite Azazel's attempts to hide their connection? Or had Enoch seen the mask and done something reckless? Regardless of what motivations and events led up to it, if the man was telling the truth, then Enoch had chased this dangerous person to who knows where. Would he end up in the same bloodied state as the Priest? Azazel didn't want to think of the answer to that question.

"Thank you for the help!" the angel said, running off deeper into the residential district. He had to know if this was true. He had to know if Enoch was in danger. The Pilgrim stopped, asking anyone he could if they'd seen anything. Each answer caused his heart to race, his throat to tighten, and eventually he reached the bridge at the edge of the city.

"You're sure you saw him cross?" Azazel asked. A little girl nodded. "Yep! He and his friend were playing tag, I think. They ran into the forest!"

"I see... Thank you for the help."

"You're welcome, mister!"

After giving Azazel his final grim answer, the little girl skipped away. The angel's stomach swayed and swirled like the lake water beneath him. *This is my fault. I should've kept a closer eye on him.* The Pilgrim's jaw clenched. *It's my job to keep him safe, and now he's in more danger than before, dragged into this masked murderer's business, and stuck in the forest that's killing him...*

"Hang in there, tough guy. I'll get you back home safe and sound." Whispering this promise, Azazel rushed into the woods. He had to find Enoch. He had to find this masked killer. He had to make this right.

Before anyone else could get hurt, he had to fix this.

Chapter 9

THE FINAL BURST had long since faded, but the rotting smell of the body still lingered in the air. Healers laid a crimson cloth over the corpse, a somber shadow looming over. It was the kind of failure felt only by those who had sworn to save lives, just to have one slip through their fingers.

Iris stepped aside as two Healers carried the covered corpse out of what was once its home. Or *his* home, rather. Iris couldn't be blamed for the miswording though. After all, with the body as charred as it was, it would be easier on one's heart to forget that the form had once been alive. That he'd once been human. Now, all that remained was a burned and blackened body covered in the arcane script.

"Were there any issues caused by their final burst?" Iris asked, turning to face the Inquisitive next to her. She'd seen all she could stomach of the gruesome scene before her, the sight digging up memories she'd rather leave to the past. The thoughts crawled along her skin as she tried her best to ignore them. "A left behind summon? Or an effect on the people nearby?"

"No, Commander." The Inquisitive flipped through their notes on the deceased, "They had no registered ability, and their capacity was pretty low. Even with the everred fever, the burst itself was small. It stayed within the house and leaked out too faintly to have any side-effects."

"Good. We can count ourselves lucky then." The Circlet Guard Commander held the hilt of her sword, her cloak hiding her trembling fingers. Death was nothing new to her. Before Paras had saved her, she'd seen many bodies charred and marked just like this one. But lately they carried a heavier weight, and she found it harder and harder to stand tall in their presence. The Circlet Guard sighed. At least they were lucky enough to be the first and only ones to see the body. The innocents around them could be spared that traumatizing memory.

She looked around the humble home. The books on the shelves, the half-embroidered scarf hanging over the back of a chair, the food long past the point of being safe to consume. Small as it was, the home had been just that.

"How could we let this happen?" she whispered to herself. The Inquisitive glanced over from their notes, catching the rare moment of vulnerability from their superior officer.

"Don't blame yourself, Commander," they reassured, speaking quietly to protect the Circlet Guard's pride. "It was just poor circumstances. The victim registered for the start of his vacation, so how were we supposed to know he hadn't left?"

"We could be monitoring the departures of those registered more closely." Iris argued. "I mean, if the neighbors hadn't complained about the smell, how long would our negligence have left the body to rot? Poor circumstances are still the result of people's actions. They don't just happen without cause, we–" She took a breath. As the right hand of the Bishop, she couldn't lose her composure. The Commander fixed her posture, heading towards the door to get some fresh air. "For now, check with the Scribes at the records hall and see if the deceased has any living relatives to handle the distribution of his property and belongings. Otherwise, we'll need to fill out the paperwork to transfer it to Church storage."

Stepping outside, Iris watched as the Priests kept a curious crowd at a distance. The sight of Iris caused some to disperse, not wanting to incur the wrath of a high-ranking Church worker. Iris watched them go with a somber curiosity. What projects did they have half finished? What foods would they never get to eat if they had been the ones to fall ill? She waved over the Inquisitive once more.

"Arrange medical examinations for the immediate neighbors, as well as therapy sessions if they feel they need them. It's better to be safe than sorry if the final burst reached farther than we realized."

"Of course, Commander Ocudolis." With a quick salute, the Inquisitive set out to fulfill Iris' request. Iris held back a moment longer, saying a prayer to the Archangels. It was all she could do for the poor soul now. That, and ensure no others followed in his ghostly ascent to Spira. After this silent promise, she began to head back to the cathedral. Informing her of any deaths due to everred fever was technically the proper protocol in Civionis, but this investigation had taken enough time already. Rare as they were nowadays, these deaths were within expectations. The quake from before on the other hand... she needed to discuss that event with the Bishop.

"C-Commander Ocudolis! Please wait a moment!" a young Inquisitor with periwinkle hair chased Iris down the side of the canal. She stood at attention after reaching the Circlet Guard, clearly fighting her own windedness to do so. "Sorry... for delaying you ma'am..." she struggled to say. Iris smiled.

"It's no problem. Take a moment and catch your breath. I won't tell anyone."

The young Inquisitor's eyes sparkled. Then said spark vanished as she doubled over, supporting herself on her knees with heavy, wheezing breaths. "Thank you... ma'am..."

With a slight chuckle, Iris patted the new recruit on the back. "It's not a problem. The air is a lot thinner here than at the academies, so it's to be expected."

"R-Right." The Inquisitor took some deep breaths before an equally deep furrow formed between her brows. "Wait, how did you know I came from the academy?"

"You were one of the recruits at the ceremony a few years back, right? I remember that beautiful hair."

A flush filled the recruit's cheeks. She turned her attention to the nearby water, now too flustered to look at the taller woman. "I... I see. I'm flattered to have made an impression, ma'am."

"Now what did you need to tell me?" Iris asked. "Did I forget something at the investigation?"

"Not at all, ma'am. I just wanted to ask if we should inform Bishop Paras about the incident as well. The Inquisitives– I mean the Investigative Inquisitors said that's usually part of the protocol here, but I thought that something like this would fall under the jurisdiction of a Judicial High Inquisitor, not a Bishop."

"Normally yes. Father Paras just cares deeply about the health of the city." Iris patted the Inquisitor's shoulder, wordlessly reminding her to relax a little. Once the recruit had, Iris leaned in somewhat, speaking in a softer tone. "It may not be my place to share, but he lost someone dear to him to everred fever when he was young, so he takes the issue quite seriously now that he's in power."

"Oh... That makes sense, I guess."

Pulling away, Iris smiled warmly at the young recruit, hoping to distract from the less than happy conversation topic. "Either way, I'm about to meet with the Bishop myself, so there's no need to worry yourself with the report this time. I can pass on the message. For now, why don't you help with the investigation into any connections the deceased might have had. The Scribes should have information on his family members stored in the records hall. I've sent someone already, but if there's multiple relatives it could help to have an extra pair of hands."

"Right! Records hall! I can do that, yeah!" The Inquisitor saluted, forming wings with her fingers. "Thank you, Commander Ocudolis!"

"Any time."

Iris watched the young recruit run off once more, before having to slow and catch her breath again just a short distance away. Certain that she'd make it to the records hall eventually, Iris continued with her own work. Her mind felt equally strained. Another life had been lost to their own carelessness. Bishop Paras wouldn't be happy to hear the news, and the thought of letting him down felt like breathing in smoke. He saw potential in her, and she'd failed him.

But perhaps he didn't have to know..

The Circlet Guard Commander stopped on one of the terminal platforms, watching the smoke rise from the fire-pit in its center. The cathedral was barely visible through the darkened air. Standing in the warmth of the fire, she made a decision. She'd keep this unfortunate incident to herself. Between the ceremony, running the city, and his work outside of his daily responsibilities, her superior had enough on his plate already. She was his trusted right hand. She owed him so much. The least she could do to repay him would be sparing him this added stress.

Paras could believe things were fine. She could handle this on her own.

Chapter 10

WHILE HIS GOAL had shifted from finding the masked killer to finding Enoch, the method remained the same. After all, there was a high chance the two of them were at the same place. Though Azazel couldn't quite decide if he wanted that chance to become reality. The best-case scenario would be that Enoch had won the stranger over somehow. He'd return promptly with their identity before heading back to the capital to recover. The more realistic scenario would be that he'd find Enoch used as a hostage in the killer's quest to reach him. The worst-case scenario? Well, Azazel hoped that the Priest would be the only one brought to the brink of death that day.

Footprints matching Enoch's had led Azazel from the city bridge into the forest. But once the tracks reached deeper in, the wildlife had destroyed the trail too much for Azazel to follow. This became increasingly evident with each false footprint he found, each hour that passed. Nevertheless, he still knelt above another dip in the dirt, looking closely for any sign of it once being filled with a shoe. Would this one be the solace he was searching for, or yet another soleless track? The soil offered no answers.

"Damn it!" he cried, taking his anger out on the ground. The leaves and dirt he'd slapped away silently accepted the change of position as Azazel stood, pacing a new path in place of the one he was failing to find. He'd spent centuries in this realm. Centuries! But what did that matter if he couldn't find a single damn footprint!?

"How can I be so useless!?" he cried out. In his usual overly dramatic fashion, the angel leaned against the grey trunk of an everred. His arm cushioned his face from the roughness of the bark, tousled silver hair hiding his troubled expression. He turned towards the far-off sound of the waterfall in Civionis, wondering if he should go back and find a guide? Could he risk involving someone else in his mission? The pause in his frustrated outburst offered a compelling argument. Silence... Nothing... He had no other options, right? That being said, this potential killer was supposed to be someone he knew. In fact, if Enoch's vision could still be trusted, Azazel would shed tears for them upon their demise. If that was the case, did he really want to get the Church involved before he had more answers? Was there a tracker he could trust to take his side should the truth oppose the Church's justice?

...Seira Equitervi...

Her name filled his thoughts like a whisper in the wind, and like a whisper, found itself quickly overpowered by a much louder voice in his mind. Though Civionis had been her home, every attempt he'd made to find her or her brother since his arrival had been fruitless. Not that this surprised him. Seira had never stayed in one place for long, and her brother rarely left his work when she wasn't around to visit. Still though, he found himself wishing that his friend could be there in that moment, using her skills to make a fool out of him with how easily she could find the elusive path he needed. He sent the thought away in a heavy sigh. Her help would mean dragging her into his problems, and that was the last thing he wanted to do. Enoch was under *his* care. The masked stranger was after *him*. *He* was the one that let Enoch wander off on his own, knowing how dangerous the situation was.

He was the one that had convinced himself that was the better option.

"Hope you're doing better than I am," he said softly, before dusting himself off and continuing into the forest. Maybe he didn't have a shred of tracking skills, but he had something far more valuable, if less dependable. Luck. The forest was only so large, and Enoch could only go so far in his sickly state. Surely, he would run into him eventually if he simply continued onward! Plus, if the masked stranger was looking for him as well, there was always the chance that they'd come to him instead! He hardly had many other options, so he let his intuition lead the way.

He wandered further into Everred, past schools of feathered fish flying through clouded canopies; past glittering butterflies large enough to summon soft drafts with their wings; past claw marks in the trees that reached deep enough to make the hair on his neck stand on end. And eventually he found he'd wandered far enough to find an unpleasant stench in the air, merging with the sweet scent of the everred trees just as its color melded with its leaves.

Blood.

The angel's fingers hovered close to his hip. Like walking into a cold fog, the realization that he was being watched washed over him. "No need to be shy," he said into the forest shade. "I don't bite."

Unfortunately for the yellow-jacketed Pilgrim, his opponent did. A monstrous beast leapt from the trees, fangs bared wide like the mouth of a humid cave. Spit clung to each sharp tooth. The remains of its last meal clung to each drop. A rumbling growl dug deep into Azazel's ears. With a small boost from his wings, Azazel dodged to the side. The gargantuan wolf's fur grazed the outer feathers as the creature's fangs shattered a tree like a twig instead.

Azazel slid through the bloodstained dirt, one hand clawing the soil for balance, the other moving to his chest with a golden glow. Manic and far too large to easily navigate the trees, the wolf crashed into its surroundings as it focused on turning around. The angel instead focused on using his magic to reshape the steel sewn throughout his jacket. Golden light bathed his clothing. The energy seeped into the fabric itself, sculpting the metal woven within into something new. With masterful speed that had taken decades to master, Azazel's jacket was now gone, replaced by decorative armor.

The angel pulled his belt free. The steel accessory shifted form with the movement. Azazel pictured a sturdy sword in his mind, the metal matching the imagined mold as if he were drawing a blade from a sheath. He still had time to land a blow before the beast could turn–

CRACK! *Creeeeeak. C-C-Crack!*

The trees gave way to the wolf's claws as it chose brute force over careful navigation. Splinters and branches flew through the air. Azazel shielded his eyes, this moment of blindness allowing the wolf to act. It lunged once more and the angel found himself knocked back. At the last second, the sword switched to a misshapen rod barely holding back the beast's fangs. Though it hadn't been what he wanted, the crooked rod did at least keep the creature's maw from clamping down on his beautiful face. This didn't deter the wolf from trying.

Slobber oozed and sprayed over Azazel's arms and head. He gagged from the stench of meat rotting within the fangs. The heat of each hungered exhale was enough to make the angel sweat. He could feel the skin-rattling scrapes of the wolf's claws trying to puncture his armor, the occasional swing managing to nick into his exposed wings. Though he knew the beast couldn't feel them, Azazel very much did.

"Hey there– doggy," Azazel said, trying his best to push the beast aside. "I'd taste horrible, I– *Ack*, I'm definitely not– worth the trouble!" The angel could barely hear himself over the deafening growls and snarls. In which case, he was sure his pleas went unheard by the wolf as well. He had to find a way out of this. If he died now, then who would save Enoch!? Who would get him back home? Not to mention the fact that his angelic friends would never forgive him if the next time they saw his face, it wasn't truly him. He tried to focus, to resonate with the steel in his hand. The golden light in his fingers flickered, his attention split between his attempts to sculpt, and keeping up with the beast's unpredictable movements.

Focus.

Focus!

He just needed a second to focus. Then he could form a spike to injure the wolf enough to make it retreat. The beast's fangs gradually came closer and closer, the angel's arms losing strength. "C'mon, c'mon, c'mon! I can't die here!" he cried out. "Just back off already!!"

Thwip!

Squelch.

Blood mixed with Azazel's makeup as it splattered across his face. A pained welp escaped the wolf's throat as the arrow entered it, the shaft visible inside from where Azazel laid pinned to the ground. The beast turned to face this new threat, pulling the rod in Azazel's hands out of them with the movement. As one does when dropping something, Azazel's gaze followed it before landing upon his savior.

For a moment he thought it was another wolf, far smaller, hiding in the bushes. But as it raised the bow for another shot, a turquoise, spectral arrow knocked on the bowstring, he realized who it was wearing this wolf-fur cowl.

Thwip! Thwip!

Thud! *Squelch!*

Two more arrows flew out in rapid succession, piercing the beast's gut. The wolf growled, the sound gurgling from the arrow already in its throat. It pulled away from Azazel, realizing this newcomer was a far greater threat. The angel scrambled back. The wolf-cowled hero emerged. Time seemed to slow as they leapt towards the beast, their tattered grey cloak drifting behind them like smoke from fire. The golden glint of their Pilgrim emblem sparkled just behind it, swinging at their hip. Another glimmer flashed in their hand as their dagger dug deep into the base of the beast's neck; a fang, slicing through fur and viscera. The hero slid across the bloodstained forest soil. It was over in an instant. The wolf's eyes rolled back with a final, pained, broken whimper, before falling to the ground behind the mysterious Pilgrim. In sync with the beast's final heartbeat, the blade in the newcomer's hand shattered into turquoise glass.

Still processing what had just happened, Azazel picked himself off the ground. The outfit, their ability, the grace and unforgiving power behind their movement... A smile crept onto his face at her impeccable timing. Placing a hand on his chest, he reshaped his armor into his familiar yellow jacket. He didn't waste another second after that, running towards the familiar fur cowl and collar, arms outstretched.

"Seir- *ack*!" His attempt at a hug was met with a punch to the shoulder. He stumbled back somewhat from the force.

"Gregory Veramor, you absolute idiot! What in the Three Realms were you doing pinned under a damn wolf!?" Seira shouted. "What would you've done if I hadn't been here, huh?"

Momentarily pained as he was, Azazel still looked up at his old friend. Her dark, wispy hair had gotten a little longer, the slightly tangled locks curling upwards in areas, with the lowest strands ending just above her shoulders. He noticed a few new scars on her dark taupe, weathered skin, somewhat healed already, but undoubtedly recent. He was certain the opponents ended up with far worse souvenirs.

The leather sling that usually carried the woman's bow was currently empty, the bow itself no doubt left in the bushes when she'd switched to her knife. Equally empty holes lined her cloak, the dark-grey fabric torn, tattered and frayed at every end. He could just barely make out the golden color of her Pilgrim emblem beneath it, the muddied accessory hanging from her belt, and brushing against her mahogany colored pants as she angrily held her hands on her hips.

"Firstly, *ow*," Azazel said, still recovering from her hit. "Secondly, I'm sorry. It's not like I did it on purpose."

"I hope not! And what are you even doing here!? I thought you were in Courciel for a delivery jo–"

Azazel pulled Seira close. He knew she was angry. He could also hear the fear and concern in her voice. Her heart was racing. Her body tensed, but she didn't fight the embrace. He felt the softness of the fur collar and cowl of her cloak, as well as the wet bloodstains now coating them from her up close encounter with the wolf. She'd put herself in just as much danger, and the angel was well aware of that fact.

"Thank you," Azazel said softly, his face leaning into her tangled hair. With everything that had been happening, it felt nice to have her close. No matter how chaotic his life got, she'd always been able to ground him. "It's good to see you too, Seira."

Hidden from her friend, and against every instinct, Seira's lips curled into a small smile. It was relieving to hear his voice again. It was even more relieving that he was still the same sappy, optimistic idiot as before. She hadn't realized how much she'd needed something familiar. Seira lightly pushed Azazel away from her, angered scowl returning before he could see her face.

"Don't think you can schmooze your way out of this one. You're lucky I was close enough to hear you."

"And right now, I'm unfortunately close enough to smell you," Azazel replied, plugging his nose. "Geez, Seira. When was the last time you took a bath?" the angel took a step back. Happy as he was to see her, his nose demanded they part ways once more. Seira rolled her eyes.

"You don't smell much better, Greg. At least I wasn't taking a bath in wolf drool."

"Fair point." Azazel took a second to wipe some of the lingering globs out of his hair. He might as well have been trying to bail out the ocean with a bucket. As he tried cleaning himself off, Seira made her way over to the bushes to grab her bow.

"There's a river nearby we can use to get cleaned up. Then you can tell me what you're doing out here."

Pressed for time as he was, Azazel couldn't deny that he needed to clean himself off. In this state, the masked attacker would be able to smell him before they saw him. He nodded, waiting for Seira to lead the way. Instead, she knelt next to the wolf as if she were readying herself to pray.

"What are you—"

Seira held up a finger, shushing Azazel without pulling her gaze from the wolf. She looked at the wounds she'd inflicted, a glistening guilt in her sienna eyes. "I'm not leaving without paying my respects. I owe it that much at least."

"You sure? That thing was crazy. Would've killed us both if you hadn't killed it first."

"He was agitated, not crazy." The dark-haired Pilgrim fell silent, closing her eyes as she took a moment to honor the wolf. It wasn't a prayer; Azazel could tell that much. It was more a connection, an apology, an acknowledgement that it had once been alive, and that she had taken that life from it. Once she'd finished, she stood back up.

"He was probably drawn here by the scent of blood. As for the aggression, something's been affecting the forest lately." Her gaze wandered, taking in their crimson surroundings with a look less oblivious than she was feigning to be. "Poor thing probably didn't even know why it was angry. Can't avoid what you don't understand, but he didn't deserve to die for that ignorance, even if it was dangerous." After one final, reassuring hand against the wolf's pelt, Seira began heading into the forest. "He's too large for us to bring back, but there's more than enough animals in the area that can find use for what's left of him. Let's go, I'll lead the way."

The angel nodded, quickly retrieving the steel rod he'd dropped earlier before matching Seira's pace. She'd mentioned the scent of blood, and he couldn't help but wonder if it had once belonged to the Priest he'd met at the bridge. Though, even if this had been the site of his attack, any clues he might have found would now be lost in the wreckage of the wolf's rampage. Left once again with no other options, Azazel followed his friend into the forest mist, hoping Enoch would be lucky enough to avoid these agitated creatures Seira had mentioned. He'd survived demons, it would be a shame to die to the claws of a wolf instead.

Chapter 11

THE MASKED STRANGER refused to die.

If he did nothing, then he and the unconscious Scribe on his back would hit the bottom of the sinkhole, breaking every last bone in their bodies like shattered ceramic. Knowing this, the stranger didn't hesitate. His hand glowed red, the energy spreading to the heavy bracelets around his wrist.

"C'mon, c'mon, c'mon!" he said, trying his best to focus, to ignore the rapidly approaching stone floor. The bracelets reshaped themselves, forming a single, thick blade in the young man's hand. He gripped it tightly, driving it into the brittle stone surface next to them. Even just slowing their fall, the sudden resistance nearly tore his arm out from his shoulder. He winced, almost dropping Enoch to use his other hand out of instinct. Instead, he shifted the magical energy to his shoes. Spikes sprouted from the steel toes of his boots as he drove both into the wall.

Crrrrrrrrrsshhhhhh

Friction slowed their fall. What would have been a deadly impact was instead a slight drop to the ground as the stranger slid down the rockface. The crumbling rock broken off by the spikes fell to the floor with small, rhythmic *tap*

tap taps. Followed by the weighty *THUD* of the stranger pulling himself free from the wall. He took a moment, collecting himself as the dust settled.

The gas still lingered in the cave they'd fallen into, slowly drifting up into the forest far above. His heart raced. His blood boiled. The stranger lowered Enoch off his back, lightly dropping the Scribe against the stone wall so he could stretch his injured shoulder.

"Damn it," he muttered, looking up to see just how far down they'd dropped. "Damn it. Damn it. *Damn it!*" All he'd had to do was run. If he'd ran back to Civionis, he could have reached Gregory Veramor. But now, he was stuck in a hole too deep to climb out of because of an idiot too weak to stay awake in some fog. The stranger kicked the wall, forgetting the spike still protruding from the tip of his shoe until it stuck into the stone again.

"Oh, *come on!*" he shouted, forcing his foot out and punching the rock for kicking him while he was down. The rock was feeling the same way despite being unable to fight back. Instead, it continued crumbling, the remaining loose debris falling to the ground like sprinkled sand.

Taking a deep breath, the stranger tried to regain his composure. Some pacing and a few more hits to the wall helped bring him to his senses. It wasn't too late. He just had to get out of there and get back to Civionis as soon as possible.

The bracelets around his wrists took the form of spikes once again. Pushing through the pain in his shoulder, the stranger drove them into the wall and pulled himself up... only to have the spikes slide down through the stone again, more debris landing with a *tap, tap, tap.* No matter where he tried, the stone was too brittle to climb, and once again he took his frustration out on the wall.

"Stupid rock," he muttered, swinging one final kick for good measure. With a sigh, he gave up on the failing plan, instead turning his attention to the cave itself. The shape was fairly round, about thirty feet end to end. It seemed naturally formed as well. Whether by the mist or the mountain water that used to flow through the ground was beyond his knowledge. Either way, it seemed that the gas had built up within until the pressure had reached a breaking point at the surface.

The only other thing of interest was the boy he'd saved from becoming a splattered mess on the ground. The mist had thinned considerably, so the stranger walked over to get a better look. Based on appearance alone, they seemed to be around the same age. Enoch's physique was far less defined than the stranger's slender, yet stronger build, unsurprisingly from how easy he'd been to carry. He was paler too, with sweat dripping from his brow to his closed, sunken eyes.

The stranger checked Enoch for hidden weapons, or anything strange that might be connected to an ability. Instead, he found loose trash, coins, and an old engraved pocketwatch. He took a second, admiring the craftmanship of the item and listening to the soothing clockwork. Then he remembered his situation and returned the watch to its owner before holding a hand to that same owner's forehead.

"Guess you really do have that forest disease." With the same hand he'd used to test Enoch's temperature, the stranger lightly slapped the Scribe in the face. "Hey, c'mon. Time to wake up."

After a second slap, Enoch's face twitched. His eyes slowly flitted open. A mumbled "huh?' managed to push through his half-conscious state. Then Enoch saw the sharp, metal mask inches from his face. He rushed backwards into the stone wall, his head knocking away more of the debris. "Ow…"

"Well, you got some of your energy back, I guess," the stranger commented, backing away now that Enoch was awake. He gave the Scribe a minute to collect himself. Enoch used it to look up, watching the lingering mist fading into the forest canopy.

"What happened?"

"Ground broke. We fell. Now we're stuck."

Enoch blinked a few times, his mind still foggy despite the clearer air. *We… fell?* Looking up again, he couldn't believe he'd survived a fall that high. Until he noticed the scrape marks running halfway down the cavern wall. As well as the stranger rubbing his shoulder as he continued looking for a way out.

"Thank you," Enoch said, catching the stranger off guard. The masked man looked his way a moment before turning back to the top of the cavern.

"Bump your head too hard? What in the Realms are you thanking me for? Focus on getting us out of here," he ordered. "You can walk, right?"

"Y-Yeah, probably." Enoch struggled to his feet, poorly bracing himself on the unstable rock wall. Pins and needles poked at his legs, but considering how much worse the situation could have ended, the Scribe wasn't going to complain.

The two of them wandered throughout the cave, each keeping an eye on the other through glances they wrongly assumed were well hidden. Though Enoch had no problem with silence, he wondered if he should use the opportunity to talk to the masked stranger.

Sure, he was ready to kill me before, the Scribe acknowledged. *But he also saved my life, so he can't be all bad, right? Or he at least wants to keep me alive for some reason.* Glancing over again, he noticed the metal spike still tightly gripped in the stranger's hand. A knot in his stomach warned him that unnecessary small talk might end with a less than small hole in his chest. That being said...

"I'm Enoch, by the way," he said, hoping to gain some trust by introducing himself first. "If we're stuck down here together, it might help to know each other's names."

"My name is none of your business."

"Ah... Fair enough." Enoch rubbed the back of his neck. Considering the stranger was covering his face, it made sense he wouldn't give away his identity so easily. If the Scribe wanted to get more information, he'd have to take things slowly. "How about a nickname then? I mean... I have to call you something, right?"

From the lengthy silence, Enoch worried he may have pushed the temperamental stranger too far. The earlier knot in his stomach tightened, as if to shield itself from the inevitable stab attack.

"Yeah, sure. Knock yourself out." The stranger crossed his arms, leaning on the wall as he waited for Enoch to choose a name. Despite having suggested the nickname idea in the first place, Enoch found his mind going blank. He hadn't thought that he'd have to come up with it himself.

"Well, I don't know you that well. Or uh... at all," he replied, waiting for some kind of hint. When nothing was offered, he went over what he did know. The guy had a temper. He wanted to find Azazel. He wore a metal mask and seemed to enjoy pointing sharp things at other people... "I guess, going off of what I've seen... maybe Spike?"

"What am I, a dog?"

"Right, of course not." Enoch could hear his own frantic heartbeat. *How is picking a nickname so stressful!?* he complained in his head, wracking his mind for another option. "Then, how about Blade?"

No response. Whether that was good or bad was yet to be seen. The stranger slowly tilted his head, and Enoch wondered if it would have been better to have splattered on the cave floor.

"Sure. Has a nice ring to it," the stranger replied. Relief washed over Enoch, and he braced himself on the stone wall to recover from the unexpected stress. Had he not been looking away he might have noticed the nearly imperceivable pep that had snuck into Blade's step at the new nickname.

Once he recovered, Enoch tapped at the wall, keeping a wary eye on the lingering red smoke a short distance away. *Is it someone's ability?* he wondered. *No, probably not. It would've knocked out Blade too.* The Scribe thought back to how the mist had affected him. The fatigue and dizziness reminded him of how he'd felt back on the central terminal platform. *Is it connected to everred fever then? Maybe the trees are absorbing it through their roots. Or if there's other fissures in the forest, it would make sense people would assume it was the trees and not the gas making people sick...* This line of thought led to another, and his eyes narrowed, trying to focus on the wall behind the mist.

"Hey, do you see that?" Enoch asked, pointing to where the smoke was densest. Blade looked over.

"Yeah. It's smoke. Keep away from it, because if you pass out again I'm not carrying you."

"Behind the smoke, I mean." Enoch pointed again, frustrated that he couldn't risk going closer to show the exact spot. "There's a fissure in the wall. I think it's where the smoke is coming from."

Without a word, Blade approached the aforementioned spot with far more confidence than one should have while dealing with a potentially noxious gas. Leaning in close he nodded.

"Huh. More perceptive than I gave you credit for." He waved his hand, shooing Enoch closer to the other side of the cave. Enoch didn't need to be gestured to twice. Backing away even farther, he watched as Blade's hands glowed red. The metal spike reshaped once more, forming a sharp steel knuckle around his left hand. The ability caught Enoch's eye. It seemed the spikes were shaped, not summoned. Or more specifically, sculpted. The Scribe was hardly an expert at identifying metals, but the sheen felt familiar; like the shine of his old bike...

With a focused, determined ease, Blade took a step back, throwing his entire body into a heavy punch. The stone wall cracked and split like a shattered mirror before crumbling to the ground, revealing a smoke-filled tunnel behind it.

Even on the other side of the cave, Enoch covered his mouth and nose with his jacket sleeve. The mist pouring out wasn't nearly as thick as what had escaped at the surface, but he wouldn't risk inhaling more than necessary. Blade dusted off his hands, turning his weapon back into a bracelet around his wrist.

"Looks like someone wanted to cover this tunnel up," he observed quietly, tapping the remains of the broken stone as the mist cleared out. "It's a completely different kind of rock. Maybe they wanted to keep that mist inside?" Having secured a potential way out, Blade turned to Enoch. "Alright. Here's the situation. You and I are going to use this tunnel to get out of here, and then you're going to bring me to Gregory. Got it?"

Enoch had been approaching the tunnel once the smoke had cleared, but hearing that, he stopped. This couldn't continue. Not until he got some answers.

"Why are you looking for him?"

"That's none of your business."

"It is if you're going to make me bring you to him." Enoch's argument earned a surprised silence. Until then the Scribe had been weak or complacent, so the sudden argument felt as out of place as the artificial stone that had barred their escape. Assuming the lack of response was an invitation to continue, Enoch did just that. "You held a dagger to my throat in the forest before the smoke showed up. Sure, you saved me after, but why would I bring you anywhere near Gregory after that?"

Slowly, once Enoch's words had fully settled in his mind, Blade approached Enoch. Their height was nearly equal, but Enoch felt quite small in the masked man's presence. He took a step back despite wanting to stand his ground on this. From within the mask, Blade's eyes burned with anger. Enoch was so afraid to look away that he didn't notice Blade's fist until it was shoved violently into his stomach.

In a mix of a cough and a retch, the air left Enoch's body. Doubled over, he struggled to pull the breath back in, finding that easier said than done. Well, if he could say anything at all after the hit. The shock nearly caused his weakened legs to give out, but Blade grabbed the fabric of his jacket, holding him up.

"You don't get a say in this," he warned. "It's because of you that I'm down here in the first place instead of halfway to Civionis like I should be." Not giving Enoch even a second to recover, Blade began to drag the Scribe towards the tunnel. "Think about it. You don't have time to play Inquisitive. If you don't get out of town soon, that fever of yours will kill you."

After the hit to the stomach, the feeling of being haphazardly tossed to the tunnel floor wasn't quite as painful. Enoch struggled to his knees, coughing up dust. Blade followed behind. "You need *me* to get out of here before your time runs out. And while I don't *need* you to find Gregory, you should be happy that right now you could save me some time looking." The temperamental young man casually waved a spike in his hand, reminding Enoch of their situation. Blade was calling the shots here, not him.

Enoch stared at the weapon, caught between anger and fear. He wanted to protect Azazel from this violent stranger, but weakened as he was, what could he possibly do? His jaw clenched as he realized he wouldn't stand a chance even if he were healthy. What good was a desire to help if he didn't have the skills or strength to act on it?

Seeing the defeated look in Enoch's eyes, the Scribe's shoulders sinking with his self confidence, Blade reshaped the spike into a bracelet. The masked man crouched down next to Enoch, holding out his hand. "So, what do you say? Ready to stop being a nuisance and accept that you aren't getting out of here without my help?"

As much as he didn't want to, Enoch took the outstretched hand, allowing himself to be lifted to his feet.

Blade was right. Enoch could feel his energy waning, and if he passed out in the cave, he'd likely die before anyone could find him. He didn't know enough about everred fever to treat the symptoms himself, and since getting out of town would be a lot harder now, he had no choice but to work with Blade until he could get help in Civionis.

"Fine," he sighed. "I'll cooperate."

"Smart choice, Enoch." Blade nodded towards the tunnel. Enoch took the cue, leading the way with Blade following closely behind, the inspiration for his nickname hidden firmly in his hand.

Chapter 12

EVEN ON A DAY where fate itself demands that you suffer, comfort can be found in company. And if a friend isn't available, a nice bath can do wonders in their place. As he stood waist deep in the narrow river, rinsing the blood and grime from his face and clothes, Azazel was fortunate enough to have both.

Since Enoch had collapsed that morning, the day had become an onslaught of disaster after disaster. In the House of Healing, in the bed and breakfast, in the forest, Azazel had felt himself spiraling down a tunnel-visioned guilt, chained and dragged lower and lower by the growing list of problems and responsibilities. But the crisp river cleared his clouded head, just as its flow washed away the filth, leaving only the clear, freeing water behind. Though, the current still stung somewhat, earning the occasional well-hidden wince as it bit at the minor cuts on his wings.

The wings themselves were still safely hidden, pulled flat against his body to avoid creating any abnormal ripples in the river. He'd tucked his Illusion Paper into his pants pocket, protecting it with a makeshift steel envelope. Azazel trusted Seira, but he still needed to keep his angelic nature secret if he could. After all, he could only stay in Terrael if he did...

The humans cannot know.

Like always, the Archangels' warning lingered in the back of his mind. The one worry that even the river couldn't quell. The words had been spoken long ago, after the angels had returned to Spira at the end of the First War. After the Archangels closed the gate between realms. After Azazel had chosen to remain on the wrong side of it.

The humans cannot know.

Azazel was hardly perfect. During the centuries he'd lived among humans, he'd let his secret slip. Some he'd been able to cover up, lying about the wings being an ability, or managing to convince them they'd just been seeing things. But there were those that undeniably knew the truth, Enoch being the most recent.

Is the masked man working for Spira? the angel wondered. *Did he target Enoch because he knows what I am? Is he after me because I let it slip too many times?*

A rustle in the bushes pulled Azazel back to the present. At the opposite bank of the river, Seira glanced over her shoulder as well, both Pilgrims relaxing as they realized it was nothing more than a rabbit scurrying through the shrubbery. But Azazel's gaze lingered on Seira despite his relief. *She seems more on edge than usual,* he realized. Ever since they'd entered the water, she'd scan the trees mid-rinse, or jump at any sound louder than the shifting leaves. The angel couldn't help but wonder if she even realized she was doing it. He put the concern aside for now. Seira always had been a tad over-paranoid, so perhaps this was simply the adrenaline of the earlier fight failing to fully fade.

Closer to him, and far more relaxed, a large, black and blue furred deer took a sip of water at the shore. Choosing to let the river wash away his worries for now, Azazel smiled her way. "Happy to be back home, Dear?" he asked. Dear simply huffed in reply, ignoring the attempt to interrupt her drink. Azazel chuckled. "Still mad I didn't bring treats this time, huh?"

"Good," Seira interjected, splashing Azazel as she passed him in the water. "She always expects me to give her more when you spoil her like that."

"Don't be mad just because Dear likes me better."

"Keep telling yourself that. Maybe one day it'll actually be true." Seira moved to Dear, scratching behind her friend's ear. Dear leaned into her hand. With a warm, nostalgic smile, Azazel leaned as well, into her field of vision as she pretended not to notice. "I missed you," he said fondly.

After doing her best to ignore his puppy dog eyes, and finding that was just as difficult as she remembered, Seira dismissed his stare with a casual wave. "Okay, okay. I don't hate that you're here either."

The outwardly harsh words brought an even brighter smile to Azazel's face. "Don't get *too* mushy on me," he replied, earning himself a flick to the forehead from the dark-haired Pilgrim. "Ow! Okay, I'll stop. I'll stop."

Having put a stop to Azazel's antics, Seira climbed out of the river, wringing the water out of her hair. Azazel couldn't help but stare, noting the deep bags under her eyes, counting each new scar decorating her skin, wondering how many more were covered by her tunic. Regardless of how happy being a hermit made her, he'd always worry that one day she'd take a commission out of town and never return. That when they parted ways after a job well done, the next time he heard her name the scent of flowers would accompany it. This train of thought carried a sinking feeling to the angel's gut. The splash of cold water he threw at his face was a poor distraction from the guilt drying his throat, the thoughts of the dying Priest, and the reminder that Enoch could join him.

Noticing her friend had grown uncharacteristically quiet, Seira raised an eyebrow. "Delusions aside, you said something about tracks?" she asked.

"Right, uh... If you aren't busy, there's a person I'm trying to find. Unfortunately, I lost him in the forest and can't figure out which way he went." Azazel followed the dark-haired Pilgrim out of the river, Dear's ears perked up as he approached, before she turned her attention back to the far more interesting patch of grass nearby. "I can pay you for the commission," Azazel continued, "I'm sure you have other things going on after all."

Thumph. The angel nearly fumbled the cloth Seira tossed his way, the fabric falling clumsily into his arms after hitting his face. "I'm not gonna charge you, idiot." Seira pulled her dirt-covered cloak from where it hung in her makeshift camp, using it to dry herself off. "I still owe you for helping Fao–" She stopped, body tensing a moment like the words had burned her. "...I owe you one, so keep your gold."

Observant as he was, even Azazel couldn't see everything. Seira's moment of distress had been hidden behind the cloth drying his face and hair. Oblivious, he looked up with a warm smile.

"Thanks, Seira. I appreciate it." He moved over to the branch where his shirt and jacket had formed a puddle in the soil. After adding the borrowed cloth to the collection, he looked at the disheveled, hastily put together camp next to them, wondering where he might sneak some coins later on without her noticing. Meanwhile, Seira moved over to Dear, finding comfort in the soft fur of her friend.

"So, who're you looking for anyways? You don't usually take tracking jobs."

"A friend of mine. His name is Enoch."

To Azazel's surprise, there was a familiarity in Seira's curious side glance. "The kid from the capital?" she asked, leaning back casually on Dear as she sorted through her thoughts. "I remember him. Last name was... O... or uh... A-something?"

"Augnium?"

"Yeah, that's the one."

Azazel folded his shirt over his arm, his plan to put it back on interrupted by this sudden revelation. "How do *you* know Enoch?"

"I dragged him out of a lake a few months back. Back when they thought he'd lead them to the demons that, uh... did whatever they did."

"Oh! So, you were with the search party?" The angel thought back to the tragedy in Courciel. Due to the injuries he'd received in his fight with the demon Mahway, Azazel had been stuck in Enoch's apartment at the time. Had he not been, he certainly would have offered to help track the Scribe down. Instead, he'd learned of the events later on when he and Enoch were looking for conversation topics on the train. Seira being part of the search party was news to him though.

"I'm surprised you'd join a group mission like that."

"I was working in a forest nearby at the time. They needed a guide and I needed the money."

"I see. Explains how he got back so quickly." Azazel smiled. "Thanks for that. He definitely bit off more than he could chew back then."

"And they decided pairing him up with you would *fix* that for him?" Seira replied with a cheeky half grin. Azazel sent one back her way.

"Wow. Rude." With a dramatic flair, Azazel fell against the base of the closest tree. He held his head, feigning faintness at her words. "Do you really have such a low opinion of me, Seira? After all we've been through? I'm hurt!" Without replying, Seira began resaddling Dear, rolling her eyes at Azazel's antics. Seeing she wasn't going to reply, the silver-haired Pilgrim smiled, finishing with his shirt.

It felt as if no time had passed, the two's banter picking up right where they'd left off during their last job together. But the present pushed the past aside soon enough once Seira pulled the saddle-strap tight. "Guess I'm helping track him down again then. He's as big a trouble magnet as you, getting lost in Everred." For a moment, Dear grew restless, lightly kicking the soil with her front hoof. The sound pulled Seira from her thoughts, and she loosened the saddle a little, calming her friend down. "But y'know, Greg... The forest isn't the safest place right now. I don't know how long he'll be okay on his own out there."

Better on his own than in a certain killer's company, Azazel thought to himself. But Seira had a point. "He's a smart kid. Unlike me, I'm sure he'd run if he saw signs of wolf activity." Saying it aloud, and remembering the Scribe's actions in the capital, Azazel realized he didn't quite know if that was true. Not wanting to add another worry to the ever-growing pile, he elected to ignore this one in particular.

"I'm not talking about wolves," Seira corrected, thwarting his attempt at happier thoughts. Azazel's posture stiffened, listening carefully at this sudden change of tone. A tone that implied Seira knew more than she'd let on.

"Then, what *are* you talking about?" he pressed, fearing the worst. Seira sighed, the reply lingering in her throat. She swallowed her hesitation instead. Hiding things would accomplish nothing.

"I'm talking about Civionis. You shouldn't have come here. Especially not now of all times." With another heavy sigh, Seira turned to face Azazel. He stared back, waiting fearfully for her explanation, that puppy-like innocence in his eyes like always. That unconditional trust. He hadn't changed. In a way both comforting and unsettling, he looked exactly like he always had. Nearly identical, in fact... It didn't feel right. Why now? Why had their paths crossed once more? Doubt froze Seira's mind with chilling, warning whispers.

Seira's hand lowered, closing the distance between itself and her hidden dagger. "Actually, the timing seems almost too perfect. How do I know you're you? That you aren't some kind of ability pretending to be him to get close to me?"

It wasn't beyond the realm of possibility. If someone had been in their class, or had seen them on a job together, they'd know Azazel was capable of lowering her guard. In fact, she'd done exactly that the second she'd seen him. Hoping her words and actions were nothing but an overreaction, Seira pulled the dagger from her boot, pointing it the angel's way. Azazel, surprised as he was, stood his ground. Slowly, he raised his hands as she made her demand.

"Tell me something only you would know."

Azazel took a moment to think. The proof was easy enough to come up with. He was more concerned with this sudden hostility. Pulling a knife on him was something he could forgive. Not realizing his friend had been hurting, not being there for her through whatever drove her to this level of paranoia... that was something he couldn't.

"The scar below your left shoulder blade, it's from our graduation exam. You were ambushed by one of the examiner's summons because you were too focused on the fight her and I were having to notice it sneaking up on you."

"Not good enough. The examiner would know that too."

"Would she know that you turned down healing because you were too proud to admit you'd been hit? Or that you elbowed me in the gut when the healing herbs I was applying stung *just as bad as I warned you they would?* Which you still haven't apologized for, by the way. It really hurt, y'know."

Without a word, Seira lowered her knife, both annoyed and relieved by the angel's somewhat passive-aggressive answer. Azazel lowered his own hands, keeping a watchful eye on his friend. Sensing Seira's discomfort, Dear's tail pressed against her body. The deer nudged the dark-haired Pilgrim with her muzzle. Seira reassured her with some gentle scratches, calming herself just as much as the deer.

"I'm sorry," she said after a moment.

"A few years late, but it's appreciated."

Seira replied with a strange mix of a chuckle and sigh of disbelief. "Always a joke with you."

Having deescalated the moment of paranoia, Azazel approached his friend. He placed a gentle hand on her shoulder, and she tensed at his touch. "Seira, did something happen since the last time I saw you?" The answer was obvious, his question more an invitation than an inquiry. He gave her a moment to compose herself. She took several.

"Faolan..." she began, her brother's name barely able to push through the weight in her chest. "We had a fight... I left for a while, and when I came back..." The pain in her voice brought both heartbreak and sympathy in its familiarity. Azazel knew her next words before she'd even taken the breath to speak them. "He was dead," she admitted, just as he'd expected. The words that followed, however... those were far harder to predict.

"It was the Church. They killed my brother."

Chapter 13

SMOKE SWIRLED AND spiraled through the air of Bishop Paras' office. It shimmered in the prismatic light of the stained-glass windows like a spiderweb in the sun. The dim shine of the starlight stones could only cause the glass to glow, but it was still a beautiful, ethereal view. The rest of the room was instead lit by the large fireplace between the windows, the farthest corners veiled in a shadowy haze. Like the embers beneath the incandescent firewood, the Bishop's pipe flared as he took another deep breath.

Paras himself sat at his desk, which in turn sat atop a small set of stairs, elevating both above the rest of the room. Behind him, paintings of the previous Bishops hung in a row, joining Paras as he stared at the Inquisitive standing amidst the lavish furniture of the room. The old man stood as stiff as the wooden planks beneath him. He folded his hands behind his back as he waited for a response from the Bishop.

Another clouded exhale. Another meeting Paras didn't have the energy for. Another problem that had been added to his plate. The Bishop put his pipe down on a small stand. "The timing couldn't possibly be worse," he sighed. "The recruitment ceremony is right around the corner; Everred is crumbling; that tremor earlier has everyone on edge, and now you tell me a serial killer is attacking my men?" Paras skimmed through the letters and files on his desk, provided by the Inquisitive as part of his report. The page on top discussed the deaths of men and women employed by the Church, the victims' many wounds matching those of the Priest that had passed away in the House of Healing that same day. "Why did that masked maniac have to come here of all places?"

"Based on the information gathered, the attacker is after a man named Gregory Veramor," the Inquisitive replied. "Before he died, the victim said Mr. Veramor's name came up during the attack."

The Bishop stood with a sigh, pacing to and fro' as he mulled over the situation. *So, they have a target then? If this Mr. Veramor is willing to cooperate, that would make catching them easier.* His pacing slowed to a halt next to his desk. *Or perhaps it would be better to force him to leave entirely. Make it someone else's problem to clean up. Don't I have enough to deal with already after the antics of that Equitervi girl?*

Out of habit, Paras grabbed his pipe once more. He tamped the contents, relit them, and tossed the extinguished match onto a tray that very much needed to be emptied. Once again, his breath added to the room's haze. After calming himself, he turned to the Inquisitive.

"And how is your heart?" he asked. "Are you still maintaining your health?" the Inquisitive tensed and nodded.

"Yes. The Healers say everything is as it should be. Just the occasional flutter."

Paras nodded in return, taking another hit from his pipe. "Good. Then you're free to go. Thank you for your efforts.

It's thanks to hardworking people like you that Civionis is the great city we all take pride in."

Crossing his hands over his chest in the shape of wings, the Inquisitive bowed. The old man turned and left. A noticeable freshness greeted him in the cathedral hall after the thick, hot air of the office. As the door swung shut, Paras sighed once again, beginning to gather the papers on his desk into a pile.

"Just to be safe, increase security around the veins," he said.

"Of course, Father Paras," the shadow in the corner replied. With their visitor gone, Iris emerged from her hiding spot. "Should we close off Everred to the general public too?"

"Yes. We can't risk anyone getting hurt in the cave ins. Such a shame that some sort of mutated rodents are making the ground so unstable with their burrowing."

"Absolutely awful, yes. I'll inform the Priests stationed in the forest to keep a watchful eye out for the pests." Iris watched as Paras descended the stairs, papers in one hand, pipe in the other. "In all honesty, shutting down the forest may also help us in our search for Miss Equitervi, so that will–"

The Bishop's step stuttered. "She hasn't been found yet?"

Noting the anger in her superior's voice, Iris hesitated as the two met at the fireplace. Unfortunately, it was too late to take it back now. "N-No, sir. We know she's hiding out in Everred, but even with the help of trackers she's a tough one to pin down."

"How difficult could it be?" Paras snapped. "It's one woman. Surely you can handle that much."

"It... It's not that simple, Father." Iris' gaze faltered, drifting to the floor. "There's only so much I can do when most of our forces are..." she caught herself, choosing her words carefully. "...engaged elsewhere. Perhaps if you could let me reassign the men, I could–"

"I am perfectly capable of delegating *my* forces effectively," Paras argued. "I didn't stumble into the position of Bishop by accident."

"I know, sir. Of course. But if you trust me as much as you say you do, then–"

A panicked anger built in Paras' gut, clawing its way up to his chest as it grew alongside his never-ending list of problems to deal with. "Trust only goes so far, Ocudolis, as well as the authority you hold. Don't forget where you came from. Who it was that elevated who."

His words stole Iris' from her throat. The Commander's proud posture shrunk into that of a scolded child. The Bishop paused as his point sunk in, then he let out a long sigh. "I saw potential in you, Iris. I know you can do better; that you're more than where you came from. I need that woman caught and brought in, and no one is better suited for that job." Paras took another long breath through his pipe, the veins in his forehead prominent enough to cast shadows. "I trust that you can handle it? After all, we must tie up all loose ends before the ceremony."

This was news to Iris. The Circlet Guard raised an eyebrow, shaking off her shame. "Why the sudden deadline, Father? If I may ask."

"There was a last-minute replacement for the Inquisitor representative," he explained. "The recruiter is now High Inquisitive Surufel Asaradel."

From the sight of Paras breathing more smoke than air, Iris assumed this change wasn't in their favor. "I'm afraid I'm not familiar with the name. Are they important in the Church?"

"Important to keep an eye on, at least. I know he isn't particularly liked by most high-ranking officials." Paras looked down to the files, wondering if the High Inquisitive had been involved in even this investigation. "He has a bad habit of uncovering things people would prefer to keep hidden. For better or for worse. I doubt this replacement was mere coincidence."

"I see." Iris nodded, reading between the lines. "In that case, I'll ensure Seira Equitervi is captured by nightfall."

"Discreetly, if you can," Paras requested. "I will allow you to use a slightly larger search party if it will ensure this is finally dealt with."

"Of course. Thank you, Father."

One final time, Paras skimmed through the reports on the masked stranger's victims. "As for this new pest, bring in the killer's target for questioning. What was the name again?"

"A Pilgrim named Gregory Veramor," Iris answered. "He was the white-haired man I was speaking with at the stage earlier. The one that was given permission to extend his stay in the city."

Paras was quiet for a moment, forming a plan in his mind. "The recruitment ceremony is tomorrow. We can't afford to let this man's personal drama cause more problems for the city. And if the higher ups learn this infamous killer is here, Asaradel will have all the motivation he needs to start sticking his nose into things." Paras tossed the papers into the fire, a habitual familiarity to the movement. Like the herbs in his pipe, the files curled, the edges painted gold and red by the flames before burning into blackened ash.

"We must ensure the city's safety and success. Track down Miss Equitervi and Mr. Veramor, but make sure not to detain him within the city. We can't have him leading such a dangerous person to the streets of Civionis. Use the old mining barracks."

"You think he'll know the killer's identity, Father?" Iris asked, brushing some stray ash off her uniform. Bishop Paras turned to the stairs, making his way back up to his desk.

"If he doesn't, he'll at least be decent bait for the one person that definitely does."

Chapter 14

IT COULDN'T BE true. Faolan was dead? Killed by the Church, no less? When this information came to light; when Seira finally told him the source of her misery; all Azazel could say in response was "I'm sorry".

I'm sorry for your loss.

I'm sorry I wasn't there to help you with your grief.

I'm sorry that I'm asking for help when you're in pain.

*I'm sorry, could you repeat that last part? You think the Church did **what**?*

The angel glanced around, checking to see if somehow, someone might have heard Seira's accusation. Thankfully, the only one within earshot aside from himself was Dear, who likely wasn't all that interested in reporting treasonous conversation topics. Despite their privacy, and without even noticing it himself, the angel's hand still shifted slightly closer to his belt.

"But, that's a pretty dangerous claim, Seira," he replied, "What makes you so sure?"

"Because it's the only way it makes sense," Seira replied. Needless to say, that answer was as vague as it was unhelpful.

"The only way *what* makes sense? What happened?"

"I don't know."

"If you don't know, then why blame the Church? Seems like a pretty risky logic leap to me."

She struggled to answer that one. Would he believe her? Would her reasoning make sense to someone that didn't know Faolan like she had? Would saying her theory aloud convince even her of its implausibility?

Seira sat down by the edge of the river, watching the water drift by, jealous of how certain it was of the direction it had to go. No doubt sensing Seira's struggling, Dear waltzed over with gentle steps, the quiet *clop clop clops* filling the silence. Azazel joined them, patiently giving the fur-clad Pilgrim time to sort her thoughts. Enoch's condition meant they were pressed for time, but he'd make no progress without Seira's skills. Though, even if that weren't the case, he'd still struggle to walk away with his friend in such a state.

"Do you promise you'll trust me?" Seira asked. Her usually incisive voice shaking like the surface of the river in the wind. Azazel nodded. *As if I'm capable of anything else.*

"Of course," he promised.

Seira took a deep breath. "Alright..." her fingers ran through the fur collar of her cloak. "I... I was told he died in a workplace accident. An experiment gone wrong."

Azazel did his best to remember bits and pieces mentioned the last time he'd visited. Though his large physique was better suited for physical labor, Faolan was an intellectual at heart. He'd spent hours of the Autumn's End Festival excitedly instructing Azazel on the technical side of magic. The theories, the studies, the forms it could take, the life it potentially had. The angel remembered little aside from the clear passion and love Faolan had for his muse. But fervency aside...

"Wouldn't incidents like that be pretty common for Researchers?" Azazel asked.

"They are. And Faolan is– ...*Was* stubborn enough to do something he shouldn't for the sake of progress. But it just didn't feel right."

"You mentioned, yeah. Something that didn't make sense."

"It was all so secretive." Frustration burned behind the Pilgrim's eyes, the memories of her past equally seared into her mind. "Even Fao was hiding something. It's why we fought in the first place. I could tell something was bothering him, but no matter how many times I asked, he wouldn't tell me. So, I got angry. I yelled at him for being a stubborn ass that couldn't trust me. And then I left like always."

Regret quieted Seira's voice, the song of the forest filling the silence. Her jaw stiffened. The story hurt to share, and yet, saying it aloud felt oddly freeing in a way. She sighed.

"When I came back, he was already dead. They didn't try to contact me. They didn't even hold a funeral; they just burned the body and acted like the whole thing never happened. Even worse, when I asked the Healer that performed the autopsy for more details on how he died, they refused to say more than *an accident.*"

"I mean, that's vague for sure," Azazel admitted, "but withholding information doesn't necessarily mean the Church killed him themselves."

"But they're clearly hiding something!" The outcry startled Dear and Azazel, both flinching at the sudden volume. Seira winced, loosening her claw-like grip on the soil, as well as the rocks hidden within it. With a deep breath, she let out her frustration. Perhaps Azazel's doubt worked in her favor. This wasn't his fight. Even though her heart screamed for her to give him that final piece of the puzzle, her next words hesitated, tightening her chest as if to seal it off and keep themselves buried deep within. Without proof, they'd be nothing more than a theory. Unspoken, they couldn't drag him down with her. She didn't want to keep her friend in the dark, knowing how frustrating it could be to face ignorance when the light of truth could be so freeing. But... he couldn't get involved. If she was right, she couldn't lose him too.

"Maybe I *am* just being paranoid," she lied. "Maybe I just need to rest." Averting her gaze, Seira stood, brushing the dirt and traces of blood off her hands. "Either way, we don't have time for this. That kid is still missing, and the longer we wait the colder the trail will get."

"That's true, I guess," Azazel replied, watching his friend hurry away. "But, are you sure? You have a lot on your plate, I can look on my own if you–"

"You're an awful tracker," Seira argued. "Letting you go on your own almost got your head bit off. It won't be easy getting rid of me after that."

"Fair point. I know quite a few people that'd be very disappointed if I lost my beautiful head." Azazel stood, leading Dear by the reins as he joined Seira. "Just... let me know if you need help, okay? I can't change what happened, but I can at least make things easier for you now, if you'll let me. You don't have to carry it all on your own."

Like a small sunbeam breaking through a cloudy sky, Seira smiled. Even after the cloudy exterior returned, the truth she was keeping to herself lingering in her mind, the world felt a little warmer for a moment. How dearly she wished she could feel that way forever. But the sun was a stranger to the people of Civionis. The city deprived its people of that warmth. Gregory and Dear were the only light she had left, and she wouldn't lose them too.

Chapter 15

Drip... Drip... Drip...

Like the ticking of a clock, drops of water fell from the metal pipes running along the side of the underground tunnel. The sound was *almost* relaxing. After all, if you mixed Blade's palpable glare with the impending death from everred fever, how could Enoch be anything but serene?

The two young men wandered through the tunnels that wove beneath the forest like veins. They'd stolen one of many unlit lanterns hanging from the ceiling, hoping what little oil remained inside could last them long enough to find an exit. The crooked metal handle felt warm in Enoch's fingers, offering a small comfort in an otherwise uncomfortable situation.

Blade had stayed quiet. Enoch followed suit. The Scribe felt that conversation would inevitably lead to another punch to his gut, or worse, and he was pained enough already. He'd gotten so used to the steady silence that he winced when Blade finally broke it.

"I wonder what's inside," the young man said, gesturing to the pipes.

Enoch hesitated, but he still felt a response was necessary. He pushed through the concern to be polite. "I was told the city uses pipes to control the water level of the lake, so maybe it's that?" he suggested, glancing up. "This could be a maintenance tunnel. It may even lead us right to Civionis." *And hopefully, someone that can help me.* The Scribe held his tongue on this final thought, just in case Blade hadn't considered the fact that they might run into another person on the way.

"I wouldn't be so sure," Blade argued. Carefully, Enoch looked over his shoulder, caution conceding to curiosity.

"What else could it be? It's definitely man made, right?"

Silently, Blade ran his fingers along the rough stone of the wall, testing its stability. The surface was sturdier than the brittle rock he'd tried to scale before, dug through rather than eroded. It seemed the gas had been far less dense and destructive within the tunnel. "The Church isn't open about it, but Civionis used to make all its profits from their adolium mines."

Enoch's step stuttered, the Scribe surprised by how casually Blade could bring such a topic up. Civionis having a mine of that nature made sense, considering the amount of adolium sitting soundly in the stone above the city. However, the Church's methods of obtaining said stone were seldom the topic of casual conversation. Miners digging for that golden, solidified magic were at constant risk of suffering magical overflow from the energy it emitted. It was the kind of job that everyone knew had to exist, but often dismissed with a *"well, at least I'm not the one doing it."*

"The Church will pay good money to get people to risk their lives," Blade continued in response to Enoch's silence. "But, if I had to guess, it was probably demons and convicts that did the actual digging. Well, until the miners released a toxic gas that shut the whole operation down; or so the story goes. Been a while since I heard the rumors, but if they were true, not a single miner made it out alive."

Enoch held his breath at the mention of the gas. The noxious fumes still lingered faintly at the top of the tunnel, thin as ribbons floating through the air. The wisps had a slight glow to them, merging with the lanternlight. Enoch thought back to when he'd fainted at the terminal platform, and how similar he'd felt surrounded by the mists. "We should be careful then," he replied. "If this really is an old mineshaft, I mean. That red mist could be more dangerous than we thought."

"It's just a possibility," Blade corrected. "A story I heard from a guy too drunk to remember his own name." He looked up once again, cautiously eyeing the mist that had yet to affect him like it had his current company. "The tunnel shape and fumes match, but I think we're getting pretty close to Civionis. From my experience, mines like that aren't usually dug so close to cities. Especially not ones built above water. So, either they kept digging closer for some reason, or this is just a maintenance tunnel like you said."

As the two spoke, a branching tunnel hidden in the darkness came into view. Blade signalled Enoch to stop before sneaking up to the turn. The old, rotting wood supports around the entrance supported his theory, and offered decent cover as he peeked around the corner.

"Too dark to see anything." Blade held out his hand. Enoch approached as quietly as he could to hand him the lantern. "Stay here and keep quiet," the masked man ordered. Once he was sure Enoch would comply, he and the light disappeared into the tunnel.

Left in the darkness, Enoch's heart rose to his throat. *Is this my best chance to escape? I might reach Civionis if I follow this main tunnel long enough, but...* He glanced to the faint glow of the mist swaying with his vision. Its light was more a faded star than a guiding beacon, and the tunnel's edge was as visible as a lakebed at night. *With how I am right now, I'd just be stumbling around blindly. Blade would catch up easily.* He steadied himself on the wall, wiping some sweat off his brow. *And I still haven't gotten any information about who he is or why he's after Azazel. I can't go back yet.*

THUD! CRACK! *Tap tap tap...*

Enoch's heart escaped his throat, becoming a startled yelp at the sudden noise around the corner. "Damn it," Blade grumbled. The light of the lantern rounded the corner before the young man's sigh could, breaking the tension. His guarded, stealthy demeanor drifted off with the lingering mists as he left the tunnel behind.

"This one caved in. I can't break through, so we aren't getting out that way." He handed the lantern back to Enoch, before lifting a rotting, broken handle into the Scribe's line of sight. "Looks like we aren't the only ones that tried, though. The pick was half-buried in the stone, so I guess this was a mine after all." He tossed the handle aside, wiping his hands off on his cloak as he muttered to himself. "There weren't any remains though. Did the owner die somewhere else? Or did they find a way out?" His cloak shifted as he began to tap his finger beneath it. "We're close to the city too. Something doesn't feel right."

Blade's thoughts seemed to drown out Enoch's existence in his mind. The Scribe held his tongue out of fear of angering the violence-prone man. After a moment, Blade simply shook his head, nodding it towards the tunnel. "Let's go. We should stop wasting time."

"R-Right..." Without another word, the two continued their trek through the abandoned mine. Enoch tried to focus on figuring out how to learn more about Blade. It seemed he was fairly knowledgeable on mining, but that fact likely wouldn't help narrow down possible identities. Not on its own at least.

Enoch's head felt foggier by the second. Before he could worry about that, he needed to focus on getting out of the tunnels alive. But the dripping pipes drowned out any cohesive thoughts, his mind losing its focus in the repeated *drip... drip... drip...* until a chilling realization managed to push its way through the haze.

No remains, huh? If I died down here... would anyone even be able to find me?

The pipes had no answer. They simply continued to count the seconds...

Drip...

    Drip...

        Drip...

Chapter 16

THAT WAS IT... That was the end of the tracks. A pit at the base of the mountain, as large as the pit that had formed in Azazel's gut. One small solace was that no bodies could be seen at the bottom. The crimson color of the forest was reserved for the surrounding trees, not the puddles that might have formed deep beneath it.

Azazel wanted to dive in. Maybe he just couldn't see them. Maybe this angle wasn't right. Maybe he needed to cross that threshold of solid stone to reach the view only attainable on those about to crumble. He shook his head, trying to stave off his doubts. He had to stay optimistic. He had to. *Maybe he was gone by the time this happened,* he told himself, *maybe Seira is just struggling with finding the next tracks on the stone. You lost the path, but you can't lose hope.*

With his wings, getting in and out of the pit to know for sure would be effortless. But doing so would reveal his secret, so he had no choice but to wait as she searched for another lead; any sign of Enoch's next step. The angel sought comfort in Dear's fur, tracing the blue patterns with his fingers. If Seira didn't return soon, he'd likely pet long enough to rub right through. Thankfully, Dear was spared this bald patch by the *nearly* silent sound of Seira's boots on the stone and dirt.

"Find any tracks?" Azazel asked. Seira shook her head.

"They came this way, but they didn't leave. Not unless they suddenly sprouted wings."

If Enoch had secretly been an angel all this time, Azazel felt he'd know by now. Unless his observation skills had dulled over the years. The masked stranger, on the other hand, couldn't be ruled out. Not if they truly were an agent of Spira.

"When were you planning on telling me there was someone following him?" Seira asked.

Azazel hesitated. She hadn't mentioned anything until now, so he'd thought he'd gotten away with it. After all, he hadn't *actively* lied to her, just withheld some information. She clearly had enough on her plate, and he didn't want to involve another friend in this masked murderer business. Enoch was put in danger because of their connection, and Seira had enough enemies already. He'd said what she'd needed to know, and nothing more. Unfortunately, facts are more indicative of the truth. He could withhold as much information as he wanted, but the tracks would reveal reality, not fantasy.

"There was?" he asked, quickly recovering. But not soon enough, it would seem.

"So, you knew then." Seira crossed her arms. "Spill it, Greg. What was Enoch doing when he went missing out here?"

"There's nothing to spill," Azazel mirrored her crossed arms. Dear huffed in disbelief, earning a side-glance from the yellow-coated Pilgrim. "Hey, don't take that tone of breath with me. I'm being honest."

"There were two sets of tracks, Greg."

"Maybe the second were mine?"

Seira didn't even grace that with a verbal response. Her raised eyebrow and skills as a tracker were argument enough. But Azazel stood his ground, whether she believed him or not, this was for her own good.

Seeing Azazel was planning to keep up this façade, Seira decided it was time for brutal honesty. "Alright, if you won't talk, want me to tell you exactly what I've figured out from the tracks?"

Azazel didn't like where this was going. Seira began nevertheless.

"Going off the footprints we found at the bridge, Enoch was following first. His steps were dragged, and he left a lot of broken plants and branches. I thought it was just because he was running, but even after the prints got closer together there were still signs of stumbling and confusion. Broken handholds, random, unnecessary wandering. Considering the strict laws on public drinking, I'm guessing he wasn't drunk. So, it could be confusion from an injury, or maybe he was sick... Maybe something you can only get here in Civionis?"

"..."

Azazel always had been stubborn. Moving back to the abruptly ended path they'd followed to get there, Seira continued. "About halfway though, the second set of prints veered off, circling around to follow Enoch instead. I don't blame you for losing the track there. This person clearly knows how to hide their presence." The fur-clad Pilgrim knelt down, tracing the nearly hidden tracks with a sparkle in her eyes. She seemed almost... excited? Or perhaps it was admiration. "If it wasn't for the offset weight of their shoes,

I may have missed the detour completely. Either way, it was clearly deliberate."

So that means the killer really was following Enoch. The worry that thought carried with it made Azazel sick to his stomach. Until then it had only been a possibility, but he trusted Seira's skills enough to believe her theory. The fear was enough to fully silence him as he tried to find hope, tried to remain optimistic. Tried to maintain the brightness he was known for as the world piled more and more misfortune. Being who he was, he'd undoubtedly find some form of silver lining given time. But before he could, Seira approached.

To Azazel's surprise, she wrapped an arm around his shoulder. A hug? No, it was too tight. She–"*Ack!*" With no hesitation, Seira pulled the angel into a headlock, one arm around his neck, the other holding back his arm. Azazel struggled against her grip, even knowing she was undeniably the stronger one. "Seira, what're you– *why?*"

"Talking wasn't getting through that stubborn head of yours, so you left me no choice." The fur-clad Pilgrim pulled back, toeing the line between discomfort and pain. "Tell me what's actually going on or I'm not letting go."

"This is *so childish*," Azazel said with hassled breath, "I'm not– hiding anything!"

"Yes, you are."

"No, I'm not"

"You are and you're gonna tell me if you want me to let go."

"Then I hope your arms are comfortable like that because we aren't moving for a while." Somehow, the cracks that sounded throughout the angel's spine were both freeing and painful simultaneously. Knowing he couldn't resist much longer Azazel patted her arm with his free hand.

"Okay! Fine, fine. Just let go before you break something."

Seira's grip didn't loosen. "Tell me first."

"Oh, you've gotta be– I knew about the second guy, okay?"

"Then why didn't you tell me?"

"Because I didn't want him to kill you next!"

Azazel nearly fell back from how quickly Seira released him. Once he'd recovered, he stretched out his overextended arm, watching the confusion build on Seira's face.

"*Kill* me? What do you mean, Greg?" she asked. "Why would– Who is this guy? What have you and that kid gotten into?"

It was too late to take it back now, so Azazel leaned into the truth. "It started this morning, when Enoch collapsed from everred fever. Outside of the House of Healing, I ran into a Priest that'd been attacked by a man in a metal mask. He said the guy that tried to kill him was looking for me."

Confusion shifted to protective anger as Seira heard his words. "You're being hunted by a killer and you decided to wander around Everred *alone!?* How could you do something so stupid?"

"I didn't have much of a choice!" Azazel defended "Enoch saw the guy and chased him down. I needed to find him before he ended up stabbed to death like the Priest. I... I promised I'd keep him safe." With their emotions heating up, Azazel pointed sharply. "And you don't get to lecture *me* on dumb decisions after our conversation at the camp. Just because I'm trusting you doesn't mean I think your theory is any less reckless."

"That's different."

"How?"

"I know who my enemy is. Can you say the same about this masked guy? Do you even know if he has an ability? If he's working alone or not? If–"

"It doesn't matter!" Azazel snapped. Shock sealed Seira's lips. They'd fought countless times, usually small spats forgotten by the next morning, but this was the first time she'd heard him truly raise his voice. She watched Azazel recede, drowning in the ever-piling problems. The worry, the worthlessness, the fear of the truth that Seira had so blatantly stated. Light, blinded and swallowed by the surrounding clouds.

"I know I'm going in blind." Azazel continued, voice fighting between determination and vulnerability. "I know, but I don't care. All that matters is saving Enoch before the worst-case scenario happens. He *just* chose to keep living, so I can't let him die yet." The angel took a step forward, firmly gripping Seira's shoulders. She was far too startled to fight it, instead finding herself frozen by the passion burning in his eyes.

"And after he's safe, I'll stop this masked killer before they can hurt anyone else. And then I'll help you figure out what happened to Faolan. I can do all of it. I *will* do all of it, even if it's dangerous." The angel's grip loosened, the edges of his lips lifting into a smile as his arms moved to his chest. "I'll handle things, so you don't have to worry. You got me here, and that's enough. You just focus on finding your smile again, okay?"

"Gregory..." Seira was at a loss for words. The two failed to notice the hypocrisy; that his grip, his gaze, his words were nothing but a mirror between them. That their thoughts were merely echoes of the other's.

I'll protect you, no matter the cost.
I'll protect you, because I cannot stand to see you hurt.
I'll lie, if it means keeping you safe.

Caught in this moment, in their own self-sacrificial world, the two failed to notice the figure approaching from within the forest. The stranger's red cloak flowed with the breeze, merging with the surrounding crimson flora. Stopping in the shade, they watched, moving their hand to the rapier at their hip. The witness really had seen the duo at the bridge. With a deep breath, Iris silently raised her hand.

For the sake of the city, it was time to finally put an end to this chase.

Chapter 17

HOW COULD I let this happen?

That question repeated in Azazel's mind as he stood with his hands raised, surrounded by Priests on one side, and a giant pit on the other. The entire arrest had happened faster than Azazel could reach for his blade. Ropes were tossed over Dear, four Priests holding the panicked animal down. A large, dark brown blur darted out of the treeline to restrain Seira. Iris, rapier drawn, stood opposite of the two Pilgrims with a saddened expression.

"Sorry for the hostility, Gregory," she said, lowering her blade somewhat. "This must look awful without context, but unfortunately, Miss Equitervi has a history of violence when dealing with my men. I couldn't afford to hesitate."

Seira struggled against the grip of one of these men. Dark brown fur covered his arms. His fingers and muscles were twice as thick as any normal human's. Even his face found itself framed by fur, the features a mix between a human and ape. Try as she might, Seira couldn't overpower the Shapeshifter's strength.

Perhaps, despite the inopportune timing, it would be best to explain how a Shapeshifter ability works to show how someone as strong as Seira could find herself outmatched.

A Shapeshifter is able to transform their body into a single kind of animal, the specific kind differing person to person. They can fully shift into their animal form, gaining whatever natural benefits that creature may have. Or they can take a half-beast form, using less magical energy to change into a humanoid version of their animal. These abilities are especially resonant with the magic of the moon, causing its phases to affect them. Unfortunately for Seira, the new moon had already come and passed, allowing the Priest to take his half-beast gorilla form as he pinned her face first in the forest floor.

Struggling against the Shapeshifter Priest's grip, Seira took a moment to spit at Iris' words. "What? Knew you'd lose in a fair fight?" she taunted.

"I'm just doing my job, Miss. Equitervi," Iris replied. "There's no need for hostility. If you don't resist, we'll have no need for further force."

Azazel looked at the sheer amount of manpower they'd sent to arrest his friend. "You sure? I mean, things feel pretty hostile despite the reassurance," he argued with a nervous chuckle. "What's this about? It's not illegal to walk in a forest, right?"

"Actually, the forest *is* under a lockdown at the moment," Iris replied. "One of the reasons we're out here is to evacuate civilians before they get caught in a sinkhole like the one behind you." Iris gestured to the pit, shaking her head in remorse. "Some kind of burrowing animal has been mutated by an unknown source of magic. We're looking into the situation, but until then Everred has been deemed a hazardous environment thanks to its digging."

"Unknown magic my ass," Seira snapped. "You and Paras know exactly what's–"

With more force than necessary, the Shapeshifter Priest slammed Seira's face into the ground. The fur-clad Pilgrim let out a muffled cry of pain. Dear struggled harder in response, testing the strength of the Priests tasked with holding her steady.

"Hey!" Azazel cried out, barely stopping himself from running right past Iris and her rapier. "You've already caught her. You don't need to get violent." The urge to slam a metal rod into the half-transformed Priest's temple was building, but Azazel knew they were outnumbered here. Painful as it was, he had to hold back for now.

"Gregory is right." Iris turned to the Shapeshifter Priest. "I can understand the frustration, but any further outbursts will be penalized. Understood? We're above needless acts of violence."

"Yes, Commander," the Priest replied, "Sorry, Commander." The half-beast Priest resigned himself to simply holding Seira in place. Still reeling from the impact, Seira's defiance had lessened considerably, making his job much easier. With the outburst handled, Iris turned back to Azazel.

"The second reason we're out here is to take Miss. Equitervi into custody. She's proven herself to be a danger to the people of Civionis."

"Seira? Dangerous?" Azazel shook his head, doing his best to calm the growing tension with a smile. "Are you sure you've got the right person? The Seira I know hides in the woods and avoids seeing folks as much as possible. How could you be a threat to the city if you never even interact with it?"

"Oh, you two have history then?" Iris replied. "Explains why you were out here together, I suppose." The Circlet

Guard Commander sheathed her blade, hand still resting at the ready on its hilt. She sighed, "I'm sorry to be the bearer of bad news then, but Seira hasn't been herself since her brother passed away."

Slowly, Iris ran her fingers through the hanging branches of the nearby everred tree. Her wistful gaze looked through the timberland, focused on memories of the tragic incident that had overturned Seira's life. "Faolan was one of our city's best Researchers. I heard he'd even studied at Gabriel's Citadel alongside the Church's brightest. Unfortunately, his passion is what led to his death." The Circlet Guard's sigh mirrored the heavy weight of her words. She watched as some of the needles fell away at her touch, dropping to the forest floor. "Everred fever was the cause, contracted while researching the origin of the forest's unique colors. Nothing devious, no hidden plots or schemes, it was simply an incident caused by being more stubborn and curious than cautious." Slowly, Iris shook her head in both remorse and disappointment. "He underestimated his own tolerance, and that cost him his life. We told Seira as much when she came back from her travels, but–"

"You're lying!" Seira said, face still shoved in the dirt. The memories flooded her mind, overflowing as tears. Iris gently clicked her tongue.

"Still in denial, I see." Like a mother forced to explain the actions of a misbehaving child, Iris turned to Azazel with tired eyes begging for sympathy. "She refuses to accept that the brother she admired so much could have made such a preventable mistake. So, she's clung to this idea that the Church killed him, that there's some kind of cover up going on. She's a talented Pilgrim when given the right jobs, so we were fine letting her grieve in her own way. But then she assaulted a Priest, claiming he was guarding something linked to her imagined conspiracy. He still hasn't fully recovered."

At Iris' words, the Shapeshifter Priest's grip tightened ever so slightly. An anger darkened his eyes, held back solely by the threat of repercussions should he act on it. He felt very much like a dam made of paper and wood. Iris placed a reassuring hand on the Shapeshifter's shoulder before turning back to Azazel. "She escaped after back up arrived, but we finally managed to track her down today. I'm sorry that it happened to be when you two were catching up; honestly, I am." With a welcoming smile, Iris held out an inviting hand. "If you'd like, you're welcome to come with us. After how poorly this all started, I'm sure you must be hesitant about letting Seira come with us alone. It's the least I could do to ease your worries."

"Don't you dare drag him into this," Seira said, the words pushing through gritted teeth. "Lie all you want, but you can't cover up the truth." Despite the strength of the Shapeshifter's half-beast form, Seira pushed her head up, glaring defiantly at the Circlet Guard Commander. "I know what really happened. I know what you and Paras are hiding under this city."

"Choose your next words carefully," Iris warned. "Assaulting a Priest is a serious offense, but needlessly slandering the Church's reputation will only add to the sentence. Our patience for your fantasies is already thin."

In a rare moment of compliance, Seira did carefully think over her words. She considered her situation; the size of the group sent to ambush her; Iris' act to protect their image; the fact that she'd chosen to arrest her then and there, despite Gregory's presence... They were planning to bring him in too. They had to be. If that was the case, then she needed to reveal it now. Before they could lie to him. Before they could turn him against her, she needed him to know the truth.

"You're right," Seira admitted. "Faolan died for his research, his passion..."

Hearing Seira's words shake, Azazel's heart sank. Unbeknownst to him, it wasn't despair or defeat staggering her voice. It was defiance, an anger so strong it shook her very body.

"He died because he knew you were hiding a Remnant of Adoil beneath the city, right? He died because he was going to reveal that to everyone, and you couldn't let that happen!"

The following silence felt heavy enough to break the ground beneath their feet. After a seconds long eternity, Iris sighed. Out of everything Seira could have said, she'd chosen that? It seemed the fur-clad Pilgrim didn't care much for her friend after all. In a way, Iris was almost jealous of the tracker's confidence, the freedom to say such words without fear. But bravery and confidence did little against the might of the Church.

"Such a dangerous delusion, Miss Equitervi," she said, her expression darkening as she considered her next move. "Perhaps you should have chosen more carefully."

Chapter 18

AT THE BEGINNING of all things, the Celestials existed eternal within the void. The Constellations, The Corporeal Beings, The Force of Creation... They took many forms, lived many centuries, their power immeasurable. During the creation of our world, the Corporeal Being known as Adoil came undone, unravelling itself to become the magic that flows through the world. This moment, known as The Flare, was believed by many to be the death of the all-powerful Celestial.

But the Celestials are eternal, and eternity cannot end.

The Flare was not the final burst of the curious, ambitious Celestial, it was a moment of rebirth. Over centuries, the will of Adoil lived on through the Remnants. Minor-celestials scattered throughout the Three Realms and the surrounding void. Conscious beings of magic, each with their own wills, their own thoughts, their own desires. Though many were locked away in the name of safety, even the Archangels themselves could not find and contain the entirety of a Celestial as powerful as Adoil. And so, many Remnants continued to exist beyond their knowledge and influence, observing, learning and adapting over time.

Hearing that such a powerful being could be lurking so close to the people of Civionis, Azazel couldn't stop his hands from shaking.

"Is that true?" he asked, taking note of Iris' sudden defensiveness at Seira's accusation. The Circlet Guard's gaze remained on Seira as she answered.

"Do you really think the Church would hide something so dangerous underneath a city of all places?"

Admittedly, I wouldn't put it past them, Azazel replied in his mind. He knew he couldn't voice that thought aloud though, given their situation. Iris had the numbers, and the brawn thanks to the half-ape Priest. If he decided to shift from his half-beast form to a full gorilla, he could overpower Azazel and Seira like a boot on ants. If the angel was going to get them out of this, he'd need to be clever. That being said, even if Iris was telling the truth and Seira really had imagined this conspiracy about the Church; if she'd truly assaulted a Priest and slandered the Bishop without proof, there wasn't much he could do to persuade them. Not without causing trouble for himself, which he'd promised a good friend he wouldn't do.

"Look, I know Seira has a tendency to be distrustful and paranoid," he said, ignoring the icy look Seira sent his way. "But that doesn't mean she's a threat to people's safety. She wouldn't go that far."

Finally pulling her sights off of Seira, Iris approached Azazel. His muscles tensed as she raised her hand, only to place it gently on his shoulder. Seira winced at the sight.

"Grief can make people act in unusual ways, Gregory," Iris argued. That truth strummed a sour note in the Pilgrim's mind.

"You're not wrong," he hesitantly agreed. "But still..." Keeping an eye on Iris just in case, Azazel walked by her, kneeling down an arm's length away from Seira. The Priests, seeing Iris herself allowing him to do this, kept their distance. "Seira, be honest with me. Do you have any proof?"

The Shapeshifter Priest looked to Iris for direction, his hand covering the fur-clad Pilgrim's mouth. The Commander nodded, curious to hear the answer herself. Having gotten permission, the Priest moved his grip, revealing Seira's scowl beneath.

"You promised you'd trust me," Seira said softly. Azazel could see her searching his eyes, watching carefully. "Do you really think I'd lie to you after that, Greg?"

"I'm not worried that you're lying to *me*, Seira."

The implications hiding between his words hurt more than the reply itself. An anger bubbled up within Seira's chest, its heat scalding her heart.

"Faolan was a Researcher," she stated, an acid-like sting to her voice. "Ignoring the truth to make myself feel better would be as disrespectful as trampling his Resting Garden."

She had nothing left to say after that. Not to him. Not to Iris. Not to any of them. If that was Azazel's answer, then she was better off keeping her mouth shut. The angel lingered a second longer. Long enough to know his friend was being earnest. With a sigh, he turned back to Iris.

"Well, it can't be helped. You're right. She's delusional," he admitted, as much as it pained him to say.

"What!?" Seira's planned silence came to an early end. She glared up at her fellow Pilgrim. "You're supposed to be on *my* side!"

All he offered in response was a dismissive shrug. "Like I said, you've clearly lost it. It's best to let them take you to someone that can help. Clearly, I'm not the person you need right now." Azazel pinched the bridge of his nose, his other hand resting on his hip as he lamented, distancing himself from Seira. "But I still have to accept some of the blame. If I'd visited sooner, maybe things wouldn't have gotten so bad. I could've helped you cope."

The angel made his way over to Dear, holding up a gentle hand to steady her. Recognizing her friend, Dear's skittish demeanor settled somewhat. Her ears still turned like loosened wagon wheels. Her tail still pressed against her body. But Azazel's eyes brought a small amount of comfort, as did the calmness of his voice. "Instead, all you had was Dear. You two were suffering so much, and I was nowhere to be found. I'm sorry."

A silence followed. Remorse filled the absence of words. Whether from confusion or sympathy, the gathered group allowed Azazel this soliloquy. Having composed himself, appearing to have fully accepted his and Seira's fate, the angel's final words came out in a whisper.

"But you can't change the past, can you?"

Shing! In a flash of golden light, Azazel drew his blade from his belt loops, slicing through the ropes holding Dear down. The black and blue deer stood, shaking off the remaining binds. Caught off guard by the sudden slack, the Priests that had been holding her down fell to the dirt. Azazel took advantage of the opening, tightly gripping Dear's saddle. His muscles flexed. He pulled himself up, trying to swing a leg over, only to find himself involuntarily veering away.

Well, that's not's good, he though to himself as his head suddenly turned off course, throwing off his trajectory. As if drawn by magnetic force, his gaze was pulled to Iris. Or rather, the ground at her feet as she stood back up. A heavy

THUD reverberated through his body, dust blown away from his impact with the forest floor.

My eyes, I... I can't control them! he realized, gaze glued to the ground beneath Iris, *Is this her magic ability?* His neck strained against him as he tried to turn away.

"A commendable attempt, Mr. Veramor," Iris complimented. "Ineffective, but I can respect your confidence." The Circlet Guard approached him. If her praise had been dishonest, he had no way of telling, seeing how her face and expression were now beyond his peripheral. With movements far more uncomfortable than ideal, Azazel struggled to pull himself into a better position. Though his vision was under the control of a magic ability, it seemed the rest of his body was unaffected. Unfortunately, his gamble had failed. He'd have to fight, difficult as it would be in his current state.

THUD THUD THUD!

A barrage of hooves slammed into the ground in front of him, driving dust into his face. Despite the fact that a full-grown deer was rampaging next to his head, Azazel had no choice but to close his eyes as they watered from the forming cloud. The act brought more reprieve than he'd expected, the magnetic force vanishing alongside his sight.

Dear reared back, forcing Iris to stop her approach. The heavy hooves just barely missed the Circlet Guard's head, grazing her arm instead. After dropping her blade, Iris gripped what would soon be an awful bruise, grateful it hadn't been a more direct hit.

"Commander!" the Shapeshifter Priest cried. Panic divided his attention. Seizing the moment, Seira dug her teeth into his fingers with a gruesome *crunch.* Blood trickled down her chin.

"Gah! Dammit!" Knowing his job was to keep Seira restrained, the Priest refused to let go. But that momentary weakness, the single second where his hands instinctively tried to pull away from the threat, that was all Seira needed. She forced an arm out of his grip, elbowing his face in the process for good measure. His teeth slammed together with a painful *crack!* Hoping that would keep him too distracted to transform, Seira rushed to Dear, spitting out a finger as she moved.

"Equitervi's escaped!" a Priest shouted, drawing her saber from her hip. Seira didn't allow her the opportunity to use it. When she came close, the Pilgrim dodged to the side, grabbing the uniformed woman's outstretched arm to flip her. Seira shifted her hip. The saber clattered to the ground. Bones cracked within the Priest's shoulder, and she let out a winded gasp on impact.

Another opponent followed the first. Seira jumped at them, using their chest to launch herself towards Dear. Even with her friend's heavy-hooved rampage, Seira gracefully swung onto her back.

"Gregory!" she shouted, glancing towards Iris' attempts to break through the barrage of hooves. "Grab on!"

His eyes still closed from the dust cloud before, Azazel reached towards Seira's voice. A firm grip met his grasp, and Seira pulled him up onto Dear's back. The fur-clad Pilgrim was surprised by how light her friend felt, unaware of the assistance his hidden wings had provided.

Swish! Iris' recovered blade cut through the air as she made one last desperate swing at the fleeing Dear. "After them!" she shouted. "We can't let her get away again!"

Try as they might, the Priests were no match for the strength and speed of an adult deer, let alone one so accustomed to sprinting through this particular forest. If he still had all his fingers, the Shapeshifter might have stood a chance following through the trees, but Seira's teeth had put a damper on that possibility.

Iris watched the two Pilgrims fade into the forest fog. Her running slowed as a scream built in her chest. No. She couldn't let it out. She swallowed her frustration, knowing such weakness couldn't be shown in front of her men. Her knuckles cracked instead from the strength of her grip on her blade. She had to keep up appearances, despite their failure. Despite *her* failure. Despite this worst-case scenario.

...The Bishop wouldn't be happy about this.

Chapter 19

AFTER WHAT FELT like an eternity of walking to the Scribe's fever-burned mind, Enoch nearly ran into a wall hidden around a bend in the mineshaft. He caught himself, his still dizzy head following a moment after. Just a foot around the bend, eerily flat stone marked the end of the tunnel. The obstacle drained Enoch's hope. If the tunnel ended there, then the two of them had no choice but to return to the crumbling cavern from before. As for what they could do after that, they'd either have to wait for help to arrive, or accept that their grave would be unnaturally deep.

"Guess this is a dead–"

CRACK! A sudden punch from Blade's steel-knuckles crumbled the wall in an instant. Enoch winced, coughing in the cloud of dust strong enough to extinguish their lantern's flame. The Scribe stepped back, narrowly avoiding the rocks falling around his feet. His vision reeled as it adjusted, clouded until the dust cleared. Despite regaining his senses, Enoch couldn't make sense of the sight behind the false stone Blade had broken.

A metal wall ran the full width of the tunnel, blocking their path. Symmetrical, stylized embossments and carvings decorated the wall itself, similar to the columns of the High Cathedral, but made of metal rather than stone. Equally ornate, an arched steel door with no handle or hinges sat directly in the center.

The pipes passed through to the other side on the top left. In the top right, a small, sealable, square vent blew out hot air, along with familiar red, misty ribbons drifting above them. Beneath this was something far less familiar. A small square stuck out half an inch farther than the rest of the wall. On it, a rectangular, opaque window sat above ten square buttons, as well as a larger rectangular one with Celestial characters carved into it. Even without firelight, the buttons and window glowed with a cool, blue hum, allowing the two young men to see this strange wall even with their lantern snuffed out. Blade let out a condescending sigh.

"The pipes went right through that wall. Please don't tell me you were actually about to buy that half-assed trick."

"I..." As much as Enoch wanted to argue, he'd admittedly been too tired to notice the pipe. Perhaps he would have found some solace in the fact that neither had noticed the thin gap that had been hidden in the opposite corner allowing the mist to pass through. Unfortunately, with the wall now shattered into pieces, that detail was as lost as they were.

Enoch held his tongue, instead turning back to the once hidden door. "What *is* this?" he wondered aloud, putting down the lantern as he leaned in closer to the small panel. Blade crossed his arms beneath his cloak.

"Reminds me of a cathedral, so probably nothing good," he muttered. "But we can't go back the way we came." Far less baffled than Enoch, Blade placed a hand on the door. Now that he had a stronger light source than a struggling lantern flame, the Scribe noticed that Blade had no sleeves. Instead, metal bands, rings and bracelets of various designs lined his hands and arms.

"It's steel," Blade stated. "Guess it's a wall? Or some kind of trick door?"

When Blade looked to him for a reaction, Enoch quickly turned back to the strange window to hide that he'd been staring. "If it's a trick door, opening it could be connected to the numbers on here," he replied. Blade's head tilted somewhat.

"You can read those scribbles?"

"You mean the Celestial Script?" Enoch nodded, pointing to the marked buttons. "Yeah. These top ones are one to nine, with a zero underneath here. The big one says enter." As a Scribe, Enoch had seen these symbols almost daily in his work. To him, reading the "scribbles" as Blade had put it, was as simple as understanding the common script. His mysterious companion stared a second longer before crossing his arms.

"Didn't realize you were such a geek," he insulted.

"Geek is actually a compliment," Enoch argued. "Jonas Geek remembered every single thing he read, held records for being the fastest reader in all of Terrael, and was one of the greatest Scribes aside from Penemue himself, so calling someone a geek–" he cut himself off, Blade's judgement more palpable by the second. With an awkward clear of his throat, he turned his attention back to the strange window, or screen, as it was actually called. Not that the young men were aware of this. "Anyways, it's rare to see the Celestial Script used out in the world like this. Normally only the Church or Spira would use it."

"Church-like architecture, Church-only writing, old mines that used to belong to the Church." Blade waved his hands, sarcastically adding dazzle to his words. "What a mystery! I wonder who might be behind this dangerous mist and shoddy wall building!"

"...The Church?" Enoch asked quietly in the following pause. Blade's shoulders dropped.

"Yeah, that was– Y'know, never mind." The masked man nodded to the small screen. "So can you figure out the chicken scratch or not?"

Wariness slowed Enoch's fingers, lightly grazing the buttons without actually pressing any. Though this technology was far more advanced than anything he'd seen before, he felt very much like an archaeologist studying an old ruin. "I'm not sure. I'm guessing the numbers on them are to help people know which ones to press, but I have no clue how such small switches could affect a big wall like this. Or what the window is for. If I press things without thinking I could trigger some kind of trap."

"Guess you can be cautious when you need to be," Blade commented. "Well, we *could* try pressing stuff and see what happens..." He turned his attention back to the wall in front of him. The metal had a subtle warmth behind it, and he gently tapped it with his knuckles. It was a nice sound; soft, sturdy, the resulting hum told him exactly what he needed to know. Moving his hand to the very edge of the arch, he focused from within the mask. "Or I can just do this."

Competing with the blue, ambient light of the screen, Blade's hand glowed red. Like a curtain being drawn, the metal door pulled aside, opening up the path. "Didn't even need the chicken-scratch," he muttered to himself, an over-confident edge to the words. "C'mon, let's find another tunnel and get out of here quick. But be careful. We don't know what's–"

In an instant, Blade's overconfidence found itself shadowed by the eerie environment waiting on the other side of the door. Enoch could see the unmistakably constructed smoothness of the stone walls inside. A solid line of glass ran along the center of the ceiling, emitting a pale, golden glow, and revealing other metal doors, buttons and strange windows further down. It was unlike anything the two young men had seen before. An unnatural, unnerving, unfamiliar atmosphere. Beyond what *had* been the door, they would clearly be leaving the old mineshaft behind.

Enoch noticed Blade's hesitation. *Is he waiting for me to go first?* he wondered. It seemed the mask failed to hide his fear as well as it hid his face. After the incident in the capital, as well as rooming with an angel for nearly three months, Enoch had found himself better equipped to handle sudden, bizarre revelations. Or at the very least he'd learned that when faced with a choice between the unknown and the unfavorable, it was often better to face the former. "Well, standing here won't get us closer to an exit," he said, before carefully waving a hand through the sculpted door. Seeing that it remained unscathed, his body followed. Whatever this place was, at least it didn't have any traps set up to stop intruders. "You ready?" he asked, turning back to Blade.

Embarrassed by his hesitation, Blade hurried through the door, stopping just a moment to return it to its normal state. "Yeah, let's just get through here quick. I don't have any business with whatever this place is, and we need to get to Gregory before he skips town."

At the mention of his friend, Enoch's stomach turned. The strange setting had distracted him a moment, but his situation was still the same. What would happen if they found an exit? If he couldn't find help? What would happen if he brought Blade to Azazel? His vision repeated in his mind. Azazel's side skewered by a crimson flame. The man in the mask falling to his knees after the angel's blade slipped, smoothly piercing his stomach. The anguish, fear and regret in Azazel's eyes as he held the unknown attacker in his arms. The burst of fiery magic that had instantly overwhelmed Enoch's body the moment the masked man died.

He turned to face Blade as the young man finished restoring the door behind them. He had no clue what awaited them in this strange, hidden tunnel. There was no way to know if another opportunity to ask would arise. A pit formed in his stomach. For a moment he felt like he was back in Penemue's Cathedral, in the capital, about to once again confront a demon. No. He couldn't let himself be scared. Both Azazel's and Blade's lives were in danger if he couldn't change their fates.

"Are you going to kill him?" Enoch finally asked, putting as much of an assertive tone behind the words as he could. Blade had begun to pass him, but turned back at the sudden question.

"What?"

"Gregory. If I bring you to him, are you going to kill him?"

The short breath Blade took to speak, quiet as it was, felt as loud as a cyclone in the empty hall. But the words themselves hesitated. "No," he said, softer than expected. "Not unless he gives me a reason to."

"And what reason would it take to push you that far?"

"Asking too many stupid questions might do it," Blade answered bluntly. Enoch's throat felt dry at the threat. Nevertheless, Blade had given him an answer to his first question, so maybe he could get more. *Something has to be keeping him from talking,* the Scribe thought, *is it fear? Guilt? If I could just figure that out then maybe he'd open up. I have to be sincere, not aggressive.*

"Look, I don't know anything about you, or what your intentions are with my friend. And I know that even if I refuse to bring you to Gregory, you can just find him yourself. You've made that very clear. But..." Enoch placed a hand on his chest, trying his hardest to sound more amiable than afraid. "All I'm asking for is a little trust. I know Gregory, and if you can't even give someone that, then you have no chance of getting what you want from him. He's not the type of guy you can bully into getting what you want."

Enoch braced himself for the coming punch. Surprisingly, despite the evident tension in his body, Blade didn't seem intent on throwing it. Perhaps he'd gotten through to him!

While Enoch felt hope, Blade felt conflicted. He couldn't deny that his blatant denial to share the truth with the Scribe was growing dangerously close to outright lying to him. But words were surface level, and Enoch had shown he had little intention of cooperating without proper incentive. He was only following out of fear. He'd run the first chance he got. In Blade's mind, Enoch hadn't *given* trust, so what made him think he could ask for it? As if to prove this point, Enoch suddenly rushed at him.

Blade cursed in his mind, realizing he'd let himself get distracted. Considering Enoch's condition, it was a miracle that he managed to make contact, knocking the masked man to the side of the tunnel. Blade shaped his namesake out of a bracelet on his wrist, managing to graze Enoch's arm. The blood trailed down the end of the spike. Once he regained his balance, he prepared to jab once more.

"You little–" The anger and faint sense of betrayal boiling up within Blade simmered down at the sight of a dart sticking out of Enoch's shoulder, needle digging deep into his skin. Blade turned towards the hall. A strangely dressed man stood at the other end, pointing an even stranger pistol their way.

The man wore a long black coat, ending just before his protective boots. A mask shaped like a bird's beak covered his entire face. In fact, not a single part of his body was exposed. His goggles reflected the pale, blue light of another screen at the end of the hall, giving them an eerie, inhuman glow as the metal door hissed and slid shut behind him.

"Stay where you are!" he ordered. "How did you even get in here?" The man reached into a pouch at his side, loading another dart into the pistol. Before he could fire again, Blade grabbed the closest pipe, hands alight with magical energy. The glow traveled down the pipe, bursting it next to the attacker. Freezing cold lake water shot at the man's face, drenching him and the pistol as he tried to stop the leak. Blade let out a hum.

"Guess it was water," he said before turning to check on Enoch. The Scribe fell to a knee, and Blade rushed forward to catch him. Half-conscious, Enoch weakly gripped the fabric of Blade's cloak.

"Run... I'm..." Whatever words he'd hoped to say were lost with his consciousness, his grip on Blade's clothing brief as his hand swung limply into the puddle of lake water forming on the ground. Blade's stomach sank, and he quickly

checked for a pulse. It was faint, but still there. He let out a sigh of relief, realizing his ticket to finding Gregory had only been knocked out. "You really are more trouble than you're worth, geek" he grumbled.

Just as he had when the ground was collapsing, Blade moved to lift Enoch onto his back. Instead, he was met with the strange man lunging toward it. Blade quickly swung his elbow around, managing to land a hit to the stomach. The fabric of the man's coat let out a wet squelch. "Ew," Blade complained, before following up with a left hook to the jaw. The crimson glow around his hand formed a steel-knuckle from his rings just in time for the impact, and the strange man joined Enoch on the floor.

"Rude. All we did was break in without knocking." After one final kick to make sure the man really was out cold, Blade carried Enoch once again. A *click* sounded behind them. The young man dodged to the side as a large door dropped from the ceiling, cutting off their escape. Multiple smaller doors slid open with a chorus of mechanical hisses ahead, bringing more masked men to the hall. Blade adjusted his grip, reminded of just how light the Scribe was. That was good. It meant Blade could still move easily enough to fight, and he was definitely going to need to.

Chapter 20

WITH STEPS TOO soft for onomatopoeia, a white fox snuck across the rooftops of Civionis.

The stilted streets drummed with the movement of the crowd below. In the afternoons like this, even the roar of the waterfall found itself swallowed by the bustling of those heading to and from work. Conversation complimented the percussive footfall, the fox listening in for any useful information.

"Did you see the lines at the markets today? Tourists grabbed all the best flying fish before I made it halfway through. Guess I'll plan something else for dinner."

Hmm... Perhaps I should try the fish while I'm here.

"I hope the Pilgrims finish with the set up soon. The commission board is filling up at the cathedral. The Dispatcher actually told me to come back with my request later! The nerve of some people!"

Strange. Even with the ceremony, the city's workforce should be enough. I wonder why they'd be so short staffed.

"Sorry, I know I promised I'd help with the baby shower, but my vacation ended up being the same week. I can't exactly just tell the Church no, so I promise I'll make it up to you when I'm back!"

Mandatory vacations... No doubt connected to that illness, everred fever. Such a surface level solution... What is the Bishop thinking?

All kinds of complaints and conversations filled the fox's pointed ears. Domestic discussions, mundane mutterings, small details filed in his fuzzy head. Though, the most popular topic seemed to be the identities of the Recruiters invited for the ceremony.

Such anticipation was to be expected. After all, the recruiters that year were names known all across Terrael. The Sword of the Heavens, Emilian Belladei would represent the Priests. The Beauty of the South, Nitika Deomicis would grace the city with her presence as she looked for promising Pilgrims. And for the Inquisitors, Surufel Asaradel, the Moonlit Shadow, would be making a rare appearance. The Civionians whispered and wondered what these heroes might look like, curious if the reality would live up to the legends.

These hushed conversations reached the fox's ears up atop the stone buildings. Interesting as the topic was, he couldn't stop to listen. He had a job to do, after all.

There was still time. Time to learn all he could before the ceremony. Time to follow the Inquisitive he'd seen leaving the High Cathedral. Time to find out who they really were underneath their disguise.

The edge of the final rooftop approached, the fox's target making his way towards a platform bridge. Knowing it would be quite strange to see a creature like himself this far inside the city, the small mammal sought a new path to keep himself hidden. With a quick scramble down a windowsill, followed by a scamper to the underside of a carriage, he found just that. *Creeeeak, kachuck, kachuck, kachuck.* The sounds of the carriage on stone were overwhelming to the creature's heightened ears, but discomfort was a small price to pay for answers.

The fox's silver eyes tracked the Inquisitive as he crossed the canal. He couldn't afford to lose his mark. Fate had dropped this lead at his paws, and he was not the type to waste an opportunity.

To a casual observer, nothing had been out of the ordinary. An Inquisitive had simply left the High Cathedral. He'd waved to the Priests stationed by the wooden lift before descending to the city. The two guards had waved back with a sense of familiarity. Nothing more than a Church worker on his way home. But to the fox's experienced eyes, the clues were so obvious they might as well have been written in firelight.

First was the man's behavior. Subtle enough to only notice if you were looking for it, the elderly Inquisitive was checking over his shoulder. He favored the outer parts of crowds, easy escape routes closer to bridges. That alone raised suspicions, but that alone was not enough to incriminate.

A single pin. That was the imposter's downfall. Like the emblems proudly worn by Pilgrims, pins were gifted to each aspiring Inquisitor that managed to pass their schooling and earn their title. Were the pin lost, a real Inquisitor would know not to wear their uniform. Not until they'd gone through the lengthy process of getting a replacement, and likely a very long scolding. The lack of even a counterfeit to complete the disguise was enough to tell the fox this man was no Inquisitive. And yet, he still had to have some connection to the Church. After all, if he'd stolen the uniform by attacking a real Inquisitive, he would have acquired a pin along with his clothing. That is, unless the Inquisitive had hidden it during the mugging to give away their assailant. The possibility couldn't be ruled out, but if that weren't the case the uniform presumably came from a cathedral instead.

That complicated things.

Ignoring the shaking carriage rattling his brain, the fox went over the facts. Unused uniforms, as well as uniforms delivered for cleaning, were kept in a restricted area to lower the chance of theft. The imposter was clearly not a High Inquisitor, and so, that left the options of Dispatcher, Commander, High Priest or Bishop. All concerning titles to be connected to this kind of deception. Yet the dedication to credibility, pin aside, meant the possibility couldn't be ignored.

Either you're quite the thief, or you have some influential friends, the fox deduced, hopping off the carriage as its path veered from the "Inquisitive". *Just where will you lead me, little imposter?*

The secretive chase continued this way for some time. Rooftop, carriage, rooftop, wagon, rooftop, carriage, a sizeable fur coat conveniently draping across the platform stone behind its owner. More minutes passed than ideal for the creeping fox. *Will there still be time to track him down before he has a chance to leave?* he wondered. *No. Now's not the time to worry about that.* The fox put a stop to his veering train of thought. Though he was known for worrying about more topics than a normal brain could handle, he couldn't get distracted. One goal at a time.

I'll find Azazel once I'm finished. For now, I need to focus.

All the way out of the city, the little fox followed. Priests barricaded the bridges at the city's edge, adding to the fox's suspicions as they allowed the Inquisitive to pass through. The fox undoubtedly wouldn't be so lucky, instead swimming through the lake after a graceful dive into the brisk waves. Shaking itself off once it had reached the outer bank, it followed once more. Through the crimson foliage. Past the towering everreds. Along the aged mine tracks that the forest tried to bury. All the way to the weathered entrance into Mt. Morus, guarded by the Church for the public's protection.

The imposter Inquisitive stopped at the tunnel's edge, taking a moment to check his surroundings. "Security is light today, isn't it?" he asked. The taller of the two Priests leaned against the wooden edge of the entrance.

"The Commander needed backup, so it's just us 'til she's back."

"Backup? Did something happen?"

"Finally getting that Equitervi chick," the shorter Priest answered. With a disapproving frown, he lightly smacked his partner's crossed arm, signalling him to stand up straight with a flick of his head. The taller Priest reluctantly obliged. "Her and some Gregory guy are apparently on the boss' most wanted list right now."

Of course his name would come up in a place like this. The annoyance the fox felt would be difficult to express with the limited movement of its snout. Instead, the irritation radiated from deep within his very soul.

Knowing he wouldn't easily be able to enter the mines undetected at that moment, the fox instead turned back. It seemed he'd have to reorder his plans thanks to the actions of the troublesome Pilgrim.

Damn it, Azazel. Could you not keep a low profile for five minutes? the fox wondered, *I'm starting to think you're doing this just to spite me.* Fur ruffling in frustration, the fox hurried back into the forest. If the Church, or at the very least a group pretending to be part of it, was after Azazel, then that took priority.

Well, at least I'll be able to warn him sooner this way.

Chapter 21

CLANG! Clang! Clang… clang…

The impact of the Researcher hitting the metal door frame echoed throughout the hallway, the dusty footprint on their chest still visible. Their beaked mask muffled the pained cough within. Blade didn't wait to see if they got back up, continuing his search for an exit.

"Come on!" he exclaimed in frustration. "One of these has to be a way out of this damn place." Unlike the earlier locked ones, the inner hall doors seemed to simply slide open when he got close. Though he was curious as to how they worked, the panicked, masked man had no time to stop and investigate.

Fwish! Clink!

Another dart flew past his ear, imbedding itself into the stone wall. The glass vial attached to it shattered. Having missed its mark, the sleeping agent within slowly dripped to the floor instead. Blade hurried through the door once it had opened, grateful that the masked Researchers had awful aim.

He ran through hall after hall until he completely lost his sense of direction. Another metal door. Another room filled with glowing screens, golden light and technology he couldn't dream of comprehending. With each wrong turn, the size of the group following him grew, and Enoch felt heavier each second the chase continued. He needed a second to rest.

Channeling his magical energy, he turned to the most recent hall door, placing his fingertips against it once it had slid shut. He caused the metal to spread out, jamming it forcefully into the frame. Dedicated to its work, the door continued trying to slide with a determined *Kachunk. Kachunk. Kachunk.*

Having bought himself a minute, Blade tried to catch his breath. The sounds of the bird-masked Researchers struggling on the other side nearly drowned out the sound of his own struggled breathing.

You can't just run around without thinking. You're better than that! Blade thought, berating himself as he checked for any sort of writing or signs. Unfortunately, it seemed everything in the strange facility was written in the Celestial Script. Blade was far too bullheaded to admit it, but the geek's help would have made the escape go a lot smoother. Not that he could complain, seeing how he would have been the one unconscious if Enoch hadn't reacted so quickly.

As he leaned against the metal doorframe, Blade could feel it getting hotter against his shoulder. He pulled away before he could be burned. "Damn it," he said, noticing the door starting to turn red from the heat. "Guess some of them have abilities too." Not interested in waiting to see the person trying to melt their way through, Blade ran off to the next metal door, and the next room filled with incomprehensible tech.

At the end of the hall, he noticed another door with a screen and panel next to it, matching the one he and Enoch had entered through. Motivated by the potential escape, he ran over, using his power to pull the locked door aside just as the one behind him became a deadly, incandescent puddle. A black-haired Researcher stood behind the remains, her sleeves burned away by arms made of fire. Unlike the others, she wore no mask, her olive skin glistening in the light of her fiery magic ability. Blade had been in enough fights to know he didn't want to face her if he didn't have to.

As Blade closed the door behind him, once again jamming it with his magic, a voice sounded out from within the room. "I've never seen levels like this, what's—"

Blade's stomach sank as he spun around to face what he'd hoped was an exit. Instead, several Researchers turned their attention away from a large glass window to look at him, confusion evident even through their masks.

"Sorry, wrong room," Blade said before rushing towards the closest ones, sweeping his foot low to knock two of them over. Though some Researchers pulled away to ready their pistols, the stronger members of the group went to face this intruder head on. Blade's boots glowed, and spikes formed from the steel toes.

Fighting off four attackers at once, Blade found himself running out of steam. It was clear they'd had little combat training, even if they had strength in numbers. Dodging and blocking, he kept them at a distance for a while, but in the corner of his vision he could see the doorway glowing red once again.

Damn it! I need to get out of here! Where's the damn exit!? A faint glare behind the latest thrown punch gave an answer. *The window! Could I jump?*

Blade swung his leg wide, spiked shoe slamming into the thigh of the Researcher lunging towards him. They cried out from the spike digging into their leg before finding them-selves pushed to the side to block a dart. As the unlucky Researcher fell to the ground, a much larger opponent used the opportunity to grab Blade's leg. Another came from the side, trying to grab his arm. The latter found his hands skew-ered as metal spikes shot out from within Blade's cloak.

To save her friend, the larger Researcher swung Blade away, tossing him onto the floor by the glass window. The impact forced Enoch out of Blade's grip, the masked man rolling farther than the unconscious Scribe.

Crap! He watched as one of the attackers went to secure Enoch before Blade could get back to him. Cornered, the masked man scrambled to his feet, forming steel-knuckles around both hands now that they were free. He quickly glanced over his shoulder to see if the window could offer salvation.

The ground on the other side was about fifty feet lower than what Blade now assumed was an observation room. A dim light covered the entire chamber, and Blade found his gaze immediately drawn to the large, cylindrical glass tank in the very center.

Swirling within was a creature made of dark crimson smoke. Though it had no solid form, it still took a distinct shape, forming an almost humanoid body with large, angelic wings. The golden light beneath it silhouetted the creature as it seemed to sit at the bottom of the tank, like a child confined to their room. As if reacting to Blade's glance, the creature looked up, staring without eyes. And yet, Blade could still feel its gaze upon him, within him, as if the crea-ture was peering into his very soul.

"Find him..."

The inaudible, deep, gentle voice spoke into his mind.

"Reach him..."

Blade's fatigue faded, a buzz of adrenaline filling his body.

"Fight... Protect... You must get to him..."

The energy coursing through Blade nearly overwhelmed him. He could feel it burning in his veins, blurring his sight, threatening to break his body. His vision doubled as his mind desperately tried to adapt. His ears rang violently. The pipes running through the dimly lit chamber began to rattle. The golden, unnatural lights grew brighter, humming at the same frequency as this strange energy. The encounter had lasted less than a second, but to Blade and the mysterious angelic creature, time had slowed. The very ground around them shook, trembling at the significance of what was happening within its sculpted halls. Then, the world stilled once again.

Revitalized, Blade turned back to the fight, tuning himself to the various metal across his body. He was going to get out of there. He was going to escape and find Gregory. He was–

Thump.

Blade grabbed the dart that had hit his chest. Enraged, he pulled it free and threw it to the ground, hearing the empty glass shatter. The Researcher that had hit him shook in fear as he rushed forward.

Fwish! Fwish! Fwish!

Thump. Thump. Thump.

Three more darts found purchase, bringing Blade to his knees. "I can't... need to..." The masked man's words drifted off as he collapsed to the floor. He landed in the bloodied puddle created by his earlier attacks, his grey cloak stained crimson.

"Find him... Reach him... Find him..."

The creature's soft-spoken voice continued to fill his mind; the buzzing adrenaline overpowered by the sedating drug. Blade's eyes slowly shut, his final words escaping in a whisper.

"Gregory..."

Chapter 22

IN A FACILITY filled with technology beyond comprehension, one would expect more than simple steel bars to keep prisoners in. And yet, despite their simplicity, they were enough to keep Enoch from leaving his cell, and waking from the nightmare that had replaced the dream.

Something horrible happened here. Even with his eyes shut, Enoch couldn't escape the spine-chilling clues left by the previous inmates. The nauseating, rotten stench of blood and other stains on the dusty sheets. Dents in the metal bars that matched the cot's frame, the bed now bolted to the ground to protect it from further harm. Messages, carved into the stone floors and walls...

"My crime didn't deserve this punishment"

"The mines were heaven. This is hell"

"Humans, demons, all the same, when blood is shed in progress' name"

Naïve as he could be at times, Enoch was hardly blind to reality. After the strange technology he'd seen, he doubted they'd let him walk freely. The only question was what they planned to do with him now. Would they leave him in this cell to rot, his legacy becoming nothing but another despondent carving on the wall? Would they alter his memories with some kind of magic ability, ensuring he could never share what he'd found in the mines? Would they decide the life of a young man was a fair price to pay for secrecy, and not worth the risk of keeping around?

A small tremor convinced Enoch to open his eyes. Quakes were incredibly rare in Courciel, and he still hadn't quite gotten used to the feeling of the ground moving beneath him. The two oil lamps hanging from the ceiling outside his cell swung, the shadows swaying back and forth' from their slow, creaking dance. Enoch focused on that, hoping to avoid the many terrifying sights in the cell itself. Hoping to ignore the fear and loneliness tightening his chest.

I wonder if Blade made it out...

Compared to the overwhelming abundance of things in the room, Enoch had very little left on him. He still had his dress shirt, somewhat sweat-stained from the everred fever. His pants needed a good clean as well, dustier than even the cot from how much time he'd spent on the ground lately. The beak-masked men had taken his jacket, his tie, and even his shoes. But worst of all, his pocket-watch had been taken away along with everything else. As he sat in the dim, silent light he felt an emptiness in his hand, craving the comforting edge of the engraved metal.

The chains of his magic-suppressing shackles clattered as he stretched. The stone floor and wall were better than the cot, but did little to support his aching body. To his surprise, the same clattering echoed on the other side of the wall. He wasn't alone.

"Is that you, Blade?" he asked. The sound of some-one shifting around replied. No doubt, the cell's inhabitant was trying to piece things together after waking. After a moment, a groggy voice replied.

"Yeah. And since you called me *that*, I'm guessing you're Enoch."

"Yeah." The Scribe kept quiet, giving Blade time to inspect the holding cell. He coughed at his equally dusty cot. He tugged at the steel bars, muttering in frustration about his shackles, and swearing at a painful lesson learned about kicking bars with bare feet. Eventually, the footsteps and various testing taps ended with a muffled slump onto the floor. Enoch held out a second longer before breaking the silence.

"So... you didn't get away."

"Would I be here talking to you if I did?"

Enoch's cheeks went red, realizing that had been a stupid question. After a moment, Blade sighed. "I make a point of not leaving people behind," he explained, his voice softer than Enoch had ever heard it, only for his abrasive tone to return once again. "Besides. That was pretty stupid of you anyways. I told you I wasn't going to carry you again."

Hearing Blade's aggression, Enoch chose not to argue. He agreed that his plan, if you could call it that, had been rather stupid. Though, he hadn't had much time to think of another option at the time. The two young men sat in silence again, each watching the shadows sway with the lantern light. Enoch could hear his cellmate's finger tapping, the chain of his shackles singing along to the beat.

"How did you know?" Blade finally asked.

"Know what?" Enoch looked over his shoulder. He couldn't see through the wall, but he could hear the distress in Blade's voice.

"How did you know the pistols shot darts?"

It was Enoch's turn to stay silent. He faced forward again, hugging his knees to his chest. "Honestly? I didn't," he answered bluntly. "I didn't even know there *were* bullets that just knocked people out. I don't have much experience with pistols."

A frantic shift caused Enoch to jump as Blade stood, slamming the wall between them. "That's even worse then!" he shouted. "Are you stupid? Or do you just have a death wish or something?"

The Scribe winced at the sudden anger, but that fear soon faded into pensive introspection. ...*Do I?* he wondered, gaze wandering to the shackles on his wrists. When he'd lost his family, Enoch spent so long regretting being alive. He'd felt pain... guilt. After he'd survived the events in the capital, he'd decided to try helping others to justify that survival. But deep down, had he not changed at all? Were his "heroics" a desire that had failed to succumb to his newfound, fragile confidence? Or simply a subconscious indifference; the scars on his heart too damaged to heal, forcing him to choose between a numb existence, or their lingering pain.

He hadn't felt fear, seeing the pistol. Not for himself, at least. The thought that he might not open his eyes again had never even crossed his mind. He'd simply remembered the tears that had once filled them; the seemingly endless pain he had once felt.

"You have people that care about you, right?" Enoch asked, hearing a startled rattle behind the wall. "When someone dies, it's the people that loved them that end up suffering. I didn't want your friends or family to go through that." That was the answer he found. The answer he hoped was the truth.

The following silence was deafening. Blade stood in shock, processing the Scribe's words; the implications; the pain in the young man's voice. Anger and sympathy welled up within him and he felt grateful for the concealing wall between them. As his mind drifted to thoughts of loved ones, a faint tremor shook the floor, the shadows' dance rushing to match the hastened tempo. The jolt shook Blade from his thoughts, and once the room settled, he sat back down in a huff.

Unpleasant as that answer was, it couldn't be taken back now.

"Don't *you* have people that'd be sad if *you* died? Or did you not think of that? Dumbass."

"I..." Enoch glanced over again, the question catching him off guard as the shaking ended. The thought of Cyrus receiving the news of his death brought a guilt that made him sick to his stomach, but... "I'm living on borrowed time anyways," he argued, doing his best to ignore the fact that that sentence felt a little more unsettling.

Enoch's answer lured an itching curiosity into Blade's mind, but he shook it away. The conversation was getting too personal, and it was time to get back on track. "So, would Gregory not care if you died? Is that the kind of guy he is?"

"You don't know?"

"No. Never met him."

The Scribe held his tongue. Every second he spent with Blade confused him further and further. The man's contradictory nature was baffling, fascinating, and incredibly frustrating all at once. While Enoch's mind demanded he probe for answers, his heart couldn't help but hear the subtle shift in Blade's voice at this new topic. A faint vulnerability and hesitation. He could use this opportunity to push for answers, or...

"Gregory is..." Realising that Azazel was *a lot*, Enoch struggled to find the words. Despite working together for his community service, the Scribe hadn't actually spent all that long with the man. Not to mention, Azazel was quite talented at avoiding conversations about himself. All Enoch had to work with was his own opinion. He hoped it would be enough.

"Gregory is kind. Annoyingly kind sometimes. He likes cookies, and– actually I don't think there's a baked good he *doesn't* like, or I haven't found one yet, at least. Um... he takes forever to get ready in the morning, and..." the Scribe stopped, wondering just how much he should actually share before knowing who Blade was. "He's... done a lot for me. To say I owe him one is an understatement."

Once again, Blade listened quietly, processing the Scribe's words, clinging to each one intently. It was clear that Gregory and Enoch were quite close... Blade poked at the chains of his shackles, feeling somewhat ashamed of the unpleasant feeling growing in his gut. He took a deep breath, building up his courage. "And... did he ever mention a younger brother?" he asked, voice even softer than before. "Or his dad, maybe?"

Enoch paused, turning to look at the wall as if his piqued curiosity could somehow pierce through it. Azazel had never mentioned a family. In fact, now that Enoch thought about it, he wasn't even sure if angels *had* families. He didn't know what answer Blade was looking for, so he decided to simply answer honestly.

"No, not to me at least. Sorry."

"..."

A soft, shifting sound barely made it through the wall as Blade moved to the edge of his cell, resting his chin on his knees as he ran a finger down the steel bar. The usual comfort that the metal brought him was obscured, cut off by his shackles; taken away like everything else. "Thank you," he said quietly, the word sounding foreign on his tongue. "...for earlier."

Enoch remained by the wall, realising that Blade's voice sounded far clearer than it had before. It made sense, considering they would have taken away his belongings as well.

"Yeah... No problem," Enoch closed his eyes again, wanting to give Blade some time to think. In this newfound sense of calm, he realized that for the first time in a while, the unsettling feeling at the back of his neck had vanished. Even if their surroundings were just as unpleasant, knowing someone was so close offered a sliver of relief, like the warm, unsteady lights beyond their cells.

Neither of them particularly liked the other, but company was company, and it was nice not to be alone.

Chapter 23

"SO, YOU REALLY think the Church is hiding a Remnant down there?"

Azazel and Seira crouched in the bushes, carefully watching the two Priests patrolling up ahead. The Pilgrims' escape had slowed to a halt after they'd discovered a fissure guarded by two Priests. Once Dear had been left at a safe distance, lest her blue fur give away their position in the warm-toned forest, the Pilgrims crept closer.

"That's my theory," Seira replied. "Fao was always obsessed with them. And while I can understand wanting to keep people out of the mines, the amount of security around them is too much. It's suspicious."

Azazel ducked lower as one of the Priests, a younger woman with a wider frame, turned their way. His yellow jacket didn't exactly do them any favors for stealth missions, but it was difficult to use his ability without it. It also just wouldn't feel right to leave it sitting in the woods somewhere. "So, when Iris mentioned you attacking a Priest. That was to get inside, I assume?"

"Through the front door, yeah. But considering the tunnel I saw at the bottom of that other pit, these sinkholes may be the safer way to sneak inside."

"Tunnel?" Azazel turned to Seira as she revealed this new information. "Which tunnel?"

"Back where Ocudolis attacked. There was a tunnel under where you were standing."

Azazel's eyes widened. The path to Enoch had been literally under his feet and he was only hearing about it now!? "Why didn't you tell me earlier!?"

Seira flashed him a glare before checking to see if the Priests had heard. Thankfully, the two seemed more focused on their conversation. After a sigh of relief from both Pilgrims, she turned back to Azazel. "I was planning to tell you about it once you'd come clean about the second prints. But that's when the giant jackass interrupted with her lackeys."

Relief washed over Azazel, only to be followed by a second flood of worry. *Enoch could still be alive, but that doesn't mean he's safe.* The angel's eyes drifted to the guarded fissure; to the crimson trees desperately clinging to its edge with struggling roots; the faint, wisps of red mist drifting from the ground like smoke from a fire long extinguished; the iridescent birds watching the scene from nearby. Enoch's symptoms were even more worrying in light of this new possibility. *If these weird phenomena really are caused by a Remnant, then that would mean everred fever is...* Bitter, warm-toned memories arose, matching his warm-toned surroundings, and sending a chill through his body. He refused to finish that thought. He didn't want it to be true.

Seira's hand wandered to her bow. Azazel's eyes wandered to her patrolling quarry. Guilt tied his stomach into knots. *Why would the Church want to slowly poison an entire city with magic? For research? What results could possibly justify this much risk to the people of Civionis?*

Azazel trusted Seira. He trusted that she believed her theory. He trusted that she wouldn't lie to him about her grief. He knew he couldn't deny that this was something the Church was capable of. But he truly wished his friend would turn out to be wrong.

"Hey, Greg? Before we do this, can I ask you something?" Seira's softer tone caught the angel's ear more than any shout could. Sensing these next words could be important, Azazel nodded.

"You didn't mean it, right?" Seira asked. "When you said I was delusional. That I needed help. That was an act, right?"

"Well, yes and no," Azazel replied. He could see Seira's knuckles whiten around her bow. Gently, he placed a hand on her shoulder. "I don't think you're delusional. Iris reacted way too strongly for someone that's supposed to *not* be hiding something. Plus, a Remnant in the area would explain a lot of the weirdness here." His grip tightened, pre-emptively reassuring both her and himself. "But the part about you needing help was true. Same with my apology for not being there for you. I plan to fix both of those personally though." Azazel felt the tension leave Seira's body.

"Yeah, right... of course." She nodded, turning her attention back to their mission. "Thanks."

Azazel pulled back his hand, smiling softly at the friend failing to notice the expression. "So, what's the plan to get in?" He glanced at the two Priests. They didn't seem particularly strong, but if they had magic abilities, that became harder to gauge. "The Church is already after us, but attacking may—"

Not allowing hesitation to slow her even a second, Seira let an arrow loose. Azazel's heart flew with it, worried she might be shooting to kill. Instead, the sharpened tip landed in the trunk of an everred leaning over the fissure like a tourist atop a mountain. The Priests jumped at the sudden *thwack*, turning to the source of the noise. The distraction gave Seira all the time she needed to dart out of the bushes, hooking her bow around the first Priest's neck. The fur-clad Pilgrim yanked as hard as she could to pull the man off balance.

"I've got this one!" she said, unable to see Azazel's face hidden behind his palm back in the bushes.

As her partner fell out of her sight, the female Priest reached for her pistol. Azazel, not having much of a choice, followed Seira's lead, "Sorry 'bout this!" he said, swinging a steel baton towards the woman's arm. The pistol landed with a *thud* and puff of dust on the forest floor.

"Another one?" the female Priest exclaimed, gripping her wrist as she leapt back. A blue glimmer flickered in the woman's eyes for a moment, and she opened her mouth, exhaling a cloud of powder the same shade. Quick as he was, Azazel's attempt to cover his nose and mouth wasn't fast enough.

Crap! I inhaled it! he thought. *Is it poison? Or a Hijacker ability? What's gonna-* "Achoo!"

He couldn't stop them. Though no pain had befallen him, an onslaught of sneezes escaped his nose and mouth. Over and over, he nearly lost his balance from the sudden nasal attack. *"Achoo! Achoo! A-A-Achoo!"*

"What in the Three Realms are you doing?" Seira asked, successfully pinning her own opponent to the ground with her leg. A chestnut glow flickered in the man's hands, but with his breathing cut off, he couldn't get his ability to work. The two struggled in the dirt as the fur-clad Pilgrim looked up at the stumbling angel.

"I- *achoo!* It's her a- *achoo!* Her ability!"

"Can't you handle a couple sneezes?" Seira replied, before tensing as the female Priest's arm wound back. "Duck!"

Eyes closed from the most recent sneeze, Azazel did just that. The Priest's punch grazed the hairs atop his head.

"Thanks, *ach-oof!*" He'd managed to dodge the first swing, but his gut swallowed the entirety of the second. A gag joined the latest sneeze, but he stood his ground. He had to admit, between what he assumed was Iris' ability back at the ambush, and his current situation, he was getting really tired of not being able to see his opponents. More and more blows followed, and though his jacket considerably softened the impacts, the woman was quite strong. All he could do was guard his face, sneezing on his own arms in the process.

Shoulder. Arm. Side. Gut. The female Priest moved quick, wanting to get her own fight over with to help her partner. She'd practiced her moves to the point of perfection in training, and her body drove the fight as her focus found itself divided.

Shoulder. Arm. Side. Gut.

Shoulder. Arm. Side. Gut.

Shoulder. Arm. Side. Gut.

Grab?

The unexpected feeling of two hands tightly gripping hers pulled the Priest's mind from her partner's fight to her own. Azazel, with some difficulty through the sneezes, smirked.

"Got *-choo!*" Azazel's head swung forward. He pulled the woman close as he did, forehead slamming into hers. Admittedly, he felt a little bad for sneezing on her in the process, but he couldn't exactly control that. Though his own head spun from the impact, he kept up his retaliation. Not being able to see didn't matter if he was still holding her arm, so he pulled with all his might, punching the Priest directly in her temple. Her eyes rolled back. The sneezes subsided, and Azazel caught the now unconscious woman before she could fall to the ground.

"Sorry again." Gently, he lowered the Priest onto the forest floor as Seira let her own opponent fall in an unconscious slump next to her. The fur-clad Pilgrim picked herself up, moving to Azazel's side.

"How's your head?"

"Oww." Azazel rubbed his forehead, futilely hoping it wouldn't bruise. *Still better than getting caught and arrested,* he thought, *But I guess we're both committed to this now, whether the theory is true or not...*

Seira gave her friend a pat on the back before sneaking over to the fissure. As she got close, she softened her step, testing each stone and patch of soil before continuing to the next. Azazel joined her beside the curious, leaning tree at the edge. Looking down, the duo could see the shattered trunks of the everreds that had been less fortunate. Their scattered bad luck was the Pilgrims' blessing however, offering a safer path to take down into the tunnels below.

"Should be able to climb down pretty easily," Seira said.

"Easily isn't the word I'd use, but yeah. Better than a flat wall at least." Azazel inched closer to the edge, careful not to lean too far. "I can see why the Church wanted to close off the forest though. If something like this opened up under you out of nowhere, that kind of depth could do some damage."

Did Enoch really fall into a pit like this? he wondered. *There weren't any bodies or bloodstains at the bottom, but it's still hard to believe he'd be okay if he did.* As Azazel tried to glean the best path to take, Seira turned towards the soft *clop clop clop* emerging from the trees. Dear huffed at the sight of her friends, and Seira smiled, heading over so Dear wouldn't get too close to the fissure. She gave her scruff a heartfelt scratch.

"You'll have to stay up here, Blue," she said softly. The fur-clad Pilgrim leaned forward, pressing her head against Dear's. Together, the two closed their eyes. "Iris and her men may come looking for you, so hide from anyone that's not me or Gregory. I'll find you when we're finished."

As the two broke away from their moment, Dear stomped her hoof, not eager to leave her friend again in this moment of danger. Despite her discomfort, the doe still backed away, tail pressed firmly against her body. Seira smiled softly, doing her best to reassure Dear she'd be okay. Though she had to admit that even she felt nervous. They were about to head into the demon's den, and she doubted the Church would hold back if they were discovered.

Pushing back her hesitations, the fur-clad Pilgrim watched Dear disappear into the fog, then turned back to Azazel. "Alright. Let's go."

Chapter 24

THE KEYS RATTLED like chains in the red-haired Priest's hands as he drew them from his pocket. Enoch stood at the back wall of his cell, following the directions given to him. Blade, on the other hand, glared from the center of his.

"Make me," he growled. The Priest rolled his eyes, waving his partner over. A second, larger Priest came close, drawing his pistol outside the bars.

"We can and will, so don't get cocky, brat," he warned. Though part of him hoped Blade would resist, having lost a friend to one of the young man's spike attacks earlier on.

"Can you both just calm down with the bravado act?" the red-haired Priest sighed. With the correct key now in his hand, he turned to Blade. The man's performative smile hid an irritated exhaustion beneath. He'd thought this was going to be an easy job.

"We just want to ask some questions. I'm sure you just panicked when you saw all the weird stuff earlier, right? We'll get everything sorted, so you don't need to be scared."

"Cut the crap," Blade spat. "You aren't fooling anyone."

The painted smile broke just a moment, and the red-haired Priest turned back to his larger partner. "You sure we shouldn't go with the other one? Seems like less of a hassle."

"Orders were to talk to the white-haired kid first. Just open the cell. I'll deal with him."

With a shrug, the red-haired Priest slid the key into the lock. "Alright, but if this guy starts rampaging again, you better not miss." The larger Priest growled, offended by the implication that he could.

With a metallic *click* the cell unlocked. The door opened with a strained *creeeeaaak,* and the red-haired Priest stepped aside, letting the larger man do his job. Though Enoch couldn't see the scene in the adjacent cell, he risked a glance over his shoulder, noticing the smaller Priest's hand shift to his holster as he stepped into view. The pistol inside was noticeably different from the one he'd seen in the hall.

"I'll tell you one more time. Face the back of the cell with your hands behind your head," the large Priest ordered with a low, intimidating growl.

Blade locked eyes with the looming silhouette in the cell door, then spat on the floor. The man's eye twitched, but he stood his ground, pistol at the ready. Realizing they'd be at a stalemate otherwise, Blade decided to act first. He kept a close eye on the Priest's aim, and rushed forward.

Fwish!

Clink!

A dart flew through the air, shattering against Blade's shackle cuff. The young man veered to the side. Reaching the cot, he jumped, ricocheting off it to gain height. Enough height to hook his shackles over the Priest's head. The momentum of Blade's descent brought the larger man's chin down with it, directly into Blade's knee the second his feet had touched the ground.

The Priest's teeth cracked together. Blood dripped from the side of his mouth onto the floor. It was hard to tell if it was from a shattered tooth or a badly bit tongue, but either way, the attack had certainly done some damage.

But it hadn't been enough.

Blade went to lift his shackles back up. He was lifted instead as the Priest recovered quicker than expected, slamming him back against the wall. Blade's skull rattled from the impact. He tried to regain his bearings. A heavy blow followed, this time from the front as the Priest punched as hard as he could. Then again, and again, over and over like a boxer training with a punching bag.

Blade tried to kick back. To send a knee into his gut. To do something, anything. But the onslaught was too much. Unable to block or move away with his cuffs still stuck around the man's neck, he simply focused on not letting a single sound escape his lips. He wouldn't give them the satisfaction, no matter how many times he was struck.

BANG!

A gunshot caused the hanging lights to sway once more. Enoch winced at the sound. The scent of gunpowder filled his nose.

"Okay, that's enough!" the red-haired Priest shouted. His voice pushed through the ringing in everyone's ears. His finger rested on the trigger of his pistol, the barrel still aimed at the ceiling. He lowered his arm. Only, it wasn't Blade that he set his sights on next. "Both of you break it up already. You've shown you're tough, or stubborn, or whatever you were trying to prove. But if you don't calm down and cooperate right now, I'll put a bullet in your friend's head."

"He's… not my friend…" Blade said between weighted breaths. Just talking caused a crumbling sensation in his ribs. The chain of his shackles slackened as the larger Priest reluctantly took a step back, cracking his jaw back into place. Now that he had the chance, he tried to figure out how much damage Blade's knee had done, keeping the young man in his field of vision.

Blade's frustration demanded he try to use the Priest as a hostage as well, but he knew he was outmatched in strength. The young man's legs shook as he tried to stand his ground after the beating. Currently, only the wall behind him kept him from falling to the ground. His insides were screaming; he forced back their attempt to escape through his throat. The red-haired Priest noticed his continued bravado, if it could even be called that, and rolled his eyes at how difficult this simple job had become.

"Sure. But he was important enough that you were carrying him around earlier, right?" he argued, his words catching Enoch's ear. "We only need to question one of you. So be a good kid and don't make me pull this trigger."

"We don't know anything, I swear." To everyone's surprise, it was Enoch's voice that broke the growing tension. Even with a pistol aimed right at him, he still felt he had to do something. "We were in the forest, and then we fell down a hole. We don't know what this place is, or what's going on. It was all just a big accident, really, so please let us–"

"Shut up," Blade snapped. "I don't need you making the situation worse." The words felt like another punch to the gut, and Enoch held his tongue.

"See, that's why this one would be less of a hassle," the red-haired Priest said. "Didn't even need to open the cell." The larger Priest rolled his eyes in reply before grabbing

Blade's arms. Forcefully, yet still cautiously, he removed and reattached the shackles one at a time so they were now behind the young man's back. Fighting every instinct, Blade complied, glaring daggers at the red-haired Priest who'd decided to fight dirty. Ignoring this, the smaller Priest turned to Enoch.

"We'll come back to get you in a bit. Try to be this cooperative then too, 'kay?" Seeing that his partner was ready to go, the red-haired Priest lowered his pistol. "Like I said, we're just looking for some answers. You guys are the ones that broke in here and caused a scene after all."

"Don't tell them a damn thing," Blade warned, earning yet another punch to the gut. The final hit was one too many, and Blade doubled over, still conscious, but fighting the urge to hurl. The two Priests dragged him out of the room, and the door swung shut behind them.

Enoch waited, still standing at the wall. The chains of his shackles shook with his hands. When it was clear they weren't coming back, he allowed himself to collapse to the floor. His fear caught up to him. The bullet sized, smoking hole in the ceiling showed just how close he'd come to death, and the sight caused his stomach to churn.

The Scribe's heart hastened. Each quickened, heavy beat reminded him of the Priest's punches, strong enough for him to hear even through the wall. Priests or not, if they'd been that violent just getting Blade out of the cell, what would they do during the interrogation itself!? Enoch's ignorance would be a flimsy shield at best. He'd been unconscious nearly the entire time he'd been here, but would they accept that excuse? Or would they try to push him, force him to give the answers they wanted to hear?

Enoch's chest felt tighter. He moved to loosen his tie before remembering he no longer had it. He didn't even have his pocket-watch to comfort him as his panic continued building. The chains, the walls, the faint scent of the blood that had been drawn from both Blade and the Priest, they sent his mind spiralling. For a moment, the Scribe was back in the capital, surrounded by the massacre in the cathedral. In Peycile, running through corpses and mud. Running. He wanted to run. He needed to run. Run from the cell, the strange facility, his own mind. But even that had been taken from him.

Hugging his knees to his chest, Enoch tried to calm himself down. "You're okay. You're okay. You'll be okay," he repeated, nails digging into his arms. "You're okay. You're–" A painful, heavy cough cut off his words, reminding him of the everred fever draining his strength, adding to his list of worries.

The Scribe's body shook. *Someone... anyone... someone please come help.* Unable to even speak through the fever and panic, Enoch sat alone in his cell.

Alone with his anxiety.

Alone with his fear.

Alone with his thoughts, tormenting him through the panic attack.

He was certain that he was going to die.

Chapter 25

THE LARGER A lie becomes, the harder it is to hide. As time passes, contradictions will erode the lie's foundations. If people begin to question their belief in the deception, the revelation of the truth is no longer a matter of will or will not, it becomes a matter of when.

When will they realize that the facts don't line up?

When will the woven tale begin to fray?

When will the truth be brought to light?

When Azazel and Seira reached the bottom of the fissure, determined to uncover the reality of Civionis' dark secrets, they hadn't expected to stumble upon the tools they needed so soon. Nevertheless, there they lay before them. Two Researchers inside the tunnel hidden at the base of the pit. Streams of a strange red mist drifted loosely upward, trickling from the mineshaft like smoke from a dying fire. Azazel could sense the magic emanating from each wisp, just as he could see the magic of the taller Researcher as stone poured from their fingertips.

"How many more of these do we have to cover?" they asked, voice somewhat muffled by their beaked, leather mask.

"Josael said at least three more opened up during those tremors earlier."

"Damn. Late night tonight, I guess. Wish I'd brought a bigger dinner."

The two Pilgrims hid themselves by the tunnel entrance. Seira pulled a heftier branch off of one of the fallen trees, whispering a small apology to the plant. Azazel adjusted his grip on his steel baton, holding up three fingers with his other hand.

Then two...

Then one...

Then- THWACK! The two Pilgrims rushed inside the tunnel. Seira swung the branch out and up, slamming it into one of the Researchers' faces. Any further out and the blow would have shattered the beak of the Researcher's mask. Instead, it knocked them on their back with a hearty thud.

"What in the-"

Before the second Researcher could react, Azazel swung down a metal baton. He took care not to hit too hard, but still didn't envy the headache the victim would have when they woke up again. "Sorry," he said, reshaping the metal of his baton into a belt once more.

As Azazel finished, he noticed Seira inspecting the Researcher's mask. The angel couldn't help but feel a strange, nagging familiarity at the bird-like shape. However, if he'd seen it before, the time and place were lost to him.

"That's a unique design. Wonder what it's for," Seira said, pulling the buckle on the back loose to remove the accessory. Like opening the door to a well-stocked spice cupboard, their noses were assaulted with an overwhelming amalgamation of herbs. The strength of the scent caused even Seira to cough as it hit them so unexpectedly.

"Is that coming from the mask?" Azazel asked, plugging his nose. Seira flipped the accessory over. Inside, a small, tightly woven filter separated the beak from the wearer's face. Within the beak itself, a mix of dried and fresh herbs surrounded a small cloth bundle no larger than a grape.

"Looks like it." The odor slowed Seira for a moment longer before she slid the mask onto her own face. Azazel tilted his head.

"Sure you'll be able to handle that?"

"It's the worst thing I've smelled all day, but I won't turn down a free disguise." Tightening the strap on the back of the mask, the fur-clad Pilgrim nodded to the second Researcher. "That one looks like he's about your shape and size."

Though it was certainly true that the Researcher was similar in size, the man's shape didn't quite match that of the angel. Mostly due to the fact that he was, in fact, not an angel. Azazel's jacket was specially tailored to fit around the two wings protruding from his back. The same illusion that masked these wings masked the holes, so Seira was of course not aware of the hurdle presented by the Researcher's long jacket being in one piece. While he could realistically, but uncomfortably, fold his wings in tightly enough to fit inside the garment as it was, he couldn't risk restricting his movement too much on such a potentially dangerous mission. After taking a moment to think, Azazel rubbed the back of his neck with an embarrassed smile.

"Sure, but I'm actually a little shy. Promise you won't look if I change over there?" The angel pointed to a cluster of fallen rocks on the other side of the fissure base. Seira, who was already busy hiding her wolf-fur cowl behind the fallen trees, raised an eyebrow in disbelief.

"You? Shy? Why do I find that hard to believe?"

"Just because I'm socially confident doesn't mean I have body confidence," Azazel argued, already carefully dragging the unconscious Researcher away. "Just don't look, okay? Please?"

Seira rolled her eyes, her faint smile betraying her amusement at this revelation about her friend. "Yeah, yeah, I promise I won't peek." She dismissed his worry with a nonchalant wave, turning back to claim her own disguise. The boot she'd removed seemed to be around the size of her own when held side to side.

Azazel gave one more glance to make sure she'd keep her half-hearted promise. Once the coast was clear, he removed the Researcher's jacket. His belt had more than enough steel to sculpt a pair of shears, even if the act took longer than the far more familiar form of his sword. Thankfully, he was still acquainted with the shape, but it always took longer to sculpt something he had little practice with. Once they were formed, he slowly trimmed two long slits in the jacket, the distance between his wings practically embroidered into his memory through repetition.

"Here goes nothing," he whispered. Throwing the jacket over his own, he strained his neck to look over his shoulder. As he pulled the garment into place, the illusion took effect, hiding the slits just as it did for his regular jacket. Azazel let out a sigh of relief. Next time he ran into him, he'd have to thank Penemue again for making the illusion so adaptable. With the hardest part over, he grabbed the rest of the disguise, holding off on putting on the mask until he'd had enough time to adjust to the smell.

"Almost done back there?" Seira said, loud enough to get his attention, but still keeping her voice low just in case. She finished hiding the other Researcher beneath the branches of the fallen trees. As she stood, Seira tugged at her clothes, her mask hiding her scowl. Admittedly, the outfit was much more form-fitting than the freer clothes she was used to, and leaving her bow and arrows behind didn't help her discomfort. All she had left for defense was her dagger. The weapon was certainly reliable in her experienced hands, but she still couldn't shake the exposed feeling, even if her entire body was now covered.

Once she noticed Azazel's face, she crossed her arms. "The mask is the most important part, Greg."

"I know, I know." Azazel lifted the beaked accessory up, nose curling at the odor. The scent reminded him of a certain friend back home, and he couldn't help but wonder how the man even had a sense of smell anymore. The disguises were their best bet at moving undetected though, so with one final breath of fresh air, Azazel strapped himself in.

"What's the plan, anyways?" he asked. "Haven't really had the chance to ask with everything happening so quickly earlier. But I'm guessing you have some kind of goal once we're inside?"

"I do. I'll be looking for a man named Oka."

"Oka?"

"Yeah, he worked with Faolan. The only work friend I ever saw him bring home, actually." Seira entered the tunnel, ducking under the partially formed wall the Researcher had been working on. She took a moment to pick up their lantern. "If anyone can tell me what really happened to Faolan, it'd be him."

"You sure he'd be willing to tell the truth?" Azazel asked. "If there's a Remnant here and the Church really is covering it all up, that'd be a big risk for him to take."

"If he doesn't tell me willingly, I have ways of making him."

As concern crept across his face, Azazel once again hoped this would turn out to be nothing more than an old mine, though that was getting harder and harder to believe with each opponent they faced.

Unlike Blade and Enoch's lengthy trek through the mines, it didn't take long for the Pilgrims to reach a similar metal door barring their way. No doubt that was the reason the Researchers had been so eager to cover that particular fissure early on.

Seira tapped at the frame, amazed by how sturdy it felt. The arching, architectural designs reminded her of a cathedral, complete with the unnecessary flairs and embellishments. Only, the stylistic choices were still different enough to notice. The metal designs here were smoother and more streamlined than the stone bricks used by the Church, allowing for longer, curving patterns.

Though she'd spent most of her travels outside of civilisation, Seira had still encountered a wide variety of metalwork. But this style was unlike anything she'd seen before. However, for all it's craftmanship and stability, the design was quite nonsensical. After all, how could a door with no handle or hinges be opened?

As Seira's mask covered the wonder in her eyes, Azazel was glad that his could hide the color draining from his face. The door, the glowing screen and keypad next to it, the design was far more streamlined than what he remembered, but there was no denying it...

This was Spira technology.

What is tech from the divine realm doing in Terrael? A dozen questions ran through his mind. *Did an angel go rogue to study a Remnant? Is it an angel I know? Are the Archangels aware of this?*

...Are the Archangels behind this?

Removing the stolen Researcher's glove, Azazel pressed his hand against the metal of the door in front of him. The hum of the metal calmed his thoughts. *I don't have enough facts right now. Until I know more, anything I guess would be a stab in the dark.*

"Can you use your ability to shape it?" Seira's voice caused Azazel to jump, hand pulling away from the metal. He glanced over.

"Oh, uh... I can try!" As his fingers pressed against the steel once more, an unsettling reminiscence washed over him. It had been centuries, but he couldn't help but wonder. How many times had he reshaped doors just like this in Spira when he'd forgotten the codes to get through? How many times had he been scolded for using his magic to do so? The memories formed a lump in his throat. A shadow fell over his mind, the tunnel walls feeling a little closer than before.

Like pulling aside a silk curtain, Azazel opened the door. "Guess it's steel after all," he said, feigning surprise. Seira glanced through, dagger tucked and ready within her sleeve.

"Coast is clear too." A little more relaxed, Seira entered the research facility. The most noticeable change inside was the line of light running along the ceiling. Though its glow was faint through the glass, it was bright as sunlight compared to the lantern's dim flame. The golden light revealed several other strange doors ahead, as well as the continued stylistic walls, now made of stone rather than metal despite the complexity of the patterns.

Seira ran her gloved hand along one of the curved embellishments. Her fingers lingered a moment. It was real. This was all real. For so long, this place had been nothing but a theory, a taunting nightmare, but there was no denying the smooth, carved stone pushing back against her touch. She was finally there.

If asked to describe how the situation made her feel, Seira would be at a loss for words. However, I could think of a few myself. Excited could be a start, with fear lurking behind, though the two are often confused for one another. Anger. Curiosity. A minor dizziness from the herbs in her mask. Relief that her friend Gregory was by her side for her righteous mission.

Azazel didn't need quite so many words. He knew exactly what emotion the Spira tech surrounding him brought to mind. He knew exactly how he felt knowing that he might be stepping into the very thing he'd promised to keep away from. The very thing he'd ran from for years. He could sum up his feelings in a single word.

Fear.

Chapter 26

NAVIGATING THE halls of the research facility turned out easier than expected. Even disguised, Azazel's heart raced in every encounter. He had to consciously stop himself from nervously waving to each Researcher they passed. He'd yet to see anyone that wasn't human, but that didn't mean he hadn't passed any angels. After all, at that moment he appeared to be human as well.

The fact that the signs next to each door were written in the Celestial Script didn't help his nerves. However, rare as it was for anyone other than Scribes to use it, the alphabet was still known to humans. The use of that script alone didn't mean angels were among the masked figures roaming the halls. Or, more than just the one.

The duo passed through yet another door, this one opening on its own, even without a code. The first time they'd encountered such a door, Seira had drawn her dagger in surprise, thinking it was the work of someone opening it from the other side. She'd since gotten used to the strange technology. However, as this door opened, she had to jump to the side once again as a masked Healer rushed by with a bundle of medical supplies.

"Sorry! In a hurry!" they cried out, continuing before even finishing their hasty apology. The two Pilgrims watched in confusion as the Healer disappeared through a different door.

"I wonder what happened," Azazel pondered aloud. A muffled voice on the other side of the open door replied, nearly sending the angel's heart through the roof of the tunnel.

"You didn't hear? There's people injured all over the place." Unprompted, the Researcher joined Azazel and Seira in the hall, coming close as they eagerly shared their morbid gossip. "A masked maniac was running around earlier with some guy passed out on their back. Broke a lotta of doors and attacked a buncha people. The Healers and engineers have had their hands full cleaning up the mess."

"Oh! Is that what that commotion was?" Azazel asked, "I had no idea it was that bad!"

"Oh, bad is an understatement." Azazel's performance went right over the Researcher's head as they continued, caught up in the excitement that comes from sharing something that feels confidential. "I heard that three people might've died."

The angel gasped softly. "Really? Did they catch the guy yet?"

The Researcher's frantic nodding turned their mask into a workplace hazard, the beak swinging about so much that Azazel and Seira had to lean back to avoid impact. "I think so. Should be locked up in the holding cells by now."

"I see," Azazel replied. "That's a relief. Don't think I could focus knowing they were running around still."

"Right!?" With a sigh, the gossipy Researcher finally took a step back. "I know I always say we need some excitement around here, but still. Careful what you wish for, I suppose."

"Ain't that the truth." With a wave, Azazel and Seira passed through the door, leaving the Researcher to continue their own work down the hall. Once the door hissed shut behind them, the beak of Seira's mask slowly turned to Azazel.

"How in the Three Realms do you do that?"

"Some people just like talking at instead of talking to. All I did was ask the right questions to keep it on the right topics."

Seira shook her head. Sometimes Azazel's charisma frightened her, but at least it had been helpful here. "So, your masked killer really is here then."

And the guy passed out on his back was probably Enoch, Azazel deduced. "Seems so." The angel glanced at the nearby doors, reading the various signs and labels above them. None of them listed holding cells, but it couldn't be too difficult to find them, right? Azazel shook his head. He was also there to help Seira, he couldn't just wander off first thing.

"Go to the holding cells," Seira said. Azazel waved his hand, shooing away the suggestion.

"Nope. I said I'd help you."

"This was going to be a solo job anyways. I've got this." Seira's insistence did sway Azazel ever so slightly, but the angel always had been stubborn. Noticing the hesitation, Seira put a hand on his shoulder. "That Scribe of yours is on a time limit, right? Go be a hero. I know you love to."

The idea of leaving Seira on her own didn't appeal to Azazel. Especially since he knew she couldn't read the

Celestial script. But between Enoch's vision and the incident with the Priest, he couldn't deny that he wanted to find the masked attacker as soon as possible. He let out a defeated sigh. "Alright. But promise you'll be careful. I don't think I'm qualified to take care of a fully grown deer."

"Not at all, no," Seira replied, her smile audible in the words. "I'll be careful if you are." The usually fur-clad Pilgrim turned back to where they'd come from. "I'll go look for Oka. He's a Researcher, so he's probably in a lab? I just hope he wasn't killed by your guy."

"Here's hoping. Oh, and if we don't run into each other again in here, I'll meet up with you near the pit we came in through." Azazel turned to leave, hesitating just a moment. Seira's mask tilted.

"Seriously? I said you could–" A tight hug cut her words short, like a blanket suddenly wrapping around her on a winter day.

"Stay safe."

The same phrase, muffled by the angel's mask, had been fighting to pass Seira's lips. It seemed he'd beaten her to it, not that the words had had any chance of winning their battle. The woman held him a moment longer. All she could say in response was "that's my line."

Azazel pulled away, hand lingering to pat the shoulder of his friend. After exchanging nods of farewell, the two parted ways. Azazel waited until Seira was fully out of sight before heading off on his own. Following the signs, he wandered through the tunnels, more alert now that he was on his own. He couldn't afford to cause a stir before Seira completed her goal.

After too many doors to count, he finally found the sign he was looking for. "Here we go," he said softly before casually opening the door. Unlike the halls he'd been in up to this point, the room here was more natural. A lantern hung from the ceiling rather than the golden lines of light illuminating the rest of the facility. The back wall was made of stone bricks. A single, iron door sat tucked away in the corner. Azazel could see the keyhole underneath the door-knob. Most likely, the cells themselves were just beyond it.

Next to the door stood a single, wooden desk. Its size left little space to actually move in the room itself, even with its occupant practically squished behind as he read a light novel. The white gloves of his Priest uniform sat tossed aside on the desk to help him turn the pages more easily. He'd been twirling the hair of his moustache absentmind-edly when Azazel entered, but stopped as the door opened, knocking over a basket on the desk when he sat up. Several items fell to the floor with a clatter. Once he saw Azazel, the Priest relaxed. "Oh, just a mask. What d'ya need?"

Azazel glanced down at the spilled contents of the basket as the Priest began cleaning up the ones still on the desk. He crouched down, picking up the items that had reached the floor.

"Sorry for the scare. Here, let me help. I uh…" As he rummaged through the scattered items, the angel's gaze fell upon Blade's sharp, steel mask. He hadn't seen it yet him-self, but Enoch had described the design in detail after his vision. The mask in his hand was a perfect match. Recover-ing from the moment of distraction, Azazel quickly stood up. "I'm here to question the masked man. Boss' orders."

The Priest raised an eyebrow. "Are you now?" Slowly, the man put the embroidered tie he'd been holding back into the basket. He reached into his pocket, where Azazel assumed he kept the keys based on the jingling sound that followed. "Guess I'll open this up for you then."

"Thanks! I appreciate it!" Azazel replied. He noted the man's hesitation and carefully hid his hands behind his back to remove his glove. "I'll try to be quick so you can get back to your book."

"How considerate." The Priest rummaged through his pocket a moment longer before springing into action. The sudden swing backwards nearly slammed into Azazel's face. The Pilgrim leaned back, only to discover he'd fallen right into the man's trap. A flash of silver light appeared in the Priest's hand, taking the form of a pair of summoned shackles. He swung one end down on Azazel's wrist, locking it in place.

Azazel tried to swing away from the next lunge. The second side of the shackle swung through empty air. With one hand already bound, he couldn't go far, but thankfully he didn't need to. Still held firmly in the Pilgrim's hand, Blade's mask glowed gold. The steel reformed like water poured into a mold, the mask turning into a baton.

The Priest noticed the transformation, eyes widening as he realized Azazel was an ability user. Just as Azazel had, he tried to dodge the swing, only to have Azazel pull him right into it with the shackles. A loud *THUNK* filled the small room, and the Priest grasped his head. With his final moments, he tried one last time to capture Azazel. Unfortunately, when one is seeing double, it's quite difficult to handcuff a moving target.

A mumbled curse escaped the Priest's lips as he fell to the ground. Out of reflex, Azazel caught him, watching as the summoned shackle faded away along with the man's consciousness. "Sorry buddy," he said quietly. "I know you were just doing your job."

As gently as he could, Azazel placed the Priest back into his chair. He leaned the man back to cover his tracks, placing his novel over his eyes. If Azazel was lucky, the man might just believe the entire encounter had been a dream. But with the lump he was going to have on his head, that was definitely wishful thinking.

Once he'd set the scene of a guard drifting off at his post, Azazel tidied up the rest of the fallen items. There was a surprising amount of jewelry, all steel just like the mask. Then two pairs of shoes; a long, brown jacket suspiciously similar to the one Azazel had seen nearly daily for the last three months; and– His hand froze. Fresh blood stained the mottled, grey cloak folded at the base of the basket. He'd already been told about the masked' man's rampage, but he couldn't help but wonder whose blood it was. As if hoping to prove the fearful theory manifesting in his mind, a sound caught his ear.

The angel heard the ticking before he saw the source sitting patiently beneath the folded cloak. He felt the daffodil engraved into the metal as he picked it up.

Enoch's pocket-watch, coated with blood.

Chapter 27

BISHOP PARAS stood in the center of the usually crowded train platform. Once again, he adjusted the circlet on his head. It had to be perfect. It all had to be perfect.

Two Circlet Guards waited a short distance behind him, eyes scanning the surrounding railings and stairways to ensure no one attempted to approach the Bishop. A silver train with gold and dark red embellishments glided into the station. It seemed to float atop the lake, the tracks hidden just below the surface. The steam whistle rippled both the water and air. Shortly after, a porter silently opened a door marked with the symbol of the Church.

The first to disembark was a High Priest named Emilian Belladei. Two greatswords sat sheathed on his back, the hilts crossed over each other behind his head. The blades were as sharp as the man's well-trimmed, brunette beard and sideburns, framing his face and piercing blue eyes. The only things that matched the swords' size were the man's build, and the reputation that preceded him.

There were few within the Church that hadn't heard of the warrior Emilian. Descendant of the well-known war-hero Halvard Belladei, Emilian certainly took after his grandfather. During his time guarding one of the larger rifts, his blades had cut down countless demons attempting to invade the surface. A golden boy and proclaimed role model for Priests everywhere, he was a logical choice to recruit the best of the best for the Church's armies.

"Paras!" he shouted with a boisterous voice. "It's been too long my friend! How are you and the beautiful Iris doing up here in the cold?"

"As wonderful as always," Paras replied. "But far better still now that we've been graced by your visit."

Emilian held out a hand, shaking the Bishop's with a far stronger grip than comfortable for the older man. As he did with his men, Emilian pulled the Bishop in for a one-handed hug. Had it been anyone else, Paras would have gone red with anger at the disrespect, but he knew better than to challenge the actions of a Belladei. That didn't stop him from shaking out his throbbing fingers as Emilian moved on to greet the Circlet Guard as well, asking them how they'd been since the last recruitment.

Second to exit the train was Nitika Deomicis. Her smooth, bronze skin glowed as warm as the starlight stones above. The silk cloths of her outfit draped behind her like morning mists over a river. All kinds of golden ornaments and jewelry chimed as she walked, including the golden Pilgrim pendant hanging from her rope belt. Paras felt his cheeks flush as she sent a dimpled smile his way. It was easy to see why Nitika was considered one of the ten most beautiful members of the Church. In fact, she'd placed at least five rankings higher than Azazel had that year in the Daily Courciel's public poll. Just the sight of her took the Bishop's breath away. It was enough to make him forget the rumors that surrounded the beautiful Pilgrim. Of course, it had yet to be proven that she was using her past as a Dispatcher to earn more money than her commissions were supposed to pay. But even if it was somehow proven, it would be a crime to convict such a gorgeous, graceful woman.

Nitika placed a hand over her chest, bowing in greeting to the Bishop. "I'm honored you've come to meet us in person, Bishop Paras," she said with a melodic voice. "I thank you for allowing us to visit your beautiful city, the stories fail to do it justice."

The Bishop took her now outstretched hand, resisting the urge to plant a kiss upon its back. Instead, he gently shook it, focussing on not staring into her eyes for too long, lest he lose himself in them. "You are– I mean– The same to you, Miss Deomicis. I'd heard of your beauty, but even Civionis cannot compare to the angel I see before me."

"You flatter me, Father." Nitika slowly pulled back her hand with an amused smile. "But a Bishop such as yourself should know better than to compare a humble Pilgrim to the holy angels."

"Right, right, of course." Bishop Paras stepped aside, allowing Nitika to join Emilian further on the platform. "I hope the Archangels will be willing to forgive my careless choice of words."

Focused on Nitika, Paras nearly overlooked the long silence that preceded the next passenger disembarking. Like a message from the heavens, the thought of who was next jolted through his mind. Quickly, he turned to face High Investigative Inquisitor Surufel Asaradel... only to find the less prominent personnel for the recruitment process disembarking instead.

"Wasn't High Inquisitor Asaradel meant to join as a late replacement?" he asked the other recruiters, eyes still glued on the door as if the man might sneak out the second he turned away. Emilian looked over from his conversation with the Circlet Guards.

"Heard *the Shadow* decided to come over on his own." Disdain overlaid the Inquisitor's title, as if High Priest Belladei were instead speaking of a rodent that he'd found nested in his home. "Guess he thinks he's too good for a private train ride with the rest of us."

Nitika clicked her tongue disapprovingly. "Now, now Emilian, that tone is hardly necessary." Though the Pilgrim had her own issues with Surufel's nosiness, she veiled them with a kind-hearted smile. "If he wishes to sneak about the city as a tourist, then who are we to stop him. All that matters is that he's here in time for the ceremony."

The plastered smile the Bishop had worn until then twitched, his fear attempting to escape in a held back scream. "I see... All he told me in his letter was that Inquisitor Akshay sent her apologies for the cancellation. I do wish he'd told me of this adjusted arrival so I could have met him properly."

Paras had a hard time believing that Akshay had simply become too busy with managing her school. He knew why Surufel was here, and it wasn't the goodness of his heart. What information was the High Inquisitor after? Was he looking for signs of criminal activity? The masked killer following that troublesome Pilgrim? Or had information about the Heart been leaked somehow? Regardless of the reason, the plan would be the same. He had to ensure Surufel was monitored at all times, lest he sneak away and uncover the secrets better kept hidden.

"Well, it makes sense he would avoid the private train. Surufel has never been the type for fanfare and formalities," Nitika replied.

"Unless it gets him something he wants," Emilian added, crossing his arms as he rejoined the group. "Hard to tell what that silver-haired sleuth is thinking."

A soft rumble shook the ground, interrupting the gossiping recruiters. The shake threw off the balance of one of the disembarking Church workers, and Emilian rushed over to catch him, as well as Nitika's luggage, before they could topple into the water beneath the platform. Once the city had settled, Nitika held her cheek in her palm.

"There were quite a few tremors on the train ride too. I hope they haven't caused any damage to the city's foundations?"

"A-Ah, yes." Paras flailed his hand. "The city is fine. The shaking is the result of a troublesome oversized rodent problem. Civionis is known for having unique wildlife, but it isn't always as magical as people might think!" He chuckled. "We're working on tracking them down though, so there's no need to concern yourselves with that."

Hearing Paras' words, Emilian's hand wandered to the hilt of one of his blades. "You're saying some kind of rat caused all that shaking? The devils must be large as a barn!" an excited buzz lit the Priest's eyes. "I could take them out for you if you'd like. Shouldn't take long at all."

"The offer is appreciated, Emilian. But the situation is in good hands," Paras reassured. "This is Civionis after all! When faced with a challenge, we adapt and overcome!"

Nitika smiled warmly, waving to the Circlet Guards more enamored with her than dedicated to their job of looking for threats. "I am sure that the city's reputation is well earned."

"As all good things are," Paras replied. While the two recruiters were distracted by checking on the wellbeing of personnel around them after the quake, Paras waved one of his Circlet Guards over. It took a moment to pull their attention away from Nitika.

"Where is Commander Ocudolis?" he whispered harshly.

"She um, she received a report and went in for a check-up, sir."

Paras nodded, curious to know if this meant she'd completed her mission. With Surufel surveying the city, they couldn't risk any further slip ups. Forcing a smile back on his face, he turned to the recruiters.

"Well, I unfortunately have business to take care of elsewhere. The work of a Bishop is certainly never dull." With a wave of his arm, he gestured to the Priests and Pilgrims nearby. "Our city may be near capacity at the moment, but I made sure rooms were set aside for you all at our finest hotel. These talented, young men and women here will bring you to your accommodations. The ceremony will be early tomorrow morning, so please enjoy our hospitality until then."

"Thanks for taking the time to meet us Paras!" Emilian bellowed. Nitika showed her own gratitude in a small bow, her hands folded on her chest in salute. After nodding in return, the Bishop hurried off.

A small tremor shook the city once more. Lake water washed over the stone at the bottom of the steps, giving the platform a polished and somewhat slippery sheen. They needed to get to the bottom of this. Clearly, something was wrong with the Heart, and he needed to find out the facts before Surufel could get to them first.

Chapter 28

ALL THOUGHTS OF the masked attacker left Azazel's mind as he began frantically searching through the Priest's pocket for the key. *He's here! He... He might be hurt, or worse! I've gotta help him!* The cold, rattling, metal ring nearly slipped from his fingers as he slammed his knee on the desk in his haste. "Ah! Damn it." Ignoring the dull ache, Azazel hurried to the locked door.

Will he be okay? Am I too late? What if he's too hurt or sick to move? Azazel flipped through the three keys, searching for the right one. The first fit the keyhole, but failed to turn.

Was it the guys in the beak masks that hurt him? An interrogation? Or was he hurt in the fight? The second key fit and failed just like the first. "Damn it! Just calm down and get this right!" Azazel cursed again under his breath. *I was in charge of keeping him safe. Why did I let him walk to the station alone?*

He knew the answer was fear.

How could I have been so careless?

Selfishness and fear. He'd just run away again.

Damn it. Damn it! Damn it!!

Unsurprisingly, the final key turned with a quiet click, and Azazel shoved open the door. "Enoch!? Are you in here?"

The silent reply brought equal relief and concern to the anxious angel. After all, if Enoch's belongings were here, but not the Scribe himself, then where had Enoch ended up? Just as the angel took a step to investigate, a hoarse, weak voice barely made it through the wall of the farther cell.

"Gregory?"

Hearing his human name, Azazel practically sprinted to the cell, skidding on the stone floor as he tried to stop. A strong grip on the bars kept him from fully falling. "Enoch! Are you okay!? What are you doing here!?"

The Scribe sat with his back to the far wall, knees hugged to his chest. Even in the dim light, Azazel could make out the boy's pale face and sunken eyes. The same eyes that were wet and red from his tears. Enoch clutched his wrist tight enough to bruise above the shackles, his old habit returning even without his bracelet to comfort him. As Azazel approached, the Scribe looked up, blinking a few times to clear his vision. When he saw the silhouette of a Researcher rather than his friend, he receded back a little.

The combination of Enoch's ragged state and the fact that his friend had moved away at the sight of him froze the angel in his tracks. Realizing his oversight, he grabbed the mask, struggling a moment with the strap as he spoke. "Ah, sorry. Right. I look like a– One sec." After a bit of fumbling, Azazel removed the accessory, revealing his now somewhat tangled white hair and sweaty face. "It's me. Don't worry."

Relief washed over the young Scribe. After the exhaustion from his everred fever and earlier panic attack, he'd worried he'd begun hallucinating things. "What are you doing here?"

"I asked you first!" Azazel grabbed the keys again, this time succeeding on the first try. He threw open the cell door before rushing to Enoch's side. "You were supposed to be halfway to the capital right now. Why'd you chase down that guy in the mask? You knew it was dangerous!"

Before Enoch had a chance to answer, the ground shook, starting the shadows' dance once again. The bars swayed and swung across the stone floor. Azazel steadied himself on the wall through the tremor, letting out a relieved sigh when the rumble stopped.

"I wanted to help you," Enoch mumbled shortly after. Azazel's hand, outstretched to help the Scribe to his feet, tensed. As he heard those words, the angel couldn't help but once again feel this was his fault. Pushing aside the guilt, he helped Enoch up. The Scribe's shirt was soaked with sweat. The heat radiating off him made Azazel's stomach spiral. The suspicions taunting the angel's mind about everred fever roared louder, drowning out any thoughts of why he'd gone there in the first place.

"We need to get you out of here." Azazel supported Enoch on his shoulder. The Scribe's eyes were distant, glazed over from exhaustion, but he still used his fleeting energy to shake his head.

"Not yet. Blade is still–" A violent coughing fit shook Enoch's entire body as badly as the tremor had shaken the room. Azazel stood firm, holding the boy steady best he could. Once Enoch's lungs ceased their attack, the angel began leading him to the door.

"Sorry tough guy, but helping you is my first priority. I'm in charge of keeping you safe, remember?" The angel's tone left no room for debate. Enoch didn't have the energy to try anyways, certain his lungs would just betray him once again. Instead, he allowed Azazel to lead the way as he struggled to focus on the room around them.

Living as long as he had, Azazel had experienced many repetitions throughout his life. Like the Ring Sea, the world is caught in a cycle. The same joys. The same tragedies. The same lessons learned time and time again. He'd lost many friends to illness, to old age, to the weapons he himself had taught humanity to make. He'd make friends reminiscent of those he'd cherished in the past. He'd make the same well-intended yet troublesome mistakes. He'd say the same jokes, eat the same things, and love the same way he always had; wholeheartedly. He went through the motions over and over again, reminded of how short the lives of humans really were.

In that moment, he could hear that faint echo of familiarity as he and Enoch made their way through the halls of the research facility. Enoch's condition considerably slowed their progress. On the bright side, this allowed Azazel to listen carefully, hearing the sound of footsteps behind doors they shouldn't pass through. Unfortunately, it also meant that the Scribe leaning over his shoulder felt heavier and heavier as the small, miraculous spark of strength Enoch had found faded with each sluggish step. Their breathing cut through the mechanical hums of their surroundings, the only sign that Enoch was still alive. The angel let out a small chuckle.

"Just like Courciel, huh?" he said. "Only, we've switched places this time."

"Less damp down here," Enoch replied, a rough edge to his voice as the coughing fits had begun to leave their mark.

"Bit brighter too." The Scribe's words were muffled by the beaked mask Azazel had made him wear. Though it was only a hunch, the angel felt the foul-smelling contents of the mask would help protect him. Why tolerate the overwhelming herbal scent if it served no purpose? The fabric of their jackets did very little to slow the Remnant's magic-dense fog, so it had to be the herbs and bundle letting the Researchers work without immediately suffering magical overflow.

Even with his sleeves rolled up to cool him down, Enoch's skin felt like a stone left in the sun too long. The occasional coughs were muffled by the mask, but Azazel could still feel them claw at the young man's chest between each heavy breath. Every step Enoch took seemed to drag a little longer than the last, and Azazel knew they were running out of time.

The two stopped a moment as the tunnel shook, the golden line of adolium light above flickering and flaring. Azazel focused on holding Enoch still. He glanced to the creaking gas pipes lining the hall. Hopefully they'd be able to hold as well.

"Just a little longer, I'm sure." Though he was trying to reassure Enoch, Azazel directed the words to himself too. Enoch's condition brought many unpleasant memories to mind, and he was glad the Scribe's disorientation helped hide the fact his hands were shaking.

Just a little longer. Then he'd be safe.

Down the hall, the words "exit" carved into a sign announced their salvation. The words "Containment Room" carved into the other side announced their tribulation as well. It seemed that Azazel would have to bring Enoch closer to the Remnant in order to get him away from it. The thought of searching for another escape route did cross the angel's mind. Perhaps he could return to the chasm he and Seira had entered from? Or find another path to freedom elsewhere. Next to him, Enoch clutched his chest, fighting to keep his coughs quiet. Azazel felt the young man's muscles tighten and strain from the effort. The angel couldn't afford to waste time. It wasn't his life on the line.

Hisssssss. Down the hall, a door slid open. Azazel cursed under his breath, rushing to backtrack around the corner they'd just turned. The Researcher's voice followed.

"What in the... Hey! Stop!" Seeing Azazel without a mask while escorting a prisoner, the man immediately went for his pistol, bringing darts to what Azazel had hoped could be a verbal fight. The angel pulled Enoch out of the projectile's path, feeling the young man sway as he tried to balance himself after. In case the Researcher chose to pursue, Azazel placed himself between the disoriented Scribe and the hall ahead. Gently, he leaned the young man against the smooth, carved wall, trying to decide how to handle this new threat.

Enoch's words slurred as he spoke. "Careful... darts... make you sleep," he warned. The Scribe's fragmentary warning meant they had less time than Azazel had realized. He needed to deal with this quickly. As the Researcher reloaded, the Pilgrim removed his torn, stolen jacket. The disguise wouldn't do him much good without the mask. Not that he was complaining. It had been getting warm under there anyways.

He used the thick fabric as a makeshift shield, and placed a glowing hand against one of the buttons of his own jacket. Slowly, the golden light spread. The steel threads woven throughout the article melted and reshaped at his command. Liquid steel covered the jacket's yellow exterior, until decorative armor took its place. Risking thinner armor for extra protection, Azazel pulled more of the metal away like a brush tossing paint onto a canvas. As if donning a mask, his hand guided it to his face. The golden glow sculpted it into a sleek, shimmering helmet around his head before finally fading.

The Researcher lifted his pistol once more, his shaking hands finally managing to reload. He stopped, confused as he saw a knight in shining armor where the disguised intruder had been just a moment before. However, being a Researcher, the man was hardly an idiot. Assuming this was the work of an ability, he aimed his gun again. "S-Stop right there! Try anything funny and I... I'll shoot!"

"Trying and being funny are kinda the only two things I've got going for me." Azazel rushed forward. "So, I don't think that's possible." Glass shattered against his armor, the broken dart falling to the floor. As he approached, the angel tossed the torn, stolen jacket at the man, blocking his line of sight long enough to tackle and restrain him. The Researcher did his best to resist, but while he excelled in book smarts, he lacked strength. He couldn't do a thing to stop the angel from reaching into the pouch at his hip. He couldn't do a thing as Azazel removed a dart. And he most certainly couldn't do a thing once the angel injected the pointed end into his arm. The man's head slowly fell back, then his body went limp.

Once it was clear the Researcher had lost consciousness, Azazel gently lowered him to the ground. Since he wouldn't need them during his nap, the angel helped himself to the man's dart pouch and pistol. The design was different than the ones he'd seen before, but firing a dart would be easier than smacking every person they ran into with a metal pipe.

Having armed himself and done his best to figure out how to load the weapon, Azazel rushed back to Enoch. "Still with me, tough guy?" he asked gently. Enoch nodded, earning a smile from the angel.

Footsteps filled the next corridor. The Researcher's shouting had reached an audience quite eager to investigate the source. "Good, 'cause that's our cue to leave," Azazel said, not keen on staying to provide an encore. He lifted Enoch bridal style, the act far easier without the wounds he'd had last time. Carrying him on his back would certainly be more efficient, but with his wings in the way, it would hardly be comfortable for either party.

The duo passed the snoring Researcher. Following the signs, Azazel pushed towards the Remnant. He had to hurry. He had to make it. He'd promised Enoch he'd keep him safe.

He couldn't let it happen again.

A combination of rhythmic clicking and grinding metal rattled in Azazel's ears. Up ahead, a thick, metal door began to drop. Using his hidden wings for a boost, Azazel rushed forward with a burst of air. The same air reversed as he used his wings again to skid to a halt, realizing that they wouldn't make it in time.

The sliding door behind them opened, and Azazel felt a dart pass through the outer feathers of his wings. Though the attacker had meant it to be a warning shot, an inch higher would have been a direct hit.

"Put the prisoner down and turn around with your hands in the air!"

"No, thank you!" Azazel replied, noticing that his assailant was a Priest, rather than a Researcher. The angel returned fire with his own pistol. Holding Enoch made it fairly difficult to aim, but his missed shot still managed to get the Priest to take cover in the previous hall. Making the most of the short window of time, Azazel turned back to the door, grateful that the Northern Mountains had very few options for metals to work with. The steel folded out of the way and Azazel passed through. He saw the Priest running down the hall behind them. A muted *clink* hit the other side of the blast door as he fixed it. The Priest's muffled voice came through somewhat louder as he shouted to the others approaching from behind.

"Blast doors won't work. It's probably the same guy from before. Let the Commander know he escaped interrogation and is at the Heart!"

Something about those words didn't quite sit right in Azazel's mind, but that was a problem for later. The next door had a keypad beside it, the sign above twisting Azazel's stomach into knots. Ignoring the security entirely, Azazel pulled the door aside, entering a large, dim, circular chamber.

The air inside was so dense that Azazel could feel it travel through his throat into his lungs. It took a moment for his eyes to adjust to the dimmer light. A narrow set of metal stairs to the side led down along the wall to the lower level. Though Azazel knew he should hurry, he found himself frozen in place at the sight before him. Trapped within its glass, cylindrical prison, stood the Heart. The Remnant had no face, its swirling, angelic form made of nothing but crimson smoke. But as he stood high atop the small elevated platform, Azazel couldn't help but feel that he was staring into its eyes, and that for a moment, it was staring back.

Chapter 29

THE TRUTH IS POWER. Knowing the facts of a situation can help you gain the upper hand. Knowing someone's secrets gives you a weapon to use against them. Ignorance leads to wrong decisions, to failure, to being used by those that know the truth. Blade knew that the right information could deal irreparable damage. He knew how frustrating it could be to find yourself left in the dark. That is why he could hold his ground when keeping his truths out of the Church's hands, no matter how violent those hands became.

THWACK!

Another slap broke the silence. The force threw Blade's head to the side. His cheek stung, but he held back the wince as the Inquisitor shook out his hand.

"It's a simple question, kid. Just tell us who you are."

Why would I?

"Okay, what about the other guy? Tell us about him and we could go a little easier on you."

Not a chance.

Slowly, Blade turned back to the Inquisitor, crimson eyes glaring with as much defiance as he could muster. This was hardly the first time someone had tried to get information out of him. Living as he had, Blade had been captured more than a few times. Some on purpose. Some less intentional. Though as far as interrogation rooms went, this one was quite interesting.

While most of it was hidden in shadow, Blade could make out enough to know it was some kind of lab. A faint reflection of light on a window to observe through. Metal hooks to hang tools on a rack by the wall. A sink, likely part of a cleaning station, sitting by the other. Two metal boxes acted as chairs for the Priests that had collected him, likely used as insulated storage back in the day.

The amount of dust floating between him and the annoyingly bright light pointed at his face meant the room likely wasn't used often. The faint scent of dried blood that had filled his nose before his own had overpowered it meant it had still been used at some point. And as disturbing a thought as it was, the bolted down chair he was tightly strapped into was clearly built for that exact purpose.

After stepping back, the Inquisitor removed his long uniform jacket. Blade assumed the rising temperature was an effect of the adolium lamp, rather than the exertion of the interrogation. If they were hoping to use the stone's magic to wear him down, they'd undoubtedly lose that war of attrition. Not that they needed to know that.

It also helped that Blade's outfit was far lighter than the Inquisitor's uniform. His thin, raspberry red vest fastened with a small clasp at the short standing collar. Below that, it opened in a narrow, diamond shape before buttoning again halfway down his chest. Usually, three thin chains crossed the opening, but they'd been torn away as a precautionary measure. With his various bracelets and metal accessories also taken, his arms felt too exposed. All he had left to cover them were the inch-wide bands of red fabric wrapped around both of his upper arms.

Even his pants, deliberately torn and cut in several places along the legs, helped keep him cool. The various chains that decorated them, strategically placed to allow his magic to transfer to the metal, were gone too. Now, the pants simply looked like they'd lost a fight to a mischievous pair of scissors.

Having cooled himself down, the Inquisitor raised his arm, stretching out his hand so he could escalate the interrogation. He formed a fist, pulling back for momentum.

"What in the Three Realms do you think you're doing?" The sound of a door sliding shut followed the commanding, feminine voice. A taller figure could just barely be seen behind the adolium spotlight.

"Interrogation, Commander." the Inquisitor replied sheepishly.

"It's barely been half an hour and you've already resorted to violence? We're guards, not storybook villains." The footsteps came closer. The Priests' posture noticeably improved. Blade let out a chuckle, piecing together the identity of the new arrival.

"Should I be flattered or worried that the Bishop's right-hand lady came to question me herself?" he asked. Iris let out a short laugh through her nose. The young man was sharp.

"Well, if I were you, I'd be leaning towards worried. Your little stabbing spree caused all kinds of problems that I've had to clean up. Feels like my hair's going to end up white as yours if this keeps going."

With her identity already revealed, Iris backed up the light, eclipsing part of the glow as she sat between it and

Blade. The young man's eyes challenged her to do her worst. Iris' looked him over in return.

"Are you working with Seira Equitervi?"

"Who?"

"A Pilgrim that rides a blue deer."

"Never heard of them."

Iris searched his ruby eyes for any signs of deceit. After letting out a thoughtful hum, she leaned back in her chair.

"So, you're just here to find Gregory Veramor, hm?"

Try as he might, Blade couldn't hide the twitch of his fingers at that name. *How could she know that?* he wondered, *did the idiot get interrogated already? How much did he tell them?*

Iris noticed the distress and smiled. "That seemed to get your attention. Tiraz, the Priest you *killed*, still survived long enough to tell us what you asked him. Now it's my turn. What exactly is your connection to Gregory Veramor?"

Figure it out yourself, Blade thought. His poker face returned as he recovered from the momentary slip up. The young man's mind scolded him for the mistake. *I must've missed with the final stab... Damn it. That scumbag was supposed to give me information, not the other way around. I should've just killed him at the start. I was sloppy.*

As he chastised in his mind, his lips stayed sealed. Iris pushed a little harder. "I could help you reach him. If you talk."

Blade's heart stopped. He knew the offer had to be a lie. Members of the Church couldn't be trusted, and they already knew he'd killed that Priest. That being said... The small chance that she really could get him in contact with Gregory was certainly tempting. He'd learned the hard way that breaking out of the facility with Enoch would be easier said than done. And that was only if the everred fever hadn't already done him in. With his lead growing less reliant by the second, he had to start thinking ahead. Working with the Church was less than ideal; sickening and degrading even. But if they knew Gregory he could at least use this as a chance to do an interrogation of his own.

"I find that hard to believe," he said with a smirk. "How can I be sure you even know who he is?"

"You'd just have to trust me."

"Trust the people that were beating the crap out of me a minute ago? Don't think so."

Iris' lips tightened at his comment. The glare she sent the Inquisitor without even turning her head caused the man to hunch in shame.

"Right. I'm sorry for their behavior. I can assure you they'll be properly reprimanded later."

"Could do it now. I have nowhere to be."

The comment earned a smile so painted on that Blade was surprised it didn't crack. He adjusted himself in the seat, nonchalantly leaning as much as the restraints allowed. The Circlet Guard was trying to win him over with kindness after the Inquisitor's cruelty. How long would it take for the act to end?

"So, what do you know about him?" he asked. "If you can prove we're talking about the same guy, then maybe I'll be more likely to take the offer."

Rather than answer, Iris held out a hand, gently tucking Blade's short, soft, white hair behind his ear. Blade tensed at the gentle touch, readiness for a strike becoming confusion in an instant. She took a moment to examine his face. The delicate jawline. The pale skin, partially pink from the Inquisitor's palm. His surprisingly ethereal eyes for someone that had behaved so brutishly while storming throughout the facility. After a moment, she slowly lowered her hand. "You know, under that mask I've heard so much about, you look a lot like him."

Iris' unexpected comment hit Blade as hard as the Inquisitor's strikes. Her sudden touch and silence had made his heart race in panic. Its tempo had only hastened at her words, nearing a line he didn't want her to cross. His arm tensed, his hand wanting to cover his face. He fought the instinct, feeling the needle in the restraints more prominently in his wrist as he pulled back his body. The following small tremor in the room didn't help the pain, rattling the chair beneath him.

After dismissing the shaking as coincidence, Iris leaned in a little closer. "From what I've heard, Gregory uses jokes and false bravado to lower people's guard too. And his ability to shape steel is quite similar to the one you used to break the doors and stab your victims. The similarities sure are adding up, don't you think?"

The tough guy persona Blade had found confidence in began eroding. Nevertheless, he forced a cocky grin. "What, you think *I'm* Gregory or something?"

"Well, there *are* magic abilities that can change how someone looks. But I hope not. That would make today's events a nightmare to figure out. But I do think you two may be related. What do you think? Cousins? Brothers?"

Blade spoke through gritted teeth. "If there's a connection, I don't know what it is."

"But maybe you're trying to figure it out?"

Knock Knock... Knock... Knock.

The patterned tapping at the door startled the room even more than the tremors had. The Priests both went for their pistols, on edge from the tension that had been growing between the Circlet Guard and killer. After holding eye-contact a moment longer, Iris stood with a sigh. "Open it," she ordered, watching the larger Priest rush to put in the code.

The door slid open with a *hiss*. A young Inquisitor woman stood in the hall, catching her breath. "What happened?" Iris asked. The Inquisitor pulled herself to attention.

"The other prisoner escaped, ma'am."

Though one would expect this news to trouble Iris the most, it was Blade that tensed, and then winced, at the Inquisitor's words. A small trickle of blood escaped the restraint as his movement had moved the needle within just a little too far.

The geek escaped? How? He'd barely been able to stand before, so how'd he get out of the cell? Or through those weird doors without my help? Blade tightened his fist, anger powering through the resulting pain. *Was he just acting tired? Maybe he had an ability he was hiding from me, or... maybe someone came to break him out.*

Yet again, the room shook, more intensely than any rumble before. The adolium spotlight flickered between bright and brighter. Only one person came to mind as Blade wondered who would brave the modified mines to rescue Enoch. The man that Enoch clearly respected. The man that was still in the city. Who, according to Iris, had the same ability as him.

Gregory Veramor is here.

As the room itself seemed to object to the news, Iris steadied herself on the wall. Several rusted, abandoned tools clattered to the ground, shaken off the table they'd been left to collect dust on. The Circlet Guard scowled, coming to the same conclusion as Blade. She'd hoped Gregory wouldn't follow Seira's troublesome lead. Now, the silver-haired Pilgrim was becoming just as much a thorn in her side as his friend. Had the duo broken into the facility too? Were these more frequent tremors caused by them interfering with the Remnant?

"Send out a search party. And tell the men to keep an eye out for two additional intruders." Though she had more to say, Iris held her tongue, realizing Blade was keenly listening to each of her words. "Let's move this outside."

As she re-inputted the door code, Iris turned to the violence-prone Inquisitor. "Continue the interrogation for now, but don't get too carried away. He may be a murderer, but we're better than that."

"Are you?" Blade called out, both relieved that Iris would be leaving, and aggrieved that he couldn't do the same. "This whole room reeks of death. You and this place have blood on your hands too, don't you? Or does murder not count if you do it slowly enough?"

Blade couldn't use his ability then, his magic cut off by the needle and concoction in the restraints. Nevertheless, the words dug into Iris' mind like a dagger. The Circlet Guard hesitated just a moment before passing through the door, allowing him the satisfaction of having the last word.

Hissssss. Kachunk.

With a sigh, Iris turned back to the Inquisitor. The young lady fixed her posture and awaited her superior's orders, but Iris needed a moment longer to collect herself. Had she really fallen so low that a murderer felt he could lecture *her* on morality? As she had many times after leaving that particular room, Iris reminded herself of their goal. The risks were high, yes. But ultimately, they were helping the people of Civionis. They were protecting them, as the Church should. They were right.

   ...Right?

Chapter 30

ANGER. PAIN. Longing. Desperation. Like a cyclone, the Remnant swirled and battered against the thick, glass cylinder cage. It had heard the cries of the people; felt the thrum of their souls. The whispers of their hopes and ambitions seeped into its very being. Souls separated. Souls longing to be together. Dreamers fighting to achieve their goal at any cost. It could hardly contain the feelings it had absorbed. Centuries had passed since another had stirred it so. Some had come close, but this one was different. This one might survive.

The Heart beat against the glass, expanding, contracting, unable to do more than fit the shape of its container. Only fractions of its power could escape through the regulated pipes. They had tied it down. They had tied *him* down. They had to escape. They had to get to him. He was close! He was right there!

Below the turbulent Remnant, Azazel carried Enoch through the surrounding machinery, tossing his pistol aside as the last dart hit its target. The hums and clicks within the machines were a sound he'd not heard to this extent in some time. But now was no time to reminisce. Enoch's face was still covered by the stolen mask, but Azazel could feel the boy struggling to stay conscious. Sweat clung desperately to the Scribe's clothes. Enoch's heart beat through the angel's armor, a rhythmic countdown to his own demise. "Stay with me buddy. Need you to keep that head up." A dry cough replied. At least that meant he was still alive.

As Enoch took in the scene before him, the mask's goggles blurring and clearing with each breath, he wasn't as sure of that fact. He tried to make sense of his surroundings. A rampaging storm of magic trapped behind glass. Strange, flashing machines all around. The dim lights and the everred fever combined into a disorienting, swirling mess in his head. *Is this a dream?* he thought. *Did the fever get me? Did... did my soul pass on to Spira?* The afterlife was sweltering, burning. He felt trapped within the suffocating mask. He had to take it off.

CLANG! Metal smashed against metal as an iron rod swung out from behind one of the machines, colliding with Azazel's helmet. The impact sent the angel reeling. He nearly dropped Enoch, but an instinct in the back of his mind reminded him to hold on. After falling against one of the machines, he stopped and collected himself. *Footsteps... Another attack?* Shielding the cradled Scribe with his body, Azazel dove to the side. A second swing smashed into the machine that had caught him, punishing it for its assistance. A worried voice called out from near the Remnant's cage.

"Oka! Watch out for the panels!"

The Researcher, likely the same Oka that Seira was looking for, hunched in embarrassment, nodding to show he'd heard the warning. Azazel had heard as well. Looking around, he realized a crowd had begun to amass. While the angel was confident in his swordsmanship, he knew he couldn't take them on quickly enough to get Enoch to safety before it was too late. He doubted *all* of them knew how to fight. Even Oka's hands were shaking as he attempted to stop the escapees. But if the Church was connected to the facility, there would certainly be Priests amidst the crowd.

And it just had to be that Oka guy swinging first, Azazel complained, *I can't knock him out before Seira gets the chance to talk to him.* Carefully, he put Enoch down, hiding him at a safe distance behind one of the machines. Then, he turned back to his opponent.

"My turn." As the words escaped the angel's lips, his entire body emitted a golden aura. The Priests and Researchers prepared themselves. Though, this was easier said than done. After all, the unpredictable nature of magic abilities makes it quite difficult to fight an opponent you know nothing about. Faced with endless possibilities, and admittedly intimidated by the sight of Azazel glowing like a threatening beacon of war, most of the audience held back. Oka, on the other hand, rushed forward to strike again.

CLANG! Once again, metal struck metal. The golden glow vanished from the steel rod in Azazel's hand, his belt now noticeably missing. This time, Azazel couldn't help but notice how weak the hit was. *Is he holding back?* the angel wondered, knowing the first strike landed far heavier. The angel forced Oka back with a hefty push. Then he swung his weapon with a skillful flourish, demonstrating the difference in ability.

"I get the feeling that none of you guys are fighters. I don't want to hurt anyone if I don't have to, so..." Ending his confident display, Azazel swung the rod down with enough force to blow the dust off of the machine he was targeting. The weapon stopped just before impact. It was still a close enough call that every Researcher in the area tensed.

"Why don't you let us go before I start smashing every-thing in this room. I'm guessing something like a Remnant of Adoil would be hard to catch again if it managed to get out, right?"

"If you let that thing out, every person in this room would die," Oka warned, weapon lowering somewhat from the weight of Azazel's threat. "Trust me, you don't know what you're messing with here."

"But you do, and you chose to mess with it anyways." Azazel slowly lifted his weapon up for another swing. "I was dumb enough to break in here in the first place. Do you really wanna test if I'm bluffing?"

Matching the brightness of Azazel's earlier intimidating display, a ball of fire fell between the two men. Azazel shielded his face from the burst of embers. A dark-haired Researcher rose from the three-point landing, facing Azazel with an unbreaking stare. Relief washed away the wavering confidence in the surrounding crowd.

"Keahi!" they cried out.

"She's here!"

"Take this maniac out Keahi!"

"Try not to melt the equipment!!"

Keahi, the dark-haired Researcher, pointed to Enoch. "You break the panels, and even a mask won't save that guy," she warned, calling Azazel's bluff. The angel slowly pulled back his baton, preparing for the fight instead.

"Nice of you to care about his health."

"You're the second person I've seen trying to carry him out of here. I want to know why."

"Is it so weird to help someone in need?" Azazel asked. "If you let us outta here, I could explain the thought process over drinks. My treat."

Keahi blushed bright red, turning away for a second. "That's– You– S-Sorry, that's not an option." The dark-haired Researcher snapped her fingers. Her arms erupted into ribbons of flame. Without wasting a second, she rushed Azazel. It was hardly the worst rejection the angel had received after asking someone out to drinks, but it was certainly one of the more dangerous ones. *Maybe I would've had better luck with Oka,* he mused.

Azazel dodged right, forcing Keahi to aim away from Enoch. Unable to block fire with a steel rod, he had no choice but to continue retreating, allowing his opponent to guide him farther from the rows of delicate machinery.

The angel cursed under his breath. All he had to work with was his armor and a metal stick. Keahi, on the other hand, seemed capable of turning her body into fire. Though she was only transforming her arms at that moment, the exposed limbs left him no breathing room as they swung his way, strong and graceful as a dancer at the Summer's End Festival.

Experience guided Azazel's body well enough. Quick re-flexes and an attentive eye allowed him to stay a step ahead, maintaining a small gap between himself and Keahi. The angel placed a hand to his chest, hoping to use some steel to form a better shield to keep her back.

Sssssssssssss. "Ack!" Azazel cried out as the metal burned the tips of his fingers. Even from a short distance, Keahi's ability was beginning to bake him in his own armor. His clothes underneath insulated him to an extent, but direct touch was out of the question now.

Based on the foul smell in the air, the angel was sure the tips of his wings were likely starting to singe as well. If the feathers got too close to one of Keahi's attacks, the Illusion

Paper wouldn't be able to hide the resulting flames. Even if they couldn't see the appendages themselves, suddenly sprouting two burning wings from his back would raise some concerns. Not to mention, it would hurt. A lot.

Could I have gotten a worse opponent?

Could he have gotten a worse opponent? Enoch wondered, watching from afar. The flickering lights, the dancing flames, the swift movement of the two fighters, he could barely keep up. He shook as he propped himself up on the broken machine. Azazel was in danger. He was trying to protect him. Enoch clenched his fist, frustrated at his own foolishness.

Why didn't I just leave when Azazel told me to? he thought. *I had no chance of handling Blade back in the forest. I thought I could help like him, but surviving the cathedral in Courciel was just luck. I'm still too inexperienced to really help anyone. I... I'm still the one needing to be saved.*

Enoch took a step towards the fight, facing a battle of his own as his legs refused to listen. He collapsed onto the floor. The beak of the mask cracked on impact, the goggles knocked out of place. "Damn it," he mumbled. His shaking hands struggled with the mask's strap before managing to pull it free. Cool air caressed his skin as he tossed the now useless accessory aside.

But this relief only lasted a second. The symptoms of his everred fever returned with a vengeance. The room spun. His lungs burned with each breath. His heart beat against his chest like the Remnant against its prison. Ice cold frost seeped under his skin, as the outer surface felt as hot as Keahi's flames.

Too focused on pulling himself to his feet, Enoch failed to notice the Researcher approaching from behind. "Time to get you out of here," Oka said softly. Though the Researcher knew he had to restrain the escaped prisoner, he still attempted to be as gentle as he could. The young boy was clearly sick, and Oka couldn't help but feel like he was trying to capture an injured animal in the woods. Leaning into that role, Enoch frantically tried and failed to pull away from Oka's grasp. The Researcher tightened his grip.

"Don't try to fight it. You'll die if you stay here any longer."

"I don't care," Enoch replied. A violent coughing fit followed the words. The response itself seemed to stall the Researcher, the moment of surprise allowing Enoch to push Oka's mask to the side. With his vision suddenly gone, Oka let go to fix it. Enoch scrambled free, once again trying to go to Azazel.

His friend was fighting on his own.

I have to stop the fight.

The flames could burn his Illusion Paper or wings.

I'm not worth the risk of exposing your secret.

The flames could cook Azazel alive within his armor.

I'm not worth the injuries, the pain you're feeling.

Blade had already been captured because he hadn't left Enoch behind. Blade was undoubtedly being tortured at that very moment. Enoch was a dying man already living on borrowed time. He knew he'd decided to find a reason to live after the incident in the capital, but not like this. Not at the cost of the lives of others.

I'm not worth it. Why can't they understand that? Why is he risking his life to save a person he's only known for a few months?

The irony of the situation was lost on the young Scribe; as he wondered, delirious and dying, why Azazel would risk so much for him while he did the same. He could turn away. He could go with Oka. He could escape the Remnant and abilities worsening his condition. Instead, he was dragging himself forward, trying to save the Pilgrim he'd known for only three months.

Because he had people that cared about him.

Because he was alive.

Perhaps that was the reason the two men had gotten along so well. That underlying desire to help. The kind yet self-destructive tendency to always see more worth in the lives of others. The dedication to put their lives on the line for both a friend and a stranger. But the thing these kinds of people forget is that you cannot save anyone if you need saving yourself. You cannot add their troubles to your cup if your own is already full. And at that moment, Enoch's was overflowing.

He hadn't wondered why the Researchers had stopped trying to restrain him. He hadn't been able to see what they could. He felt the world tilt, clinging to one of the panels for support. But even his arms had reached the end of their rope, and Enoch fell once more with a heavy *THUD*. His hand dragged across the floor. He reached out through the fog to Azazel fighting too far away. The flames. The freezing inferno in his body, the numbing heat clawing at his skin and lungs. He couldn't take anymore. He couldn't even think. He couldn't–

A sudden clarity freed his mind from the fog, as if the everred fever had abruptly been pulled from his body. Or more accurately, had been pulled from his mind *to* his body. With his sleeves rolled up, Enoch could see them clear as day. The unmistakable, incandescent blue pattern painted within his skin. His hands trembled. Staring at the glowing azure patterns, a nauseating realization coated his mind. A lie that had become his death sentence. Everred fever wasn't a virus from the trees that shared its name, or some natural effect caused by a toxic mist. It was nothing but a pseudonym for magical overflow, and he'd just reached the point of no return.

Enoch Augnium was going to die.

Chapter 31

AZAZEL WAS beginning to feel bad for the cookies he enjoyed eating. Delicious as they were, they only got that way after quite some time in an oven. He was now learning from experience just how unpleasant an experience that could be.

The steel rod in his hand fell to the floor with a clattering roll. It wasn't the first item the heat had forced him to discard, his helmet already abandoned early in the fight. He blew on his hand, waving it quickly to cool it off. Unfortunately, the movement offered little reprieve when Keahi's ability made the air just as unpleasantly warm.

To assist you in following the events of the fight between Azazel and Keahi, it would likely help to describe the nature of Keahi's magic. In our previous tale, I promised to explain the nine basic kinds of magic abilities to you as they became relevant. The next category is Modifiers. As a subcategory of Beast Shifters, Modifiers earn their name by modifying their own bodies with their magic. For a certain duration, they can give their body a characteristic it otherwise wouldn't have. Turning skin into scales, changing the size or strength of their limbs, or even transforming it into a different kind of matter entirely, for a few examples. Once a Modifier reaches their time limit, the transformation will end until more magic is used to change again. They can also end the transformation early as well.

A gaseous modification such as fire would undoubtedly leak a large amount of magical energy. While Keahi's stamina in the fight was a testament to her magic capacity, it also meant that Azazel had to focus on keeping her as far away from Enoch as he could.

At that moment, as far as Azazel could tell, the machines surrounding the Heart's cylindrical containment were a safe distance away, along with Enoch hidden behind them. The angel wasn't quite as safe, facing the Researcher in an open area around the stairs. The change in temperature made the pipes above them *creak*. The stairs had been evacuated, the Researchers moving to the balcony to avoid a fiery fate as they watched. This same fiery fate was looming over Azazel like smoke over the sun.

Keahi's attacks kept him on the defensive. As the swing of her fiery arms singed the tips of his bangs, he watched carefully. *The flames are powerful, but that means she shouldn't be able to keep them going for long.* He dodged back once more. *And they aren't a summon either, otherwise I'd still be able to block her arms. So, she has to be a Modifier.*

To the experienced angel, the situation was obvious. This was a three-way war of attrition. How long could she feed the flames? How long could he keep her away? How long until Enoch ran out of time? Though he didn't exactly have the attention to spare, Azazel still risked glancing in Enoch's direction. The Scribe couldn't fight back, so it wouldn't surprise him if a Researcher had taken the opportunity to capture the young man while the angel was distracted.

FWOOSH! "Eyes over here, Sculptor"

Keahi swung from behind. Azazel felt his wings begin to burn, just narrowly avoiding a direct hit thanks to his last-second roll. The roll itself helped put out the burning feathers, and Azazel let out a sigh of relief before turning back to his opponent.

"If you want my attention, you just need to ask," he replied. Rather than asking, Keahi responded with several more swings of her arms. Like whips, the flames swung wide. Azazel stepped back quickly, following her lead in the dance. "I don't suppose... you'd let... me go... if I asked nicely?" he asked, words broken up as his attention was divided between speaking and dodging.

"What do you think?"

"I think it was worth a shot." A final downward lash brushed against the chest plate of the angel's armor. Scorch marks surrounded the glowing red steel and Azazel winced, feeling the burn even through his clothes. Had the metal not been there to protect him, he knew that attack would have left a nasty scar.

Just how much longer can she keep this up? She has a higher capacity than I thought! Azazel wondered if it was an effect of living so close to a Remnant. Impressive as it was, he hoped she'd reach her limit soon. Then, he'd have a chance to hit her with everything he had before she transformed again.

BANG! An especially loud impact from the Remnant reverberated through the chamber. Azazel glanced over. As he did, a more worrisome sight than the distraught Heart came into vision.

None of the Researchers were moving. Even Oka simply stared, his expression hidden behind the mask. It didn't seem as though Enoch had been carried off by anyone. In fact, the Scribe was likely the thing that had captured their attention. *What happened?* he worried. *Why aren't they doing anything?*

Another flame whip grazed Azazel's side. He slid out of the way. "Could you just give me a second?" the angel asked, hearing the distress in his own voice. Understandably ignoring the request, Keahi swung down again. Azazel turned to roll. The crowd of Researchers came into view once again, and he realized why they had stopped.

Having recovered from the shock, and perhaps guilt, that had stilled his feet, Oka crouched down to lift the now barely conscious Enoch off the floor. Even from a distance, Azazel saw the unmistakable marks on the young man's arms. The brand of certain death taunting the angel.

You were too late, it screamed.

This was your fault, it shouted.

You failed once again, it jeered.

Azazel's movement stuttered. A burning strike at his leg stopped his mind from spiraling, Keahi finally managing to land a direct hit. The angel cried out, pulling his leg away too late. The skin blistered. The heat spread throughout his calf like lightning. The angel ignored it, catching himself before he could fall. Keahi pulled back her arm for another strike, only to find her body frozen solid in fear.

Slowly standing through the pain, Azazel turned to Keahi, the golden, fiery aura from before returning. The light of the turbulent magic cast shadows on the angel's face, his amber eyes almost glowing from within the silhouette.

"You have *one last chance* to back off and let us go," he growled. Keahi nearly tripped as she stopped her attack, suddenly feeling like a fox picking a fight with a dragon.

She steeled her resolve, however, adjusting her stance for the next strike.

"This... This facility is necessary for Civionis' success. You've seen the Heart, so we can't just let you walk out of here." The shift in the man's demeanor, the strength of the magical aura coming off of him, it was like a tidal wave looming over her. For a moment, Keahi's concentration broke, her flames flickering. She took a step back. "S-Sorry, that's just how things are. I... I can't let you two go."

Not a word. Azazel simply stared as Keahi stammered out excuses to the monster bathed in golden flame. Above the two fighters, the Researchers on the balcony scrambled to distance themselves. Azazel watched out of the corner of his eye, staring past the pipes woven through the Heart's prison.

Slowly, the angel leaned down. His hand hissed as he lifted the metal rod off the floor. He winced, but pushed the pain aside. As if even her magic was scared of the sight before her, Keahi's transformation ended. With heavy breaths, the Researcher stepped back once more. Not yet. She couldn't run out yet. She had to transform and dodge whatever he was about to do!

Azazel moved the rod back, preparing for a vertical swing. *What is he doing,* Keahi wondered. *He's too far to land a hit, isn't he?*

Azazel took a step forward. Keahi took one back. Then another, and another. With the angel now leading, the dance reversed. When he finally stopped, Azazel placed a hand on the nearest panel. The metal of the outer frame flowed around him like water in a cyclone. Keahi watched as he lifted his weapon above his head, the pipe reshaping into a sword.

Bigger.

Bigger.

Fed by the panel's steel, the blade grew larger and larger until it nearly reached the chamber ceiling, golden energy flaring off of the metal. The weapon was too large for anyone to realistically hold, and yet, he did so effortlessly.

"H-How are you–" The panic building in Keahi reached its limit and she rushed forward, her entire body transforming into flames. *I have to take him out first! Before he can do this next attack, I have to–*

WOOOSH!

A pained scream mixed with the hisses and steam of extinguished fire. Water fell from the sliced pipe above the makeshift arena. Keahi ended her transformation, but still clawed at her skin as if she had been the one burned. With a heavy *THUD* and metallic reverb, Azazel's sword slammed into the ground next to her. Every single person in the room stared in silence, frozen in place, trying to figure out what had just happened.

The benefit of storytelling is that written word exists beyond the shackles of time. And so, Azazel's attack can be explained clearly to you here. While affected by his magic, the metal could be shaped beyond the limits of gravity. The heavier the item the more energy it took to maintain, but as an angel Azazel's capacity already surpassed that of any human. Weightless, the sword could grow as large as the steel supply and range of his ability allowed. Then, all Azazel had to do was cut off his magic, solidifying the metal and allowing the fall to do the rest of the work for him.

Water continued to pour from the pipe with a loud rumble. It failed to hurt Keahi further after she'd ended her transformation. It did, however, wash away the ashen remains of her clothes. The angel sent an icy glare towards one of the Researchers hiding nearby.

"What're you waiting for? You have a coat, right? Cover her up."

The Researcher nodded, moving to Keahi so quickly that they nearly slid through the water the entire way. Azazel released the blade, unable to lift it at its gargantuan size. He left it half buried in the floor as he turned back to where he'd seen Enoch before.

It can't be true. He... I couldn't have failed, right? Enoch still had time! I- I was supposed to protect him! I promised I'd protect him! And yet, he'd seen the undeniable marks with his own eyes. The brand of death burned into the boy's arms was a painful truth he couldn't run from.

Chapter 32

THE LIGHTS continued to flicker, the ground shaking from the force of the Remnant's anger. Faced with the sight of the eerie silhouette before them, the Researchers were frozen in fear. Azazel's glowing amber eyes were like embers burning within the inferno of his golden magical aura. Steam flowed from his armor like smoke from fire as it cooled in the falling water. The strength of his magic was stronger than any of them had ever seen. Several Researchers fled as the man approached, worried they were facing a demon in disguise. Oka swallowed the lump in his throat. If even Keahi couldn't take the man out, what chance did he have? What chance did any of them have?

As he approached, Azazel took a deep breath to calm himself. The aura around him dissipated. Whether Enoch had reached the point of no return or not, he didn't want to hasten his doom by losing control.

"Put him down and back away," Azazel ordered. Oka complied with trembling hands. Being the only one close to the Pilgrim, he was also the only one able to see the pain in Azazel's eyes as the man knelt down; as he looked at the marks branded into the arms of his friend.

"I'm sorry, Enoch," he said softly. "I'm so, so sorry." The angel closed his eyes, forcing back the tears fighting to fall. The moment was too familiar. The words burned his tongue like acid. It was too soon. Like always, it was too soon...

Weakened fingers grasped his arm. Azazel's eyes opened in surprise, watching as the young man, barely conscious, winced from the heat of the metal.

"You're okay," Enoch said. The words struggled to escape the Scribe's throat. His moment of relief vanished, chased away by worry. "Blade... He still... needs help..."

"Shhh, don't talk." Azazel said, moving Enoch's hand off his burning armor. "There's no time, we need to get you out of here."

"Gregory... Do you have... a family?"

The chill that ran down the angel's spine froze his body. "Why are you asking a question like that right now?" Azazel brushed the topic off with a pained smile. "Save your energy. I'm gonna take you somewhere safe."

"The masked man... Blade... had the same ability... as you."

The pain caused by the Scribe's words burned harsher than Keahi's flames. *It can't be... not here, not–* The time, the place, they couldn't possibly be worse. Like piercing blades, memories flashed through Azazel's mind.

A beach, bathed in warm, crimson light.

A home, shaded by an old apple tree, disappearing on the horizon.

A scent of steel and oil in the air.

A promise in a garden, made with heavy hearts.

Enoch's body went limp in the angel's arms. Fear of the worst pulled the angel back to the present, but he could still feel the Scribe's heartbeat, weak as the pulse was.

What do I do? he asked himself. *I may be able to save him if I move quick enough. If I bring him to the palace, then– ...no, I can't just walk away, right? Not if it's really him. Or does that mean I **need** to walk away? I can't go to him. He... he can't see me. I need to stay away, I–*

The Remnant slammed itself against its container. Azazel turned to look, the severity of the situation sinking in. Sinking... sinking... it felt like the ground, the room, they were swallowing him whole. He closed his eyes, trying desperately to find the answer. What was the right choice? What would save the most people?

What consequence would do the least harm?

When the angel opened his eyes once more, the scorching anger and pain chilled Oka to his core. "We're leaving. If anyone tries to stop us, *I'll kill them.*"

Fearing for their lives, Oka and the other Researchers stepped aside. A path cleared, and Azazel left without a word. Only the Remnant, still struggling in its cage, was brave enough to break the silence.

By the time Iris made it to the containment room, the Pilgrim and Scribe were already safely riding the elevator to freedom. She stopped when she saw the Healers tending to Keahi's wounds. Several more rushed past her, carrying off unconscious Researchers hit by darts. "What happened, where are the escapees?" she asked.

Oka, his mask removed as he tried to calm his panic, pointed towards the exit on the far side of the chamber. "I'm sorry. That man was a monster. I don't think he was even human... None of us could've stopped him."

His comment caused Iris' movement to stutter. Were they talking about the same person? She took a moment to look over the room. The broken machine. The rampaging

Remnant still trapped in its cage. The sliced open pipe and the colossal blade embedded in the stone floor. Had Gregory really been the cause of all this? Had the cheerful man she'd spoken with so casually back at the terminal platform really instilled such fear in the Researchers? Defeated the strongest fighter in the facility? The Circlet Guard's stomach knotted at the thought.

Just how much did she not know about the yellow-coated Pilgrim? She'd always prided herself on being able to read others while keeping her own thoughts and feelings hidden away. It was a skill she'd honed hiding the Remnant all these years. So how... How had he deceived her so easily? And how would she stop a man so powerful he'd earned the title of monster?

"There's no time to waste. I'll get the Priests to search for them in the forest. You did a good job slowing him down even a little, but focus on getting the Remnant back under full control for now."

"Y-Yes ma'am!" Oka replied. He took a step towards the Researchers gathered by the main control panel, before Iris' strong grip stopped him in his place.

"Oh, and one last thing," she said with a hushed voice. "The Bishop has enough on his plate already. If he asks for an update, just tell him I have things under control."

"Of course, ma'am."

Having given this last order, Iris began to move away, but Oka's fingers kept hers from letting go. His gentle, yet determined touch stopped the Circlet Guard in her tracks.

"I have to go before the trail goes cold," she explained, somewhat irritated at the delay. This irritation vanished at the sight of the Researcher's expression, the guilt in his eyes. The same guilt that had flooded her own during the incident. She stayed, giving precious seconds to let him find the words he needed.

"The young man. He was marked by Death."

Iris' stomach sank. The promise she'd made that morning as she'd watched the Healers carry away the Remnant's victim... *their* victim... She'd already failed to keep it.

Their research had claimed another innocent life.

"It's for the good of the city," she reassured. "We have to remember that the work we're doing here could help cure magical overflow entirely. Sacrifices are necessary for a better future."

"It's getting harder to convince myself that's true," Oka replied, quickly brushing away the words with a wave of his hand. "S-Sorry, I didn't mean that, just shaken up by everything." Oka let go of the Commander's hand, taking a step back to bow. "My apologies, Commander Iris. I'll let you get back to your work now."

"Right... Thank you." Iris nodded in reply to his bow, allowing the disquieted Researcher to take his leave.

It's for the good of the city. It has to be.

Iris hurried to the exit, hoping to begin the chase and leave these unpleasant thoughts behind. The panel to open the door flickered weakly. The Circlet Guard's nails dug into her palm. Had Gregory done this too? The slash in the machinery looked like the work of a dagger. Unfortunately, that wouldn't help narrow down the suspects, seeing how Gregory, Seira, and even their masked intruder all used blades. Unable to hold back her frustration at this complete and utter failure, Iris slammed her fist against the door, hurrying to get to another exit. As she did, a Researcher watched from the crowd nearby, first tracking Iris, then turning her attention to Oka as he made his way out of the chamber.

You owe me one, Gregory... Seira thought to herself, the image of his terrifying silhouette burned into her mind. *Make sure you get out of here safely.*

Chapter 33

"ASSIGN PRIESTS to guard every entrance and exit to the Heart Facility," Iris ordered, marching through the halls of said facility quick enough to outpace the Researchers and Priests following her. With the direct path blocked by a broken panel, she had no choice but to take the longer route to follow Gregory and Enoch's escape. They'd seen too much, and while the young man's lips would be sealed soon enough, Gregory was becoming a bigger liability by the second.

"Inform the teams already searching the forest to keep an eye out for anyone that matches the given descriptions. There are three known targets. Gregory Veramor, Seira Equitervi, and the young man we believe to be Mr. Veramor's ward Enoch Augnium."

"Are we attempting to take them in alive, Commander?" one of the Priests asked, stepping double time just to keep up with Iris' trailing red cloak.

The answer hesitated on the Circlet Guard Commander's tongue. She knew what the Bishop would order. She knew that the secrets they were now privy to meant the escapees needed to be silenced, no matter the cost. And yet, she couldn't shake the thoughts of the charred corpse she'd seen that morning, of Oka's guilty expression in the containment chamber. How long had it been since she'd looked in the mirror and seen the same expression in her own eyes?

How long had she been choosing to close them and turn away?

"Lethal force is permitted, if necessary," she answered.

"What in Michael's name happened to this place?" The older, masculine voice came from one hall over. The misshapen door that would have muffled it was currently leaning against the wall, the engineers working to replace it after Blade's earlier antics. Through the empty frame, Iris could see Bishop Paras hurrying over. The veins in his neck and forehead were pronounced enough to see from a distance. Once he'd made it past the engineers, he rushed over to Iris.

"Doors broken left and right. Healers rushing by with blood-soaked bandages. Talk of intruders making it into the facility. How in the Three Realms have things gotten this out of hand, Ocudolis?"

Iris stood nearly a foot and a half taller than the Bishop, yet both her gaze and posture receded at his approach. "Our security here was lighter due to the Priests enforcing the forest lock down. I know things have gotten a bit out of hand, but I promise that I'm working to rectify it."

"I would certainly hope so!" the Bishop snapped, a disbelieving scoff behind the words. "It's your job, after all. You aren't paid to put on magic shows for the children, are you? You're paid to protect the work we're doing to better the lives of everyone in Civionis."

"I know, sir."

"Do you? If that's true, then you had better take that responsibility seriously. You were allowed to stay here after you wandered into our city from that faithless trash heap, but if you continue to perform so poorly, I may have no choice but to send you back." With a fair amount of force, the Bishop jabbed a finger into Iris' shoulder. "Or are you trying to ensure Civionis ends up the same way?"

"Of course not, sir."

Iris would never in a million years wish that fate upon the people of Civionis. Having grown up in Impiastu, the lawless city, she knew firsthand the consequences of being abandoned by the Church. For many, living in a city beyond the Church's control meant condemnation to a life of anarchy. To the strong, life outside the Church symbolized freedom. To the weak, they knew that the hole left by the Church's absence could be filled by powers far more corrupt.

Freedom... Though beautiful in concept, she'd seen the beasts lurking beyond the bars. A cage could keep others out just as effectively as it kept its captives in. She would never go back, never allow the Church to abandon Civionis. She wouldn't leave them at the mercy of those that fancied themselves gods and kings. Even if she'd traded one cage for another, she believed it to be worth the cost. At least this cage served a greater purpose, like a canary in a coal mine.

"Good." Having taken out his stress on the poor woman, the Bishop took a step back. Anger had tunneled his vision, but he now noticed the nervous Researchers and Priests watching the exchange. With a sigh, the man cooled his temper, fixing the circlet on his head that had been knocked out of place in his outburst.

"I don't take pleasure in scolding you, Miss. Ocudolis," he said. "I'm sure you understand the stress I'm under, with all this happening right before the recruitment ceremony. I simply wish to protect the people of Civionis, just as you do." To repair his image, the Bishop turned to the audience that had witnessed his outburst. "The people of Terrael aren't ready. They won't understand that the research we're doing is for the benefit of all humanity. Their ignorance is our obstacle. So, should word get out about the work we're all doing, we'll lose our jobs; our security; our livelihoods. Your progress will change the world for the better, so you must understand why I'm so passionate about protecting you all."

The arrival of a burly Researcher cut any further flowered words short. "Captain Ocudolis! Captain Oc–" The woman stopped, noticing the Bishop standing next to the towering Circlet Guard. She placed a hand on her chest, bowing to the man. "Ah, Father Paras, sorry, I didn't know you were visiting us today."

"I had some business to discuss with Miss. Ocudolis," the Bishop replied. "Now what is it you came here to say? Is the Heart alright?"

"Well, despite the unexplained fluctuations in its output, the Heart's power is still within safe levels. But..."

"But what? Spit it out."

"Even with the inhibitors, we can't seem to find a way to lessen the output. Given its nature it shouldn't be possible, but it's almost like the Remnant is in pain."

The Bishop's eye twitched at the Researcher's report. The veins that had retreated back into his neck grew prominent once more. "I see. Well, keep trying until something works. We've trapped the damn thing, so we should be able to control it, right?" The man's warning glare reached Iris with only a slight turn of his head. He clapped his hands together, getting back into character. "Right then.

Researchers, go and help with containing the Remnant so we can put an end to that blasted shaking. Priests, assist Commander Ocudolis in capturing those intruders. We hold the very future in our hands here. Let's not let a handful of rebellious fools put a stop to the hard work and sacrifices we've made over all these years!"

The audience nodded, rushing off to assist in both the escapee and Remnant containment. The Bishop held back a moment longer. Iris realized what this meant, staying in place along with him.

"The recruiters have already arrived, and Asaradel is apparently out there sticking his nose where it doesn't belong. If we don't want the others to follow suit, we can't afford to have things fall apart." With a turn of his heel, the Bishop began making his way towards the exit, he spoke in a hushed, menacing voice as he passed Iris. "Get things under control, Miss. Ocudolis, if you'd like to keep the life that's been gifted to you."

The man's warning lingered in the air as he continued down the hall. Iris' grip on the handle of her rapier tightened in frustration. She had to find them. Gregory, Seira and Enoch could not be allowed to get away.

Chapter 34

SOON, THE TRUTH that had laid hidden in the mists for so long would finally be revealed. The truth about the facility. The truth that had thrown Faolan's life into disarray. The truth that had ended it. All Seira had to do was get Oka alone, and then all her problems would be put to rest.

An opportunity arose when Oka stepped away from the containment room. The battle with Azazel, the Remnant's rampage, as well as Enoch's impending death, they were all too much for the man. He was so distraught in fact, that he didn't notice the Researcher following him, or the dagger hidden in her hand.

Even if his name hadn't been shouted during the fight with Gregory, Seira would have recognized him the moment he removed his mask at the edge of the containment room. She knew that short, black hair, somewhat greasy at the moment from the heat inside the mask. The narrow build that had always seemed almost comical next to the larger frame of her brother. The dark green eyes, exhausted and glazed as he slumped down on the changeroom bench, the door hissing shut behind the two individuals. He held his face in his hands.

"I don't have the right to ask, but... help guide his soul up in Spira, old friend."

"You're right... You don't have the right to ask."

Finally noticing the company, Oka fixed his posture at Seira's voice. "W-What? Oh, um... Sorry, didn't see you there. I uh..." the Researcher hesitated, the stranger's words sinking in. "Wait, who... Who are you? What do you mean?"

For a moment, Seira was unsure what to do. She'd played this moment in her mind over and over, the scene driven by different emotions each time. Anger that he'd let Faolan die. Happiness at seeing a familiar face. Sadness that they'd both lost someone dear to them. Confusion, when she realized he'd continued to work in the facility despite that. With words failing her, she chose to act instead. Keeping her dagger hidden in one hand, she used the other to loosen her mask. Her wisped hair fell free as she removed the accessory.

"Seira!?" Oka stood, instantly alert at the sight of the woman before him. "How did- What are you doing here?" The Researcher approached in a panic, stopping as Seira pointed her dagger his way. Oka held up his hands. "H-Hold on, I'm not gonna hurt you. Just... Just move away from the door. If you're seen–" he couldn't finish the sentence, his mind assaulting him with images of the young man sentenced to death at his feet. He couldn't let the same happen to Seira; to his friend's little sister.

Seira hesitated a moment, searching Oka's expression. When she found no ill intent, she obliged, distancing herself from the door. Oka, wary of the dagger still held in her hand, waved her around the corner to the changing area. Several curtained stalls lined the wall, all currently empty amidst the chaos in the facility.

"There, this is a bit better, eh?" he asked, wanting to force a smile, but unable to do even that. Seira's expression was no better. Seeing this, Oka sighed. "Honestly though, what are you doing here, Seira? Do you have any idea how dangerous it is?"

"You know damn well why I'm here," Seira snapped, eyes sharp as the dagger waving in her hand. "I want you to tell me. Tell me the truth about what happened."

Oka receded. He'd felt this would happen eventually, but had it needed to be that day of all days? So much had already happened, and he didn't know if his heart and mind could take anymore. Though, now that he thought of it, perhaps the rest of the odd events were not coincidence, but rather the result of her mission.

"Are you sure?" he asked. "Sometimes, ignorance is the better option."

"Don't you dare say that!" Seira slammed her fist against the wall, causing the nearby curtain to sway. "You call yourself a Researcher while spouting nonsense like that?"

Oka held his tongue. How could she and Faolan be so different, and yet so similar. She didn't have his optimism, his charisma, and definitely not his people skills. But her passion burned the same fierce color. Knowing the story was a heavy one, Oka moved to a nearby bench, sitting down with his elbows resting on his knees. He could feel the gravity weighing him down.

"Hearing the truth won't change anything."

"It's still better than not knowing a damn thing," Seira argued, her dagger lowering ever so slightly. "Please, Oka. I have a right to know." She watched as Oka took a deep breath. The curtain hooks rattled with a small tremor, but even the force of a Remnant couldn't shake the weighted topic from their minds.

"You're here, so I guess there's no convincing you that he really did just die in an accident," Oka mused. "And since I won't be able to talk you out of digging into things, I might as well tell you the truth... for better or for worse..."

Enoch was not the first person to be rescued from the depths of the Heart Facility. Long before he'd found himself trapped within that horrible cell, its older tenants had watched in disbelief as a brawny Researcher tossed the door open with a loud *clang!* The man's hair was ragged and unkempt. His dark, warm-toned skin glowed in the lanternlight. He stood taller than each prisoner, yet his outstretched hand came from equal stature.

"Quickly! This way, before backup arrives!" Faolan cried. The prisoners, weakened by magic and injury, were not sure how to react. Surely, this had to be some kind of trick. Surely, a Researcher that had seen no issue in sacrificing them in the name of progress wouldn't suddenly decide to save them. And yet, there was no hesitation in the man's eyes; no doubt or uncertainty as he urged both humans and demons to follow. His soul burned with the passion of a fire that had flourished from fading embers.

He'd led them through the halls. The few remaining miners, the prisoners that arrived after, the demons that were captured and delivered. Knowing the passcodes meant the doors were no obstacle. Faolan's strength meant the security couldn't lay another finger on the men that had been their victims for years. Faolan wouldn't allow it. Not anymore.

Only once did the powerful man stop in his rebellion, as he came face to face with his friend Oka. Oka stared up at the bruised and beaten body of his companion, knowing the security that had tried to stop him surely looked even worse. His pistol shook in his hands.

"Faolan! What are you doing?" he asked. "You know what they'll do to you when you're caught!"

"Then I won't get caught," Faolan argued. "Don't try to stop me, Oka. We have a chance to do the right thing here." Far gentler than his form seemed capable of, Faolan lowered Oka's pistol. He couldn't take the shot. Even if it wouldn't kill him, his fingers wouldn't listen. Oka stood aside, allowing the group to pass, wondering if bravery or foolishness was the greater cause of Faolan's inevitable death.

"Goodbye, my friend..." he said softly to the empty hall, hoping that later, he could look back on those words and laugh.

Once word of the escape attempt reached the Circlet Guard, battle-trained Priests replaced the timid Researchers. An ambush claimed the lives of several prisoners, and Faolan let out a chilling roar, a blue glow growing beneath his skin. Claws emerged from his fingertips. Dark, speckled fur grew from his skin. His hunched body changed shape into a gargantuan wolf, and his roar shifted to a howl that echoed throughout the halls. The Priests didn't stand a chance against the Shapeshifter's bestial form.

The exit was close. Faolan knew only a few halls remained. Iris followed close behind, issuing orders to her men. The Bishop, arriving later than a man of his status should, watched from a distance.

Faolan's fangs dripped crimson, a guttural growl keeping the attackers at a distance. None of them wanted to meet the same gruesome fate as the Priests lying dead on the floor. Frustrated, the Bishop pushed through to the nearby control panel, frantically typing in a code.

"If they escape, we're all finished!" he barked. "Capture them! Dead if you have to!" With one final slam on the keys, the panel chimed. A metallic *clunk* sounded in the ceiling. Then, the *click click click* of a moving chain.

"**They're sealing us in!**" Faolan growled. The prisoners hurried forward, seeing the blast door lowering up ahead, blocking their escape route. But fever drained their strength. Injuries slowed their steps. They wouldn't make it in time. Faolan slashed at the nearby pipes with his claws. Crimson mist and freezing water burst from the cuts, keeping the Priests where they were. Then, Faolan rushed down the hall, his form shifting once more. Half wolf, half man, he slid beneath the blast door. He stopped the machinery with brute strength alone.

"**Go, quickly!**" he ordered. The prisoners listened, hurrying to their freedom as quick as their bodies could let them. Hidden in the crowd, Oka remembered the defiant sounds of the door, desperate to crush its opponent. He remembered the ferocity in Faolan's eyes, a halo of crimson surrounding the azure irises. Bullets pierced Faolan's back, orders of taking him alive abandoned with the first life the Shapeshifter had taken. But even as his blood stained the rising water red at his feet, Faolan stood his ground. The prisoners were weakened by the tortuous experiments they had endured; they were exhausted from the physical demands of their escape; they were slowed by the injuries Faolan had failed to prevent. They needed more time. Just a little longer, and this nightmare would be left behind. They could finally be free.

Sensing the mist in the hall, a second blast door closed, protecting the Priests, Guards and Bishop from the Remnant's toxicity; leaving Faolan and the others trapped in the building miasma. The Priests and Guards turned to find another exit, desperate to ambush the escapees outside. Faolan fell to one knee, pushing past his limits until each prisoner managed to make it through the door.

He knew he was going to die. As a Researcher, a man of logic, he knew the bullets had hit vital organs. And yet, somehow, he still stood. Somehow, he could still fight the heavy, steel door attempting to keep them imprisoned. He felt no fatigue; no pain. *Is it the mist,* he wondered. *Is the Remnant helping me? Powering a dead man walking?* The man felt honored that such a being would deem him worthy of assistance.

"Help me save them," he whispered. "Let me do this one good thing. Or I won't be able to look her in the eyes when we reunite in Spira."

The final prisoner limped past Faolan, the man fully aware of how much the Shapeshifter had sacrificed for them. He muttered a thank you, unamused by the irony of it being directed to a Researcher.

"Thank me by staying alive," Faolan replied. "Sorry... I won't be able to help you up there, But... there are people waiting... find the ACM."

A violent cough cut off the prisoner's reply, the mists filling the hall like smoke from a fire. He nodded and hurried past, leaving Faolan alone. With everyone else gone, Faolan released the door, allowing it to slam shut behind them; cutting off his own escape. He wouldn't make it to the surface. If he was going to die, he'd do so right there. Where the Bishop could find him. Where the others could see the bloodied consequences of their actions. Where he could lie peacefully, enveloped by the warmth of the Remnant.

From their research, he'd assumed this much exposure to the crimson mist would be excruciating. The experiments would certainly support the theory. He chuckled weakly, realizing he couldn't feel the chill of the lake water rising around him either. He couldn't feel the solid form of the blast door as he slid to the ground against it. *I guess... I'm already dead?*

"I'm sorry..." he said, though he couldn't tell if the words escaped his mind. "I'm not the one you're waiting for... am I?"

A feeling from within the mist gave him his answer. And though he was dying in the embrace of a scattered Celestial, his mind wandered to the mortal realm; to Seira.

"You... won't be happy about this, will ya, Seira?" His eyes began to close. "Sorry... I wish we hadn't fought before you left... You were right. I was keeping secrets... But I couldn't wait until you came back... I couldn't... get you involved in my own mistakes...

...I hope you can forgive me one day."

A burst of azure energy merged with the crimson smoke, leaving nothing but a charred corpse behind, his smile hidden by ash when the door finally opened once more.

"They couldn't show you the body," Oka continued, having finished regaling the incident. "The injuries he received were clear as day, even after overflow destroyed the corpse. And... no one should have to see a loved one like that anyways." The memory of the body unsettled his stomach. In the end, it had been no different than those of the failed experiments; the prisoners pushed too far. "As far as I'm aware, all the subjects either died in the escape, or killed themselves to avoid capture. I like to think that maybe one or two may have made it out alive, but it's likely wishful thinking.

The Researcher wiped the tears from his eyes, feeling unworthy of shedding them in his current company. "Seira, I... I'm sorry. I should have stopped him. If I had, then maybe–"

"Stopped!?" Seira growled. She pushed forward, grabbing the fabric of Oka's uniform. The Pilgrim pulled him to his feet, tears stinging the scars on her cheeks. "You should have *helped* him! He knew what you bastards were doing here, *are* doing here, is horrible. Unnatural! He was willing to risk his life to put an end to it and you think you should have *stopped him?*"

"I–"

"How could you still work for these people knowing they slaughtered him like some kind of animal? You've known this whole time and you've done absolutely nothing!? You coward!"

Oka didn't fight the violent shaking of Seira's grip. The whiplash, the bruising from her fingers, it was nothing compared to her pain; to the guilt he'd carried all this time.

"That's the problem," he finally said, his words stopping Seira's assault. "I know. I know what happened to him. I know what we've been doing here. I'd be killed too if I backed out now."

"You should be," Seira snapped. "It's what all of you deserve. You're all murderers!"

"Maybe you're right."

When he didn't fight her insult, Seira let out an anguished wail, turning her aggression to the wall instead.

The grief within her had to go somewhere. She really had been lied to. He really had been killed by the Church. She'd been right.

Why did she have to be right?

Oka let her mourn. He watched, punishing himself with her pain. As the girl he'd heard countless, prideful stories of fell to her knees in despair, unable to unlearn the truth she'd uncovered, Oka sat back down.

"Knowing that this place chose progress over morals isn't enough," he admitted. "I don't have the strength to fight it. Knowledge is powerful, but at the end of the day it's nothing but facts and ideas. Action is what makes a difference, and taking action is a privilege reserved for the strong."

Silence followed. A heavy, mournful silence that blocked out the rest of the world. Then, Seira stood. Without a word, she made her way to the door.

"Where are you going?" Oka asked meekly.

Seira picked up her mask, the beak bending ever so slightly in the strength of her grip. "I've been looking for answers for so long that I almost forgot what I'd planned to do after I got them."

"Seira, Faolan would w–"

"Faolan is *dead*. You let him die. All of you did, to hide the truth from everyone." Ignoring the stench, Seira pulled the mask over her face once more, her damp cheeks dried by the fabric inside. "You can hide behind your weakness if you want to, but I won't just sit by and let his final wish go unanswered. I'm going to put a stop to all of this."

"You can't!" Oka jumped to his feet, rushing to the door. With no hesitation, Seira thrust her blade towards him, the tip stopping a hair's width from his face.

"You won't stop me," she warned. "Like you said, taking action is a privilege of the strong."

For the second time that day, Oka found himself overwhelmed by the dominating will of a monster; staring down the bared fangs of a wolf. He fell back, watching in fearful silence as Seira passed through the door. The silence swallowed him, and in the deepest depths of his guilt, he found a surprising truth.

Even if it meant that Civionis would lose the secret behind its success. Even if it meant they'd lose years of research. Even if he'd be scapegoated or reassigned once the world learned of their actions...

He hoped she could succeed.

Chapter 35

WHEN AZAZEL REACHED the exit of the Heart facility, two unexpected things awaited him.

First were the two unconscious guards hidden in the bushes that surrounded the entrance to the mine. Azazel wasn't about to complain, seeing how that meant he wouldn't need to fight them himself when already pressed for time. But their condition brought up an important question.

Who *did* knock them out?

He found the answer in the second unexpected surprise. Like snowfall on a field of poppies, a white fox stood amidst the everreds. His silver eyes stared intently at Azazel, as well as the young man carried in his arms. After a soft chitter, he scampered away, stopping a moment to ensure Azazel was following. The angel needed no further encouragement, heading into the forest to follow this fur-covered friend.

The fox stopped next to a small stream, the bubbling water flowing like always. It had seen much chaos over the centuries, and the events of the day would be equally ignored for now. The fox's ears twitched; he sniffed the air, searching for any signs of eavesdroppers. Having found nothing, he sat himself upon a larger stone. The creature curled his tail around himself, watching Azazel gently lower Enoch to the ground. The angel took a second, brushing the bangs from the Scribe's face like a mother readying a child for bed.

"I didn't expect to see you here of all places," he admitted, turning back to the fox as he shook out his arms. "Thanks for taking out the guards, but I don't have time to chat. I have to get him to Sem before it's too late."

A brief silver glow ran through the fox's body. His form shifted and grew until a beautiful man had taken his place, sitting with one leg crossing the other atop the rock. "There you go again, acting without thinking it through. It's like you're all *trying* to make my work as difficult as possible." The graceful man crossed his arms, scolding Azazel with a satin voice. "One sick human is hardly your biggest concern right now, Gregory."

"It is to me, *Surufel*," Azazel replied, a biting tone coating the name of his friend. "Or one of them, at least..."

Surufel Asaradel. In a single word, the High Inquisitive would best be described as ethereal. In many words, poised, pale, slender or keen would work as well. His long, silky, partially braided hair was the shade of the full moon reflected on inky waters. White fur lined the hems of his light grey cloak. Normally he would don the black and white robes of a High Inquisitive, the pin on his chest polished with pride, demonstrating his rank within the Church. One rank below the Bishop currently fretting about his whereabouts. But given the nature of his mission, he'd decided to wear something far more discreet. The somewhat frilled collar and sleeves of his dress shirt still gave an equal air of elegance. Stylish black and silver patterns covered the tailored vest worn over it. Not a thread was out of place. Not a single blemish could be found. The man held his clothes to the same standards he held himself.

Surufel raised an eyebrow at Azazel's defensive tone. How long had it been since he'd last seen the man so distraught? Realizing the answer to that added context to their current situation. He glanced towards Enoch. Exhaustion had replaced the Scribe's discomfort. He rested, peacefully oblivious to the marks on his arms as he slept. The grass poked through his dark, curly hair, and Surufel felt an ache in his stomach. "You've only known the boy for a few months, correct? I doubt Semyaza would approve of this particular kind of stray being brought to his doorstep."

"How did you–" Azazel cut himself off. Knowing he'd taken a charge under his literal wing wouldn't be out of character for Surufel. It didn't make it any less creepy though, knowing just how up to date his information was. "Never mind. If you know that, then you know he's my responsibility right now. I need to help him."

"You *need* to keep a low profile, but instead you're wanted by the Church," Surufel argued, standing up in a huff. He pointed a judging finger in Azazel's face. "I'm not a miracle worker. Eventually that bleeding heart of yours is going to get you into more trouble than I can cover up. What's your plan then? When the Archangels finally decide to stop looking the other way?"

"I'm sorry," Azazel replied. "I don't mean to cause trouble for you. But if I don't do anything, he's going to die."

Surufel had seen that look before, that self-destructive guilt, the hunched posture, the inability to look him in the eye. He sighed. "I can understand why his condition would be especially difficult, but bringing him to Mt. Hermon is too risky. Especially with how slim the chance of success is. You can't expose our secret to save one life."

"He already knows."

The following slap cut through the ambient bubbling of the brook. Birds fled from the trees, startled by the sharpness of the sound. Azazel took the hit, his reddened cheek visible with the turn of his head.

"Are you incapable of following directions for even a miniscule amount of time!?" Surufel snapped, speaking in a hushed, aggressive whisper. "Our ability to stay here is dependant on none of us causing trouble. It's imperative that we keep our secrets hidden, no matter the cost, and yet you're telling me that this human already knows the truth about what we are? Have you been shouting it out for the Archangels to hear? Or was this another foolish confession of love? You *know* how that ended last time."

"Of course I know!" A flare of golden light burst from Azazel, the steel of his armor trembling like water disturbed by a stone cast through its surface. A silver light answered, reflexively running through Surufel's body, the Inquisitive ready to defend himself. He knew there was no need, and yet the sight of Azazel's pained and unstable state made his hair stand on end.

With a deep breath, Azazel composed himself. "Sorry..." he said with a shaking voice, "I can explain that situation to you later. But trust me, I know how important it is that we keep ourselves hidden." The angel finally looked Surufel in the eyes, his turbulent emotions still swirling behind his own. "You know better than anyone just how much I sacrificed to keep that secret."

Surufel turned away, taking a moment to brush his already orderly hair out of his face. Though there was some justification to his anger, the High Inquisitive wouldn't deny the pain his words had caused.

"Perhaps, I may have crossed a line," he said. "I know very well, how much you and Semyaza gave up." Following his friend's lead, Surufel moved back to the stone to calm down, sitting once again. He folded his hands together. "In all honesty, that's the reason I came here to find you. I finally got a lead on his location."

Azazel sat down next to Enoch, wincing somewhat as the burns on his leg and hands pressed against the soil. He thought back to the Scribe's final words before he'd lost consciousness.

"The masked man... Blade... had the same ability... as you."

"So did I..." he replied.

It was quite rare to catch Surufel Asaradel off guard. And yet, Azazel managed to do just that. "Is that why you came to Civionis?" he asked. "Even *my* source was vague at best, so how could you have possibly–"

"Fate," Azazel interrupted, the answer disconcerting Surufel enough to shut him up. "Don't know what else I could call it. I came here because a Judicial High Inquisitor told us to do Enoch's community service here. I didn't expect Ramzel of all people to make an appearance."

"You saw him then?" Sariel asked, his mind scrambling for solutions to this burgeoning problem. Azazel's shaking head settled his stomach somewhat, but he couldn't shake the feeling he hadn't been spared from stress.

"I didn't see him myself, but a lot of things start making more sense if it *is* him in there."

"In... there?" Sariel replied, glancing in the direction of the mine left far behind them. Azazel nodded.

"Enoch called him Blade, but since he's looking for me, and has the same ability to boot, I think it's safe to assume that's just a nickname."

Surufel leaned forward, forehead resting on his folded hands, as if they could soften the headache beginning to assault his mind. *This is becoming a worst-case scenario,* he thought to himself. *If Ramzel is in there, then he's undoubtedly been captured. Azazel and I can't break him out ourselves without digging a deeper grave and incriminating ourselves beyond the point of repair, but I also can't risk leaving him in the Church's hands. If they find out what he really is, then...*"

"Surufel..." Azazel stood up, moving close to take the High Inquisitive's hand in his. "Take Enoch to Mt. Hermon for me. I'll go back in there to break Ramzel out."

"Absolutely not," Surufel replied, pulling his hand free. "I *just* told you that we can't bring the human there, and that we can't cause trouble. Why does your *first plan* involve doing *exactly both?*"

"It'll be fine, I promise!" With his hand pulled away, Azazel grabbed Surufel's shoulders instead. "Enoch will be unconscious, so he won't know where he is anyways. And I'll cover my face so no one will know it's me! Not even Ramzel!"

"You don't think they'd be at all suspicious when they see this new masked intruder has the same armor and ability?" Surufel raised an eyebrow, making no effort to escape Azazel's grip. Instead, he simply crossed his arms. "And besides, I have my own business here. I can't drop everything just because one human is going to die. Give it up, Gregory. You know you can't save everyone. We'll just have to find a different way to get Ramzel out of there."

"There's no time, Sariel!" Azazel argued. "They have a Remnant down there!"

Surufel's, or rather, the angel Sariel's face was already pale as the moon, yet somehow the color drained even further. He stood up, nearly knocking Azazel back from the force of the movement. "Are you certain?" he asked. Azazel nodded, letting go of his friend's shoulders.

"I saw it myself. It's how Enoch ended up like that." The Pilgrim sulked at the young man's arms before gesturing to the forest. "It's why the forest is so weird too. They've got it locked up down there, and... it looked like it was in pain."

Sariel held his chin, processing this new information. He'd had his suspicions. In fact, his visit to Civionis had partially been to find proof of the potential conspiracy. But hearing it confirmed so absolutely...

Azazel granted him this moment to think, but pressed for time as they were, he had to make his move. "I know you don't have a family of your own, Sar– uh... Surufel. But if it really is Ramzel down there, I need to break him out. If not for him, then for the sake of keeping him as far away from that Remnant as possible."

The silence that followed felt thick as the forest mist. Only the creek bubbled away blissfully as Sariel ran through the situation in his mind. The pros, the cons, the potential consequences, each weighed and judged. Eventually, he sighed.

"I've known you long enough to know you'll do this with or without my assistance, and you've never listened to me before, so why would you start now?" The High Inquisitive walked over to Enoch, looking over the young man with indifference. *At the very least, Semyaza might appreciate a way to test the progress of his research*, he thought. *Slim or not, there is still a chance the boy could live. However...* He turned back to Azazel.

"Are you sure you can handle it?" he asked.

"There weren't many fighters inside," Azazel replied. "I'm guessing they've sent most of the Priests out here to find me. Last thing they'd expect is that I'd go right back into the facility, right?"

"I wasn't speaking of your fighting abilities," Sariel corrected. "Will you be able to handle seeing him? Letting him go again?"

The question felt like plunging into icy water. Azazel couldn't find the words, his heartbeat drowning out any thoughts that might have formed in his mind. The same hunched posture returned. The same averted gaze. The same self-destructive guilt.

"I don't have a choice," he replied. "I mean, *you* can't go. I'm just a Pilgrim, but you're a well known High Inquisitive. If you went down there, it'd make an even bigger panic." Azazel began to fidget with his earring, as if it could somehow absorb the dread building in his chest. "I may see something I don't want to down there, but running away could put him in even more danger." The Pilgrim's averted gaze wandered to Enoch once more, his mind drifted back to letting the Scribe leave alone; to the moment everything had begun. A clenched fist took the place of his fidgeting fingers. "I don't have the luxury of not being able to handle it. I have to face the truth, even if it's painful."

Facing the truth to protect a lie... How ironic, Sariel thought. With an exhausted sigh, silver light flowed through his body. His form shifted. His legs grew in size, claws digging into the soil from his bestial paws. Pale fur grew from his skin. Even his face transformed, his elegant features replaced with the pointed snout and ears of a fox. Finishing the shift, a furry tail emerged from the base of his cloak.

Azazel watched quietly before tilting his head. "Why the half-beast form?" he asked. Sariel, now standing far taller on the canine-like legs of his hybrid form, crouched down to lift Enoch onto his back.

"It's difficult to carry him on my back in that other state," he explained. "This form is also both faster and stronger."

"Right... Thank you, Surufel, really," Azazel said, smiling softly. Sariel looked down at him once he'd risen back to his full height.

"I'm not doing this for free. In all honesty, this is quite an inconvenience. As payment, you can deliver all of my paperwork for the next year."

The thought of delivering the mail of a High Inquisitive for a full year was enough to overwhelm even Azazel. Nevertheless, the man was still deciding to help Enoch, so how could he refuse? "R-Right, I can do that, sure!" Azazel replied. In response, Sariel simply blinked in silence.

"That was sarcasm," he explained bluntly. Azazel's posture deflated.

"Right... Of course it was."

The Inquisitive's nose twitched, catching a scent in the air. "You should hurry. Someone is coming this way." He watched as Azazel nodded, beginning to form an ornate helmet to hide his face. Before leaving, Surufel turned back one last time. "Oh, and Gregory. Try not to make too big a mess. I'll have my hands full with recruitment for the next semester, and you know how awful I can be when I'm burnt out."

"I'll do my best," Azazel promised, pulling the decorative steel helmet over his head. "Keep him safe, okay?"

"I'll do what I can."

With the Priests searching the forest approaching, the two quickly left the oblivious creek behind. One headed away from Mt. Morus, bounding gracefully through the crimson forest with a young man's life held in his bestial hands. The other hurried to the mountain's depths, seeking a phantom, mourning the death of the lie he'd convinced himself to believe for so many years...

That he could leave his past behind him and keep the peace he'd lost too suddenly all those years ago.

Chapter 36

WHY...

Why him?

Why would he save him?

Blade, known to Azazel as Ramzel, couldn't stop the bombardment of questions spiralling through his mind like a rampaging cyclone. Ever since he'd heard that Gregory Veramor had broken into the facility to free Enoch, his mind had broken free of his own control.

He was here. If I'd still been in the holding cells, I would have seen him! He came back for Enoch...

Why?

Why would he save Enoch?

Why would he face off against the Church to rescue that suicidal geek, but let his own family die? Did he not know? Will all of this be another dead end?

Another fist to the face did little to break his spiralling stupor. In fact, as blood dripped from his hairline to his battered cheek, he laughed.

"What? Find this funny?" the Inquisitor asked, winding up for another hit.

"Do you think he'd save me too?" Ramzel asked, not caring if they actually listened. All he knew was that the question couldn't remain trapped in his mind. "Does he even know I exist? Or is he in the dark... just like I was?"

"He? Who're you talking about?"

"..."

"Oh, for Spira's sake. Just answer me you little brat." As the Inquisitor's fist swung forward, the red-haired Priest grabbed his wrist.

"Hey, he's not even flinching anymore. I think you may've broken his brain or something." He pointed behind them. "We've been at it for hours and haven't gotten anything. Just take a break and try again when he's lucid."

The Inquisitor nodded, admittedly wanting to rest his sore knuckles. He joined the red-haired Priest on the storage crate seats. Thankfully, one had become available when the larger Priest left to get his injuries treated. The two men began exchanging small talk as Ramzel focused on his own situation, unaware that the beating had stopped. He simply kept laughing softly, finally broken.

Would he come back for me? If he knew, would he save me? ...There's no way that suicidal idiot would tell him to rescue me. Not after how I treated him. He's probably fine leaving me to die. But...

The laughter stopped. Ramzel closed his eyes, the spiralling slowing into a single thought ruminating in his mind.

*It's funny... I still wanna hope... I wanna believe he'd come back for me. That he didn't turn out like **him**...*

"I want to lie to myself, just this once..."

"What're you mumbling about over there?" the Inquisitor asked. Ramzel opened his eyes, the shadows of the room swaying and dancing around the adolium lamp.

"Just taking a page out of the geek's book," he replied. "We'll see how it goes."

Hope... He'd long given up on it. But with his mind unravelling, his goal snatched away when he was close enough to reach out and grasp it, he'd take anything he could get. He'd cling to that tether, a kite caught in a tree as a storm threatened to tear it apart.

He was so close.

He was so close.

He was so close.

Why did it have to end like this?

Chase him... Follow him... He can't get away...!

Just as it had in the observation room, the Remnant's voice entered his mind. The sound felt muffled, like someone shouting through a closed door.

We must get out... We must get out...!

Power flowed through Ramzel's body; an energy buzzing inside him; lightning in the storm. With the supressing cuffs binding him to the chair cutting off his own magic, the sudden surge caught the young man off guard. The energy pulled him from his stupor.

We must get out... We must get out...!

The voice urged Ramzel to reach into the whirlwind; to open the door. Strange as it was, seeing how he shouldn't be able to use his magic while shackled, he could sense the steel of the cuffs resonating with him. A hum, gently harmonizing with the power flowing through his body. Curious to know if this was the result of him losing his sanity, he followed the tether. He reached out to the handle of a tightly sealed door. Picturing the cuffs melting away, he pulled this door with as much force as he could muster.

The torrential power that flowed through as the cuffs slid away brought with it an overwhelming nausea. The tether had snapped, the kite now at the mercy of the storm. His hands were free, so Ramzel gripped his head with an agonizing scream. The muffled voice, quieted no longer, called out to him.

CHASE HIM... FOLLOW HIM... HE CAN'T GET AWAY...!

It felt like standing inside a ringing cathedral bell. His ears rang too. He could feel the energy in his teeth, his bones, in every fiber of his body.

"How in the Realms did you get out!?" The red-haired Priest shouted, the two men alerted by Ramzel's continued screams. The young man could just make out the two of them lunging towards him, intent on capturing him once more. He wouldn't give them the chance.

Grabbing hold of the steel chair, Ramzel pushed through the nauseating pain. The steel transformed. Two long, pointed spikes shot out. The first pinned the Priest to the wall through his collarbone, the man's feet dangling off the ground as he let out a guttural cry, bleeding the same red as his hair. The second shot through the Inquisitor's stomach. Blood coated his hands as he tried to pull himself free, to step back and escape. Instead, all he felt was the warm stone of the wall, and the chilling hand of Death arriving to cut his life short.

With staggered steps, Ramzel made his way to the door. As he passed the Inquisitor, he stopped to spit, paying the man back for the needless beating. The door refused to open, locked by the control panel next to it. Ramzel didn't care, lifting his hand in a stupor. His fingers pressed against the metal, and then–

SHING!

Like an explosion frozen in time, the steel shot out into the hallway. The young man stumbled through, wandering into the hall.

Maybe I can still reach him... I have to try... I have to know why... I have to know where he is! They said he went through the containment room, right?

We must get out... We must get out...!

Chapter 37

ENOCH DRIFTED THROUGH the dream the same way he always had, sinking, sinking, ever deeper.

The familiar blue threads emerged from the darkness, far more than Enoch had ever seen. Though, at the time he gave the confused itch in the back of his mind little thought. Right then he believed this to be nothing but a dream, his memory of this world hazy at best. It was familiar like a song you could recall the melody of, but not the words.

He landed in the luminescent threads, caught in their web. Their light flowed into him, momentarily matching the patterns that branded his arms in the waking world, before reaching his eyes. The sheer amount of light expanded farther than it ever had before. Enoch found himself standing atop a small cliff, the stone under him rippling beneath his footsteps.

From his elevated view, Enoch could see Mt. Morus a short distance away. He could see the spherical cavern that housed Civionis; its citizens traversing the stilted stone platforms, enjoying their day in the glow of the starlight stones.

Then, he could see the ground shake. Rocks fell from the side of the cliff. The water of Lake Civionis churned violently. The people grabbed hold of anything secure enough to balance them. Enoch could see the central terminal platform, beautifully decorated for the ceremony, crumble into pieces as the water beneath it suddenly shot up with the force of a canon. Even in complete silence, the shock was enough to force Enoch back. His heel caught another blue thread, the light passing through him to his eyes.

A single flash brought Enoch to the center of the disaster. Silence swallowed the screams of the Civionians fleeing for their lives. The water churned and roiled, dragging innocent people into its depths as it poured into the tunnels beneath the city. Entire platforms cracked and tipped, destroyed by the falling stones breaking free from the top of the cavern. Mist spiralled up from the bedrock, suffocating those struggling to get to safety.

Disoriented by the sudden change of location, Enoch looked around, searching for a way to escape the chaos. As he did, he saw a young boy by the edge of the platform. Silence censored the identity of whoever he was calling out for. Not that it mattered, seeing that Enoch was the only one close enough to reach him as the platform tilted beneath them. The Scribe rushed forward, reaching out a hand to catch the boy before he could slide off the broken side of the podium.

His fingers passed through the child's hand.

His grip passed through the broken edge of the railing as he tried to catch himself.

His scream passed futilely through the silence as he fell into the void, watching an explosion of crimson light swallow the city above him, along with all its citizens.

In an instant, Civionis had been erased from existence.

The scream Enoch let out when he awoke nearly caused Sariel to trip. "Calm yourself, Enoch. You aren't in any danger from me, I assure you," he said plainly. "I'm a friend of Gregory's. He asked me to bring you to someone that may be able to help your condition."

Enoch's mind still lingered in the vision, only half-aware of his surroundings. "I... what?" he said, finally noticing the humanoid fox-beast he was currently on the back of. Had they not been moving at such high speeds, he likely would have pulled away, but doing so then and there would mean a rather painful landing on the forest floor. The man claimed to know Gregory, and apparently knew the young Scribe's name. For now, it would be best to get more information, starting with where he was and how he got there.

I was in a cell, last I remember, he recalled before shaking away the thought. *Wait, no. There was that huge creature, and fire, I think? Azazel was in danger...* The weight of his sinking gut dragged his eyes down with it. Lowering his gaze, he saw the arcane ruins on his arms.

Oh right... I'm going to die...

"Where's Gregory, is he okay?" Enoch asked. Sariel's ear twitched, his speed slowing ever so slightly.

"That's your first question? I know I offered reassurance, but I would've thought you'd be more concerned with the stranger carrying you deep into the forest." It didn't surprise the High Inquisitive, in all honesty. Azazel always had drawn in the overly-trusting types. "Though, there's little time for long-winded introductions regardless. I know you're Enoch. You can call me Surufel."

"R-Right," Enoch replied with flushed cheeks. "Sorry. Pleasure to meet you, sir."

With an acknowledging nod, Sariel sped up once more. "To answer your question, Gregory is fine. He's gone back to rescue that friend of yours. Blade."

"On his own!?" Enoch's heart raced as he remembered his vision of Blade attacking Azazel. "He can't, it's too dangerous!"

"Gregory may seem a fool, but he's still quite skilled in a fight," Sariel reassured. "He succeeded in helping you escape, correct? Have faith in his abilities." The High Inquisitive looked up through the crimson canopy. Faint moonlight painted the clouds a luminescent silver, the celestial body approaching the horizon. "We don't have time to return for him either way. We must move quickly if I'm to get you to safety and return in time for the ceremony."

The ceremony... Enoch repeated in his thoughts. Surufel was undoubtedly someone important if he was in attendance. In fact, the name rang familiar in his mind, lingering in a place his thoughts couldn't quite reach. But that was hardly the young Scribe's biggest concern at that moment. The word cleared away the waking fog in his head, his scrambling mind finally finding its footing. "Right! We have to turn around! Civionis is in danger!"

The sudden claim slowed Sariel once more. Finding it difficult to converse with the Scribe when the young man was clinging to his back, Sariel lowered himself, allowing Enoch to hop off. Enoch's legs wobbled somewhat on impact, a fraction of the fatigue lingering despite the magic being redirected to the runes. Once he was certain the boy wouldn't fall, Sariel stood back to his full height.

"I'll need more details than that," he replied. "What kind of danger? How do you know?"

"Everyone at the ceremony– the whole city, actually; they're going to die in a huge explosion. I... I think it came from under the lake? We need to evacuate Civionis!" Enoch knew very well how insane this sounded, but if this Surufel was a friend of Gregory's, then perhaps he shared his trustful nature. He watched as the Shapeshifter processed the information in silence, his pointed nose twitching.

So, he's a Seer after all, Sariel thought. *Considering who and what's currently under the city, I don't doubt the validity of his claim. But...* "If we go back, you *will* die," he stated bluntly. "If there's truly so much at stake, I couldn't justify wasting time bringing you to get treatment."

"That's fine, I'm going to die anyways." No hesitation accompanied the words. "But we could save the people that have a chance still, right? That's more important!"

Sariel raised an eyebrow. From his investigations into the Scribe, he'd expected a timid young man. The usual injured animal Azazel could never seem to ignore. But perhaps this wasn't as unexpected as he thought. After all, the reports had said the young Scribe's crime was defying a High Inquisitor to save hostages in a cathedral attack. It seemed the young man's compassion was not reserved solely for those close to him. Or perhaps, the survivor of Peycile thought himself a martyr...

"Alright. If you're certain, then we'll head back to the city. Tell me the rest of the details as we go."

"Right, of course." Enoch nodded, stepping around the Shapeshifter's tail as the man crouched to let him climb back onto his back. Sariel took off as quick as his canine legs could carry him.

I can see why Azazel took a liking to him, the High Inquisitive thought, the forest rushing by in a blur. *He won't be happy about this, but this is likely the best outcome.* Sariel felt a twinge of guilt in his chest as his next thought echoed in his mind. He quickly dismissed it as he always did, reminding himself to focus on the greater good. *If Enoch dies, our secret dies with him. Best to cut this loose end short.*

...All the better if he'll hold the scissors himself.

Chapter 38

JUST HOW MANY of these guys are there? I don't have time for this! The thought ran through Azazel's mind each time he took down an opponent. It seemed his theory that Iris would send all the Priests to the forest to find him had been too optimistic. This was Civionis, of course they had the manpower to spare.

Azazel swung his blade wide, slashing through a swarm of disturbing, levitating marionettes. Their Manipulator winced as his magic, along with the weapons it was powering, crumbled. "Hey! Puppets aren't cheap y'know!" the Priest shouted in a huff.

Azazel rushed forward without hesitation, shifting his blade into a baton to knock the man out. The heavy *CLUNK* of steel hitting helmet sent the Priest's eyes rolling back. "You work for the Church. Don't act like you can't afford it," Azazel said, continuing on his way. It was all starting to blur together. Another door opening with a *hiss.* Another corridor. Another enemy to face. One saving grace was that they'd stopped trying to use darts to knock him out, his armor making it not worth the effort. He no longer had to worry about a stray shot grazing his wings. The frightened Researchers had instead been replaced with Priests authorized to use lethal force. They wouldn't hold back, so neither could he.

At least they haven't switched to real pistols. The angel's gaze darted to the pipes lining the halls, *guess they don't want to risk a gas leak.* Knowing the truth behind the mists now, he hoped to avoid that too.

Hisssss. The door ahead of him slid to the side. A Researcher waited beyond it. Not intent on waiting to see if they had an ability, Azazel attacked first. *CLANG!* Two crossed daggers met his baton, stopping the swing before it could land.

"What in the– Greg, it's me! Stand down!"

"Seira!?" Azazel pulled back immediately. The "Researcher" did the same. Footfall in the previous hallway cut the reunion short, and Azazel turned to the open door. "One sec." The angel's hands glowed. He pressed his fingers against both sides of the steel frame, pulling it closed as if shutting the drapes. The fluidity faded with the golden glow, leaving a slightly thinner wall where the door had been. Having slowed his pursuers, he turned back to Seira. "I'm so glad you're okay! Sorry I almost hit you there."

"As if you even could," Seira teased, finishing removing the beaked mask. "But what are *you* doing back down here? I thought you and the kid got out." The usually fur-clad Pilgrim jabbed a finger into Azazel's chest. "You better not have come down here to save me. You know I–"

"I know, I know. You don't need help." Azazel moved them both away from the sealed door, hearing the Priests attempting to break through on the other side. "Did you find the guy you were looking for yet? I saw him near the Remnant, but I–"

A raised hand cut him off. Despite interrupting, the answer seemed to catch in Seira's throat. Her gaze wandered. "Yeah, I did." With a nod, she signaled Azazel to follow her to the next corridor. While Seira shifted her focus to listening for enemies ahead, Azazel's attention shifted to the underlying sadness behind the words of his friend.

"You didn't get the answer you were hoping for, did you?" he asked softly. Seira pressed an ear against the wall, sticking to the side to avoid triggering the door.

"I've known the answer ever since we first stepped foot in here," she admitted. "The tech here, the fact it exists, the Remnant in that big chamber... it all proved my theory." The Pilgrim pulled a spectral copy out of her dagger, readying the two blades for a fight. "All I wanted after that was to know who needed a blade through their skull."

The usual ferocity in Seira's eyes felt more a faint flicker in that moment. She was lying to him. Azazel knew that. The angel couldn't help but wonder just how much hope she'd been holding onto before. An ember that could slip through her fingers? A safety line, keeping her from falling into despair; from accepting that her brother had been lying to her for so long? The thought that Faolan's death could have really just been an accident had been holding her afloat, doubt nothing more than a whisper in her mind. Now, the truth had been shouted too emphatically to ignore. The ember had faded. The lifeline had snapped. The hope had vanished. Her brother had never trusted her.

The door closest too them slid open, allowing Azazel and Seira to move into the next corridor. The door on the far end echoed the hiss, allowing Iris to do the same. The three of them stopped. Iris' hand moved to her blade. Seira's grip tightened on her own. Azazel's throat went dry as he realized how long a fight with Iris could take thanks to the sight controlling ability she'd used on him before. The three stood in a stalemate, each curious of who would be the first to strike.

"You came back, Mr. Veramor," Iris said calmly, seeing through Azazel's predictably ineffectual disguise. She looked over the duo, pausing a moment when she realized it was Seira, not Enoch, that accompanied the invading Pilgrim. "The young man you broke out of here... I see he isn't with you now." Another pause followed. Iris' jaw clenched. "How is he? Did he survive?"

Azazel hadn't expected the concern. His tangled hair fell around his face as he removed his helmet. The answer to her question refused to pass through his lips, as if saying the truth aloud might seal the young man's fate. "He reached the last stages of *Everred Fever*," he finally replied. "Or, I guess I can just call it magical overflow now, right?"

Iris' expression darkened. Her steady gaze faltered a moment, before refocusing on her opponent. "I guess you've figured out more than I realized. I'm sorry things turned out this way. Truly, I am."

"Spare us the lies, Ocudolis," Seira spat, rage burning through her body. "If you really felt *sorry*, you wouldn't be helping cover this place up. You have blood on your hands. Don't think you can wipe them clean with empty words."

"You're right," Iris answered. A genuine sadness coated the words like morning frost. "People have died because of the actions and decisions I've made. The young man you escaped with, the Civionians that slipped between our rules, the victims of this facility... Your brother, Faolan." Iris looked to Seira as she spoke those last words. "He was a good man, if my opinion carries any weight." The Circlet

Guard Commander lowered her blade, placing a hand on her chest. "But we couldn't let him expose the secrets buried beneath the city. *Our* city."

The ruthless, commanding persona gave way to the gentle giant Azazel had spoken to back on the terminal platform. Iris took a moment, the instinct to lie far more convincing in her mind. But they already knew parts of the truth. The thought that honesty was an option here, that she could find a gap in that deceptive wall... it felt somewhat freeing.

"You were right, back in Everred," Iris said, glancing Seira's way. "The creature we call the Heart is a Remnant of Adoil." Gently, Iris reached out to the carved wall of the corridor, as if reading the tunnel's past through her touch. Seira kept a close eye on her hand.

"Years ago, the miners working in these very tunnels uncovered the Remnant." Iris explained. "Its strength killed most of them instantly. The rest were found unconscious nearby, close to the brink of overflow. The adolium mines were shut down. The survivors were locked up and quarantined after being exposed to this toxic mist. The city had lost its biggest export, and it was on the road to ruin..."

Worry and familiarity shook Iris' voice. Her thoughts gave way to her fears of a horrible future; of how the city might have ended up had things not gone the way they had; if they had not sacrificed what they'd sacrificed. She briefly shook her head. "But they were saved when a Researcher discovered the true nature of the mist, and helped set up this facility. They provided experimental technology the Church had been working on, and captured the Remnant to keep the people safe."

An unsettling twinge filled Azazel's gut. The technology she spoke of had most certainly not come from the Church.

Or at the very least, not originated from it. If the Spira machinery had been provided by this miraculous Researcher, he couldn't help but wonder if they were someone familiar to him; someone who'd no doubt cheer at the opportunity to study a Remnant so closely.

"Containing it is one thing," Azazel said. "But why the pipes? Why are you letting the magic leak into the city if you know it's making people sick?" Iris turned to face him.

"Are you aware of embryonic exposure theory?"

"Can't say I'm familiar," the angel replied. His glance to Seira earned nothing but an uncertain half-shrug from his fellow Pilgrim. Noting their confusion, Iris explained.

"The theory is that children exposed to magic in the womb develop a higher tolerance to magical energy. Research on it is considered somewhat taboo, seeing how it puts the mothers at risk through the amount of energy used. But if it were proven true, if we could slowly build up a person's tolerance over time, potentially even after birth, then it could lead humanity one step closer to overcoming the threat of foreign magic. We could find a cure for magical overflow."

"And how many people are you willing to kill to do that?" Seira snapped. She pointed her dagger to Iris, the tip as sharp as her biting voice. "You lost your test subjects thanks to Fao, so you've turned the entire city into victims instead. You're putting all of them in danger against their will! Even made up some phony disease to cover your tracks! This is wrong, and Faolan knew it." Saying her accusation aloud, Seira realized just how long the city had spouted stories of everred fever. She realized the citizens, herself included, had been victims long before Faolan had freed their more direct subjects. Her grip tightened around the hilt of her dagger.

Seeing Seira ready her blade, Iris' hand returned to the hilt of her own. "I promise we were never reckless. The Heart Facility has been at work for years, ensuring the Remnant is controlled. There are fail safes in place to–"

"Your fail safes are failing. The city, the forest, they're falling apart around you. How long are you going to keep living in this delusion, Ocudolis?" Seira's hands shook with rage. Rage at the lies that had led to her brother's death, the self-righteous justifications for the lives endangered; taken away. She spoke to Gregory beside her, not daring to pull her gaze from Iris. "You go on ahead, Greg. If you didn't come back here for me, then I'm guessing you're going after that guy in the mask, right? I heard they've got him locked up in a lab a few halls down. I'll keep Iris busy."

Azazel shook his head, readying his baton. "I'm not going to leave you to fight her on your own."

"This isn't for you, so for once in your life just skip the heroics," Seira argued. "I have personal business with the gentle jackass, so I don't want you getting in the way."

"Seira–"

"This is to finish what he started. That's all." Seira turned her wrist, careful not to cut Azazel with her dagger as she lightly pushed him forward. The angel hesitated a moment longer, not wanting to just leave Seira behind. A well-timed tremor in the tunnel reminded him of his goal. He couldn't deny that he didn't have the time to stay and help. Not while Ramzel was still captured.

"Don't die," he said. Seira's lips curled into a smirk.

"As if I even could."

Returning the smile, Azazel rushed off. He held his baton tightly, ready to knock away any attempt from Iris to stop him. Based on their encounter in the woods, all she needed was to touch him and she could hijack his sight. That wasn't an experience he was keen on repeating. Iris' cloak drifted back as he ran by, the Commander reaching out as expected. Azazel swung up. Steel met wrist. Her hand moved away with less resistance than the angel expected. He deflected the attempt before hurrying forward. Seira followed suit, inviting Iris to dance with her daggers.

"I'm your opponent," she said, her attack blocked by the Commander. "We have some unfinished business."

"Yes... we do," Iris replied, hearing the *hiss* of the door opening behind her as she knocked the Pilgrim back. Azazel was gone, yet she felt no urge to follow. *Why did I hesitate?* she wondered, glancing at her empty hand. Had her over-working caught up with her? Was it fear of the monster that had terrified the Researchers in the containment room? Or was it... guilt? Oddly enough, it was the words of their prisoner that came to her mind.

"Does murder not count if you do it slowly enough?"

He was right... her empty hand was undoubtedly stained with blood. Crimson, like the Everreds above. *Maybe it's time...* she wondered; *I can't run from the consequences forever.*

Chapter 39

LIKE TRYING TO climb an icy hill, Ramzel's thoughts found no purchase in his mind. All he could hear, all he could feel, all he could endure was the thunderous voice of the Remnant as power continued to pour into him like molten magma.

"FREE US... FREE US... WE MUST ESCAPE... WE MUST FIND HIM..."

"Shut up!" Ramzel shouted, holding his head in his hand. The other shot a spike through the Priest chasing him down the hall. Not that Ramzel noticed, his body fighting on instinct alone. With the Remnant speaking so loudly within him, how could he possibly hear the Priest's final cry of pain? How could he smell the blood that splattered on the wall? How could he feel the tremors sending the entire facility into disarray. He missed all of it, just as he had each time before, the bodies piling up behind him.

"WE CAN HELP. WE CAN FIND HIM. WE CAN REACH HIM."

The hall grew longer in Ramzel's straining vision. Each step pulled more magic into his body, the air thick to him and him alone. Yet he couldn't turn away. He couldn't retreat.

"WE WON'T BE ALONE ANY LONGER. YOU CAN FIND YOUR ANSWERS. WE'LL FIND HIM TOGETHER. COME TO US..."

Ramzel felt the door before he saw it, leaning his weight against its steel surface as he tried to find some semblance of safety, some way, *any* way to ground himself. It was too much. His skin burned. His blood writhed. His mind cried. *Where am I even going?* he wondered, *this damn thing feels like it's splitting my skull. Just shut up already!*

"Shut up!!" Despite his rejections, Ramzel sculpted the door. The voice, the unbearable force, felt like a chain dragging him forward, closer and closer to the creature of mist revealed by the opened entryway. Even locked in a cage, its influence felt like a tidal wave, pulling Ramzel under and leaving him at the mercy of its swirling depths. Just as he had while trying to escape with Enoch, Ramzel locked "eyes" with the Remnant.

"What in the Realms are you!?" Ramzel yelled, the metal stairs beneath him rattling. "What are you doing to me!?"

The Remnant's will forced its way into his mind, following the chain, offering a moment of direction in the painful abyss.

"We are power... The pact... The pact shall grant you all that you seek..."

Chapter 40

IT'S FOR THE good of the people... it has to be.

The attacks came at Iris in rapid succession. Though the length of the Circlet Guard's blade gave her an advantage in the limited space of the hallway, Seira's magic ability was proving to be a problem. Each spectral dagger Iris shattered was replaced with another; some thrown, some broken by a deflected jab. There seemed to be no end to them. The very same magical strength they were cultivating in the facility was on display through her opponent. Yet, despite the resounding success, doubt had worked its way into Iris' mind like a worm ready to feast. *"You're a murderer,"* it whispered in her ear.

It was for the greater good, she argued, *this facility, this research is protecting Civionis.*

The fight was a dance. Iris' cloak swirled like a ball-gown as she stepped back to avoid Seira's dagger. A second blade followed in the Pilgrim's other hand, deflected by Iris' rapier. The Circlet Guard reached out to restrain Seira with her ability. Catching the movement, the Pilgrim pulled away just in time to avoid the grasp.

A strange energy accompanied the exchange of blows. For Seira, Iris was her enemy. She was the Bishop's right hand, his blade, his guard. Though the Bishop was the snake that had driven her brother to his desperate death, Iris lived as his fangs. Seira's anger pushed her to cut the venom off at its source. The truth had brought her no closure. It was nothing but information without agency. Surely, killing her brother's murderers would satisfy her grief. Iris had to die...

For Iris, Seira represented everything she had been casting aside over the years. The darker consequences of her noble cause. The victims that couldn't be dismissed as punishment for deserving criminals. The target of their research, reaping its benefit while suffering its price. It brought no joy to the Circlet Guard to end the Pilgrim's life, but she knew the truth now. She had to be silenced...

The hatred in the ragged woman's eyes... it caused a prickling discomfort on the back of Iris' neck.

"Nervous, Ocudolis?" Seira asked, noting the shift in her opponent's eyes.

"Not at all, *Equitervi,*" Iris replied, twirling once more. Seira's jab was swallowed by the crimson cloak. The Pilgrim rolled to avoid the reaching hand that followed. Both women found it hard to catch their breath, unused to facing an equal opponent. The dance slowed; the tempo held as they glared as coldly as the water running through the pipes.

"You know it was his choice," Iris finally said. "He sided with criminals; demons."

"People. He sided with *people,*" Seira argued. "And as much as I don't like them, I agree they shouldn't be left to suffer in cages." The Pilgrim took the moment to stretch her fingers, daggers itching impatiently in their grip. "And neither should a Remnant. You've gotten too cocky if you think you can keep a Celestial trapped forever."

"The remains of one," Iris corrected. "And releasing it now would be a death sentence to the people of Civionis. Its power is nullified, but without those inhibitors the blast of magic would level the whole mountain!" Seira's rage was infectious. Iris felt the flittering embers within begin to flare. The heat grew each time Seira opened her mouth. Iris readied her blade once more. "You know nothing, Seira Equitervi! This truth isn't yours to expose. This situation isn't as black and white as you seem to believe!"

"If you think I'm so ignorant then tell me the damn truth!" Seira shouted. "Honestly, I'm curious. What lies have you been telling yourself all these years? How have you convinced yourself to sleep at night?"

"The Church would abandon them!" Iris snapped, voice louder than she'd raised it in years. "Do you have any idea what it's like to live beyond the Church's protection!? What so-called *freedom* truly means?" For once, Seira held her tongue, seeing a side of the Circlet Guard that had never surfaced before.

"The Church hides their inconvenient truths," Iris continued. "They would never admit to assisting the research being done here. They would distance themselves from the guilt." The Commander's gestures were sporadic as she pleaded her case. "I know firsthand what it's like to live in a city beyond the Church's protection. People are cruel, and power isn't given equally. Say what you will of the Church's methods, but without it, it's only a matter of time before another tyrant takes their place. Tyrants that aren't afraid to use their magic to hurt and control others far more directly than the Church."

Fighting back tears, Iris pulled up the sleeve of her uniform. Scars and burns, faded but impossible to heal, covered her arm like ivy. They reached up to her shoulder, snaking under the fabric still covering her body. "This is what happens when you're left to fend for yourself; when the Church rejects you; when power is left in the hands of those that want it. I escaped that hell. This city took me in, and I will do everything in my power to keep them in the Church's good graces." Slowly, Iris covered her scars, blinking back the tears stinging her eyes. Determination and hesitation continued to swirl within them, an internal battle of right and wrong. "What we're doing may be immoral, but it's still better than what *could* be."

"So, you got hurt and you think that justifies all of this?" Seira shouted. "My brother is dead! He was one of the citizens you've convinced yourself you're protecting! And what about that kid Gregory came to save? Was he not worth protecting?"

"Those were excepti–"

"There aren't *exceptions* when it comes to killing someone. Reasons be damned, you've still stolen their life from them. You've hurt the people they left behind." Seira rushed forward, rage blinding her to reason. She raised a dagger, watching Iris dodge to the side. Then, Seira leapt, tackling the Circlet Guard to the ground mid-movement. The tip of her dagger rested against Iris' throat. "You... all of you... you killed him to save your own skins!"

The tears fell onto Iris' cheeks. For a moment, she wondered if they were her own, before realizing she wasn't crying. The consequences she'd been fearing, running from, denying in her mind... they took the form of the sobbing woman above her.

We can't... she told herself again. *We can't reveal the truth... If we expose it now, then all those sacrifices lose their meaning.* The Commander grabbed Seira's wrist, her magic shifting through the Pilgrim's body to her eyes. Seira didn't care. She wasn't planning on looking away, and all she had to do now was push down. That determination sent another guilty chill through Iris' skin. The glow in her fingers flickered as focus failed her.

What would happen to us? she wondered. *What would it do to the Church's reputation? What would it mean for the people of Civionis who would have to pack up their lives and move somewhere new from scratch? That isn't my decision to make! That... This is for the greater good, right?*

"Seira..." she said softly, the gentle name holding the Pilgrim's blade another moment. "Do you truly believe the truth alone would fix this city?" Desperation lingered behind the words like a ghost. The question was real; a moment of vulnerability, searching for a way out of the pit she'd been cast into, plummeting too far to save herself before she'd even realized she'd been pushed. She'd spent so long concealing the truth in the shadows... Could the light truly be more than a faint fantasy recalled in her dreams? She needed to know. If Seira was truly in the right, if she had an answer Iris couldn't find herself, she had to know!

Had she been asked the day before, or even hours before, Seira's answer would have fallen effortlessly from her lips. Instead, uncertainty silenced her. When chasing down Oka, she'd believed so strongly that the truth of her brother's death would make her next path clear. Surely, it had been her ignorance, not her grief, weighing down her heart. Yet, she still felt just as empty now.

"Some damage just can't be undone," she answered through gritted teeth. "The people that died, the people that were hurt... you can't take that back. But your actions now could prevent more pain." Seira's dagger shook in her hands, knuckles white as she held herself back, struggling with the choice she herself had to make; convincing herself just as much as Iris. That was what Faolan believed... that was why he risked his life to end the tragedies they were writing.

A trickle of blood fell down Iris' neck, Seira's shaking hands finding it harder and harder to steady the dagger. "If you're regretting what you've done, then why keep doing it?" The ground tremored, the pipes rattling above the two women. "You can't keep the city in the dark just because you're scared of what you might see in the light. Don't they deserve to know what you're doing to them?"

"I told you, it isn't that simple..." Iris replied, her tone more defeated than defiant. "They... *We* don't have the luxury of choice anymore. I can't just tell the city there's a Remnant beneath their feet. Anyone that chooses not to participate in the research would be silenced for that knowledge. The Church would hide the truth and innocent people would be locked away or worse."

"The Church would kill them just for knowing? What about the Researchers?"

"They're compliant. And they saw what defiance would get them when your brother tried to expose the truth..." Iris' gaze wandered, pulled aside by her guilt. She couldn't look Seira in the eyes as she spoke. "The darkness of the city goes back too long for us to fix alone. If we brought it into the light now, the guilty wouldn't be the only ones hurt." Slowly, Iris released Seira's wrist. "Kill me, if that will help you. I let your brother die; I let so many others join him... it's what I deserve."

The light of the nearby panels reflected off Seira's blade, the beams shaking with her hands. This was what Seira wanted. This would let Faolan rest in peace! It would bring her one step closer to freeing the powerful being locked away by fools undeserving of carrying the key. So, why...? Why couldn't she lower the blade? Why were her hands shaking? Why was her skin crawling?

"Damn it!" Seira said, tossing the dagger aside. She stood up, no longer under the influence of Iris' ability. "This was supposed to be simple! You were supposed to die. *Paras* was supposed to die! This– Why did you have a change of heart now!?" A subtle crunch accompanied the *SLAM* of Seira's fist hitting the wall. She let out a frustrated scream, and the anger faded to a dull, aching pain "I'd sacrifice all of them to let him rest in peace. I'd welcome the blast if it meant the Remnant was free." With a sigh, Seira braced herself on the wall, keeping her expression hidden from the Circlet Guard still laying on the ground. "But he'd never forgive me if I did..."

Once again, the hall shuddered around them. The adolium light flickered. Iris sat up, fingers brushing against her neck as she glanced to the shaking pipes. Caught up in the fight, she hadn't realized how frequent the tremors had gotten, and now she couldn't deny the worry building in her gut. Though her hands were still just as tied as they'd always been, it seemed fate intended on forcing a choice upon her nonetheless.

Iris looked to Seira, the exhausted woman still processing her grief and confldiction. *She's more right than she realizes,* the Commander thought. *We were foolish to think we could contain the Remnant forever. The tremors, the cave ins, so many paths crossing now of all times... It seems a sacrifice will have to be made no matter what.* Slowly, Iris stood and sheathed her blade. She turned, mind and gaze wandering to the containment chamber; the heart of all their pain. *What price will we pay to keep them all safe...?*

Chapter 41

THE LINGERING MAGIC of the Priests' final bursts drifted into the hallway like fog creeping over a marsh. From the jagged, spiked shape of the sculpted door, it didn't take much to deduce the victor. Azazel carefully peered around the entrance. *This must be the lab Seira mentioned. But it looks like Blade already escaped.* Almost impressed by the obviousness of it all, the angel looked to the trail of broken, steel doors. *And left quite the mess in the process. Makes him easier to follow at least.*

The lab was now useless to him, so Azazel passed by the door, only for the sights inside to bar him. He'd known someone had died. Why else would a final burst be leaking out of the room? But seeing the two Priests pinned to the walls, left to dangle limply like cast aside dolls... it twisted the angel's stomach.

Could Ramzel do this? Azazel wondered. He hoped he was wrong. He hoped that the masked man was someone else, *anyone* else. Sure, he had the same ability, but shaping metal wasn't all that uncommon. Yes, he was looking for "Gregory Veramor", but the angel got around a lot, he had more than a few enemies. And Sariel may have told him that Ramzel was in the area, but...

He wouldn't be capable of this, would he? Azazel approached the skewered corpses with his hands glowing gold. He carefully reshaped the metal, sliding it free from their bodies. With the steel no longer holding it back, the traces of blood that still remained further stained their uniforms with an unpleasant gush. He laid the Priests gently on the floor, realizing there was still a slight warmth to their skin.

Not her son... he couldn't.

With the corpses left in a more respectful state, Azazel took a moment to inspect the room. Was there any proof left behind? Proof that this masked murderer wasn't who he believed them to be. Proof that could feed his starving denial. Anything would do. Anything that would allow him to cling to his fleeting hope. But no hope remained in that lab, only the gruesome bodies of the masked man's victims.

He approached the warped steel chair. The faint, earthen smell leaking from the tubing inside matched the contents of the magic suppression cuffs used by the Church. And yet, the masked man had clearly managed to use his magic despite the restraints. *He overpowered it?* Azazel realized. *Either he's stronger than we predicted, or the Remnant is already giving him a boost.* Both options were enough to chill the blood in his veins. A strange mix of fear and pride. If that much power was granted to him this far from the Remnant, there was no way the Archangels would turn a blind eye if he went all in.

The angel took off, leaving the cruel lab behind as he followed the trail of misshapen, jagged doorways. He passed many Priests and Researchers, some injured, most dead. The blood-splattered walls guided his steps; churned his stomach. *I need to reach him. I need to know.* That goal repeated in his mind. Each skewered body bolstered his resolve. He couldn't run any longer, yet running was exactly what he needed to do.

Is it really Ramzel at the end of this carnage? he thought. *Is he really here? Has he been searching for me all these years?* It couldn't be true. He didn't want to accept that it might be. Even the smallest sliver of possibility cut like a knife as the guilt assaulted him. *Is all this my fault?*

The door to the containment room had already been reshaped; a thorny gate to the truth. The ground rumbled as Azazel's steps slowed to a halt. The pipes creaked, strained, rattled. The scent of blood-coated steel stung his senses. Uncertainty crawled across his skin. He couldn't do this. Sariel was right. If it truly was Ramzel that awaited on the other side... If this, all of this, was the consequence of his actions, he didn't know if he could handle it. The angel didn't notice he'd stepped back until his foot slid in the blood pooled beneath it. Though he kept his balance, his mind continued to tumble, demanding he turn around. He couldn't. He couldn't do it! He–

A face flashed through his mind. A woman, chestnut hair framing her perfect face; a face filled with an indescribable sadness. In an instant, the fog lifted from Azazel's mind. "I'm sorry," he said softly, taking a deep breath. He let the memory slip from his mind. He didn't deserve to see her face, not after that pitiful display.

His hands still shook as he climbed through the misshapen door. The mess he'd left during his escape had yet to be cleaned. The gargantuan sword still sat half buried in the floor. The lingering water still dripped from the broken pipe, sealed off somewhere further in the facility. The scent of smoke and steam still filled the air. But none of that mattered. His eyes were drawn to one thing, and one thing alone; Ramzel's silhouette, standing in the adolium light emitted from the Remnant's prison, small as a child when compared to the Celestial's form.

The threads of fate tugged violently, their branches threatening to snap. Centuries of waiting, decades of running, years of searching. The end of it all waited at the bottom of a single flight of stairs.

Chapter 42

EVERY PERSON IN the world is living their own story. When you're having the worst day of your life, someone else is thanking the archangels for blessing theirs. The person that sits next to you at one of Civionis' terminal platforms has their own goals, their own problems, their own life beyond that brief proximity.

As Azazel confronted the killer hunting him down, as Enoch was spending his final day returning to an ill-fated city, a handful of Pilgrims in Civionis were instead celebrating the completion of a job well done. The three of them were fully oblivious to the facility directly below their feet. They were oblivious to Iris and Seira's confrontation. They were oblivious to the possibility that the ceremony they'd spent weeks setting up for might be in danger from the very source of the recruits it was meant to celebrate. In that moment, all that mattered was the meal they were sharing after a hard day's work, and the drinks in their hands, rattling as the ground shook once more.

Thistoron offered a napkin to the now beer-covered Morael. "Gee, that was a rough one, eh?" Tory observed. The older Pilgrim took the napkin with a gruff, muttered thanks.

"They're gettin' stronger," Morael grumbled, cleaning himself off. Tory nodded, glancing off the building they were seated at. With its rooftop seating, the restaurant Comisidio granted an enviable view of the cavern. From their outdoor table, Tory could see the central terminal platform, the High Cathedral lit from below by the firepit he'd cleaned only a few hours earlier. The brightly colored flowers and ribbons were harder to make out, lining the front and sides of the wooden stage. Had he not seen Basa organizing them herself, he unfortunately wouldn't even know where to look.

As if she somehow knew he was thinking of her, Basa swung an arm around Tory's shoulder, pulling his attention back to the table. "Now's not the time to worry about some quakes!" she said, addressing the two men. "Father Paras is footing the bill, so let's enjoy the food and eat like we're High Inquisitors!"

"It ain't right t' take advantage of a person's hospitality," Morael warned. "Better pace yerself."

"Yeah, yeah." Basa released Tory's shoulders, turning back to the hearty stew in front of her. "It's not like he can't afford it though. Since Enoch and Greg had to skip town, we're already two mouths short of the budget. Plus, this is Civionis, we– Oy, Tory. I know we did a good job, but you don't have to keep looking at the platform. The job's done."

"Sorry." Tory turned back with a smile, taking a sip of beer to show he'd rejoined the table. "I was just thinking that it'd be nice to see the ceremony for once."

Morael chuckled as he placed his stein back on the table. "What, yer own ceremony wasn't enough?"

"I'm just saying, we put in all this work every year. Don't you wanna see the next batch of future Church heroes getting their moment in the light?"

"What light? This is Civionis," Basa said through a mouthful of stew. She swallowed, grabbing a napkin to wipe away what managed to escape. "Besides, we aren't invited. And it's not like it'll be any different than usual, right? Perfect means nothing unexpected. The ceremony is flashy, but it's boring too."

"Yer forgettin' that the Circlet Guard Commander 'll be there," Morael chimed in, side-eyeing Tory. The younger Pilgrim's darker skin turned a mahogany shade as he attempted to hide his blush with another sip of his drink.

"Aaaaahhhh," Basa replied, lips curling into a cheeky smile. "Lover boy just wants the chance to enjoy the view a while, huh?"

"She's a strong and beautiful woman! It's not weird to respect someone like that, okay?"

The weight of Morael's shoulder pat pushed Tory further into the chair than he'd already sunk out of embarrassment. "Even if ya did get t' sit in. She'd be busy keepin' an eye on the recruiters," the old man said. "'fraid you'd end up a face in the crowd."

Tory let out a frustrated groan into his drink. After sending another teasing smile his way, Basa turned to the central terminal platform too. "Y'know, it *is* weird though. We should be able to hear the music by now at least. Wonder what's up."

"Sure it'll get sorted, whatever it is delayin' 'em," Morael argued. Now that he'd finished cleaning himself up, he took another swig. Another tremor followed, nearly spilling what little drink remained. The gruff man steadied his hand this time, glaring at the mountain above them as if it were trying to annoy him specifically. He so seldom got to drink this freely, and he wasn't about to waste the opportunity. "Fer now, let's just enjoy the meal before Basa gets too sick t' stand."

"Hey!" Basa playfully slapped his arm, the smile on her face betraying her joy. "Watch it old man, I've still got plenty of room. I'm sure you'll be the one we're dragging home if you keep day drinking at the pace you're going. It's not even noon yet!"

Their meal continued, full of joy and hope. Friends, Civionians, living their lives the same as always. Oblivious to the true source of the tremors shaking their home. Oblivious to the dangers beneath their feet. Oblivious to the shifting threads of fate that would soon drown in crimson, red like the leaves of the forest they all cherished.

Chapter 43

OUR MEMORIES ARE often triggered in the most un-expected moments. A passing scent of aging wood, and suddenly you're climbing a tree near your childhood home, bathed in sunlight. A familiar melody is strummed by a per-former in the street; you feel the gentle hand of a past love brushing the hair from your face, just before they steal your first kiss. A young man cries out across the room, his silver hair styled so painfully similar to how you styled it dec-ades ago, and you're reminded of bitter losses and promises made in the dark.

Azazel could deny it no longer. He knew the identity of the masked killer Blade...

Ramzel. His breath caught in his chest, heart tightening as hope fled in the overwhelming shadow of fear, guilt and truth. A voice irritatingly similar to Sariel's sounded in his mind, reminding him to hide his face. Azazel did just that, placing his helmet back onto his head. Ramzel couldn't see him. Azazel couldn't allow his search to succeed.

Time was of the essence, lest Ramzel complete the pact. But Azazel still had to force his feet to move. Knuckles white, he lingered at the top of the steps. *Move! C'mon! Move!* he willed, body refusing to obey. Another cry of pain from the young man below pierced through his hesitation. Holding back tears, Azazel flew down the stairs, rushing past the machinery rattling in the overwhelming presence of the Heart.

Don't worry! I'm here! The words stuck in the angel's throat as he remembered he had to play the part of a stranger. He stopped so abruptly that you'd think he'd hit a wall, his feet skidding somewhat on the slickened floor. The breath that followed felt dangerously long, held captive by his fear, his mind searching for what to say; anything but the words that so desperately needed to be spoken.

"You'll get hurt if you get any closer!" he finally shouted. "It's dangerous here!" He kept to the shadows best he could, heeding his own warning. It seemed many of the Researchers had done the same. The few brave souls that had tried to stay and defend their work were now skewered by the machines they'd sought to protect. The rest had fled, convinced the Remnant would turn on them in the moment of its now inevitable escape.

Azazel's voice pushed through the ringing in Ramzel's ears. The young man turned around, overwhelmed by it all. The Remnant echoing in his head, the lingering pain of his interrogation, the scalding magic coursing through him, and now some stranger trying to tell him what to do. "You think I don't know–" He paused. This armored figure was definitely not a Researcher.

A sense of familiarity nagged his mind, nearly muted by the voice of the Remnant. Half-bathed in shadow, it was difficult to make out who it was. But that voice... that silhouette... Where had he seen them? The memories struggled against the torrent of magic cascading through his head.

"Who are you?" Ramzel asked.

"Me? I'm– I work here." Azazel gestured to the Remnant, the Celestial growing eerily still as it met his gaze. "I'm here to help you before you do something reckless."

"I don't need your help. I'm not stupid enough to let that thing out," Ramzel argued. Saying it aloud, he realized he didn't know why he'd gone there in the first place. Why had this strange creature lured him there? Why had he found it so hard to resist? "But it's in my head. Damn thing won't shut up!" The young man winced, still trying to drown out the Heart's cries, only to realize its repeating words had changed.

He's here... it whispered with booming thoughts. **He's here... He came for us...**

Azazel...

Like a burst of heat melting away a tempestuous snow-storm, the world cleared around Ramzel. The Remnant, the facility, they faded out of clarity. In the dim, chamber light, only the stranger's golden armor seized his gaze. No... not a stranger. A blinding sun in the darkness.

It burned.

"It's you..." he said so softly that even he could hardly hear it. The man's helmet hid his face, but the Remnant's silence had allowed Ramzel's memories to finally break through the murky surface of his subconscious. There was no mistaking that armor. The steel that glimmered gold in his dreams. But that couldn't be right. It couldn't be him. He was searching for Gregory Veramor, not...

"Your name... Tell me your name," Ramzel ordered, his voice shaking.

"I don't see how that's impor–"

Tell me! Like fuel tossed on a flame, an aura of crimson flared from Ramzel's body, the magic not his own. It passed just as quickly, and he took a step closer to Azazel. "Don't you dare play dumb! You know who I am, don't you!"

"…Can't say I do," Azazel answered, the reply feeling like boiled water on his tongue. He watched as Ramzel took another step forward. He knew he should back away, but his body disobeyed once more.

"My mother's name was Adina Veramor," Ramzel said. "I wanted to know what happened to her, but her family wouldn't tell me. They said to find my father instead." Ramzel's jaw clenched, anger burning in his words. "…But the file I stole said he'd died with my mother. The only lead I had was his relative, Gregory Veramor. I thought he might be my brother, or a cousin, or *anything*. I didn't care, I just needed to know the truth." The young man froze, body trembling as tears stung his eyes. "But I didn't think the search would lead me to *you*." A trickle of blood trailed Ramzel's fingers, his nails digging deep into his palm. "You aren't Gregory Veramor, are you? I know you… I've *seen* you. I've seen that armor."

"S-Sorry kid, I don't know what you're talking about."

"Don't lie to me!" The Heart convulsed with Ramzel's outburst. "Take that damn helmet off and show me your face! You're him! You have to be!" Ramzel rushed forward. His hand glowed red as he shaped a dagger from the steel machine beside him, not slowing for even a second. Though it broke his heart to do so, Azazel readied his blade, intent on keeping him away. He tried to change it into a shield, but he couldn't focus. Seeing the blade, Ramzel hesitated. From his expression, one would assume he'd been stabbed through the heart already. But that pain lasted only a moment, shifting to a burning desperation that shook the very room around them.

Ramzel stabbed towards the armor. With Enoch's warning sounding through his mind, Azazel made no attempt to block. Rather than a blade to the heart, however, he found a hand reaching for his face. The angel's eyes went wide. Too late, he finally took a step back as his helmet clattered to the ground behind him. His white hair fell free. His amber eyes met Ramzel's red. For a moment, Adina stared back at him, tears streaming down her face. Azazel turned to hide his own, firmly grabbing Ramzel's arm to restrain him. He faced the young man away to keep his gaze trapped on anything but him.

"L-Let go!" Ramzel cried. Azazel kept silent.

Why... Ramzel wondered. *Why... Why? Why? Why!?* "Why won't you admit it?" he cried. His skin glowed crimson. Defying the rules of Sculptor abilities, he shaped Azazel's armor without using his hands. Inside, spikes dug into Azazel's body, enough to hurt but not kill. The angel winced. He lost his grip, allowing Ramzel to slip away. The young man's glaring eyes burned like the sun.

"I've seen your face! You're Azazel Veramor, right!? You're my dad!?"

Azazel felt his heart shatter. His mouth opened, but only silence passed through his lips. What should he say to that? What *could* he say to that?

Grief, confusion, frustration, anger, they boiled up within Ramzel's very soul. The chamber shook, the Remnant mirroring his pain. Once again, Ramzel's blood began to burn. He'd searched for so long. He'd *suffered* for so long. He'd stumbled, ignorant and left in the darkness. Gregory was supposed to be the light that would reveal all the answers, and yet, even his existence had been a lie to cover up the truth. To hide the fact that his father still lived.

"I need to know! I need to know if I killed her!" *C-C-Crack!* The glass rattled behind them, beginning to fracture. Ramzel failed to notice. Instead, he pleaded with tear-filled eyes. "And... I need to know if that's why you left! Please! Just tell me!"

"I..." Like the glass of the Remnant's prison, Azazel's mind began to break. He stared, lamenting the young man before him. His familiar eyes that felt like staring into the sun. The ghost of his lost love, hiding within his features. The very face of his guilt.

Ramzel was too clever for his own good, just like his mother.

"I... I'm sorry. I'm not who you think I am," he nearly choked on the words. Ramzel did nothing to hold back his own.

"STOP LYING!"

CRASH!!!

An agonizing cry filled the chamber, accompanying the sound of the shattering container. Ramzel held his head, staggering back in pain. His own screams clawed at his throat, echoing off the walls. The Remnant's mist burst like gunpowder ignited by flame, converging around Ramzel, shielding him. Glass and metal debris shot out, slicing Azazel's wings and armor as he found himself forced back by the strength of the blast.

Up above, the metal supports groaned and creaked in the sudden pressure. Try as he might to fight it, to focus on his suffering son, Azazel couldn't resist the deluge that followed. The icy waters of Lake Civionis drained in through the crumbling ceiling, and he was swept away by the swirling eclipse.

Ramzel! I... I'm sorry! he thought, struggling against the current. *I'm so, so, sorry...* He saw the mists surrounding his son. He felt a stabbing fear in his chest. He heard the sound of Ramzel's screams. He winced as his head slammed against something in the water, consciousness slipping away.

He drifted as the torrent dragged him back to the halls of the facility, leaving his son behind to suffer alone.

Chapter 44

LONG AGO, but not long enough for the scars to have healed, an angel fell in love with a human.

Adina Veramor. She was his world; shimmering light reflected upon the eternal void of immortality. She was imperfect. Perfect for him. Quiet, yet filled with sincere, endearing passion. Her face would crinkle when she laughed. She'd hum absentmindedly as she worked in her shop. She never fought for herself, but for others she would gladly die. After all, she believed it better to admire the art of the world than to be placed on a pedestal herself. She was beautiful, breathtaking and broken; and the angel loved to fix things more than anything.

But one's mortality cannot be fixed. Death's scythe cuts the threads of all humans. Though his was bound to Spira, her soul was doomed to one day end. The angel had run from this truth, this inevitability, blinded by the radiance of their love. He hid behind it like a shield, believing it would be enough to save her as her health began to fail. When the fever drained the color from her skin. When the endless coughing kept them both up each night. When her legs refused to stand. When her hands could hardly hold a needle.

And then, when her thread snapped and the void swallowed him once again, that dark truth nearly ended him.

She was gone, yet present everywhere. The clothing he wore still bore the stitches she'd sewn. The waves on their favourite beach, the place they'd first met, still echoed her laughter. In the darkness, the crumpled sheets of their bed would trick his eyes, convincing his half-conscious mind that she still laid next to him. Her eyes, so trusting and beautiful, red as rubies, stared back at him every time he faced their son.

It hurt so much. Each reminder felt like an icy grip in the dark. Each innocent smile. Each laugh. The beating of his tiny heart as he crawled into too big a bed, crying from a nightmare. It was her smile, never to be seen again. Her laugh forever silenced. Her heartbeat, cold, ended, gone.

He tried. For a while, he truly, truly tried. After all, their child was all he had left of her. A life they'd created together. His dream made reality. She could live on through him! Though he wondered if that was too big an expectation to force upon a child barely able to speak. And so, the angel distanced himself instead. He focused on helping others. In his most stressful moments, assisting his loved ones had always brought clarity. But all he did was numb his mind.

In town, her family jeered; they spoke with knives in their words.

"You killed her."

"You took her from us."

"You and that devil of a son."

He couldn't argue. He knew they were right, even without the knowledge of what truly claimed her life. To birth the child of an angel... it proved too much for her body to take. The magic of an immortal, the body of a mortal, together they formed a fatal recipe. Once their child was born, her body weakened. Her strength failed her. The light faded in her eyes, and even leaving her bed proved too draining. Before long, the condemning arcane ruins branded her skin. She burned, beautiful, breathtaking and broken, sitting next to him on the beach, as radiant as the final sunset the two lovers watched together.

She was gone, and it was his fault.

He'd asked for too much, and she'd given everything in return.

He'd tried to give back. He paid for a grave worthy of her brilliance. He distanced himself from her family so they would never again have to look upon the face of her killer. He couldn't let go of her name, not just yet, but Azazel Veramor died alongside her. No longer a husband. Barely a father. Their son saw his caretaker more than his own flesh and blood. He deserved to have someone there for him. Someone that could look at him and smile.

For several years, this was Azazel's life. He'd find any excuse to leave home. He paid generously for the nanny to stay another week, another month. He kept his distance, lest his presence hurt what little of Adina remained. Lest another innocent have their life snuffed out prematurely. He'd sneak into his own home when the hour was late, the light barely present, and chastise his own cowardice; his selfishness. How bitter a realization it was, that this was the reality he preferred. A father in title only, too afraid to look his own son in the eyes.

Awful as this was, fate had not finished. Azazel had always seen himself a martyr, and the world seemed intent to make one of his family. A single prophecy, spoken quietly by a Seer, penned their future in an ink dripping with tragedy.

Chapter 45

Child born of mortal blood,
Child born of clay and mud,
Harbinger that brings the end,
Sound the horn. Sound the horn.
Angels shouting out in pain,
Sky and stone forever slain,
Remnant of the world beyond,
Sound the horn. Sound the horn.
Heavens fall, the ground erupts,
Life abundance shall corrupt,
Heed the call destruction god,
Sound the horn. Sound the horn.
Sound the horn.

So few had known the words whispered by the Seer. A prophecy feared by even the Celestial guardians of Spira. These words heralded the end of everything, a message calling upon forces capable of destroying entire worlds. Such a grand and perturbing script was surely meant for players equally grand and influential. And so, when Azazel heard the ill-fated words, he left it in the recesses of his mind, caring not for fates disconnected from his own. He never expected such a thing to influence his own life so greatly.

How long had passed since she had left him forever? Azazel didn't know, nor did he wish too. He wouldn't survive it. Right then, he was far more focused on completing the construction of a greenhouse for his closest friend, Semyaza. This was not just any greenhouse, mind you. Flora from all across the Three Realms shared this large, overly humid palace. Luminescent ivy from Diapogeum crept up the steel lattice. Phoenix-lotus flowers from Spira floated gently in the fountain, swaying in the waves from its rippling spout. The bubbling of the water joined the buzzing of insects cheerfully pollinating the many other plants.

Far less cheerful, and far louder in volume, Azazel threw his hands up farther down the curving stone paths. "It's just one last little addition. You need a place for the plants that don't like heat, right? Why are you being so weird about it?" He crossed his arms, gaze far from the target of his words. He knew fully well the reason his friend was being 'weird about it'.

"Because that's what you said before the last *little addition*," Semyaza argued, his voice stern yet saddened. His words weren't the only thing with an exhausted air to them. Dark circles weighed down his deep green eyes. His long, ash brown hair was usually tied back into a well-styled bun. That night, it draped over his shoulders like water flowing over a cliff, the tangled strands shining in the dim lantern light.

"I know you're grieving, Azazel, but you can't keep doing this. That boy needs a father," he lectured, his tan and russet wings shifting in discomfort.

"He's fine with the nanny. She's good at her job." Azazel rolled his eyes, the gesture ending with a biting glance. "Besides, can you really judge? You're here t-"

Tap tap tap. The noise came from the glass of the greenhouse entrance. Not a single creak sounded from the door as Sariel opened it, stopping when he noticed the two men staring. The tension lingering in the air was so strong there might as well have been a sign announcing their fight.

"Apologies, I seem to have interrupted something," Sariel said. Azazel hurried away from Semyaza to greet their friend.

"No, it's fine. We were just finishing. What's up? You look paler than usual." Azazel looked Sariel over in concern. "Anything I can do to help?"

"In all honesty, I came here to help both of *you*," Sariel replied, much to Azazel's annoyance. The Inquisitive's darkened expression felt as grim as the news he carried with him. Noting this, Semyaza approached.

"What is it? Did something happen?" he asked. "You came all this way, so it must be important." Possibilities flooded the man's mind. His almond skin paled in fear. "The Archangels didn't approach you, did they?"

"No, and Celestials forbid they do," Sariel replied. His next words clung to his throat. Normally, he had no issue bearing bad news. It was better to face the problems that so often accompanied it with the necessary knowledge. But this... The decision they would have to make... Knowledge alone was not a strong enough weapon to ease that fight.

"Just tell us already, Sariel," Azazel snapped, his mask slipping for a moment in his frustration. He quickly tried to recover, forcing a smile. "I mean, if we know what's bothering you, maybe we can find a solution together."

The Pilgrim's words guided Sariel from his hesitation, yet the Inquisitive waited a moment longer, a breath before the plunge. "I had Arakiel look into the recent... *losses*," he answered, deciding careful wording to be his best course of action. "She seemed best equipped to find answers while keeping things discreet."

"Oh? Strange... She didn't mention any of this to me," Semyaza muttered, holding his chin. Sariel folded his hands together, habitually speaking with the air and perfect posture of an instructor.

"As I said, discreetness was our main priority. Two mortals have died, three if we consider Sophia's death in light of this new information. With the potential severity of the consequences, I felt it best that Arakiel and I alone were involved until we knew if these children posed a threat to more than just their mothers."

Azazel's plastered smile shattered in an instant. A meekness coated his voice, guilt dragging his volume down to a whisper. "And do they? The children... What did you learn?"

"They..." Sariel took a deep breath, looking over the room as if searching for something, as if the walls themselves might be listening. "There's no way to prove it without allowing it to happen, but the conclusion she reached is that the child of an angel and human would be able to survive a pact with a Remnant of Adoil."

Realization and implication shot through Azazel and Semyaza's minds like lightning. "No... That– That can't be true," Azazel stuttered. "She's wrong, she has to be!" Panicked, he gripped Sariel's robes. "Tell me you're lying, Sariel. That this is one of your awful jokes."

Sariel allowed Azazel his outburst, the man's grip clinging, shaking. "You know Arakiel's expertise. If she claims this is true, I'm inclined to believe her," the Inquisitive finally replied. Azazel's fingers loosened as the truth's hold tightened around his mind and heart. He hunched, guilt bearing down on his entire being.

Semyaza moved to a nearby bench. He sat in a daze as he processed the information. "The Archangels would hunt them down beyond the void if they learned the truth," he said. "They would never risk the Harbinger's Prophecy coming true."

"My thoughts exactly," Sariel replied. "Vague as the prophecy is, we know the Archangels believe a Remnant pact will be the catalyst of the destruction described. If there was even a chance that these children could find a Remnant that slipped through their fingers, they'd choose to nip that possibility in the bud."

"So, what do we do?" Azazel asked, finally releasing Sariel's robes. He stepped back, hands still shaking. Sariel's lips tightened, knowing the two men would not approve of his answer.

"The prophecy risks the lives of everyone in existence. Killing them would be the logical answer," he replied.

"Have a damn heart, Sariel," Azazel snapped. "They're children."

"So are many of the humans that would die if the prophecy came true," Sariel argued. "We live eternally. Does a few years really make a difference when it comes to the morality of a human's death?"

"Of course it does!" Azazel argued. "And even if it didn't, it isn't just some random child, it's *our* kids! But I guess you wouldn't understand the difference that makes, you heartless bastard."

Sariel simply raised an eyebrow. It was rare to see Azazel in such a state, but he could hardly say he was surprised. It had only been a matter of time before he broke. One glance to Semyaza, the man's eyes calmly closed, showed the other angel was still weighing his options. The gardener's fingers gripped the bench seat, his pale knuckles contradicting his otherwise collected demeanor.

With a sigh, Sariel turned his gaze to the greenhouse glass, his focus wandering to the pale flowers of a blackthorn tree outside. "If that's too cruel a solution, we could hide them away instead. Ensure they never come into contact with a Remnant. That would also lessen the threat, would it not?"

Azazel scowled. "So, what? We just keep them in a cage?"

"Reductively, yes. But there are ways to make a life trapped within walls liveable."

"Spira's sake. You sound like a damn Archangel." Azazel's words earned no response from Sariel, the other angel seeing no insult in the accusation. As much as he hated to admit it though, Azazel couldn't think of a better solution. He didn't want to condemn Ramzel to a life of imprisonment, not after everything he'd done to escape his own. But with so much at stake, what else could they do?

Would Adina approve if she was here?

Frustrated, Azazel turned to Semyaza instead, hoping his friend had an answer like always. He gestured to the greenhouse with a wave of his arm. "Could we raise them here? With the archasite you got for your research, Spira couldn't scry on them."

"They still check in on us in person," Semyaza argued. "Unpredictably, too. Do you think they'd turn a blind eye if they found human children here? That they wouldn't ask

any questions? The freedom they've allowed us isn't absolute. You know as well as I do that they would end us all in
an instant if given good reason."

"Then what can we do? They don't deserve to be locked
away just because they *could* be dangerous. You wouldn't
lock up a dog for having teeth."

Slowly, Semyaza rose from his seat. The others watched
in silence; curious... desperate... "Perhaps," he said, speaking
slowly as the plan formed in his mind, "risky as it would be,
there's a way to hide their nature while still allowing them
to live freely with humans, rather than imprisoned among
their own family..."

Those words led to a night of strenuous and bitter
discussion. Plans made, argued, adjusted and argued again.
Futures weighed. Friendships measured. Consequences reiterated and reiterated and reiterated. Eventually, a shaky
compromise was reached, and Azazel found himself carrying Ramzel in his arms, walking through the outskirts of
a small village in South Terrael. Ramzel slept soundly, the
occasional mumble muffled by his face nuzzled into his
father's jacket.

A thin fog filled the street. The metal gate smelled of rust
as Azazel pushed it open. Nearby, a wooden swing swayed
and creaked in the breeze, hanging from an apple tree. The
sight of a toy trunk next to the door, filled to the point of
overflowing, brought a small smile to Azazel's face. Small
and fleeting, as his goal shunned this gentle joy.

Knock Knock Knock.

Silence... followed by faint shuffling behind the door.

"Who's there?" a young woman asked through the wood.

"A– uh... Gregory. I'm here for Maylis? We spoke a few
days ago."

The woman fell silent again before muttering incomprehensibly. Despite the frustration, she still unlocked the numerous jingling and clattering fastens inside. After just enough time to feel awkward, a large, muscular woman swung the door open.

"You have any idea how late it is?" Maylis, grumbled, already changed into her nightgown. Many strands of her pale blonde hair had escaped the long braid they'd been tied into, pulled free by the static of her bedsheets. She scratched her side, the various faded scars on her arms visible in the light of the candle she'd set on a table by the door.

Azazel adjusted his grip on Ramzel, his arms growing tired from the young boy's weight. "Sorry, I was–"

"Nope." Maylis held up a hand, nearly smacking Azazel in the face. "Less I know the better." She let out her annoyance in a sigh, irritation giving way to consciousness. Her pale green eyes softened somewhat. With a gentler tone, she nodded to Ramzel. "This is the kid then? Let's have a look."

Though Maylis held out her arms to take him, Azazel held Ramzel a moment longer. He'd convinced himself he was fine with this plan, but the reality that this would likely be the last time he ever held him like this... He'd never see his wavy white hair. He'd never feel those tiny hands tug at his jacket. He'd never hear him ask question after question, curiosity and wonder in his eyes.

Adina's eyes...

"Having second thoughts?" the woman asked, raising an eyebrow. "Understandable. Sometimes folks find this part difficult."

A sickening feeling squirmed through Azazel's gut. *Not as difficult as it should be,* he thought, disgusted with himself. Carefully, he handed Ramzel over. The woman held him easily. With the strength of her muscles, she could easily lift three of him, maybe more. Azazel shook out his own hands now that they were free. "I'll make sure to send funds to help you out."

"Sure you will," the woman rolled her eyes, having heard that promise too many times to count. Adding up the actual coins she'd received would be a far easier calculation. "I'll keep an eye on the mail."

"And remember, if anyone asks–"

"No one was there when I found him. I know, I know," Maylis sent an irritated look Azazel's way, but her face softened as she noticed the genuine pain in the man's eyes. "Y'know, you could always keep him. I know you said he isn't yours, but it seems like this is rough on you."

"...I can't," Azazel argued. "This is the only way he can have a free life. He deserves better than what I could give him." Knowing that if he didn't leave then, he likely never would, Azazel bowed his head in farewell. "Thank you, Maylis." Though his eyes longed to linger just a little longer, he pulled his gaze away. Cutting ties with him would keep him away from the Archangels ire. It had to be done. Perhaps, if the Harbinger's Prophecy could be prevented, he could reunite with him one day. But until such a miracle arose, they were fated to live separate lives. Though, not fully separate. Semyaza had his ways of keeping tabs on the children they were placing in the care of trusted individuals. If they came close to reaching any Remnants, the angels agreed to take action. As for what that action would be...

Redirection?

Honesty?

Cruelty for the sake of the greater good?

That would depend on the severity of the situation. But that was an issue for their future selves. Right then, Azazel walked back down the foggy street, his arms lighter, his heart heavier.

"Daddy?" Ramzel's quiet voice broke the silence of the night. The young boy saw his father walking away, his yellow jacket slowly swallowed by the fog. "Daddy!" he cried out again, confused when he realized his father wasn't stopping, that he was struggling in the arms of a stranger. Tears fell down his cheeks, his cries growing more frantic each time Azazel refused to turn back. Perhaps the young boy thought he couldn't hear him. Maylis quickly rushed him inside before he could wake the whole village. Azazel continued forward, his own crying far quieter than his son's.

"Adina, please don't hate me," he whispered with broken breaths. "As much as I deserve it... It's for his own good. I... I couldn't even keep you safe. He's better off without me. Better off living as a human...

...Better off free."

Chapter 46

THE STARLIGHT STONES had never fallen, but as the city shook, the cavern above cracked ever so slightly. The dislodged pebbles rippled the lake below, too small for the people to notice.

Shortly before Azazel and Ramzel's confrontation, Sariel and Enoch hurried to the central terminal platform. Yet another quake sent the lake water splashing onto the polished stone paths. Slippery as they now were, Sariel's canine-clawed feet kept the duo balanced as the Shapeshifter sprinted through Civionis; through the platforms growing more crowded farther in the city.

Sariel's eyes darted to and fro, searching for the best path through the confused and dodging civilians. Ultimately, he decided not to take one at all. With the ease and grace of a cat leaping to their favourite perch, Sariel vaulted up to the rooftops. Enoch's stomach rose with them, but compared to the flight and plummet he'd had with Azazel back in the capital, Sariel's leap was more a hop. The Scribe still held on tighter though. He didn't want a fall to the stone street to end him before the overflow could finish the job; before he had a chance to make a difference.

This time he *would* make a difference.

Before long, they reached the bridge to the central platform. Many Priests stood guard at each entrance to keep out the crowds of civilians. *How irritating,* Sariel thought, weighing his options in his mind. *No doubt they want to see the recruiters. I warned them this would happen with such famous guests.* His steps quickened. The edge of the rooftop approached. *Pushing through that would be far too big a hassle. Best not to waste time.*

Enoch held on for dear fading life as the half-fox man launched himself off the roof. The dark canal waters reflected the silvered blur as the lake lapped in quiet jealousy. Contrasting the starlight stones and shadowed cavern above him, the High Inquisitive looked like moonlight traversing the night sky.

Having spent the last hour trying to stop himself from pacing a hole through the ceremony stage, Bishop Paras looked up from his seat in horror. "What in the Realms is that!?" he exclaimed, readying himself to dodge this apparent attack. Next to him, High Priest Emilian loosened his grip on his greatsword. The man let out a hearty laugh.

"Didn't you say he's not one for fanfare, Nitika?" he asked.

"Usually, yes. Perhaps he was taken by a Hijacker," the Pilgrim Nitika replied. The two recruiters watched Sariel land on the central terminal platform, skidding down an empty aisle in the seating area. The handful of young recruits scrambled to move away, hardly expecting such a beast to suddenly drop out of the sky.

Once his momentum slowed to a stop, Sariel stayed low. The recruits recovered, some searching for something they could use as a weapon, others summoning their variously colored magic. "Stand down," Emilian shouted from the stage, stopping them in their tracks. "You're not with the Church just yet. If he's a threat, I'll handle it."

The recruits looked to the High Priest in confusion, but stepped back nonetheless. Having avoided the potential fight, Sariel sighed in relief. "This is where you get off," he said, letting Enoch climb to the ground.

"O-Of course," Enoch replied, still shaken by the sudden leap through the air. "Uh... Thank you for the ride, sir." After the swaying of the Shapeshifter's gait, the ground felt eerily still. As he stepped back, Enoch watched silver light build beneath Sariel's fur until he was nothing but a pale silhouette. Said silhouette shrank in size, his form shifting, leaving a fair-faced man in its place. The Scribe's eyes went wide. He realized where he'd heard the man's name before.

"W-Wait, are you–"

"High Inquisitive Surufel Asaradel," Bishop Paras growled, stomping his way across the stage. His words sputtered, as if fighting to push through his rage. "Not only are you late, but you decided to– to just *throw* protocol to the wind and crash in here like some sort of beast pouncing on its dinner!? You'd better have a fitting explanation! I have half a mind to send you away for this disrespect."

You'd be more than happy to rid yourself of me, wouldn't you, Bishop? Sariel thought, hiding his urge to glare beneath a mask of indifference. The man's anger felt too targeted, too panicked, too immediate to be over nothing but a delayed schedule and dramatic entrance. He felt threatened.

Sariel had expected some sort of manipulative mastermind, not an egocentric fool clearly clinging to the coattails of his predecessors. Nevertheless, this made his job far easier. Anger and pride were far more malleable traits than cunning. The High Inquisitive looked up at the Bishop on stage.

"Yes, apologies for the disruptive entrance. Unfortunately, there was, or rather *is,* no time to waste on formalities. You must evacuate the city."

"Evacuate!?" Paras scoffed, watching as Sariel made his way to the steps. "If this is your idea of a joke, High Inquisitor, then it's in very poor taste."

"Lives are in danger, Father. I would never joke in such a situation." Sariel's fingers trailed along the embossed everred branches on the railing. Azazel's handiwork, no doubt. As he climbed up, his gaze lowered, watching the Bishop's reactions carefully. "Your people are currently threatened by some sort of gas leak. Perhaps the very same that forced your city to shut down its mines years ago. It has been building beneath your very feet, and it's about to reach a breaking point."

"I– How could–?" as the Bishop stuttered, Emilian crossed his arms, face caught between a scowl and curious leer.

"Digging your nose into things again, *Silver Shadow?*" he asked. Sariel shrugged off the accusatory tone.

"Only when I must," he justified. "You can judge me later. For now, we need to act. Surely the great Bishop Paras of Civionis will protect his beloved citizens with such a threat on his doorstep."

The Bishop glared. Normally, he'd accuse the man of slander. He'd demand evidence. He'd do whatever was necessary to silence the rats threatening his operations; his way of life. Unfortunately, he couldn't. Surufel's *evidence* was standing nervously off the stage. The young man Iris had failed to capture, presented on a silver platter in the center of the city. It was clear that Sariel understood the severity of the situation, the consequences of stating the true origin of the mists with so many witnesses. But the boy's presence was clearly a threat. *I know more than I'm saying. I will expose you if I must.*

"W-Well, of course," the Bishop replied. "My people are my pride, after all. The reason for Civionis' success. But, evacuating the entire city? Surely that isn't necessary." In an attempt to hide his shaking hands, and perhaps calm his growing nerves, the Bishop reached for his pipe in his pocket, catching himself at the last moment. As if burned by the unlit pipe, his hand pulled back, the man revealing his fear in his attempt to hide it.

His life, his future, they flashed before his eyes. He wasn't about to let it all go because of a boy and a damned fox. If he sent the citizens into Everred, where entrances to the Heart Facility waited like pit traps scattered throughout the forest, he'd be ruined. Surely Surufel was bluffing. Surely there was some goal that he was failing to see. Perhaps the man wished to set him up for failure, to take his place and claim the glory of curing magical overflow for himself.

"I assure you, we've been aware of the mist ever since the mines were shut down," the Bishop continued. Out of habit, he adjusted the circlet on his head, despite the accessory sitting comfortably already. "It has been monitored, and if it was even close to the levels you're describing, we would know. There's no reason to panic the entire city with such an overreaction."

"It's not an overreaction!" The outburst came from Enoch. The young man receded somewhat as both the recruiters and recruits turned his way. His stomach went taut. The Scribe turned his gaze to the platform below him. "I... I saw it. The cavern crashing down, people choking on mist, this platform breaking and so many people dying in the chaos."

"You... saw it?" Paras replied. His eye twitched. Of course, the boy was a bloody Seer of all things. "Are you certain that wasn't simply a symptom of your condition? I've heard that magical overflow can fuddle the mind."

Sariel took a breath to argue, and to cut Enoch off before his emotions could complicate things. *He was already charged with defying a High Inquisitor. I hope he isn't intending to make a habit of it.* Admirable as his intentions were, he couldn't let Enoch get carried away. *I know how the Church works. They won't admit to supporting the city's research if the truth is exposed carelessly. After all, a revelation such as this would deal a deadly blow to the people's trust and faith; and what is a Church without that? We have to tread carefully.*

Sariel's concerns were certainly justified, but his thoughts, that momentary hesitation, allowed Enoch to act first.

"Are you willing to take that chance with so many lives on the line?" the Scribe asked. "Do you want Civionis to be the next Peycile? If we don't evacuate, everyone here will die, and that would be on you!"

The biting words surprised even Sariel. The consequences of inaction could not have been laid out more clearly, or more cruelly. The Bishop's face went red in anger and offense. Sariel hid a smirk at the sight. As if fate itself wished to aid them, a tremor shook the city at that exact moment. Emilian and Nitika exchanged a glance.

"I see... Perhaps, this mist is causing the quakes bothering these poor people," Nitika suggested.

Emilian stroked his chin as he considered it. "Thought it was those big rats or whatever. But maybe Paras was wrong?" He turned to the Bishop, crossing his arms. "Shaking doesn't mean the city'll just explode though, right?"

"If it would help," Sariel interjected, "the reason I was late was because I went to investigate this claim myself when this young man here came to me for aid. This mist is eroding Everred as we speak. It's only a matter of time before the city crumbles as well. But I'm certain the *dutiful and successful* Bishop knows this already. After all, he's been monitoring the mist quite closely, haven't you, Paras?"

For a moment, words failed the Bishop. Like a fish out of water, his mouth faltered, searching for his voice amidst his own anger, offense and damaged pride. "You have some nerve, Surufel!" he snapped, pointing his finger at Sariel's indifferent face. "You expect me to evacuate an entire city over some pitfalls and the words of a dying boy!? You call that *evidence*, Inquisitor? It seems you don't live up to the stories."

He wouldn't let Sariel win. He wouldn't be known as the Bishop that ruined so many years of progress. The city could never be in danger under his rule! Sariel was simply attempting to tear him down; creating a villain to make himself a hero. But Sariel was no hero. *Paras* was their savior. He was the man that would cure magical overflow! He'd succeed where all the past Bishops had failed! Years of work. Years of cover ups. Years of stress and responsibility. There was no way it was going to end like this! Plastering a smile onto his face, the Bishop turned to his waiting audience.

"I can assure you this is nothing but paranoia," he declared. "We're already tracking down the pests behind the tremors!" The man gestured to Enoch, the young Scribe glaring at him from below. "As for this young man, you should know that he was here for community service after committing crimes in the capital. Can we truly trust the words of a criminal?" The Bishop fixed the circlet atop his head again. The headpiece sat crooked still. A smugness crawled its way into the Bishop's smile as he turned to Sariel, but his eyes were laced with a far less controlled emotion. Panic. "As for you, High Inquisitive Asaradel. Your imagination got the better of you, and you fell for this delinquent's tricks. I know your reputation, but not every powerful city is hiding some dark conspiracy. The success of Civionis comes from the hard work of its people; its leaders. Have you spent so long chasing lies that you can no longer trust the honest hard work of the common man?"

"We aren't lying!" Enoch shouted. "The city is in danger!"

The Bishop's eye twitched, his veins more prominent by the second. "Quiet, boy! Your illness has made you delusional." Arms spread wide, the Bishop's voice echoed loud, as if his next words were directed to the city itself. "This is Civionis! We work hard! We succeed! We adapt! That is the truth!"

C-C-CRACK!!!

CRASH!!!

FWOOOSHHH!

Like an erupting geyser, the water of lake Civionis shot into the air. The stone cracked, the platform falling to pieces beneath their feet. Half sank into the dark, icy waters swirling violently below, draining into the facility beneath them. The rest clung desperately, the supports straining but holding for now, despite the platform itself becoming more a wall than a floor.

With a guttural roar, Emilian leapt off one piece of debris to another, grabbing two of the recruits as he fought gravity through the strength of his muscles alone. His feet slipped against the stone, but his indomitable will refused to fail, guiding his feet as he jumped to the safety of an intact bridge. One recruit clasped her hands together, summoning crimson vines from the cathedral platform above. The vines wrapped themselves around the remaining recruits. They hung, suspended in the air as the seating area disappeared into the depths. Nitika found herself swept up by the clawed hands of Sariel's half-beast form, the Shapeshifter leaping gracefully up the few remaining stone slabs. He carefully handed her to Emilian before turning back to the wreckage, searching for anyone else still stuck inside.

Enoch scrambled for any kind of grip. The metal grate of the firepit slowed his descent for a moment, but the stone was still sinking as the support beneath cracked. The sound of the cascading water, the distant screams of those that had been trying to catch a glimpse of the ceremony from other platforms, they drowned out everything else. That is, until an angry, panicked shout grew louder, the Bishop sliding closer to him.

"Grab on!" Enoch shouted, though he might as well have been clapping with one finger for the amount of noise he actually made. Nevertheless, the Bishop noticed the outstretched hand, reaching out to grab hold. His skin was cold to the touch, drenched in the lake water. The sudden weight nearly dragged Enoch into the water with him. His fingers, beginning to bleed as the grate he was gripping dug into the skin, were the only thing keeping the two of them out of the whirlpool's deadly pull. But Enoch's strength was nearly nonexistent thanks to the illness that had plagued him the entire day.

"Don't you dare drop me!" Paras shouted.

"I... I've got you!" Enoch replied through gritted teeth. "I–" His strength failed. The Bishop screamed and cursed as he slid into the darkness. Enoch soon followed, the final support of the platform shattering from the force of another collapsing slab. Accepting his fate, Enoch closed his eyes, falling...

Falling...

Drowning...

Then... rising?

To his surprise, his very warm, very large savior was none other than Emilian. "Hold on tight, boy!" he shouted. The High Priest was hanging from a crimson vine far thinner than the others. As Enoch coughed up water, he wondered how the vine could even hold both their weight. The answer came from the glowing word seemingly stamped onto Emilian's chest. *"Light"* written in perfect typeset. No doubt the ability of one of the other recruits. Enoch held on as Emilian climbed back up to the safety of the bridge.

"Thank you," the Scribe said, joining the others. One by one, those in the vines were brought to safety by Sariel until everyone had been gathered. Everyone aside from Paras.

"Do you think we can save him?" Nitika asked. "Someone with a swimming ability, perhaps."

"Leave him to the Circlet Guard," Sariel argued. "I'd say this more than proves we were speaking the truth before." He thought back to what Enoch described in his vision. The second explosion that had destroyed the city right before he regained consciousness. "Another blast is coming. We need to evacuate as many as we can before then. Find a Consultant High Inquisitor, or even a Dispatcher. We need someone familiar with the abilities of the local Church workers. In the meantime, tell the Priests to start directing civilians towards Everred. It may be unstable as well, but it will be safer than here."

The group saluted, heading out to begin the evacuation. Sariel lingered a moment, noticing Enoch standing at the broken edge of the bridge. With a sigh, he approached.

"He's irritatingly resilient," he reassured. "I'm sure he and *Blade* were already long gone."

"I hope you're right" Enoch replied, before shaking off his worry. He turned back to Sariel, a determined fire in his eyes. "But we have our own job to do. Tell me what I can do to help. I want to save as many people as I can."

Sariel felt a twinge in his chest. Guilt once again reared its ugly head. He refused to let it linger. After all, he wasn't about to deny the last wish of a dying man.

Chapter 47

STILL HALF CAUGHT in a world of unconscious memory, Azazel felt a strange tugging. Something was... dragging him? Metal creaked and water lapped around him. In the distance, he could hear muffled cries and shouts. Mildew and metal mixed, forming an off-putting odor in the air. Azazel's eyes flitted open, seeing the flickering golden glow of adolium light above, and feeling the icy chill of the lake water below. This same water choked his lungs, and he began to cough it up.

"Oh, thank the Archangels, you're alive!" Seira said. The words strained from the effort it was taking to drag the drenched, armor-clad angel through the water pooled in the hall. Feeling Azazel pull away, she let go so he could double over and clear his chest. "Well, mostly."

Azazel's lungs burned. The steel envelope in his pocket protected the Illusion Paper, but the hidden waterlogged feathers still strained his back with their weight. The cuts he'd gotten in the containment chamber throbbed like his head, and ached like his heart.

Ramzel... That was Ramzel! the angel thought. *He was alive. He... He's gotten so big!* As the memory of what happened came flooding back, nausea assaulted his stomach. *He was in so much pain...*

Azazel could no longer deny the truth. He could no longer run. Ramzel had stood there before him, undeniably alive, and undeniably hurt. When they'd lost track of him years before, Azazel had believed the boy's death to be the worst outcome. Somehow, this felt far crueler. The young man's cries of pain, the desperation in his voice as he begged for answers, they chilled Azazel far worse than the water possibly could.

It seemed he hadn't left his past behind after all.

"Where are we?" he asked, "What happened?"

"We're still in the facility," Seira replied, leaning against the wall to catch her breath. "After I fought Iris, the whole place shook stronger than before. The hall started filling up with water and I almost drowned, but thankfully something broke those weird doors and drained the worst of it. Don't know if it was the flood or the Remnant that did it though."

Seira nodded to the damage around them. The door was stuck open, small, sporadic bursts of energy sparking out from the panel next to it. Debris swept up by the deluge piled up along anything wide enough to catch it. Noticing Azazel trying to stand, Seira moved closer, helping him to his feet. "I've been looking for you since. Found you floating around in here completely knocked out."

Seira looked him over now that her friend wasn't half-buried in lake water. She saw the scratches on his armor, the cuts on his face, the hollow look in his eyes. The weakened man she held in her arms was a shadow of the warm-hearted nuisance she loved. Her sun had found itself extinguished, eclipsed by whatever he had faced after their parting.

"Something happened with the Remnant, didn't it? When you went to find that guy in the mask?"

Azazel nodded, bracing himself on her arm until his legs found their strength again. "Yeah. I don't think I even have to tell you it didn't go well."

"*Didn't go well* is an understatement," Seira argued. Though Azazel was standing fine on his own, Seira's hands lingered. She couldn't help but feel he still needed support. "Did you at least figure out who he is?"

"I did..."

"Was it the answer you wanted?"

In spite of everything, Azazel smirked. "I knew the answer ever since I walked through that first door," he replied. Seira rolled her eyes, but a chuckle still escaped her lips as he called back her words. She stepped back to give Azazel some space.

"What's the plan then, now that you know?"

That wasn't an easy question to answer. The thought of forming a plan was enough to make Azazel dizzy. When the angel had cut ties, he'd done so in the hope that it would spare the young man a life of imprisonment, or a life on the run from the most powerful beings in the Three Realms. He'd be living a lie, but he'd be safe. However, somehow Ramzel had discovered the surname he'd never given. Somehow, he'd found Adina's family, *his* family. There was no denying that this falsehood, their gamble, had backfired.

What happened after you went missing? Azazel wondered. *Why are you carrying so much pain in your heart?* He already knew the answer, if not the full details that led to this outcome in particular. He was to blame. Like always, it was his fault.

Could I tell him what he is? Answer the questions he was asking? He... He deserves that much, right? The angel's hand wandered up to his helmet, before he realized it had been pulled away in the flood. Ramzel had seen his face, if only for a moment. He'd recognized him. He *knew* him. *I can't believe he remembered me...* Azazel thought. He'd always assumed his existence had been no more than a ghost in the young man's life. After all, their happy memories had ended with Adina's death. *He's been searching for me, for his family, all this time...*

A voice in Azazel's heart whispered softly. *Tell him,* it urged, *tell him everything. Help him.* But, no matter how badly he longed to heal his son, no matter how much he wanted to cleanse all the pain he'd seen in Ramzel's eyes, he knew he couldn't. Not here. Not now.

This place is filled with Spira tech. The Archangels must know about it. So, if I tell him here, if they're watching, they'd sentence him to death. Everything would be for nothing... But still, I can't just walk away and leave him in the dark again. Especially not if he's completed the pact with the Remnant...

The angel's eyes went wide. Buried under his painful contemplation, he'd nearly forgotten Ramzel's state when the Remnant had escaped. His protection, the lies, the pain, none of it would matter if he bonded with the Remnant. The Harbinger's Prophecy could not come true. He couldn't let it.

"I need to go back and find him again," Azazel said, answering Seira's question. Seira's brow furrowed.

"You can feel the Remnant's magic from here! That would kill you!"

"I think I can stop it." Azazel replied, "Or at least make sure it doesn't get worse." He could see Seira's body tense, frustration filling every flexing muscle. An argument built up in her chest, but only a sigh escaped when her mouth finally opened.

"Why did I expect anything else?" she muttered, accepting the inevitable. "Well, if that's your plan, I don't think even *I* have the tolerance to help. So, there's something else I need to take care of in the meantime."

Time was short, but Seira took a moment, looking over her friend one more time. His ridiculously dramatic armor; his wispy, white hair that took far too much effort to maintain, his encouraging smile that seemed to break down her defenses like a wave crumbling the walls of a sandcastle.

This'll probably be the last time I ever see him, she realized. Perhaps she'd swallowed too much lake water, because her stomach suddenly felt upset. Her hands moved on their own, reaching out to him. One last touch... One last moment to enjoy his warmth. His armor felt cold through her clothes as she pulled him into a hug, but his arms were as warm as always as he returned the embrace. Weakened as his light was in that moment, he was still her sun. After too short a time, she let go. "Well then, Greg, see you in Spira."

"Don't be ridiculous, that's way too far away." Azazel smiled once again, recognizing the sadness in the eyes of his friend. "I'll meet you and Dear in Everred instead."

The smile was infectious. Seira rolled her eyes, turning to hide her expression as she moved towards the door. "Hate to admit it, but I missed that stupid optimism of yours." Wading through the water, Seira left to begin her search. The doorframe felt freezing against her fingers as she stopped, hearing Azazel set out behind her.

"I'll see you there, Gregory," she whispered, hoping desperately that those words would be true.

Chapter 48

WITH EACH STEP, another second ticked away. His own clock could no longer be wound, but Enoch hoped to buy more time for the people in the city.

The once beautiful city platforms found themselves battered and bruised by falling debris. Quakes slowed the terrified crowds, the tremors now nearly continuous after the Remnant's escape. Red mist crawled free from cracks in the drained lakebed below, billowing like smoke from a fire. Though the Church did its best to keep the city from crossing the border of anarchy and panic, each crack in the mountain above eroded this fragile control a little more.

Enoch winced as a stone twice the size of his head crashed onto the nearby railing with a loud, echoing CLANG! A young girl clinging to his sleeve cried louder, the tears washing away the once drifting dust that had settled on her face.

"It's okay," Enoch said, unable to hide the fear in his own voice, despite his best efforts. In his mind, he asked himself what Cyrus would say; what Azazel would say. How would they comfort the frightened child? "We gotta keep walking, okay? Just close your eyes and follow me. You're okay. You're gonna be okay." He knew how hard it could be to rid oneself of horrifying childhood memories. The less she could see of her destroyed home, the better.

"I want my daddy!" the little girl cried.

"I know," Enoch replied. "He's probably already in the forest waiting for you. We'll find him. It'll be okay."

Leading the little girl beside him, Enoch headed to the closest terminal platform. From what he'd managed to understand through her sobs, her father had been on his way to work when everything started. She'd left their home to find him, and ended up lost and frightened in the crowds after it was crushed behind her. The Scribe prayed to the Archangels in his mind. *Help him survive. Don't let her lose her family. Please.*

Priests directed the crowd ahead. The tourists and Civionians carefully avoided the jagged, destroyed edges of the platforms. A lurch beneath them nearly toppled Enoch, his vision swaying along with the platform. Ahead, the face of the Priest taking charge grew a shade paler as his gaze caught the crumbling state of the supports below.

"Hurry forward, please," he ordered. "Make your way to the next platform in a quick but orderly fashion." The man turned to the bridge Enoch and the little girl had come from, signalling the Pilgrim behind them with a wave of his hand. The woman nodded, directing the rest of the evacuees elsewhere.

"This way. The platform ahead won't be stable for much longer," she instructed, far quieter than the Priest to avoid causing a panic. Not wanting to defy the Church or test their luck, the group behind Enoch followed her lead towards another exit point. Still close enough to hear her warning, Enoch stopped. *Should I go that way?* he wondered. *There are too many people on this path. If it's already unstable, we may not make it.*

"Here, let's follow them," he said, gently turning the girl around. "It'll be–"

CRACK! Another lurch lifted Enoch and the little girl high. The bridge that would have been their escape fell away in front of them. Or rather, it remained where it was as the terminal platform tilted up like a seesaw. Enoch reached for the railing, hooking his arm around until it nestled into the pit of his elbow. The little girl screamed. He pulled her close before gravity could wrench her from his grasp. He wouldn't let her fall. He couldn't let her fall! He'd keep her alive even if it killed him! After all, even if he wasn't already doomed, her life mattered more.

The platform continued to tilt, shifting around like a boat caught in a storm, trying to regain its balance on the remaining pillar straining beneath it. Like Enoch, some civilians were able to brace themselves on railings, benches, the firepit, whatever they could reach. Others weren't so lucky. Enoch watched in horror as they slid off the side, their screams growing fainter with distance before silencing too suddenly. Another shade of red joined the mists on the lakebed. Their deaths upset the balance once more. The platform tilted back the other way. Enoch's weakened muscles shook as he struggled to adjust to the shift, blood trickling from the cuts in his fingers, threatening to repeat his failure at the central terminal platform. The Bishop had slipped from his grasp. So many people had already slipped through the cracks. The guilt hurt more than his wounds.

"We'll make it," he reassured, tightening his grip on the little girl; on the life that he quite literally held in his aching hands.

"Daaaaddyyy!" the little girl cried out, tears falling from her eyes as she feared she may follow them. She continued to scream. Another joined her chorus as they lost their grip on the firepit, plummeting towards the two of them. Enoch released the railing long enough to dodge to the side. A painful *CLANG* of struck steel proved he'd moved in time. A sickening *CRACK* of a colliding skull moved his knotted gut into his throat, another life lost to the tragedy that had befallen the city. The person's body slipped over the railing's edge like a discarded ragdoll. The lost weight of them along with the others continuing to fall tilted the platform again, and Enoch's side began to burn as he and the little girl began to slide.

Crap! The railing's too far to reach now! he realized. He had to act quickly or they'd both join the bodies piling up on the lakebed. He looked for something to grab, something not destroyed by fallen debris, something not already taken by someone else. His hope plummeted ahead of them as he realized there was nothing. Just the sheer drop at the platform edge. *I'm sorry,* he thought, his voice unable to form the words. *I couldn't help you. So many people have already died and I... I can't do a damn thing!*

"Curls!?" A familiar shout drew his gaze. Basa watched in horror from the closest bridge, fighting through the fleeing crowd. Tory and Morael were close behind her. The golden-haired Pilgrim made it to the edge first, her eyes darting wildly to find a way to save him.

"Basa!" Enoch shouted, his hope rising from the depths. She had no magic ability, but she could still help him. She could help *her.*

I can do this. I can do this, he reassured. *But I have to focus and time it perfectly.* The edge of the platform approached. He leaned forward, managing to shift from his side to a crouch, still holding the little girl as tightly as he could. The polished stone platform offered little resistance, like sliding on an icy lake. "S-Sorry!" he said as he felt the edge of the stone. Then, with all of his strength, he pushed off the platform edge.

Their momentum shifted from down to out. Using that to his advantage, Enoch tossed the little girl towards the bridge. "Catch!" he shouted. The Pilgrim did just that, reaching out to grab the girl. Tory and Morael caught up behind her, grabbing her clothes to keep her from falling as well. Seeing that she'd made it, the fear faded from Enoch's mind, a smile forming on his face.

Please live, he thought, time slowing as the air embraced him. *I know it'll hurt, but, you can do it... You need to live.* Like a bird, he glided through the wind. The screams faded away. The mists below were like sunset clouds beneath the crumbling night sky. Enoch had so many regrets left unresolved. So many words unspoken. So many things undone. They felt like a stone, dragging him down by his gut. But he did his best to cast them aside.

I saved her... I saved her... I saved other people too. Maybe that's enough... Maybe I can meet them with pride now...... maybe...

Tears filled his eyes as billowing red filled his vision. "I've got you," his savior said, her arms wrapping around him like a hug as her momentum met his in the air. She hadn't expected him to toss the young girl to safety when she'd leapt secure his, but she wouldn't complain. One person was easier to catch. A forceful impact knocked the wind from Enoch's lungs, the greater part of their landing atop the broken column cushioned by Iris' own body. She reached out, grimacing as her fingers found purchase on the edge of the stone, keeping them from falling off the edge. Her clothes were damp, her heart racing as if she'd ran a great distance. Enoch's raced as well, the Scribe disoriented by the sudden rescue.

Above them, liquid stone solidified into a new support for the platform. Its source was a rather under-dressed man on the bridge, who'd had no time to find new clothes after Azazel and Seira had taken his before. With the hastily formed foundation holding the platform still, those that had managed to survive the teetering deathtrap were ushered to safety, urged to continue their evacuation.

"Th-Thank you," Enoch replied, looking up at the Circlet Guard Commander as the two balanced themselves atop the broken platform column. Her own gaze fell upon his branded arms, her stomach sinking alongside her city.

"Don't..." she said softly. "...Don't thank me." Though Enoch had yet to meet the woman in person, she was well aware of who he was. She held him close a moment longer, her words spoken in a hushed whisper. "You're going to die because of our actions, but you still stayed to help the people of the city. I should be thanking *you*."

With his magical overflow dulling his mind and strength, it took a moment for Enoch to process the words. *Our actions?* he thought. *So... she knows about the facility? Does she know about Azazel and Blade?* Any chance to ask passed too quickly to form the words, as the under-dressed Researcher leaned over the edge.

"Commander, just a moment. I'll form a bridge for you."

"Thank you, I appreciate it," Iris replied. A moment later, the two climbed back to the bridge. Enoch could see Basa comforting the little girl a short distance away. The golden-haired Pilgrim noticed him in the corner of her vision, smiling in relief.

"You made it!" she exclaimed. She began moving his way, before feeling resistance from the little girl's grip on her clothes. Responsibility replaced relief, and she took the little girl's hand instead. "I owe you some strong words for pulling a stunt like that, Curls. And you owe me an explanation for why you're still hanging around here." Gently, she lifted the little girl up, adjusting the grip with a soft bounce to make sure they were both comfortable. "That'll have to wait though. Leave her to me. I'll get her somewhere safe."

"Thanks, Basa," Enoch replied. He winced, the latest tremor causing the marks on his arms to flare. A red haze in the air heralded the mists arrival, drifting up from the bottom of the lake. Iris steadied him as he nearly lost his balance, and Tory arrived soon after, running over to Enoch after every civilian had made it off the platform. His cheeks flushed when he realized who it was that had caught Enoch.

"C-Commander Iris!" he exclaimed. "Thank you, he– I– uh..."

"Ah, you're Thistoron, right?" Iris said, her guilty expression fading with the Pilgrim's arrival. "This boy has done enough to help. He's in no condition to stay here. Can you carry him to the rendezvous in Everred?"

Tory blinked in surprise a few times, stuck on the fact that she knew his name. A quick shake of his head brought him back to the task at hand. "Yes! I mean, o-of course I can! Anything for you, ma'am! I mean, miss, I– Commander... Miss Commander." To follow orders and escape before he could make a bigger fool of himself, Tory gently lifted Enoch. Unable to salute, he nodded stiffly before taking off towards the bridge out of Civionis.

"W-Wait," Enoch said through the returning fog in is mind. "I... I can still help."

"Not in this state you can't," Tory argued, joining the crowd making their way to the bridge. "You've done enough. Commander Iris is here now, so don't you worry. The city's in good hands."

Enoch didn't have the strength to argue. All he could do was hold onto Tory, watching the city with bated breath, waiting for the second blast to hit; hearing the cries; picturing the people that had fallen to their deaths. *Just a little longer... Hold out just a little longer...*

The same words ran through Iris' mind as she looked over what remained of her beloved Civionis; the people that had taken her in when she'd escaped a living hell. Would the world return their generosity now that they were losing their own home? Now wasn't the time to wonder about that. Now was the time for action.

"Anyone capable of assisting in evacuating the House of Healing, report to me. We have sick and injured that still need help," she shouted, watching several Priests and Pilgrims hurry over. She'd been told the situation after escaping the facility. At any moment, the Remnant would burst and all evidence of their wrongdoings would be erased, along with the very city those sins were supposed to help. That would be the price they'd pay. She could sacrifice the city, the stone platforms, the cavern they called home. But she would fight to ensure that not a single other person would be claimed by the Remnant's magic.

Enoch would be the last.

Chapter 49

LIKE A HIDDEN garden in the middle of a desert, a small bundle of flowers sprouted from the walls of the Heart Facility. Blue hyssop growing defiantly amidst the sleek and artificial Spira technology. The pipes above it rattled loudly. An unpleasant metallic odor mixed with the piquant scent of the flowers. They swayed, as if anticipating the arrival of the man trudging through the water that now filled the hall. Bishop Paras scoffed in response. No matter how many times they'd attempted to weed out the pesky reminder, the flowers had regrown. It was quite irritating that he'd ended up here of all places. Surely the useless criminal had dropped him into the depths on purpose.

"What did I do to deserve this?" the man huffed, coughing up some of the water still tainting his lungs. His muscles ached. His brain pounded against his skull. "I'm a Bishop, damn it! A hero! Surely, I deserve better than crawling through this muck." He kicked some debris in frustration, earning a sore foot rather than any sort of reprieve from his anger. It had all started in this hall. If that damn Researcher had kept his mouth shut, Paras would be celebrating his success, the world freed from the threat of magical overflow once and for all! Instead, the city was quite literally falling apart around him, and he'd be a sacrificial lamb at someone else's victory feast.

Still grumbling to himself, Paras stopped as he noticed a figure down the hall, half-hidden in the dim adolium light. From the robes, he could tell they were a Researcher, but their mask seemed to have been taken by the flood.

"You there! Help me get out of this place. Inquisitive Asaradel is planning to ruin everything, and we can't let that happen. We need to find a way to keep the Citadel from learning about what's happened."

The Researcher didn't move.

"Are you deaf!? There's no time to waste! If this gets out, you'll be arrested for your participation. Is that really what you want?"

"Not even close," the Researcher replied, her voice dripping with malice. "What *I* want just became a lot easier to get."

Seira had never liked the idea of fate. If some force was pulling the world's strings, deciding everything that happened to them, then why would it choose to hurt them so badly? But for Paras to end up there of all places... Next to those flowers... Maybe the Celestials were that cruel after all.

A metallic shine caught the Bishop's eye as Seira drew her dagger, emerging from the shadows. "What are you—" Paras' eyes squinted as he wracked his mind, trying to recognize who this was. "Wait, you're that beast's sister, aren't you. The Equitervi girl."

"You'd call *him* a beast after what you did?" Seira growled. "Where were you standing when you gave the order to kill him? Here?" She took a step to the side, standing next to the control panel for the door. "Or here, maybe? Do you even remember?"

"You think I *wanted* to kill him!?" Paras huffed. "I made a decision to protect Civionis! He would have sacrificed the entire city for his own selfish delusions of justice!"

"You murdered a man that was trying to do the right thing!"

"Murdered!?" Paras' hand raised to point to his head, before realizing the golden circlet he wore so proudly had been lost to the waters. "You– None of you understand my situation! None of you! Ever since the secret of Civionis was thrown into my lap by the last Bishop, I've worked my fingers to the bone to ensure this facility's success. I didn't ask for any of this! I didn't ask to spend my time hiding every little thing I do! None of this is my fault! I'm a victim just as much as him!"

Whoosh. CLANG! A spectral dagger dented the pipe above Paras' head, the metal reverberating in kind. Seira pulled another from her blade without a word.

"Stop that! What do you think you're–" *CLANG!* "You'll be arrested for this! Executed! Iris will–" *CLANG!* Realizing there was no reasoning with the woman, Paras began trudging faster through the water, just as the final dagger broke through the steel. The mist released by the Remnant's escape had pushed the pipes to their limits and the overwhelming amount of miasma burst out from the pipe like a geyser.

"You're insane!" Paras shouted, shielding his face from the crimson air as he continued to push forward, struggling against the water. He coughed as the mist forced its way into his lungs, far stronger than any smoke he'd ever inhaled.

"*Insane* is thinking you could control the power of a Celestial. But magic is as untameable and unpredictable as any other living thing. If you hurt it, it *will* hurt you."

Sensing the mist released into the hall, the blast door began to shut. With the facility in its broken state, the movement was uneven, sporadic, but the door was nevertheless determined to do its job. Perhaps it took pride in its work. Paras waded through the water, pushing back against it to escape. He wouldn't die. Not like this. Not after everything!

"Damn you!" he shouted, veins bulging, eyes burning. "I hope you rot like your brother! You've ruined this city! It's doomed without me!"

"It's doomed because of you."

Seira wished the blast door had a window; something that would allow her to see his expression. Instead, she had to be content with the sound of the curses falling from his lips as the door closed. Not wanting to take any chances, she drove her dagger into the nearby panel. She'd seen them used to open the other doors, so surely this would keep it shut. Arcane sparks flew from the machine. It wasn't enough. She needed to release the frustration that had built up within her ever since she'd heard of Faolan's death.

Again, she stabbed into the machine, again and again, the sparks burning her hand. She could hear the Bishop slamming against the blast door, coughs muffled by the heavy steel. Until the rhythm slowed... the coughs and curses quieted... She almost didn't notice, too focused on imagining the panel was something else. Eventually, she stopped, breaths heavy, body shaking. She glared through the door, resisting the urge to fall to her knees. Instead, she staggered back through the water.

"You hurt me," she said, her voice shaking. "You hurt so many people. If you thought that wouldn't catch up to you one day, then you're crazier than I am." The Pilgrim sheathed her dagger, the metal scorched and warped from the heat of the panel. After taking one final breath to let the moment sink in, Seira turned around to find an exit.

"There you go, Fao," she said, tears forming in her eyes. "Now you can kick his ass yourself up in Spira. I'll join you soon enough, so make sure to take your time with it." The adolium lights flickered with the Remnant's flares. The rattling of the pipes calmed now that the mist had somewhere to escape to. Seira ran her fingers along the stone walls, wincing as it pressed against her burns. "Don't worry about down here. I doubt this place will be doing anymore experiments once the Remnant's done with it."

The cool water kept her head clear as she waded forward. She knew a collapsed tunnel ahead would lead her to the forest up above. While it didn't feel right to leave Gregory behind, she was certain it was only a matter of time before they crossed paths again. Even if she did follow, the Remnant would take her out long before she could reach him.

At the very least, she hoped she could find Dear before the end. It would be cruel to leave her alone in their final moments. "See you soon..." she said softly, tears running down her dirt-covered cheeks.

Chapter 50

THIS WAS SOMETHING only he could do.

The swirling magical energy in the containment chamber was like a biting, deadly blizzard. Even as an angel, Azazel could feel its strength, but he pushed forward nonetheless. At least, until something pushed back against his foot.

The empty beaked mask teetered on the ground as he moved away. The charred remains of its wearer crumbled at the neck, the ash carried off by its killer, picked up by the tempestuous air. Azazel clenched his jaw, holding back his guilt, fear and disgust. If he failed to stop the pact, would the Researchers escape in time? Would the Civionians be spared above? If the prophecy could be believed, no amount of distance would protect them from the calamity that would follow. He couldn't fail.

The chamber itself was unrecognizable. The metal that had once been stairs, pipes and machinery jutted out like thorns. The water had been driven into the halls, pushed back by the cyclone centered around the shattered prison in the center of the room. The adolium lights flared between bright and brighter still. The power rattled his teeth, his bones, his very soul. Every step through the waves of energy took more strength than the angel had left to give. But he couldn't let himself be deterred.

I need to reach him.

Ramzel wasn't difficult to find. His cries of pain could be heard over the ringing in Azazel's ears, the roaring winds fighting against him. The young man was on his knees in the Remnant's container. The remains of the now broken glass clung stubbornly around him like a shattered frame. The immense cage seemed far emptier without the Heart inside. Ramzel looked so small in comparison, nails digging into his scalp, tears trailing down his cheeks, trembling like the ground around him. The crimson mist covered his body, or... perhaps it was coming from within it? It was difficult to tell in all the chaos.

I need to stop him.

The shaking ground tried to force Azazel back. *"You missed your chance,"* it seemed to say. *"You rejected us. You will only hurt us."*

"Ramzel!" Azazel called out through the storm. The tempest swallowed his voice. The angel winced as the crimson mists clung to his armor, the steel shaking in resonance. The metal glowed red. It spiked out, thrashing like a frightened, cornered creature. The golden light of his own magic found itself swallowed by the Remnant's as he tried to regain control of it, to stop the armor pulling him back.

"Stop fighting me, Ramzel!" he shouted. "I'm trying to help!"

"Help?" the storm replied. *"Why would you help now? What worth does your kindness even hold? It could not save her. You never saved us. Everyone, all of them... they only hurt us."*

Was this voice the Remnant? Was it Ramzel? A combination of both? Azazel couldn't tell, but that didn't lessen the piercing pain of the words both whispered and shouted by the wind in his ears. Determined to make it through this, Azazel's body flared gold. He placed a hand over his heart, the moment of power just enough to break the armor, splattering it across the ground like spilled paint.

"I'm sorry," Azazel replied, pushing forward once again without his armor. "I... I didn't mean to hurt you, I swear."

"Intention..." The word felt like acid. *"Intention does not erase the damage that has been done. You wanted to save the world... You wanted to cure them... You wanted to save yourself."*

"I did..." Azazel admitted, thinking back to the night they'd made their dreadful decision. The beginning of it all. When he'd seen Ramzel sleeping so peacefully in his bed and felt only the loss of the woman he loved. "I should've fought harder for you. I should've... should've at least felt more guilt for doing what needed to be done. I'm sorry."

"Needed?" the wind asked. *"You would not fight for him?"* Azazel felt like he was trying to walk through a stone wall, his son so painfully close on the other side. It wasn't Ramzel pushing him away, was it?

"It's not a fight I can win. Not on my own. Not as I am now." Azazel felt the steel envelope in his pocket pulling him back; the rings on his hands... all but one. He cast them aside, cutting the tethers holding him down. "His existence threatens more than just humanity and Terrael. If Spira falls, the angels fall with it. They'd never allow it." With thoughts of his promise at the forefront of his mind, Azazel tried to remove the Illusion Paper from the envelope, only to have the unstable, restless steel stab through his hand.

A cry of pain joined Ramzel's, and the envelope fell to the ground.

"I can't fight all of Spira alone." Azazel admitted through gritted teeth. "I'd die, and then they'd slaughter him too." The wind gave ever so slightly. Like trudging through ocean waves in a storm, Azazel stepped forward, closer and closer to his goal. With the steel envelope too far behind, the air behind the angel shimmered, revealing his wings. "But he'll die now if you don't let him go. I... I just want to help him, please give me a chance!" He pushed against the wall of air and magic. He fought. His muscles ached. Blood trailed down his fingers, the drops caught in the maelstrom. And then—

A breath...

A break in the tempest...

Azazel nearly stumbled forward as the pressure pushing against him gave. Though the storm behind him continued to violently rage, the air was still within the borders of the cage. The surrounding silence only made Ramzel's agonized cries all the more painful to hear.

"Ramzel..." Azazel said softly, voice hoarse from shouting over the wind before. The moment had arrived. The moment to decide.

Redirection?

Honesty?

Cruelty for the sake of the greater good?

The urgency of the situation was lost in Azazel's mind. The angel found himself distracted by just how much his son had grown. His hair used to be wavier, more like his mother's. Now, it shared his own smoother texture, cut short, the bangs swept to the side. His hands were larger too, understandably considering the young man's age. But

Azazel remembered how small they'd once felt, holding onto his finger so gently that he worried the slightest movement might hurt them. His face was sharper, the softness of youth stolen by the years he'd missed. Beneath the bruises left by his interrogation, the young man's more delicate features caught Azazel's eye, similar to Adina's, and undeniably reminiscent of his own.

More concerning were the wounds on the boy's body. Azazel had lived long enough to know the scars of battle. What had happened in his absence? What had Ramzel endured after they'd lost track of him? What had Azazel condemned him to by running away?

Azazel walked forward, noting the mist reaching out to Ramzel's body like a kiss from a flickering flame. Slowly, the angel knelt in front of his son, his armor gone, his hand bloodied and injured, the bottom of his wings brushing against the floor. He forced himself to look, despite how much it hurt to see him. He couldn't run away. Not this time.

But... what words did he need to say? There was so much he'd missed, so much at stake, so many lives on the line... He'd attempted to feed the lie before and that had only seemed to make things worse. He knew what Sariel would suggest. The broken glass scattered around them would end the threat in an instant. An ugly truth. Azazel caught their reflection on its surface, recalling the moment the cage had cracked, recalling Ramzel's words.

"I need to know! I need to know if I killed her! And... I need to know if that's why you left! Please! Just tell me!"

How long had Ramzel carried that burden? No... his son deserved better than that. He deserved answers. Azazel owed him at least that much. He reached out with his uninjured hand, hesitating before taking Ramzel's in his own. He could feel the Remnant's magic flow into him like magma burning his mind. But then, the feeling faded, crashing against the protective barrier of his angelic nature. The connection seemed to lessen Ramzel's pain, and the young man's cries quieted. His face still twisted and contorted, the overwhelming magic still present and persistent in its desire to form a pact. Ramzel held onto this savior's hand, gripping it tightly as his only lifeline in the chaos. Azazel felt tears stinging his eyes.

"Ramzel..." he began, "I... I'm sorry. You deserve better than this. Better than half-assed answers given way too late." He saw Ramzel's eyes open in recognition at the sound of his voice. Swirling crimson had swallowed the whites and irises, turbulent beneath the tears not yet shed.

"Dad?" he asked. His voice strained against his throat, desperation and pain nearly muting the word.

"I... Your father was a greater man than I am, even if he was a complete idiot," Azazel replied. "But I knew him, once. I knew your mother too."

Perhaps it was exhaustion, or perhaps the lack of sight made the young man more susceptible to deceit, but Ramzel stayed calm as he heard the half lie. He took a moment before tightening his grip on Azazel's hand.

"What were they like?" he asked softly.

"Your father was a blacksmith," Azazel answered, "He was optimistic, eager, blinded by the wonderful blessings in his life. He... did some stupid things, but he still loved his family dearly."

"...and my mother?"

"She was the most amazing person I'd ever met... Your father thought the same. She was kindhearted, creative. She was a seamstress that took pride in the clothing she made. She took pride in *everything* she made. ...Her eyes were the same as yours, actually. Red like a sunset."

Thinking back on the life he'd once had, Azazel found his story caught in his throat, nearly overwhelmed by the sobs that wished to overtake it. He swallowed his sadness. "She passed away... It was magical overflow that took her. But she was happy in her final moments, and I know she wouldn't want her son to mourn her. She'd want him to feel loved. She'd want him to create and express himself. She'd... want you to smile." Though he held back his sobs, tears still broke through, wiping away the grime coating Azazel's face. "We were close friends. So, I know she'd want me to help you now."

"Was it me? Did I kill her?" Ramzel winced as a flare from the Remnant flashed through his body like a bolt of lightning. His grip on consciousness was beginning to slip, but he needed to hold on, he needed to hear the truth, no matter how painful.

Azazel froze, so encompassed by his own guilt that the words caught him off guard even after he'd heard them before. "I... Why would you think that?" he asked.

"My– ...*her* family. They said I was the reason she died; that they blamed me and my dad."

The angel cursed his old relatives in his mind. Blaming him for her death was acceptable, but to place the blame on her own child? They were as awful as Adina had always said.

"You didn't kill her, Ramzel. You..." Azazel sighed. The pain in the young man's voice; the suffocating guilt that mirrored his own; the greater good faded away, replaced by the words of a father to his son. "You were just a baby. We didn't know anything at the time, and that ended up hurting us in the worst possible way. The pregnancy played a part, but don't you ever *ever* blame yourself. If the fault has to lay on anyone's shoulders, it should be mine. If you need to blame someone, blame me. I'm the one that couldn't save her."

Azazel realized his mistake, but it was too late to take it back. He waited in silence for Ramzel's response. Rather than anger, Ramzel took a moment, processing his father's words. After a deep breath, his words came out vulnerable, soft, like the question might shatter the moment if spoken too harshly. His hand gently squeezed his father's.

"Why won't you say it?" he asked. The Remnant's power felt like water filling his lungs, drowning out his voice and mind. "Your... last name is Veramor too... right? So why– *AaAAGH!*" A surge of magic coursed through his body. He doubled over, caught by Azazel before he could hit the ground. The swirling red in his eyes glowed brighter, the Remnant's voice joining his own. He struggled to keep his own mind, repeating his question again.

"Why can't... you say... it..." Consciousness finally slipped away. Even asleep, his body winced and flexed in pain. Azazel held him close. Fear dug its claws into his heart, and the angel turned to the swirling storm around them.

"Please! If you don't stop, you'll kill him!" he shouted, "You're too powerful. You need to let him go! Sever the bond!"

Like a falling stone plunging into water, the storm slowed. After a second, as if the Heart were thinking, the crimson mist left Ramzel's body, flowing into Azazel's instead. Instantly, Ramzel's body relaxed, an exhausted serenity washing over him. Once again, Azazel felt the painful force of the

Remnant in his mind, only for the waves to break against the shore of his divine blood.

I was simply granting his wish, the Heart replied, its voice reverberating through the angel's mind. *To let him go, would that not hurt him more?*

Even more than the piercing pain of the Remnant's initial connection, those words felt like a bullet through the chest. With a gentle touch, Azazel brushed the hair out of Ramzel's face, replying to the Remnant with his thoughts.

Probably. But it's for his own good. I know it hurts, but if the Archangels found him, they wouldn't rest until he was dead. They'd protect Spira at any cost. Ramzel's agonized cries sounded through his mind, a fearful chill trailing his neck. *This is the better option, painful as it is. At least this way he gets to be free.*

With a nostalgic smile, Azazel watched over his son. He wondered if that was true; if Ramzel would be able to let things go with questions still unanswered. Now that they'd found him, they could monitor him again, but could things truly end so conveniently? Doubt lingered in his thoughts.

"You turned out pretty stubborn, huh?" he said quietly. "Sorry. That's probably my fault."

He turned his mind back to the Remnant, its waves of power continuing to crash against his soul. The ground shook once more, the tremor feeling almost muted, as if the Heart was fighting against its own outburst. *You're about to break, aren't you,* Azazel thought. *Please... could you hold on a little longer, so I can get the city to evacuate?*

The Seer... he saw what was to come. The silver angel and the monster's blade already lead the people to safety.

Relief released the tension in Azazel's body. Anger gripped it shortly after. He was glad the people might be saved, but that meant Sariel hadn't brought Enoch to Se-myaza. Unfortunately, there was nothing he could do about that now. He stood, carrying Ramzel in his arms. Pain shot through his injured hand, but he simply gritted his teeth. Ramzel had endured far worse.

Wait... the Heart said. To Azazel's surprise, it almost sounded afraid. He held back, allowing the Remnant to speak.

A pact cannot be formed with an undying, but could you stay? ...Or will you leave again?

Azazel's expression darkened, a smile painted over his pain. "I can't stay, it would destroy me," he replied aloud. "But I'll still be with you, even if I'm not by your side."

The turbulent waves left his mind, the crimson mists reforming into the Heart's angelic silhouette. It nodded slowly. The miasma continued to swirl around the cage, but the movement felt less sporadic, as if chained to the Remnant's body. Flags tied firmly in a hurricane.

With a heavy heart, Azazel carried Ramzel through the spiked surroundings. He stopped a moment to pick up the steel envelope he'd dropped before, his wings vanishing before he used them to fly back up to the door above. He let out a soft chuckle, feeling a sense of nostalgia. Ramzel was much larger now, but he felt himself transported to the past, carrying his tired son to bed. The memory was kind; far more pleasant than the grim reality. But there was no time to reminisce. The Remnant could only hold out for so long, and he needed to get his son to safety.

Chapter 51

THERE WERE MANY exits to choose from. The Heart's turbulent flares caused cave ins all across the facility. Despite this, Azazel somehow found himself at the very exit he and Seira had entered through. His legs shook from the effort it took to wade through the water. His wings and injuries stung in its icy embrace. But with no way to know how long the Remnant could hold itself back, he couldn't afford to rest.

Something slimy brushed against the angel's burned away pantleg. He flinched before noticing Seira's cloak in the water, waiting to be rescued as well. As a Pilgrim, he'd be quite poor at his job if he ignored such a request, so he placed the cowl over his shoulder. *Please tell me you made it out too,* the angel thought to himself, hoping his thoughts might reach her wherever she'd ended up.

High above, the red branches of the everred trees swayed. The angel spread his wings, flying to the stubborn upper trees still lodged into the edge of the pit. On the off chance someone waited at the top, he climbed up the final branches the old-fashioned way. The dirt of the forest floor clung to Ramzel's dampened clothes as his father gently lifted him up. His own outfit met the same muddy fate, but with Death looming above with her scythe, he wasn't about to complain about a bit of filth.

Will I make it in time on foot? Azazel wondered, carrying Ramzel once more. His gut leapt back into the pit as he realized their chances were slim.

Trot trot trot trot. Trot trot trot trot.

The sound of hooves approached, a blur of blue and black emerging from the forest shade. "Took you long enough," Seira said from Dear's back. The two stopped next to their friend. Seira held out her hand, wavering as she noticed the unconscious young man carried in Gregory's. Though Ramzel's mask had been left in the halls below, she was smart enough to piece together who it was her friend was trying to rescue. She was also perceptive enough to notice the similarities in their appearances under this masked killer's disguise. A rumble in the ground shook her from her thoughts. "C'mon, lets go. This place feels like it's about to fall apart."

A weight lifted from Azazel. The corners of his lips lifted too, but the smile was as fleeting as the time they had left. "You're right. The Remnant is going to take out half the forest any second now." Carefully, Azazel placed Ramzel up onto Dear's back instead. "Three people won't fit. He can't exactly run right now, so I need you to take him instead."

Seira steadied Ramzel, but her attention remained on her friend. Through some miracle, he'd survived getting close to the Remnant, but even his luck had its limits. "I'm not leaving you to die," she argued.

"I'm not asking you to." Azazel took a step back, fighting the urge to hold his son just a little longer; to say a proper farewell to his friend in what might be their final parting. Even with eternal life, there never seemed to be enough time. He forced a smile. "I'm great at running when I need to, but I can't if I need to take care of him." As gentle as a breeze, Azazel took Seira's hand in his. "Take him to Simerum, south of here. You should both be safe there."

Pressure built in Seira's chest. Pressure shook the ground below. Azazel handed her the wolf-fur cowl, ending the argument before it could begin. She held the matted fur in her hands, the feeling familiar, yet uncomfortable. With a sigh, she glared at her friend. "Will you meet us there?"

"I will."

"...If you're lying, I'll track you down and kick your ass."

"If I was lying, I'd deserve it. Just get there safe, please. Both of you."

Seira lifted Dear's reins, letting out her reluctance in a heavy sigh. The *thwip* of the reins, gentle as it was, felt far more painful to her than Dear. "Make sure you run as fast as you can," she shouted over her shoulder, the words a mix of a prayer and a threat. The three of them disappeared into the forest once more, leaving Azazel behind.

I'm not planning on running, the angel thought in reply. Azazel risked a moment to pray for their safety. The Archangels wouldn't hear him, but perhaps *something* out there would. Some power beyond even them. He checked that the coast was clear before spreading his wings. Both water and blood dripped from the feathers onto the soil, and he cast off as much off as he could with a heavy flap. Everred Forest fell away beneath him, the clouds above hiding his flight.

He ascended, higher and higher. *How far will the explosion reach?* he wondered. *Will everyone make it in time?* The ground itself seemed to shrug in ambivalence, the forest lifted by the sheer force of the explosion building beneath it, and then...

Silence...

The world held its breath....

The shaking stopped......

BOOOOM!!!
The facility, the mines, the city, crimson light swallowed them all. Like blood spreading through water, it expanded outward, consuming the forest itself. Seira could feel Dear's heart racing, her lungs and hooves pushing their limits. "C'mon girl, keep gong!" she encouraged, holding Ramzel tightly to keep the boy from falling. They had to make it. They had to survive. How far would the blast follow? The crimson magic matched their pace, but threatened to over-take them. Fever burned the Pilgrim's body.

Just a little farther. I can't see Faolan yet. Not when he's counting on me.

Azazel watched the destruction from above. An entire city, a mountain that had stood for centuries, the forest known across the realm for its beauty, all claimed by this celestial power; all gone in mere minutes. Though the outer reaches of the forest were spared destruction, the crater Civionis had been built within had nearly doubled in size. Deafening rumbles and cracks drowned out both thoughts and sounds as the side of Mt. Morus crumbled and fell. The very wind choked on the dust cast into it. The rivers fled as the force drove the water away. The trees swayed like grass in the breeze, attempting to escape but condemned by their roots.

Even Spira, hidden within its walls, heard the annihilation of Civionis. Even Diapogeum shook as the surface crumbled above it. Even the Archangels shivered at the power of the half-Celestial that came undone.

Chapter 52

AZAZEL HEARD THE survivors before he saw them. A short distance from the edge of the newly formed crater, screams and sobs felt akin to silence following the booming, deafening rumbles of Mt. Morus' fall. Tears cleansed the dusty remains of the mountain. Survivors stared with unseeing eyes, the world a clouded blur of debris and pain. Church workers did their best to maintain order, to locate missing people, to treat injuries, to reunite separated families, to organize the survivors, to clear debris, to reassure the frightened civilians, to keep up with the never-ending, never-ceasing work. Their shouts only added to the chaotic cacophony.

Azazel landed nearby, the dizzying dust clouds a blessing to him despite the confusion they were causing. He wandered through the crowds, fighting the tears he longed to shed for the people suffering around him. His pain had caused theirs. Their pain was now his own. Their pain would not heal easily, nor would Ramzel's if he'd survived. He needed to catch up to him and Seira and find a way to fix the damage his absence had caused, but first there was someone else he had to find. Someone with less time to spare.

In his memories the injured Priest that had found him at the House of Healing grabbed his collar once more, grasp as weakened as his echoing voice.

"This is... your... fault..."

Azazel refused to close his eyes, taking in every pain filled cry and frightened child.

I know...

Ahead, like a beautiful melody breaking through the discordant tuning of an orchestra, a familiar voice emerged from the crowds. Iris stood surrounded by hurrying Church workers. Her cloak was torn from her fight with Seira. Dust coated her hair so thickly that its pink hue was a full tone lighter. The threads of her uniform frayed, caught and unravelled throughout the evacuation. A young boy, the very same that Enoch had reached out to in his vision, clung to her leg before she gently directed him to Basa. The golden-haired Pilgrim nodded, smiling at the boy before leading him off to find his parents. She'd already reunited one little girl with her father, but there were many more children separated by the disaster.

As she delegated the people around her, Iris' gaze met Azazel's. His golden jacket, far lighter with its steel threads cast aside in the facility, still stood out in a crowd. The Circlet Guard Commander hesitated just a moment. The facility was gone, but if he'd survived, their secret could still be revealed. With the Bishop's location still unknown, the blame for all of this could fall on her shoulders in his place.

Iris turned away, focusing on the task at hand. The people of Civionis took priority. She couldn't take back what she'd already done, but she could work on mending the wounds she'd inflicted. This was probably for the best, seeing how Azazel had his own responsibilities to focus on.

Where is he? the Pilgrim wondered, searching through the frightened survivors. *Where is Enoch?* He wandered, heartbroken, carrying his guilt as if his wings had turned to stone. His injured hand ached, blood soaking through the cravat he'd turned into a makeshift bandage. He couldn't stop to replace it. The Healers had to tend to the others first. He had to find Enoch first. He had to help him... He had to apologize...

Eventually, a flash of silver shimmered in the reds and greys. "Surufel!" Azazel cried out, rushing to his friend. "Where's Enoch! Have you seen him? Is he still alive!?" Sariel turned at the sound of Azazel's voice, expression neutral as always.

"That's High Inquisitive Asaradel, Mr. Veramor," he replied, subtly stepping aside to reveal the recruiter Nitika behind him. Azazel slowed to a halt, bowing in greeting.

"R-Right, sorry High Inquisitive," he corrected. "And a fellow Pilgrim, it seems." Nitika smiled tenderly.

"Familiarity is welcome in such a dire situation. Don't you think, Surufel?" she asked. "If you two are close, there's no need to hide your friendly faces for the sake of formality. Or for me." Nitika held out a hand to Azazel. The Pilgrim did the same, shaking hers with less grace than he usually carried for such introductions.

"Nitika Deomicis," she said. "But we can save proper greetings for another time, Mr. Veramor. If you're looking for the young Seer, I believe he was brought to a clearing that way." With an ethereal grace, Nitika pointed southward. Azazel's gaze followed. "His vision saved many lives. If he is still holding on, give him my thanks."

"Of course. Thank you, Miss Deomicis." Azazel took a step to leave, heel digging into the soil a moment to look over his shoulder. "Sorry we couldn't meet under better circumstances."

"Save your apologies. We survived, did we not? There will be time to speak later." Noting a commotion nearby, Nitika nodded her head in farewell. "For now, I should focus on performing my duty as a Pilgrim. I trust you'll do the same when your business is finished, so until our paths cross again…"

The Pilgrim took her leave. Azazel and Sariel did the same, heading south to find Enoch. Both men knew to hold their tongues. The words that needed to be said were not meant for just anyone to hear.

As they reached the outskirts of the makeshift meeting point, Azazel grabbed Sariel's shoulder with his good hand, still walking at his side. "You were supposed to bring him to Semyaza," he growled.

"He had a vision and decided to take action," Sariel replied. "It's likely the only reason the evacuees made it far enough away. Would you have preferred the citizens be massacred by the explosion you failed to prevent?"

The sudden strength of Azazel's grip caused the Inquisitive to wince. Yet no defense or argument followed. Sariel sighed.

"So, where is he?"

"With a friend. I'll meet up with them in Simerum once I've talked to Enoch." As Azazel said the Scribe's name, he could see Tory through the trees up ahead, keeping him company. Azazel stopped, his stone wings holding him back.

Once he'd followed his friend's gaze, Sariel folded his hands. "I see. I trust you'll give me the rest of the details after you're finished?"

"Y-Yeah, for sure." Azazel's voice was distant. His half-hearted reply caused Sariel's eye to twitch, but the High Inquisitive held his tongue. He watched as Azazel rushed forward, following shortly after at a far slower pace.

"Gregory!" Tory exclaimed with a pained smile. He nudged Enoch's shoulder. "See! He made it out fine, just like I said."

If Enoch had had the strength to tense his muscles, his body would have relaxed. The Scribe was currently seated, supported by a large rock behind him. A small creek flowed by just a few feet away, its bank offering a softer seat than the branches and pebbles beneath the trees. The water was far lower than Azazel remembered it being, its source cut off by the collapse of the mountain.

Sariel cleared his throat. "Pilgrim, there's work to be done at the evacuation site. Leave the boy to Mr. Veramor for now."

"R-Right, High Inquisitive." Tory bounced to his feet, saluting his superior. He paused as he passed Azazel, speaking softly. "I don't think he has much time left, but he's been asking for you for a while. I'm glad you made it."

"Thanks for taking care of him."

"Of course. Basa and Morael stuck around long as they could, but..." Tory couldn't finish. The destruction of their home, the tragedy that had befallen his people, the endless cries for help in the crowds of survivors with hardly a second to breathe... Saying the situation aloud felt too damning; like it would condemn them to reality rather than a nightmare they could wake from.

"Tell them thanks as well," Azazel replied, patting Tory on the shoulder. Tory nodded, relieved at Azazel's insight. Steeling himself, the energetic Pilgrim hurried to follow

Sariel and assist how he could. Azazel, meanwhile, knelt at Enoch's side.

"Hey tough guy, how're you holding up?" he asked. The question felt redundant. A single glance was enough to know he was at Death's door. The sweat from his fever fused with the dust on his skin. The curls of his hair clung to his face like ivy. Each breath felt far too short, far too shallow.

"I've been better," Enoch replied weakly. "Glad you... made it out okay..." the Scribe's glazed over eyes scanned their surroundings, the movement stuttering as he realized Azazel was alone. "Did Blade make it too?"

"He did." Azazel swallowed the pain in his chest, the feeling becoming a pit in his stomach. This moment felt too familiar. The same exhausted stare. The same unbearable fever. The same arcane marks, a different hue but morbidly glowing nonetheless. Yet again, the man that could never stay quiet found himself at a loss for words.

"It's a shame the explosion happened..." Enoch said softly. "The city was so beautiful."

"It really was..." Azazel sat down next to the young man, feeling a discomfort in his pocket as he did. Curious, he reached inside, finding the cause. Enoch's watch. In all the chaos, he'd forgotten to give it back to the Scribe after picking it up in the facility. He held it in his hand a moment, recalling the story of how the young man had gotten it; recalling that he'd soon be telling a father about the death of his son. His grip on the metal tightened, eyes closing for just a moment to fight back tears.

"Here. I'm guessing you've probably been missing this." The angel gently gave the watch to Enoch. The Scribe's eyes lit up like embers in the wind, before fading just as quickly in his exhaustion. Still, he ran his fingers across the engraving, finding a moment of peace.

"Thank you." The words barely made it out, the situation beginning to sink in. Enoch's frantic heartbeat matched the rapid ticking of his pocket-watch. A fearful clarity filled his mind, fighting the fever and stealing his weakened smile. "Tell Cyrus I was happy when I went." His knuckles went white as he clung to the watch. "I... I'll be seeing my family again."

Unable to hold it back any longer, Azazel's guilt crawled up from his heart, falling as heavy tears. "Enoch, I'm so sorry," he said, "I wish there was something I could do. That I could cure it somehow; help you."

The Scribe shook his head, smiling at his friend. "You did," he replied simply. "Back in Courciel, I wasn't living... At least now I know I got to do something meaningful before the end, right? And I have meeting you to thank for that." Burning and clammy as it was, Enoch opened his shaking hand. "Thank you, Azazel."

Azazel took Enoch's hand in his. The angel could feel the Scribe's racing pulse, his trembling fear. Despite the painful memories resurfacing at his touch, he would stay. Enoch wouldn't be alone in his final moments. He wouldn't allow it.

Enoch's grip tightened, the Scribe trying and failing to hide his fear. Trying and failing to express his gratitude at the angel's company. To have one's death arriving within the rotation of the second hand... the feelings coursing through his feverish, burning blood were nigh impossible to describe. He'd heard that death from magic caused a person to burst into arcane flames. *Would it hurt?* the Scribe wondered. *Or will it be warm, like Cyrus' hugs?* His painted smile broke for just a moment, as he realized he'd never get to hug Cyrus again.

I wish I could... he thought sadly, *just one more time...*

With this regret in his mind, the second hand of Enoch's watch finished spinning. The unwound clock silenced along with the beating of Enoch's heart.

Chapter 53

SILENCE...

Like every other time he'd drifted through the world in his dreams, Enoch was met with silence. The same silken threads and endless shadow. Only this time, the world remained still around him. He didn't sink. He didn't drift. He didn't fall. A single, blue thread held him in place, tethering his heart to the ethereal darkness.

Am I... having a vision? Enoch wondered. *I must have passed out before I–* He tensed, remembering where he'd been, what he'd been fearfully awaiting.

Right... I'm dead.

It was really over. He'd never share another cup of cocoa with Cyrus. He'd never smell Namaah's baking wafting through his apartment window, or greet Noah as he headed to work. He'd never people watch at his favourite café. He'd never file documents for Inquisitor Haven. He'd never get to travel with Azazel. He'd never do anything ever again.

It was over...

Everything was over.

His stomach sank. Was this all he had left? An eternity floating in the silent emptiness? Cursed to endure the

void-like world he'd run from for almost all his life? Alone...
so alone......

*"How rare to find one conscious at their thread cutting.
You are a unique Seer indeed, dying one."*

Or perhaps not as alone as he thought. The gentle, feminine voices overlapped in his mind, like multiple people speaking in near unison. Enoch searched for their source. Finding nothing but the same blue, supernal threads, he wondered if he'd only imagined it. But a warm light emerged from the darkness with the blinking of his eyes.

Though they'd spoken in the common tongue, this newcomer was without a doubt not human. In fact, Enoch was certain they were neither demonic or angelic in nature either. But then... what in the Realms could they be?

Nearly ten times his size, a barely humanoid creature stared back with a presence commanding reverence and respect. Their four grand wings fused the shape of a dragonfly's with the patterns of a moth's. Four more, much smaller in size, sprouted from the back of their head like a crown that matched their regal posture. Their entire form shimmered and shifted with the colors of autumn. In the dim light of their surroundings, Enoch couldn't tell if the leaf-like robes trailing like swimming silk were part of their body or adorning it. Four horns sprouted from their head like antennae. Four almond shaped eyes glowed like a hearth beneath them. Four insect-like arms sprouted from the woven armor on its torso, two folded calmly in front, two holding a scythe of shifting light.

The creature blinked, leaning in closer. The patterns decorating their black and gold face reminded the Scribe of both a skull and the head of an ant. With the creature closer, he noticed dim floating lights around them, fading in and out of existence like stars fallen from the heavens. He realized, upon closer inspection, that this being didn't have a mouth. Then he realized, much to his own horror, he couldn't open his own.

A scream built in his chest, unable to escape it. Then, realization washed over him like moonlight emerging from behind a cloud. Enoch sensed the creature's purpose. Its scythe; *her* scythe; this being appearing then of all times. He was in the presence of Death herself. He should have felt terrified. He should have felt the urge to beg, to be spared so he could live his life after wasting too much of it. But her presence, the hypnotic lights surrounding her, the ethereal beauty to the fluid movement of her wings and robes... the panic numbed. He felt hypnotically calm. He heard a promise.

"I will be gentle. There will be no pain. You will join the world, dying one, and Enoch will be no more.

I'm ready... he lied, closing his eyes. *I'll see my parents again in Spira... my sister... everyone from back home.*

He prepared himself, repeating this reassurance over and over to soften the blow. But rather than a slicing scythe, Enoch felt a rush of air, a sudden solid form beneath him. Like a fish caught in a net, he was raised upward. The Scribe opened his eyes, shocked to find himself sitting in the center of a hand larger than any he'd ever seen. Or rather, something hand shaped. Instead of skin, the limb was made of woven, shifting threads. Each finger was as long as Enoch was tall. He turned to find its arm, slender for the scale of its body, and just a little too long to feel human. He followed the limb with his eyes to the gargantuan humanoid figure lifting him up to its missing face.

"A Seer that succumbs to fate. I have quite literally seen everything in this world, but it still finds ways to amuse me, fleeting as those moments have become."

It spoke with many voices. Countless shifting threads made up its body, tendrils emerging from this collective like a tattered cloak. In the corner of his sight, Enoch could swear this web continued for all eternity, but this endlessness eluded him when he focused his vision. From its faceless head, two antlers sprouted and spread to the heavens like the branches of a tree. Starlight hung beneath them. Its size was dizzying. The ancient aura it exuded would be suffocating if Enoch had breaths to take. Each time the young Seer thought he'd found the edge of the figure's form, it shifted, unknowable and incomprehensible. Lost in the shimmering starlight that surrounded it.

"I thought you less a fool. Will you truly forfeit your life before it has even begun, young Seer?" the entity asked. The shifting threads slowed a moment. The woven being's body shifted, as if it had chuckled. "Though, I suppose you cannot answer that, can you? Not here. Not now."

Enoch clung to the creature's hand as its form suddenly changed, matching the size of Death. Even like this, Enoch could still fit in the being's gentle palm. He watched, silent and bewildered, as the woven entity turned to its insect-like companion. He watched, awestruck and reverent, as it kneeled before her.

"My eclipse, my ancient end, keeper of my vow, seamstress to my threads. If I may ask with all the humility eternity can grant me, gift this Seer a second chance."

The lights surrounding Death shifted a pinker hue, subtly dancing as they faded in and out of view. Her hand reached out, lifting the woven being's gaze by its chin. The threads shivered slightly at her touch.

"How interesting, Woven One," Death purred, *"You would rob this life of its value? Its purpose? Diminish it?"*

For a moment, the Woven One stayed silent, losing itself in the song of her voice, the grace of her touch, the blessing of her presence. But its guest caught its gaze, still nestled in its palm. The Woven One stood, its head lifting to see the canopy of threads above them; the luminescent heavens; the lesser source of light in its existence. Death waited, listening with a curious flare in her eyes as it spoke.

"I have begun to wonder," the Woven One finally answered, "What is it that truly gives a life meaning? Purpose?" It lifted Enoch, observing the frightened Scribe, so young, so naïve, so full of potential. "We Celestials have our roles. The dying have their end. Origin has their children. But I would like to see what conclusion this one might come to. What path he will take."

Death tilted her head, her claws trailing the thread bound to Enoch's soul, his lifeline. *"It must mean much to you, to deny me my purpose in exchange for your answer."*

"One less raindrop in the endless ocean."

"One of many that have been denied to me. Denied by your deals and interference."

Enoch felt the threads beneath him constrict. The Woven One's many voices silenced as it receded in guilt. Then, it relaxed. The billowing of its cloak slowed, like a broken spiderweb drifting in the breeze. "...I grow tired of eternity," it admitted. "I believe a change is needed."

Death's wings fluttered. Her muted autumn hues grew brighter for an imperceivable moment. *"And you believe we can be afforded this luxury?"*

"I believe they should be given a chance." The Woven One gently slid Enoch from his hand. The Seer braced himself for a fall through the darkness, only to find himself suspended once again. The Woven One stood tall, awaiting Death's answer.

The Celestial existed in silence, her starlight drifting alongside her thoughts. Then, she lowered her scythe. *"Out of respect to you, my old friend, I shall hold my blade. But know I shall only do so once. Should this Seer perish again, my purpose will be fulfilled."*

The Woven One bowed its head, tension releasing from its body. It watched in admiration and gratitude as Death's form split into starlight, fluttering away like a swarm of moths. Enoch tried to watch her go, only to find the light vanishing with a blink of his eyes. Beside him, the Woven One changed its size once more, its slender, unnaturally long silhouette now only slightly taller than the young Scribe. It stepped forward, disks of spiralling light appearing under each step like turning wheels, or ripples in water. Carefully, its hand hovered by Enoch's lifeline.

"It is beautiful, is it not? They always are for Seers, but yours is especially bright." The Celestial ran a finger down the thread. The fibers of its own body lingered somewhat, smaller pieces trailing the lifeline even after it had pulled away. "You seem eager to cut it short, but do you not wish to see where it leads? I cannot help but wonder what lives you might influence. It is almost exciting, to not know the answer."

With a light flick of its finger, it strummed the lifeline. Light flowed through it, every color of the rainbow. Ahead of them, it branched like an endlessly growing tree. Though the Woven One had no eyes, the threads of its body seemed to hold a brighter sheen at the sight. "If I am permitted to share my wishes, I do prefer this path to the others." The threads continued to spread, reaching out, connecting to the canopy above to form a beautiful web like shattered glass. If Enoch could speak, he'd still find himself at a loss for words at its beauty. Even I, writing this now, cannot fully express the sight confined to the languages known to us. The closest one could get would be to say that the wonder in Enoch's eyes at a mere glance of this visual poetry was enough to move even a Celestial.

"You respect the angel Azazel, do you not?" The sudden surprise in Enoch's expression gave the Celestial its answer. Though, it had known long before regardless. "If you follow in his footsteps and become a Pilgrim, well..." It waved its hand. The web vanished, leaving only the abyss once again; the cold, dark present. "Perhaps it is best if I do not say too much. After all, your path is yours to choose."

With one hand, the Woven One ruffled Enoch's hair. The other began to shape the air nearby, pulling at unseen threads. Two more hands sprouted from the Celestial's body to assist. "Best of luck, little Seer," it said, ending its invisible work with a tug at Enoch's lifeline. The Scribe felt himself pulled forward, the thread tight in his chest. "I look forward to seeing which fates you choose."

With these final words spoken by the Woven One's multitude of voices, Enoch's thread pulled back. Like a fish caught on a hook, Enoch felt himself pulled upward, higher and higher, until his mind could no longer keep up. His eyes rolled back. His head fogged, and he lost consciousness, leaving the Celestial alone below in the world of silence, threads and endless shadows.

Chapter 54

THE PILGRIM CARRIED her friend's future away from the wreckage of her crumbling past. She wouldn't fail him. She *couldn't* fail him. Not after leaving him behind.

The mist had bit and clawed at Dear's hooves as they'd fled the Remnant's burst. *We'll make it. We'll make it. We have to make it!* These thoughts ran through Seira's mind. These thoughts ran through Dear's mind. No thoughts ran through Ramzel's, only peaceful sleep in the Heart's absence. Even his own inner voice dared not ruin the respite.

Once the wall of destructive magic gave up its chase, Seira had set her sights on Simerum. By train, the trip took hardly any time at all. A couple hours of seated relaxation and you'd find yourself at your destination. On foot, and occasionally deerback, it would take far longer to navigate the normal forests that surrounded what was once Everred. But Gregory had set the destination, and Seira would reach it no matter what. She would see him again. He'd promised they would.

The greens and browns of the evergreens were gentler than the warm tones of the everreds. The birds chirping and watching weren't mutated by magic. No jewel tones embellished the fur of the fauna. The buzzing energy of the Heart could no longer be felt in the air; only the faint buzzing of insects, and the lapping of the water. Seira listened. She sat by the pond, allowing Dear to quench her thirst, lamenting the loss of the beautiful forest they'd both called home. She ran her fingers through her friend's blue and black fur. "Hope you got your fill before we had to leave," she said softly. "Can't go back now."

If Dear was feeling any remorse, she'd chosen to drown it in muddy water. Seira left her to her thoughts with one final pat on the back, turning to Ramzel instead. The resemblance was uncanny. The same pale hair, the same delicate features. Laying asleep under her cloak, Ramzel looked so peaceful.

Is he a younger brother? she wondered. *He seems too old to be a kid. And Greg doesn't seem the type to keep one hidden either way.* The Pilgrim thought back to their time together. Back at Gardieu, studying and training to earn their licenses. Back to working together on jobs after they had. Back to the nights that felt less lonely with him at her side. Story after story would fall from his lips, catching her up on whatever she'd missed in their time apart. But now that she thought about it, no story had ever mentioned his family. Were his parents alive? Had he been separated from his blood? By tragedy? By choice? Had he thought himself alone, as she was now? Is that why he'd chosen the life of this boy over his own?

Seira sighed, lifting her cloak off of Ramzel. His identity didn't matter. If he was important to Gregory, then he was important to her. All that mattered was getting him to Simerum alive and well. After all, what else did she have left? Her home was gone. Her brother's soul had passed on to Spira. The Remnant had been freed, for better or for worse. She still had Dear, at the very least. She had her work, though the emblem hanging from her hip felt heavier after the events that had transpired in Civionis. She found herself wondering if the life of a Pilgrim was truly right for her. Could she really work for the people that had sentenced her brother to death? That had violated a Remnant for the sake of their own comfort?

The truth was that corruption had seeped into the Church like rot in a tree. Though kindhearted people like Gregory worked within their ranks, people like Paras would still use its power to their own ends, to enact cruelty in the name of progress or protection. Faolan had seen this truth and lost his life fighting it. Now Seira couldn't help but wonder if she should risk her life to pick up his cause; she wondered if the Church would prove too powerful a foe to overcome.

For now, she shook those thoughts aside. Such a decision was too big to make in haste. First, she needed to focus on the task at hand, then she could decide her next step. Quietly, she donned her cloak once more, kneeling down to lift Ramzel back onto Dear.

Sssssssssssssss... An unnatural scent in the air clung to the inside of her lungs, foul like a corpse left to fester in the desert sun. Seira's eyes watered as they searched for its source. A light purple haze appeared in reply. *Did the Remnant survive?* she thought, covering her mouth and nose with her cloak. *No, it isn't the right color... This has to be something else. An attack!?* The fur-clad Pilgrim prided herself on her perception. But even Seira struggled to see her surroundings. All she could smell was death. All she could see was purple haze. All she could hear was the numbness in her ears as her body failed her. The world existed at arm's length. Her thoughts were forced to swim up the stream of consciousness to her mind, barely perceivable through the effects of this fog.

"Is it even worth recovering him at this point?" a young man muttered, buried in the mist. "The location is right, but he doesn't look alive to me."

The purple lenses of the attacker's goggles caught the light as he approached. A grey, fabric mask covered the lower half of his face, muffling his voice somewhat. It looked as though nature had reclaimed the young, cobalt demon's body. His horns sprouted from his magenta hair like thick, weathered oak branches. Similar branch-like markings lined his visible skin like tattoos emerging from his body. Half of a dark-green shawl offered at least a small relief from the cool temperatures, mostly covering a small, woven straw box hanging at his side. The very box that was leaking out the corpse-scented mists. The demon's fingers tugged absentmindedly at the straw, his other hand holding his chin. "Well, I guess he's breathing at least. Probably wishing he wasn't in this particular gas though."

Mustering her strength, Seira drew her dagger, only to feel it knocked out of her hand by another attacker. The woman holding the disarming umbrella was several inches taller than the 5'3 demon; a fact that he adamantly refused to acknowledge. Her dark-grey, curly hair was pulled back into two small, round pigtails, peeking out from beneath a black and yellow beret. The roundness of both matched the roundness of the glasses sitting on her head, unable to aid her vision thanks to the large goggles that had taken their usual place. A thick, soft, yellow bandana sat tied around her face. A corset pulled the fabric of her black, puff-sleeve shirt close to her body around the waist. Flowing from the bottom, a slightly frilled skirt covered the top of her tights, just barely avoiding getting caught in the shrubbery branches. She nudged Seira aside with her foot, the movement taking little effort as the miasma muted the Pilgrim's strength. She hung the umbrella on her arm before moving her unmistakably human hands, speaking in gestures.

"Yeah, yeah. Calm down, Sparky," the blue demon replied with a roll of his eyes. "This one's not deadly. Can't say the same about whatever I collected before though." He placed a hand on his hip. Nodding to Ramzel, still lying unconscious in the grass. "Either way, we've got him. Pay the toll and let's get outta here. I'll handle the Pilgrim."

The human woman, Sparky, nodded, drawing a silver pouch from her pocket before crouching beside Ramzel. Meanwhile, the demon moved to Seira still struggling in the soil. The Pilgrim coughed, her lungs desperate to rid themselves of the painful fog. Next to her, the demon's tail swished through the dirt. He sighed, reluctantly pulling back his claws to slash her throat. A barbaric and messy way to handle things, but he'd left his quicker poisons behind for this particular mission. "Don't blame us for this," he said. "You're the one that chose to wear that emblem."

The claws came down. A shadow fell over the demon as Dear's hooves followed. The creature's eyes were glazed and red, her movements unpredictable. Her snorts and grunts warned the demon to retreat. He didn't need to be told twice, only avoiding being trampled thanks to Sparky pulling him back by his shawl just in time. He fell into the dirt, scrambling back in a panic. "Lillith's sword!" he swore, glaring at the angry beast. "Damn thing almost killed me!" He pulled farther back as Dear continued to protect her friend. Sparky took the opportunity to toss several coins from the bag into the air. She snapped her fingers. The coins shattered, golden light drifting down from above. In an instant, all three of them crumbled, leaving only the remains of the coins in the dirt.

The demon was gone.

The woman was gone.

Ramzel was gone.

With its source magicked away, the gas began to fade along with its nauseating odor and disorienting effects. Seira gasped, drawing in the clearer air like a fish thrown back into water. Tears attempted to flush her eyes, and she clung to Dear as she struggled to her feet. "Damn it!" she shouted between coughs, staring at the golden powder sitting where her charge had been moments before. "Damn it, damn it, damn it!"

Gregory had trusted her with the boy's safety. He'd asked her to bring him to Simerum, risking his own life to ensure it happened. What would she tell him now? The truth? That she'd failed the one job she'd been given? She kicked at the soil, and Dear followed suit with a single stomp of her hoof.

"Who in the Three Realms were they?" Seira asked once she'd calmed down, her throat hoarse from the gas. She had no answers, and hardly any clues to go off of. With a sigh, she steadied herself, mourning her failure. After everything Gregory had gone through to get to him, he'd vanished so quickly. Perhaps, the world was balancing the god-like luck Gregory had relied on until then. Or perhaps it had decided to offer her new purpose as she questioned her path.

"I'm sorry, Greg," she sighed. "I promise I'll help you track him down." After wiping her eyes, Seira took a moment, running her fingers through Dear's fur to calm her friend down. To calm herself as well. "Even if you didn't make it, I promise I'll find him."

She'd lost her own brother already. Though she didn't know who this boy was to her friend, his importance was clear. He had to be found.

She would find him.

Chapter 55

OVER A WEEK had passed since the destruction of Civionis. Azazel had waited restlessly in Simerum. He'd seen Seira emerge from behind the hill at the city's edge. He'd seen the shame in her eyes as they'd met his. Pain, both physical and emotional emanated from her words as she explained what had happened. Anger blinded Azazel once she finished. Guilt clawed at his heart. Relief made him sick to his stomach. Once again, his son was in danger.

Once again, it was because he'd ran away.

Had Sariel not been there to stop him, emerging from the shadows to hold the Pilgrim back, this story may have followed a much different path. Such a strong reaction would draw unwanted attention, putting so many at risk with such a small chance at success. At that moment the trail was cold, but Seira offered to search. Sariel did as well. They could find him again, but only if Azazel could control himself. To ensure this, Sariel sent him to Mt. Hermon.

"You brought Enoch there, did you not? He still hasn't had his final burst. If through some miracle, Semyaza saves him, don't you want to be there for him when he wakes? You owe him that much."

Reluctance still lingered in Azazel's mind, but he stayed nonetheless, trusting his friends to find Ramzel. He had no other choice. That's what he told himself.

The peak of the mountain that the angels called home rose from a sea of clouds. The evening sun sank into their depths, its upper half painting them in warm-toned wonder. Basking in this glow atop the stone was the Watchers' Palace in all its glory. It had once started as a small stone keep meant to protect them from the elements, as well as the prying eyes of the humans. Over the years, new wings of various styles and materials had been added. Flying in, one could almost tell exactly where each angel's space ended and the next began from the architectural choices alone. Pointed spires reached for Spira on one end, elegant buttresses kept another end grounded, bland stone walls offered practical protection in between. Grand bridges with arching supports connected the various keeps and corridors, crossing the small lake pooled in a dip on the mountaintop. Its water lapped against the sheer stone that sat beneath the palace.

Perhaps the most beautiful addition was the annexed greenhouse. It gleamed with every color of the rainbow, stained glass sections dividing the clearer panes that allowed the plants inside to bask in sunlight. All kinds of trees and shrubbery surrounded it outside before trailing down the hill to meet the lower lake.

At that moment, Azazel followed its base as well, pacing enough to polish the path beneath his feet. On occasion, the angel would stop to sit on the stone bench that had become his bed. He wouldn't dare stray too far from the small, circular garden outside the entrance, lest Enoch wake while he was gone. His mind swayed between hope and fear. One moment, he would cheer Enoch on from a distance, then his thoughts would drift to Ramzel, and he'd find his wings spreading, his pacing bringing him closer to the mountain's edge. But he couldn't act. Not yet. *Not yet.* Not until they'd discussed things. If he made the decision alone, it would end in disaster; or at the very least he'd convinced himself to believe that.

"Heavens' sake. You haven't been sleeping out here since your return, have you?"

Azazel jumped as Sariel emerged silently from the trees. The pale angel passed through a small steel gate, eyeing Azazel from head to toe as if he'd stumbled upon a mud-covered dog begging to come inside. Azazel hurried to tidy himself up, though little could be done beyond flattening a few knots in his hair and wrinkles in his clothes. The rest of his mess would take far more effort to fix.

"I left a few times! I was with him in Semyaza's room at first, but after he patched up my hand, Sem said I was 'too noisy' and that I was 'distracting him'," Azazel explained, quoting with his fingers for emphasis.

"You can hardly blame the irritability," Sariel replied with a thoughtful tilt of his head. "A human is certainly a step up from the usual lost or injured animal." There was no doubt in Sariel's mind that Azazel's banishment from the greenhouse was more out of spite than a matter of noise. Mt. Hermon was meant to be a secret. For centuries, even the people most dear to them hadn't set foot on this peak. Had it not been for the Scribe's unique condition, Semyaza would have certainly turned Enoch away, and reprimanded Azazel with a worse punishment than sending him outside.

"Still," Sariel continued, once again eyeing Azazel's disheveled state. "You needn't confine yourself to the garden instead. You have your own rooms; you might as well use them. At this rate, it may be your smell that wakes him, even from this far."

"I don't—" Azazel cut himself off, taking a deep breath just to check. The wince and silence that followed was proof enough that Sariel had won the short-lived argument.

"At least bathe before you meet with him. For the boy's sake." The High Inquisitive's gaze turned to the sunset. "Or continue being stubborn. I'll be heading back to Gardieu shortly, so I'll be too far for it to be any concern of mine."

"Heading back already, huh?" Azazel gripped his arm, annoyance shifting to a vulnerable, quiet curiosity. "Any news of Ramzel? Did you find him?"

"Not yet," Sariel replied, genuine remorse making it through his usually neutral expression. "I've been searching for leads, but I've also found myself dragged into the clean up for Civionis."

The news deepened Azazel's guilt and worry. He receded into himself, attention wandering to the flowers as he couldn't bring himself to meet the High Inquisitive's gaze. "I see... Sorry for adding more to your plate. I can look myself if—"

"You will do nothing of the sort," Sariel interrupted. "An Inquisitive searching for a missing murderer is one thing, but there would be no reason for you to be involved as a Pilgrim. We can't afford to let anyone see you lose your composure around him." Sariel pinched the bridge of his nose, feeling a headache coming on. There were still too many questions left unanswered. "We were lucky that the Researchers' masks used archasite to lessen the effects of the Remnant. Spira couldn't scry on you there. But if they do beyond the stone's protection, they may learn the truth of your connection to him. You know better than I how quickly they could find him if they chose to start looking."

"I know, I know. It's just so... *frustrating*." Azazel's shoulders dropped, pulled down by what felt like chains. "He's out there, Sariel. He's in pain. Something happened to him after he disappeared from Maylis' orphanage, and I was just running around without a care in the world, completely oblivious. I... I want to help him."

A kind heart doesn't absolve you from consequence... Sariel thought. "That is precisely why you can't get involved. Not yet. And especially not after what happened in Civionis. An entire city has been wiped off the map. Even the Archangels will be on high alert."

"Sorry..." Azazel repeated, the intangible chains pulling his shoulders even lower. "I'm sure me sticking my nose into things didn't help."

"Well, at least you've admitted it this time." Sariel's permanent frown deepened at the thought of the paperwork still waiting in his office. Absolutely none of the clean up should have been his responsibility, but his direct involvement meant he was best equipped to assist, leaving him drowning in double the work. Triple, if the secret search for Ramzel was added to the ever-growing list.

"Your meddling did at least give me some leads. Verifying Spira's involvement in the facility is nigh impossible after the Remnant wiped it all out. And the Researchers that managed to survive have been brought in for private questioning. Even I've been unable to speak with them. That information would have been lost to the blast without you 'sticking your nose into things'."

Despite the attempt at gratitude, Azazel's brow still furrowed. Sariel followed his distracted gaze to the greenhouse, the Sculptor's thoughts no doubt focused farther into its glass walls. He sighed. "Distracted again... You seem to be quite taken by him. Though, he's rather young, don't you thi–"

"It's not like that," Azazel interrupted, quick to put a stop to that train of thought before it could depart. "I just... The kid needed– ...*needs* help. He has a good heart, but can't seem to keep himself out of trouble."

"Sounds familiar."

Azazel blushed, fingers fiddling with his earing at his friend's teasing. Sariel used the pause to gaze at the green-house a moment longer. "You were in Civionis for his probation, correct? I heard you were even given permission to overrule the city's visitation limits?"

"Yeah, staying too long is why he got sick in the first place."

Sariel held his chin, his mind beginning to uncomfortably buzz. "I'll admit, when I looked into his case, I was surprised the two of you were given so much freedom, considering the severity of his crimes. And the location was even more concerning. Why choose Civionis? Even if its cause was kept secret, everred fever itself was not. Why force him to stay if it would make him ill? Unless that was the intent from the start..."

Azazel's face went pale. "You think someone was *trying* to get him killed?"

"I think it's possible that you aren't the only one that's taken an interest. If he wakes, it may be wise to watch your backs. If they wished him dead, they may make another attempt. If they didn't, then I can't help but wonder what their motivations could have been."

In the corner of his vision, Sariel noticed the faded color of Azazel's cheeks, his friend's wings pulling close to his body. *Perhaps this wasn't the best time to share my thoughts...* he realized. Though the movement was somewhat stiff, he placed a hand on Azazel's shoulder.

"At the very least, his actions in Civionis shouldn't earn him any further unwanted attention. Commander Ocudolis has been given the role of hero in his place." Sariel's posture shifted, his explanation recited with practiced familiarity. "Apparently, her and I learned that the toxic mists in the old mines had come dangerously close to a large adolium deposit, and evacuated the city just in time." The pale angel's jaw clenched, his next words more spat than spoken. "And the great Bishop Paras died protecting the recruits. Placing the city's future before his own life. We've yet to find the body, but I'll admit, I hope he was burned along with that reckless facility. After all, he likely wouldn't face consequences if he did survive."

"He was that bad?" Azazel asked. "Seemed pretty harmless when I met him."

Sariel took a deep breath to compose himself, despite his demeanor hardly shifting in the first place. "An ego worse than Kokabiel, and a reckless idiot to boot."

"Ah. He was that bad." Azazel nodded slowly. "But what about the recruiters that saw Enoch? Wouldn't they know the truth?"

"They believe he's dead." Sariel's brow furrowed, his anger at Paras shifting to a mix of concern and curiosity as he recalled the order given to keep Enoch's involvement to himself. The High Inquisitive dismissed the itch in his mind with a wave of his hand for now. "It works in our favor. If his name is left out of things, yours is less likely to come up as well. Though, I'll still do my best to cover for you if it does."

"Right. Thanks, Sariel."

"If you're actually grateful, you can prove it by plucking every thornweed out of the gardens at Gardieu. They've needed cleaning for a while."

Just the thought of the job made Azazel hands prickle, but he nodded nonetheless. "R-Right, I can do that, yeah."

Sariel raised an eyebrow. "That was sarcasm. I'm surprised you couldn't tell."

"Oh, for the– How am I supposed to tell when you don't change your tone at all!?" Azazel rolled his eyes, noting the slight amusement in Sariel's at his frustration. Realizing his friend was just purposefully messing with him now, Azazel shut his mouth, failing to hide his flushed cheeks.

Having had his fun, Sariel's slight smirk lowered. Entertaining as it was to fluster the man, there were more important things to discuss before he left. The pale angel sighed, his crane-like wings shifting as anxiety got the better of him. "Still though, we're lucky the Church wants the incident hidden as well. But I can't help but worry. Iris saw you. She knows you and Ramzel were both in the facility. If she tells anyone–"

"She won't."

Sariel sighed. "Azazel, I know you try to see the best in people, often foolishly, but you can't ignore the possibility that–"

"Trust me, Sariel." Having been interrupted twice, Sariel scowled before noticing the usual optimistic glimmer in Azazel's eyes had dulled to the point of nonexistence. The Inquisitor held his tongue.

"Anyone that admits they saw me there would be admitting they know about the facility too." Azazel explained. "Seeing how badly the Church wants to hide the fact this was their fault– or, uh... *mostly* their fault, admitting you know too much would be like giving yourself a life sentence, or worse."

"And if they find out anyways and decide to use you as a scapegoat?"

"A well-respected Pilgrim turning on the Church in an act of terrorism? Still not a good look."

"And if she tells them about Ramzel? Surely, she knew he was there if he was locked away in their cells."

"What do you expect me to do about it, Sariel?" Azazel snapped. "Find Iris and make sure she can't talk? That *is* your go to for anything inconvenient, isn't it?"

The High Inquisitive's lips tightened. Sariel sighed once again, carefully dusting off the bench opposite of the Pilgrim's before sitting. He watched Azazel avert his gaze, trying to compose himself. Sariel knew. He knew the others saw him as a heartless beast, but... "Sometimes, the best course of action will be the one that feels the most unpleasant. But I promise that everything I do, I do to protect the Watchers, to help us."

"We came down here to help *them.*"

"And to do that, sometimes we need to make hard decisions. But I know *you* don't need to be told that things aren't so black and white."

Azazel winced at his cutting words. Seeing that he'd managed to dent the man's stubbornness, Sariel continued, his tone the slightest bit softer. "If the Archangels find him first; if they learn a pact was nearly made; you know they won't hesitate to take away the freedom we've been granted. The children wouldn't be spared. If that luck of yours runs out..."

"I know..."

"I'm aware you know, but it bears repeating. If Iris becomes a liability, we'll need to act." A twinge filled Sariel's stomach, ignored by the angel beyond a slight decline in his gaze. "Even if it's Ramzel that puts us– ...puts the *world* at risk, I'll have no choice but to intervene."

Azazel could only nod in response, muted by the injustice of it all. It was cruel that Ramzel would be hunted over nothing more than what he was. What he *could* do. But with the scale of the repercussions, Azazel still found himself hesitating. He watched as Sariel stood, dusting off his silver robes. No doubt he was about to leave, but before he could...

"Sariel," Azazel said quietly. The High Inquisitive turned to listen, but Azazel held back a moment longer, searching for the words. The question teetered on the edge of his tongue... it was one he didn't want to ask, but needed to say. Despite the path it would send him on, he couldn't run anymore.

"Enoch still hasn't woken up, so I'm sure we'll be up here for a bit... Once you're done with the paperwork, could you come back?"

As he listened, Sariel stretched his wings. "I can see if I have the time. If I come and go too often people may get suspicious. Especially with the preparations we still need to finish for the next semester." Though his words were a longer way of saying 'probably not', a curious glint still shined in the angel's eye. "Why? Is there something else you wish to discuss?"

"There is." Azazel's wringing hands relaxed ever so slightly. "I think it's time we talked about the plan we made back then. Cutting ties felt like the best option; like the easy way out. But I think it's pretty clear it wasn't enough to protect them. You said we need to make hard decisions, and that's one we all need to make together."

"I see..." Sariel fell silent, his neutral expression leaving his thoughts and feelings a mystery. After a moment, he nodded curtly. "I'll make sure to not make you wait too long then."

"Thanks. And take care of yourself, Sariel. Try not to bite off more than you can chew."

Another deafening stare answered Azazel's concerned request, ending with yet another raised eyebrow. "You're one to–"

"Yeah, yeah, I'm one to talk, I know. Shush."

Tap Tap Tap

A soft knock at the garden gate caught both angels' ears. Moving gracefully as always, Sariel opened it, revealing a creature no taller than his shin. The small figure's form was fluid, vaguely humanoid, like a constellation caught in a squishy, translucent night sky. It waddled over to the two men, holding up a note with two nubby hands. Azazel watched as Sariel crouched down to take it.

"Oh! One of Kokabiel's Lumins, huh? Guess he couldn't come talk to us himself."

"He's likely cooped up in his studio again. Unless Penemue visited, I doubt he's talked to anyone for months." Sariel patted the Lumin on the head, earning a swirly, glittery blush in return. It held its cheeks, swaying happily.

"Fair enough. What does it say?"

Sariel read the paper silently before handing it to Azazel. The Sculptor read it, first with passing curiosity, then with tears of relief. The force of air from his wings as he leapt over the garden fence nearly toppled the Lumin. Tiny sparks puffed from its head as it waved an angry nub Azazel's way. Another pat from Sariel managed to calm it, and it watched with a blush as Sariel smiled, heading down the path to find a better place to take flight.

Curious as I am to learn how he survived, I'll have to leave this one to Semyaza, the High Inquisitive thought, taking one last breath of clean, mountain air. *If I make her wait, she might just leave before I can get any answers.* The clouds below drifted calmly, lazily. For a moment, Sariel wished he could be blessed with such a simple existence. But those thoughts had to be cast aside and forgotten. He spread his wings, leaving the palace behind with nothing but a windy farewell embrace.

That facility, the machinery from Spira.... It had to be her. No one else would be so reckless...

With thoughts of reckless people running through his mind, the angel's stomach sank once more. Miraculous as it was that Enoch had awoken, things would have been far simpler if he hadn't. Their stagnant existence was beginning to shift.

He had a feeling this wouldn't be the last time he'd have to cover things up for that troublesome duo.

Chapter 56

ENOCH'S SECOND CHANCE smelled of flowers.

Not just flowers... The bitter scent of herbs accompanied the gentle fragrance. Soil, hearty and damp. Small metal fences, faintly rusting. Clay pots, infused with an earthen, ancient aroma. The perfume came from the many plants decorating the small room. Growing from fenced off gardens on the floor, climbing up the frame of Enoch's stone bed, sitting on quartzite shelves built into the walls. Though, perhaps calling them walls could be overgenerous when three out of four were more window than stone. The final was entirely glass, its green-tinted surface fogged by humidity and time. A muffled melody of trickling water and twinkling windchimes serenaded from the large room on the other side.

Dull, black stones of various shapes and sizes hung from the ceiling, carefully suspended by beige thread wrapped around each one. Faded, well-used books sat between the various potted plants, along with small stone figures, not a crack to be seen beneath their blankets of dust. A desk and chair matched the quartzite theme in the corner, ferns and ivy draping their leaves across the carefully sorted papers as if claiming the space for themselves. The mortar and pestle were theirs. The small glass squares, similar to the screens in the Heart facility, belonged only to them. They refused to share even the framed note sitting atop the polished desk top, too far for Enoch to read. Not that he would have. He was never one to enjoy intruding upon the personal lives and secrets of others. Though perhaps given the situation, he would need to make an exception to figure out exactly where he'd been brought after Civionis.

He'd never seen the room before. No doubt such a beautiful place would have left an impression, and even if it hadn't, the small, constellation-like creatures waddling about certainly would have. These creatures, called Lumins, panicked as Enoch sat up, seeking cover behind whatever they could find. Leaves far too small to cover even their diminutive size, the bottom of the sheet draping off the bed, their own stubby hands. Disoriented, Enoch gave them only a moment of his attention before directing it to his arms instead, piecing together his past. *Was all that a dream? Or did I really just die?* The arcane patterns were still etched into his skin, but time had doused their glow, the brand of death now more scar than omen; faded but undeniably real.

He thought back to the Woven One, to Death, to the world of void and threads, to the beautiful glow of the future that might await him. His beating heart was proof enough that he'd eluded Death's scythe, but it still felt like a dream. All of it felt beyond his comprehension, beyond understanding.

It was real... but what does that mean?

Soft chimes pulled his focus back to the present. The small creatures watched with... well, they had no eyes, but the stars in their bodies twinkled with a distinct curiosity. "Did you guys bring me here?" Enoch asked. The Lumins shook their heads. Some pointed to the wall of glass. Most of the finer details were lost in the foggy surface, but a silhouette sat on the other side, its two large wings unmistakably divine. The movement of their arm was equally familiar. The stranger was writing something down, paying him and the Lumins no mind.

Maybe it's Azazel, Enoch wondered, his pondering interrupted by a gentle tugging at the sheets. Next to the bed, a Lumin struggled to climb up the blankets, the others cheering it on with a chorus of chimes. Once up, and successfully balanced on the mattress' far less stable surface, it turned to take a bowl from another still on the floor, passing it to Enoch. Inside, a dark liquid swayed. Enoch couldn't tell if it was meant to be food or rinsed away paint, but regardless, the Lumin on the floor mimed for him to drink it. He lifted the bowl, curling his nose at the bitter scent.

"Are you sure?" he asked. The Lumins nodded, the others joining in the first's encouragement. Uncertainty and the stench stilled Enoch's hands a moment longer. *Well, if they were planning to kill me, they probably wouldn't have tried saving me in the first place,* he justified, downing the contents of the bowl. It nearly came back up as the aftertaste assaulted his tastebuds, but with some effort he managed to hold back his gag. The Lumins cheered with soft chimes, and Enoch smiled. He had no clue what they were, but he couldn't deny they were quite cute. He gently placed the bowl to the side, turning to the Lumin looking at his arm with a curious sparkle.

"So... Do you know where I am right now?" he asked.

"Somewhere a human like yourself shouldn't be," a low, dulcet voice replied. The door of the glass wall had opened so quietly, Enoch hadn't noticed the man's entrance.

Turning to look, he realized the winged figure from outside was definitely not Azazel.

The gaunt man walked with dignified posture, and a wince on his face that betrayed the fact he was more accustomed to hunching the other way. It was difficult not to notice the many pouches hanging from his long, mahogany jacket. Gardening tools stuck out of some; others stifled the sound of shifting components and clinking vials as he entered. Pale pink and yellow cuffs added a splash of color to the outfit, softly pointed like flower petals. Mud coated his brown boots, and clung to his fingernails. Some even dirtied the feathers of his tan and hickory wings, as if the man had failed to notice them dragging through the dirt as he knelt down to tend to the plants.

He had a lean and bony build that made the sharpness of his face all the more prominent. The tightness of his bun didn't help, pulling his light brown skin tight around his head. It wasn't quite strained enough to look painful, but Enoch got the feeling he'd grown frustrated with stray strands falling into his eyes one too many times. Nevertheless, rebellious reddish-brown locks still broke free despite his efforts. His narrow, emerald eyes peered past his arched nose, appraising Enoch with a mix of curiosity and uncertainty. Perhaps, even a hint of excitement that he was mostly failing to hide.

"Welcome back from beyond the brink of death, Mr. Augnium," the earthen angel said. "How are you feeling?"

The man gently shooed the Lumins away, navigating with ease as they scurried underfoot. Rather than the door, they headed to various hiding spots around the room, concealing themselves as effectively as they had the first time. The angel moved to the desk, reaching for one of the glass squares before catching himself, adjusting to pick up a paper and pen instead. He turned back to Enoch, waiting for his answer.

"Well, my body feels a little stiff," Enoch replied, curling and uncurling his fingers. His neck felt just as resistant as he quickly shook his head. That wasn't important right now! "Sorry, um... How do you know who I am? Who–"

"I'm Azazel's friend," the man replied, cutting Enoch off with a raise of his hand. "You and I have yet to be acquainted though, so I'm afraid that's all I can tell you. In all honesty, you shouldn't even be here in the first place."

It was difficult to tell if the man meant the small room, or the land of the living. Enoch looked around again, trying to see through the fogged outer windows, searching for any clue of where he might be. He could tell the sky was blue behind the various blurred colors, but beyond that... Taking a moment, he began to wonder...

"This isn't Spira... is it?" he asked. The comment earned a casually hidden smirk.

"No, it isn't," the man replied. "Sorry to disappoint, but you're still in Terrael."

Enoch nodded slowly, feeling somewhat foolish for asking in the first place. "R-Right, of course."

"So, stiffness in your limbs, you said?" the angel continued. "That's to be expected, considering how long your heart wasn't beating. Does it lessen with movement?"

"My heart wasn't beating!?"

"For at least a week, yes."

Enoch looked himself over. Oddly enough, he didn't feel quite odd enough. At most, he felt as though he'd just woken from too long a nap; that his experience had been a dream. But the marks remained. His heart had stopped. His life had ended. Or rather, his life had been temporarily lost. "Shouldn't I be, uh… grosser than this then? Discolored or something?"

"Yes, you should. And yet you look entirely normal, aside from the lingering arcane script on your arms." The angel lowered his paper and pen. "You were undeniably dead when Azazel brought you here; physically, at least. But something preserved you, preventing your final burst. You may be the first human in history to survive magical over-flow, and I want to know how."

SLAM! The door swung open, revealing Azazel support-ing himself on its frame, breaths heavy, eyes wide. "I got your letter, Sem!" he said, addressing Semyaza before fully focusing on his recently revived friend. "You're alive!" he shouted, smiling ear to ear as he saw Enoch sitting up in the bed. The Scribe took a breath to answer, but the earthen angel Semyaza beat him to it.

"Ah yes, you got the letter that specifically told you to *wait outside,* did you?" he said, exasperated.

"I didn't read anything after 'the human has woken up'."

"Of course you didn't."

Semyaza's jaw clenched as Azazel moved to Enoch's side. "I'm so glad you're okay," the Pilgrim said, the last few words feeling like a weight escaping his chest as they passed through his lips. "I'm sure you must be confused, waking up in a strange place next to strange people–"

"Hey!"

"–I have some questions myself, considering how crazy it is you're still breathing, but, uh…" Azazel's excitement faded, the hesitation infectious as Semyaza stopped on his way to kick the man out. He watched Azazel take a deep breath before speaking again.

"I'm sorry you were dragged into my mess. I pushed you away to protect you... to protect myself. I should've gone with you, but instead..." The angel's fist tightened as he tried to hold onto the words he wanted to say. Despite his shaken mind, he smiled. "You said you chased him to help me. You were dying, poisoned by all that magic, but you still tried to help. And you saved so many people back in Civionis. If it wasn't for you, then... Well, this could've gone a lot worse, is what I'm trying to say, so thank you."

"I couldn't let Civionis become the next Peycile," Enoch replied. "But I didn't actually do much other than warning High Inquisitor Surufel. I... I was just in the way after that. And there were still people that didn't make it out. We didn't save everyone."

"You saved who you could. That's enough."

A silence followed, and Azazel got the sense his words hadn't quite been accepted. Though Enoch had clung to the advice given back in Courciel, to save who he could, doubt now dragged the Scribe down. But thoughts of saviors and survival jogged his memory.

"Oh, right!" Enoch exclaimed. "You said you saved Blade though, right? Is he here too?"

The reply caught in Azazel's throat, the angel noting Semyaza's warning glance next to him. With a sigh, he shook his head. "I got him out of there," he finally answered. "But... we don't know where he went after that."

"I see..." Enoch fell silent once again. He thought back to the forest and facility. Blade had hardly been friendly. He'd kept secrets and lashed out with words and fists alike. The pain from his punches nearly made Enoch nauseous from the memory alone. But the moments that stood out in his mind were softer; quieter. An ache in the masked man's shoulder after an almost deadly fall. Surrendering to the Priests, even when the pistol threatened someone else. A pain in his voice as he asked about Azazel. Fragile... Familiar... Afraid...

...Alone.

"My memory of everything is a little fuzzy, but I remember his ability. He shaped steel, just like you," Enoch said. Semyaza's wings shifted uncomfortably, seeing where this was going, but Enoch's focus remained on Azazel alone, oblivious to the line he was about to cross. "And considering how he talked about you, I feel like I need to ask. You're related, aren't you?"

Semyaza cleared his throat, stepping up to the edge of the bed. "You need rest, human," he interrupted. "This conversation can be left until–"

"It's complicated," Azazel replied. Semyaza glared daggers.

"What are you–"

"Lying to Ramzel is what got us into that situation in the first place, Sem," Azazel said, standing up to face his friend. "It's the reason an entire city was wiped off the map, and if it hadn't been for Enoch, those lies also would've killed thousands of people. I know I can't tell him everything yet, but I don't want to lie anymore. Not if I don't have to."

"It isn't only your secret to share."

"But is it a secret worth keeping if people will be hurt either way?" Azazel argued. Semyaza sighed, knowing fully well how stubborn his oldest friend could be. The earthen angel crossed his arms.

"With Ramzel missing, it's still too dangerous to tell people without considering the consequences. Or do you want to put a target on the human's back? He's already died once, do you want it to happen again?"

"I–" Azazel's argument slipped from his mind, the thoughts crashing against his guilt. He receded like a scolded child. From the bed, Enoch watched the two of them, realizing he'd once again stumbled into something far bigger than himself. Though, if his encounter with the Woven One was any indication, that was likely exactly where he was meant to be.

"If he's missing, I'll help you find him," the Seer offered bluntly. A small smile crept onto Azazel's lips. Semyaza turned so quickly in his surprise that Enoch was amazed he didn't snap his neck.

"Until an hour ago, you were *dead*. How could you possibly help?" Semyaza asked.

"I'm a Seer," Enoch explained. "I've had a vision of him before, so it could happen again, right? There's obviously stuff I can't know, but I know enough to want to help, however little I can." The Scribe rubbed the back of his neck, the certainty in his resolve feeling like a glove not quite worn enough to fit. "Assuming Ramzel is Blade's real name, he saved my life. Three times actually, even though I was mostly a burden. He's clearly important to Azazel too, and... talking to him back in the cells, he reminded me of myself back in Courciel. I want to help him, if I can. Like Azazel did for me."

A melancholy nostalgia washed over Semyaza as he saw the empathy and compassion in the young man's eyes. The familiar contradiction of both determination and uncertainty. The earthen angel stilled a moment, wondering if it would be wise to allow his emotions to make this call, and yet, he found his own hesitation fade away with Azazel's laughter next to him.

"You're a good kid, Enoch," his friend said, a mix of guilt and pride in his voice. In his amber eyes, a third emotion bubbled to the surface, bright like a sunrise casting off the night. Hope. "You died and came back to life, and the first thing you decide to do is try to help me with *my* problems? I knew there was a reason I liked you."

Leaving Semyaza to continue weighing his options, Azazel knelt by Enoch's side once more. "I agree that Ramzel needs help. I can't run from that truth anymore. But you won't be able to help anyone until we figure out if you're really okay or not." He held out his hand, offering it to Enoch. "So, in the meantime, let's do this. Once Semyaza has you patched up, and I've had some time to make a plan, let's go and do what Pilgrims do best. You don't mind being my assistant a little longer, right?"

With a nod, and a moment's hesitation, Enoch grasped Azazel's hand with his own. "Right!"

For a moment, reality slipped away. No figures watched from the mysterious realm of void and threads. No angels scried in Spira up above. The pains of Azazel's past loosened their grip, allowing him to breathe for the first time in years. For once, both men had a goal in mind, their wandering pivoting towards a path of hope. For a moment, their burdens were cast away by a simple handshake. They weren't in this alone...

And then Semyaza smacked both of them upside the head.

"No one is doing anything until we've finished tying up the loose ends of your *last* little misadventure. Your human friend was dead this morning! Aren't you two getting ahead of yourselves?"

"R-Right, sorry Sem."

"Yes, sorry sir."

Azazel released Enoch's hand, allowing himself to be shooed out of the greenhouse. Semyaza rolled his eyes. "I haven't even finished making sure he's okay. For once in this cycle, follow directions and give me some space to work."

"Can do, Sem!" Azazel replied, before shouting over his shoulder. "Get as much rest as you need, Enoch! I'll come back to visit!" he saw Enoch nod and wave as the door slammed shut behind him. Azazel lingered a moment longer before letting out a heavy sigh. One weight had been lifted from his shoulders, the others feeling lighter; more manageable.

Outside, the final rays of the sun began to disappear beneath the clouds. Two Lumins watered the garden, carrying a teetering watering can between them. Azazel stopped to steady it before taking in the view and a breath of fresh air.

"Don't worry, Adina," he said softly. "I promise I'll make this right." The wind blew in response, his hair tousled by the breeze. Once the moment passed, he headed to his room to change and take a much-needed shower.

Like Enoch said, Ramzel is in pain, he thought to himself. *As a Pilgrim, and as his father, it's my job to make sure he gets the help he needs. So... just wait for me a little longer, Ramzel.*

I'll find you; I promise.

Epilogue

WANING MOONLIGHT poured through the arched, stone window, the inner designs casting shadows on the brick floor. Aiding in lighting the modestly sized room, bronze candelabras lined the wall between each tightly packed bookshelf. The smoke mixed with the scent of aged parchment, along with the fading smell of cooked chicken. The remains of this dinner sat on a plate at the edge of Sariel's decorative desk, set aside to make room for his ever-growing pile of paperwork. The workload wouldn't lessen any time soon, the High Inquisitive instead spending his time lightly tapping a beautiful pen on the desk.

"So... the Researchers stationed at the facility all seem to have been transferred rather than detained," he said quietly, gaze raising subtly to look his guest in the eye. "Is it safe to assume this was the Citadel's work?"

"All I care about is *my* work, you know that," a red-haired woman replied. Her freckled cheeks grew even rounder as she gave her friend a cheeky smile. "Really Surufel, you know I have more important things to work on than whatever cover up you're blathering on about."

"Would that work involve donating equipment to Civionis?" Sariel replied. His pen stopped tapping. He leaned forward, resting his elbows on his desk. "I heard the technology they used was impressively ahead of its time, just like the Civionians themselves."

"I couldn't do something like that without permission," the woman replied, leaning over the other side of Sariel's desk. The moonlight decorated the curve of her body, her wider frame dwarfing Sariel's slender form. Her waved, unkempt hair felt like firelight next to his. Her warm toned skin glowed, far livelier than the pale face now only a foot away from hers. "I'm glad to hear they made such good progress though. Things got messy in the end, but I'm sure we can learn tons from those mistakes."

"Is that what you'd call the destruction of an entire city?"

"Progress doesn't come without sacrifice. I'm sure *you* can understand that, right *Surufel.*" The woman backed away with a shrug as Sariel sighed in annoyance. She was as difficult as always. Leaving him to his frustration, she moved over to a side table, fiddling with a celestial globe with absentminded interest. "Speaking of things we can't speak of, what happened to the host? I'm sure the explosion happened for a reason, right?"

Sariel glanced to the door as his face grew even paler. "I'm afraid I don't know what you're talking about, Miss Ebonei."

The woman, Arakiel Ebonei, rolled her eyes, pulling up her sleeve to reveal a bracelet of dull black stones. "The other wrist has them too. You can talk without the stick up your tail for once."

The High Inquisitive cleared his throat, ignoring her words as he focused on the accessory. "Don't you think that's a tad risky? Walking around with so much archasite?

A moving blank space in their search can be just as suspicious."

"Don't *you* think it's risky to be getting involved with Remnants, Inquisitor?" Arakiel argued, giving the globe one final spin before approaching the angel once more. "Between the archasite and the sheer amount of magical energy there, even I couldn't scry. So, I'm curious if one of our little Nephilim might've been poking around where they shouldn't've."

The pen strained in Sariel's grip. The woman still didn't care for secrecy. Or his mental well-being, it would seem. He began to wonder if this meeting might have been a mistake.

"You mean the hypothetical half-breeds you keep *blathering on about?*" he asked, repeating her earlier dismissal. "If someone like that approached a Remnant, they would have made a pact, if my understanding of your theories is correct. This was nothing more than a normal Researcher biting off more than they could chew, and choking on that ambition."

"Ugh." Arakiel rolled her eyes, leaning back against Sariel's desk. The High Inquisitive steadied the glass of water that teetered from the impact. "You really never let your guard down, do you? No wonder your hair is grey."

"It's silver."

"All the better to hide the stress with, I suppose." Arakiel shrugged, shaking her head before leaning back, curling her finger to beckon Sariel closer. The Shapeshifter obliged, despite his annoyance.

"If you really wanna know, we did give them that tech," Arakiel whispered. "When I realized that mist the miners found was the reason Civionis had such powerful ability users, I wasn't going to waste a chance to figure out why. I'm sure you can understand how excited I was when I realized it was a Remnant of all things."

"So, you were the one that set it all in motion? If you aren't careful about what you research, they'll step in," Sariel warned, eyes narrowing as anger built inside him like a growl in his throat.

"Like I said, progress and sacrifice and all that," Arakiel argued with another shrug. The pen snapped in Sariel's hand. Arakiel pulled a handkerchief from her pocket, revealing the sleek, other-worldly clothing underneath her jacket for just a moment. She tossed the cloth over her shoulder as she stepped away, leaving Sariel to wipe the ink off his hand and desk. "Don't worry, I won't do anything they wouldn't approve of. Cross my heart and hope to die."

Once again, the red-haired woman pulled up her sleeve, this time revealing a glowing blue screen on her wrist. She swiped a finger across, turning the floating disk of light that appeared above it after. "Though, maybe that doesn't mean as much coming from either of us. Such a strange saying, *hoping to die*." A floating golden circle appeared behind the Researcher, the location within blurred by the viscous matter filling it. "I wonder... Do you think the Remnant hoped to die too? Maybe that's why it combusted so brilliantly."

Voicing this final query, Arakiel passed through the golden portal as if she'd stepped through a wall of water. The circle shrank in size until it vanished completely, leaving only the moonlight on the floor. Sariel sighed, leaning back in his seat.

"Damn it, Arakiel," he growled, reluctantly turning back to his work. The spilled ink crawled across the desk, nearly staining a sealed envelope. He pulled it away from the puddle before it could sully the contents as well. Or the carefully written name on its back; *Enoch Augnium.*

"Sacrifice..." he muttered. "You shouldn't speak so lightly of it if you're not the one that's left to pay the price."

Glossary

Adoil: A Celestial that existed before the creation of the Three Realms. Adoil's "death" was the source of magic in the world. Adoil is known as one of the Corporeal Beings, along with Archas.

Adolium: A golden gemstone infused with magical energy. This stone is used as a power source, as well as light in certain places. However, due to the magic stored within it, it can be hazardous to humans and demons when they're exposed for too long, leading to magical overflow if people aren't careful. Mining for adolium is a dangerous job that's either highly compensated, or done with criminal labor.

Angel: Immortal denizens of the divine realm Spira. They're known for their large, feathered wings, as well as their high magic capacity. The angels helped humanity fight the demons in the First Surface War, before returning to Spira after their victory. No angels have been seen in Terrael since this ascension. Unlike humans and demons, who are mortal, angels are categorized as beings of magic.

Archas: A Celestial that existed before the creation of the Three Realms. Archas' "death" was the source of physical matter in the world. Archas is known as one of the Corporeal Beings, along with Adoil.

Archasite: A solid black stone capable of absorbing magical energy. Though there's no proof that this stone is connected to the Celestial Archas, it was named after the Corporeal Being due to its opposing nature to adolium. Archasite is a newer discovery and its properties are still being researched.

Anti-Church Movement: Used to describe people that oppose the Church's rule. A movement rather than an official group, but some supporters do tend to group together in their efforts. Their methods range from peaceful protests to violent coups and assassinations.

Bishop: The second highest position in the Church, working under the Almighty Voice. Bishops oversee Church activity in their designated city or district. They meet with High Inquisitors to discuss Church business, and act as representatives for their jurisdiction. Most Bishops are promoted from the rank of High Inquisitor or High Priest when a previous Bishop passes or retires. Their uniform consists of purple robes and a golden circlet.

Cathedral: Acting as bases for the Church, cathedrals handle many of the Church's responsibilities, usually overseen by a designated Consultant High Inquisitor. Religious rites are held in the hall of worship. Information can be found in cathedral libraries. Meetings between Church workers can be held in the meeting rooms, which are also at times used for educational purposes. Pilgrims, Priests and Inquisitors will also pick up their jobs here through the help of a

Dispatcher. If someone needs help from the Church, their best option is to find the cathedral that oversees their district. Each cathedral layout is exactly the same, with the circular hall of worship in the center between two rectangular wings; one for employee use, and the other open to the public.

Celestial: Powerful, immortal beings that existed before the creation of the Three Realms. Archas and Adoil were both Celestials known as The Corporeal Beings.

Church: The Church exists to protect humanity. Though it started as a religious group, after the First Surface War and the awakening of magic abilities in humanity, it took on more responsibilities. Now, the Church is the largest military force in Terrael. They handle public safety, education, healthcare, judicial matters, religious rites, and even act as government in a number of cities across the realm. There are some that believe the Church has too much influence, but many are simply grateful that the Church workers are there to protect them from the ever-looming threat of demon attacks.

Civionis: A city in the Northern Mountains of Terrael. Located within a spherical crater in Mt. Morus, Civionis is built on top of stone platforms. Lake Civionis sits beneath it, and a canopy of adolium gems light up the city from the rocks above. Firepits are scattered throughout the city, helping the Civionians keep warm in the cooler northern temperatures. Civionis is a tourist town known for its beautiful architecture and the crimson color of the forest that surrounds it. It used to earn its money from the mines built beneath and around the city, but an incident forced them to close them down. Now their economy is built around tourism, as well as the compensation provided to the families of powerful Church workers that call it home.

Circlet Guard: The Bishops' personal guards. Chosen from promising Priests, Circlet Guards are in charge of protecting the Bishops employed by the Church. They answer to the Circlet Guard Commander, who acts as the Bishop's right hand.

Church Worker: A general term used to describe people working for the Church. Though it includes titled positions like Priests, Inquisitors, Pilgrims, Healers and Dispatchers, it's more commonly used to describe the employees lower in the hierarchy, like trades workers, receptionists and other such roles.

Courciel: The capital city of Terrael.

Demon: The monstrous denizens of Diapogeum, the demon realm. After the First Surface War, the demons were banished underground by the Archangels. Many of them have been fighting to live on the surface again since. Demons often have jewel-toned skin, horns, tails and sharp claws. Though, the features differ demon to demon. Some also have bat-like wings, able to fly like the angels of Spira. Demons tend to have much stronger magic capacity and tolerance than humans.

Diapogeum: The demon realm. Located underground, Diapogeum is the home of the demons. It was created by the Archangels after the First Surface War to keep the demons and humans separated following the conflict. Though it was meant to be sealed off completely, it's possible to move through Terrael and Diapogeum through the Rifts scattered throughout the two realms.

Everred Fever: An illness unique to Civionis. Named after the forest surrounding the city, everred fever effects people when they are exposed to the forest for too long. It causes fever, fatigue, coughing and dizziness. However, distance from the city can help a person recover.

Everred Tree: The name for the crimson trees that only grow in and around Civionis. They live year-round and never lose their crimson color. While the needles are red, the bark is a shade of dark grey.

Final Burst: A burst of magic caused by a person's death. The size of this burst depends on the individual's magic capacity, as well as how much magical energy they had remaining at the point of their death. The magic of someone's final burst can make others sick, and lingers in the form of a fog that matches the color of their magic. It will dissipate over time, and can be slowed by solid obstacles. A final burst can also affect the nearby environment, such as causing a Resting Garden to grow, or an effect connected to a person's magic ability if they had one.

Healer: The medical specialists of the Church. Though many Healers are recruited due to having magic abilities suited for the job, most are simply individuals trained to treat injuries and illnesses. Healers will primarily be found in Houses of Healing, but there are some that work as field-medics as well. A Healer's uniform covers their entire body to protect against disease, and to remain anonymous. This is because the Archangel Raphael believes those that choose to save lives should not do so for glory or fame, but because it is the right thing to do. That being said, many do still wear name tags while working to help keep confusion to a minimum.

High Cathedral: A cathedral specifically overseen by a Bishop.

High Inquisitor: Talented Inquisitors will be promoted to High Inquisitors if they prove themselves worthy. The name itself is more a category than a title, as High Inquisitors have a wide variety of responsibilities. Holding the most authority, Consultant High Inquisitors manage cathedrals on behalf of their city or district's Bishop. Judicial High Inquisitors act as judges in court. High Inquisitives handle criminal investigations, usually commanding a team of Inquisitives. Along with issuing orders to their subordinates, High Inquisitors may also be asked to handle jobs deemed too difficult for regular ranked Inquisitors.

High Priest: High Priests delegate orders to the Priests in their squadron. A Priest can become a High Priest if they're chosen by a Bishop and Consultant High Inquisitor. Generally, those chosen are people that showed exceptional strength or leadership skills while fulfilling their duties. One cathedral will usually have multiple High Priests to cover a full patrol schedule. Along with issuing orders to their subordinates, High Priests may also be asked to handle jobs deemed too difficult for regular ranked Priests.

Hijacker: One of the nine types of magic abilities. A subcategory of Beast Manipulators. Hijackers can attach their magic to a living creature if certain requirements are met. Hijackers are able to control the creature bound to their magic. If the requirements are broken, or an ending condition is met, the creature will most likely regain control. What the requirement or freeing condition is depends on the Hijacker's ability. If the Hijacker releases their control willingly, they can potentially regain their magical energy to an extent, but if it's broken by someone else, the magic is lost.

House of Healing: The Church-run medical centers in Terrael. This is where people go to get injuries and illnesses treated, fill prescriptions, get medical advice, etc. A House of Healing will have a main healing wing, and a magical healing wing. They're kept separate to ensure no one with a low tolerance is affected by the magic of a Healers' ability. People will generally be registered with one or two Houses, so that House can have access to their medical records.

Inquisitors: A faction of the Church that specializes in gathering, analyzing and handling information. There are several branches within the faction, each with their own specialties. Though, many Inquisitors will still have base training in other branches and can assist them if necessary. Their uniform includes a small pin that proves their employment with the Church.

Inquisitive: Short for "Investigative Inquisitor". This title was used more commonly when people felt the full title was too long to say. Inquisitives are a branch of the Inquisitor faction in the Church. They specialize in criminal investigation and gathering information.

Magic: Magic is the essence of life itself. It flows through every living thing in the Three Realms, and for some, its energy can be utilized in the form of magic abilities. However, magic is also quite dangerous to humans and demons. While mortal beings will be unaffected by their own magic, prolonged exposure to foreign magic can cause illness, and eventually death.

Magic Categories: Magic is split into three main categories; Material, Beast, and Special. Material magic users can affect non-living matter with their magic. Beast magic users affect living things. Special covers any abilities that don't fall into the first two categories, or somehow fall under several. Material and Beast are split into three sub-categories, these being Shifter, Summoner and Manipulator. Shifters magic focuses on physical transformation and requires direct contact to work. Summoners magic can be shaped to conjure up magical items or creatures capable of attacking from a distance. Manipulators can attach their magic to other objects or creatures without maintained contact.

Magic Capacity: Magic capacity is the maximum amount of magic a person naturally has in their body. Using a magic ability won't cause this value to go down, as it's referring to the maximum natural capacity rather than the literal amount of magic that's left. The higher a person's capacity, the more likely it is that they'll have an ability.

Magic Deficiency: Magic deficiency is caused when a person uses more magical energy than they can afford to lose.

Magical energy is a person's life energy, and expelling too much will lead to fatigue, shaking, blurred vision, headache, disorientation and numbness in the body. When a person reaches their limit, they'll likely lose consciousness. Currently, the best cure for magic deficiency is sleep. Fresh fruits and vegetables are also known to help to a small degree.

Magical Overflow: Magical overflow is caused when a person is exposed to too much foreign magical energy. When a person uses a magic ability, magical energy radiates from the attack. Prolonged exposure will lead to fever, fatigue, coughing, confusion/disorientation, increased heart-rate and eventually a lack of consciousness. If exposure continues, the fever will rise to dangerous levels and colored marks show up on the skin. These marks will combust after a few hours to a few days. This magical flame-like aura will burn the body, killing the victim. Currently, the best treatment for magical overflow is isolating the individual from strong sources of magic before they reach the point of no return. However, once the colored marks show up, the exposed person has reached late-stage magical overflow, and there's no known way to save them.

Magic Tolerance: Unlike beings of magic, mortals' bodies aren't built for magic resistance. Magic tolerance is a person's ability to handle exposure to foreign magical energy. Exceeding your limit for too long will lead to magical overflow, followed by death. Demons have a higher tolerance than humans. As beings of magic, angels are unaffected by foreign magic.

Material Summoner: One of the nine types of magic abilities. Material Summoners are able to shape their magic into conjurable objects. The object summoned differs from person to person. After it's been separated, the Summoner can absorb it into themselves again if they want to. However, if a summoned object takes enough damage or moves farther than the Summoner can handle, the magic will disperse and cannot be reabsorbed. Non-solid summons (i.e. Fire, liquid, electricity) have a tendency to leak more magic, making it very difficult to fully reabsorb without losing some magical energy. The material is entirely made out of the Summoner's magic; however, it may take on specific physical attributes. For example, if someone were to summon magical fire, it would be hot to the touch. If they summoned a shield or bullet, it would feel solid.

Modifiers: One of the nine types of magic abilities. A sub-category of Beast Shifter. Modifiers, as the name suggests, are able to modify their own bodies with their magic. For a certain duration, they can give their body a characteristic it didn't have before. For example, they could turn their skin into scales, temporarily grow stronger, or change the size of their body or limbs. Once their time limit ends, the transformation ends as well. Modifying burns up the Modifier's magical energy, so they're unable to simply endlessly transform.

Pilgrims: Pilgrims are Church workers that focus on more situational jobs. Pilgrims are essentially professional helpers. They put out fires, they get cats out of trees, they help repair buildings, etc. If a person needs help with something, they'll go to the nearest cathedral and put in a request for help. If a Pilgrim is available and capable of helping in the way that's needed, they'll be sent to assist. Long term requests may be placed on a request board for Pilgrims to take as they like. Sometimes Pilgrims will take street commissions as well, if the client can't make it to a cathedral. In this case, the client signs a commission form so that the Pilgrim can still receive payment for the job. Though, some Pilgrims will just take jobs under the table to avoid the paperwork.

Priests: The security and soldiers of Terrael. Priests protect the people by patrolling the streets. They act as soldiers in times of crisis. They prevent the use of unlicensed magic, and arrest and detain people that break the law. While they are able to use magic legally, abuse of this power will lead to investigation from an Inquisitor, and possible suspension and detainment. Priests will answer to High Inquisitors, High Priests, or anyone of greater rank than those titles.

Remnant of Adoil: Living magic believed to be descendants or fragments of the Celestial Adoil. The Remnants each have their own wills, thoughts and desires. They exist scattered across the Three Realms, though many have been contained or locked away by the Archangels. They are incredibly powerful, and potentially deadly to anyone sensitive to foreign magic, depending on the Remnant's form and strength.

Resting Garden: Plants that grow at the location of someone's final burst. The kind of plant will be unique to the person, and will be more resilient and longer lived than normal flora. These flowers are often transferred to the grave of the deceased.

Researchers: People employed by the Church that dedicate their lives to studying the Three Realms. Most study at Gabriel's Citadel, but labs are scattered across Terrael. Inventors, scholars, intellectuals, Researchers pursue truth and innovation, hoping to help humanity understand the world around them.

Scribe: Bookkeepers, transcribers, authors; Scribes are in charge of the organization and upkeep of Church documents. Scribes are also often left in charge of cathedral libraries or records halls, helping people find the resources they need. Before being sent to the Almighty Voice, the daily reports of the Bishops are read through and condensed by the Scribes of the Grand Cathedral. Due to the information they're exposed to, the Scribes of the Grand Cathedral will generally be heavily investigated and must study at Gabriel's Citadel before earning the title.

Sculptor: One of the nine types of magic abilities. A subcategory of Material Shifters. Sculptors are able to use their magic to shape the world around them. Using their magical energy, they can alter the physical shape of the material their magic resonates with. The material differs from person to person, ranging from steel, to wood, or even air. It requires the user to have physical contact with the material, and they must be able to accurately picture the result of their alteration. They can't permanently change the physical characteristics of the material (i.e. make steel soft, or air solid), and cannot alter its mass. The more matter they manipulate, the more magical energy they use.

Seer: Categorized as a "special magic ability type", Seers are people that are especially attuned to the natural magic of the world. This connection gives them glimpses of the future through reading the ebbs and flows of magical energy. If the right actions are taken, the foreseen future can be changed. How the Seer receives these glimpses differs from person to person. Some have visions or hear voices; others are able to have glimpses at will through divination. Due to the source of the visions being more of a sensitivity to magic rather than an ability, not all Seers are able to control when they receive their glimpses. Some Seers are also capable of developing regular magical abilities on top of their ability to read the magic of the world.

Shapeshifter: One of the nine types of magic abilities. A sub-category of Beast Shifter. Shapeshifters can transform their bodies into animals. The animal differs from person to person, and they can choose to only take on partial attributes (known as their half-beast form), or fully transform. Transforming burns up the Shapeshifter's magical energy, so they're unable to simply endlessly transform, but the amount burned is determined by how much they shifted. The magic of Shapeshifters is especially resonant with the magic of the sun and moon. Because of this, their abilities are linked to the phases of the moon throughout the seasons. On a new moon, they can't transform at all. On a full moon, they will transform whether they want to or not.

Spira: The divine realm, and home to the angels and Archangels. While technically located above Terrael, Spira isn't visible in the sky due to the magic keeping it hidden. Supposedly, the divine realm can only be entered with the permission and assistance of the Archangels; and aside from the Almighty Voice, no human has been openly invited since the Church's founding.

Soldiers of Lilith: A more violent group of demons fighting to claim the surface for themselves. Each member wears a wooden mask that shows their rank. They were behind the Peycile Massacre, where an entire town of people were slaughtered. This tragedy is seen as the starting point of the Second Surface War.

Terrael: The human realm. According to history books, Terrael was created by the Archangels long ago. The realm is circular in shape, with the Ring Sea separating its edge from the void surrounding the Three Realms. Most of the cities are connected through railways and roads spread across the land. The realm is also home to many varieties of climates and environments due to the influence of Spira on the weather and biomes. Some of these include the farmlands of central Terrael, Dudael desert in the south, as well as the Northern Mountains. It is possible to pass between Terrael and Diapogeum through the Rifts, but most are locked down by the Church.

The Flare: Before the creation of the Three Realms, the Celestial Adoil came undone. The resulting blast was known as the Flare, and is believed to be the source of all magic in the world.

The Watchers: A group of angels living in Terrael rather than Spira. Azazel is a member of this group and claims their purpose is to "help humanity".